behind
our lives

Behind
Our Lives
A Tale of Life and Love in Three Parts

BOOK ONE OF THE BEHIND OUR
LIVES TRILOGY

CHARLENE CARR

Published in Canada by Coastal Lines
www.coastallines.ca

Library and Archives Canada Cataloguing in Publication

Carr, Charlene, author
Behind our lives : a tale of life and love in three parts / Charlene Carr.

(Book one of the Behind our lives trilogy)
Issued in print and electronic formats.
ISBN 978-1-988232-05-8 (softcover).--ISBN 978-1-988232-06-5 (HTML)

I. Title.

PS8605.A77285B44 2016   C813'.6   C2016-907708-X
C2016-907709-8

This novel is a work of fiction. Names, characters, places, and incidents either are the product of the author's imagination or are used fictitiously. Any resemblance to actual events, locales, organizations, or persons living or dead is entirely coincidental and beyond the intent of the author.

Typography by Charlene Carr

First Edition, December 2016

For more information and a chance to join the author's Reader's Group visit:
www.charlenecarr.com

For Dave,

In honour of all the nights we walked the city and grew our somewhat odd, but cherished friendship.

P.S. I stole your grocery bags.

All these things we hold onto will one day be tossed away: the framed pictures, the old bottles of hotel shampoos, the little scraps of writings—of thoughts and ideas captured tenuously—will pass onto other hands or pollute landfills, just as we'll pollute the earth, leaving our medicated and genetically modified cells to leach out of us.

And yet we hold on.

We hold onto it all, as if by doing so we hold onto ourselves.

We tell ourselves a story: We matter. This matters.

What uselessness.

What beauty.

CHAPTER ONE

Lincoln lay on a patch of grass in the sunken yard just outside the Halifax North Memorial Library. Romper snored beside him. It was one of those days when the sky made him dizzy—the way the clouds zoomed on by like that. Racing. Time seemed to stand still, stuck in a world moving far too fast.

But time never stood still. Like the clouds, it raced. The weight of it all a sea upon his chest, he lay there, half-drowned by all the hours still to be lived. The seconds. Minutes. Days.

He breathed deep the scent of truck exhaust; coughed, sputtered, sat up. Romper let out a startled bark. The mutt looked both ways, seemed to roll his eyes at Lincoln, then settled back down.

A woman pushed out of the library door, a large bag and a small boy trailing behind. *Her.*

She seemed everywhere lately: invading the streets, invading his thoughts. She strode past him with steps that seemed too long, too forceful, on a person so graceful.

The first time he saw her, he'd thought, 'Foxy Brown.'

Was that racist?

He was a fourth black after all, though no one would know to look at him. So, racist to say it, but not to think it.

The woman raised a hand to someone across the street—barely an acknowledgement, barely a smile—and walked on.

Lincoln had been wrong. Not Foxy Brown—a Nubian goddess of ancient times. Transported here, to Gottingen Street, to the year two thousand and fifteen.

He collapsed again, but a relaxed fall this time. The grass seemed friendlier. Welcoming. If she could transport to another time and place, maybe he could too. Escape.

Beautiful. Clean. With no guilt or uncertainty. Without hurting anyone.

Lincoln ran his fingers through his beard, scratching, pulling, contemplating. He could go inside or stay here. Return home or stay here. Close his eyes and be swept away. He'd stay, just a little longer. He had time.

When Lincoln opened his eyes he convulsed. His hands were damp. His clothes. The sky had darkened. The clouds stood still. He propelled himself forward—up the steps, over the railing—and leapt toward the library doors. Locked. How long had he slept? Hours, obviously. The library closed at nine p.m.

Stupid. A waste.

With his hands against the glass, Lincoln caught a movement. Cheryl. He pounded three times. She jumped and turned, her brow furrowed.

Lincoln grinned.

She pointed to the clock above the desk. 9:01.

"It's fast," Lincoln shouted. "I swear."

She turned her wrist. Shook her head. Pointed to the watch.

"Please." The grin again. He always put a grin on for Cheryl, and it always worked.

She walked to the door and stood staring, her hands on those big ol' hips. But he saw the twinkle in her eye. Lincoln turned to Romper, who had sidled up beside him, and gave the dog a nod. Stay. Romper looked away with a huff and settled onto his front paws.

Cheryl turned the lock and opened the door. She didn't step aside. "You know our hours."

"I don't have a watch."

"And that's my fault?"

"I fell asleep on the lawn."

"You fell—?" She shook her head. "Lincoln, we're closed."

"But the door is open." He pushed past her to the stacks. "My stuff is on hold. I'll be 20 seconds."

"Ten."

"Ten. Okay."

A minute later Lincoln dropped a pile of books on the desk. Cheryl jumped, then reached for the first. "You don't deserve this."

Lincoln nodded.

"What are you doing, anyway? All this stuff … architecture, woodworking, solar energy?"

Lincoln beamed. "Learning."

"I know, but—" She shook her head, her gaze on the books, and then at Lincoln. "What are you up—?"

"Your husband's waiting, isn't he? John, is it?"

Cheryl huffed and scanned the books. She pushed them to Lincoln, her brow furrowed once more. "Go on, then. Get."

He grinned and stepped outside. The night wouldn't be wasted. He would dive into these books, devour them, then go through again slowly, making sure he understood every concept and had thought through every application and possibility. He cocked his head at Romper and turned toward home.

No, not home. Home was a ten-minute drive. A forty-seven-minute walk. A thirty-minute bus ride, with transfer. Not that knowing these numbers mattered. In eight months he hadn't made the trip once. Hadn't even told his family he'd returned.

Lincoln walked past the community garden, the church that had been there longer than anything he could see, the greenhouse the local kids were so proud of.

Halifax wasn't a big city. But it was one you could get lost in—if you wanted. And where he was headed wasn't home. It was just a place to be lost.

ONE-TWO-THREE, FIVE-SIX-SEVEN. One-two-three, five-six-seven. Clomp-clomp-clomp, clomp-clomp-clomp. Lincoln was at least four buildings away and already he could hear the words and sounds that filled his life, invaded it. Five evenings a week and every other weekday afternoon.

He hoped the music would start soon—drown out the incessant sound of those heels, of the instructor's booming voice. The music, though not his style, was a reprieve after the clomping. A gift ... for the first few minutes.

Several women in dresses with swishing skirts and high heels rushed past Lincoln, chatting with high pitched, laughing voices.

He couldn't figure out the appeal. The dance? He doubted it. Salsa was supposed to be passionate, freeing, not this regimented counting and clomping the studio seemed to advocate.

Didn't the women get that?

More likely it was the idea of the dance. The idea of something exotic and freeing and full of life. That, he supposed, he could understand.

Maybe he'd pop in one night. Get a closer look at who, exactly, had the wool pulled over their eyes. New lovers awkwardly trying to impress each other? Seasoned lovers aching to fill the empty, silent hours of knowing everything there was to know and yet still being strangers? Or singles?

A man strode past in khaki's and a tucked in dress shirt; he flipped his key fob then clicked it. A horn sounded just behind Lincoln, making him jump. He shook his head, then followed the man with his gaze.

The studio accepted singles, a big sign made sure no one missed the announcement. Hello, lonely soul. This too, is for you.

The man jogged up the studio steps.

Maybe it was all singles, a myriad of people hoping there'd be some kind of magic in those numbers, those steps—one-two-three, five-six-seven—that would mean they didn't have to be alone anymore. Two buildings away now, the sound dominated the street.

Lincoln held the library books to his chest, envisioning their promise—silence, solitude, a life apart.

He felt sorry for the dancers. For their blindness, their searching after something they could never have. We were all alone. That was the truth. Born that way, we die that way. The big lie was that the years in between could change that.

One building away, and he could feel the music thumping

in his chest.

All the windows were open. That's why the sound had travelled so far. Warmer weather. The window would be open all the time now. Lincoln sighed.

A slew of hopefuls poured down the studio steps. Laughing. Chatting. Arm in arm. He walked past them, through them. They spread wide as if he were Moses parting the sea.

Almost there. Almost home. He'd close his windows, no matter how hot it was.

Romper ran ahead, past a car in front of Lincoln's steps, past the long toned leg attached to the woman stepping out of it.

Lucy.

Lincoln stood frozen, his back against a tree. Flee? No point; she'd see him run. A door slam. *They* were here. What could they want? How had they found him?

Lucy laughed as Joseph took her arm. That tinkling laugh. The laugh that made him first notice her, made him turn his head in a crowd and see.

Lucy.

She was beautiful as ever. Slim. Blue eyes flashing under lashes long with mascara that never clumped, not once in their four years together, that never ran or smudged. Not when she cried. Not when she was slick with the sweat of lovemaking.

The mascara of every other woman he'd ever been with had clumped.

Her eyes met his—Lincoln braced himself to say something, anything, but her gaze flitted away. She gripped Joseph's arm tighter. Joseph, who barely looked at him, who walked on as if Lincoln were nothing more than a bum on the street.

Lincoln watched them pass. Her in her red dress and black heels; Joseph in khakis and a wrinkle-free shirt. They weren't here for him. The dance. They were here for the dance.

Lincoln slumped against the tree, his heart thumping against his chest like a mallet. He looked down at his loose and aging clothes. Not the crisp suits and perpetually shined shoes Joseph and Lucy were used to seeing. Instead, Lincoln wore an old flannel button-up and torn jeans. His hair hung in greasy clumps, inches longer than it had ever been.

He raised a hand to his beard. He hadn't intended to grow it, had never had more than stubble before. But in those first few weeks, which quickly turned into those first few months, he couldn't bother shaving. What was the point? Then one day an old classmate approached. Lincoln walked on, dreading each moment the distance between them shortened, the questions that would come, the explanations he'd have to give. He braced himself, steeled himself, readied ... and the classmate walked on with only a casual glance. He hadn't recognized him. More than that, he dismissed him. In that moment, Lincoln decided the beard would stay. And he hadn't bothered to cut his hair once in the eight long months since he'd seen them. But he never thought ... Joseph. Joseph not recognizing him. Joseph not *seeing* him.

Lucy had, though. Whether or not she'd known for sure it'd been him, there'd been a flicker of recognition. And then she walked on.

Lincoln kept his back close against the tree. What time was it? After nine? Nine-fifteen, maybe? Classes started on the hour. So they were late. Typical. Of Lucy, at least. That magical mascara took time to apply.

Thursday at nine. He wouldn't be outside at this time again.

CHAPTER TWO

Lincoln stood against the tree a moment longer. He refused to turn his head, see Lucy staring back at him, *them* staring back, discussing—*Is it him? No. It can't be. But Joseph, it's him. I would know. No, I would know.*

Lucy knew it was him. She saw. Lincoln could almost hear it, the conversation they'd be having. The conversation they must be having. Any minute now, Joseph's voice would boom. He'd stride over like he owned the street. Owned the world. Owned Lincoln. Any—

Lincoln opened his eyes—when had he closed them?—and turned from the tree. The salsa studio's steps were bare. The sidewalk was bare. They'd gone inside like he didn't matter. Like he was nothing. No one.

He should be happy.

Lincoln turned to his own steps. Romper's head was cocked to the side. His eyes curious. The red bandanna around his bushy black neck flapped in the breeze.

Swallowing, Lincoln took the steps two at a time. Stupid. Pathetic. He almost laughed. He should laugh. If she'd seen, known, she would have said something. She wouldn't walk by. Couldn't walk by. She'd always been a person to want the last word and he hadn't let her have it.

He should have said something. Anything. Not stood there like a frightened child, back pressed against a tree just to stay standing.

He unlocked the door to his building and trudged up the old wooden steps to his apartment one at a time. If he didn't, Sandy from unit 1a, hating the noise, would bang her broomstick or golf club or whatever she used against the ceiling the second he stepped through his door.

Inside, Lincoln dropped the books on a crate and rammed his fist into the wall. Hard enough to hurt, but not to break anything—flesh or plaster. He could only be so stupid in one night. He punched again, near the door frame this time so he could punch harder. Tingles of pain radiated through his arm. The broomstick banged. Lincoln cursed under his breath. Enough.

He'd wasted enough hours today. He scooped up the books and took them to the couch. He flipped through the first one. Diagrams. Diagrams. Lucy.

Lucy laughing. Crying. Yelling.

He pulled over a crate and kicked his legs up. Was this normal? The way his stomach twisted? The ball that felt like an actual presence within his gut?

He clenched his eyes shut—trying to force away the words and images that flew at him.

"I won't do it," she had screamed. "I won't." A bottle of coconut scented lotion soared across the room, aimed at his head.

"Calm down." He'd held his hands out. Supplicating. Wearing the half smile he saved for the office war room. The smile he'd seen on Joseph since they were children. "Be reasonable, Sweetie."

"Reasonable?" A tube of toothpaste this time.

Yes, reasonable. Practical. Logical. Lincoln had just started to make a name in the company, to earn respect that didn't come from his family name: all the things Lucy wanted, all that she had pushed him toward. "We're not ready. Not yet. Our lives aren't—"

A laugh. He hadn't known what it meant. Hadn't even guessed.

"*Our* lives?" She'd looked at him with disgust, like he was the pathetic one in the situation, like he was the one not capable of seeing the larger picture, and left.

Lincoln's stomach growled, bringing him back to the present. His library-lawn nap had meant no dinner. But he couldn't cook, not tonight. Not when, nowadays, cooking meant Kraft Dinner or Ravioli or cereal and toast. A glance out the window told him the rain had come. No matter. He'd get dry again eventually.

Lincoln slipped into his make-shift galoshes. He chuckled. What would Lucy think of these?

Romper came to the door expectant, tail wagging. Lincoln shook his head and the dog sidled away—snout hung down—then looked back, reproachful.

Outside puddles were forming. Lincoln walked in the opposite direction of the salsa studio. He had a good thirty minutes until class was over. Plenty of time to make it to Kut Korners Pizza and back—with time to spare.

When Lincoln pushed through the door, the kid with the shifty eyes and puffed out chest stood at the counter. "Usual?"

Lincoln nodded. He perched on the stool and swivelled back and forth as the kid rambled on his cell phone, as the rain came down in torrents.

Lincoln paid in cash, double knotted the plastic bag holding his dinner, and stepped into the onslaught. He guessed he'd sat in the shop ten to twelve minutes. Five to seven to get home, depending on the lights. He was cutting it tight.

A whooshing sound rose up. Lincoln turned to see a typhoon of muddy water coming straight at him. It ran into his eyes. It soaked through his shirt and pants. He should get angry. Yell at the driver, scream expletives, give him the finger. Do what any normal person would do.

Lincoln sighed. That lump, knot, whatever it was in his stomach, grew heavier. He walked on, skin sticky, clothes thick. Yet his feet were dry. He looked down at his favourite pair of loafers, the left one opening at the toes, flapping like a mouth, revealing the 'b' in the Sobeys grocery bag he'd stuffed inside it. What would Lucy say? He couldn't come up with an answer for that one. Lucy's Lincoln wouldn't have thought of such a thing. Grocery bags in his shoes. Ridiculous. But Lucy's Lincoln, new loafers or no, would have wet feet right now. A smile crept across his face. Life had its positives.

Lincoln continued down the busy street. In this city, if rain kept you inside you'd be a hermit. Some walked as casually as him, but these had umbrellas and rain boots to shield them. Others dashed past, holding a purse to block the rain or a jacket, raised up like a tent. Pointless. This rain flew in from the side as much as the sky. And wet was wet.

Wet was wet. Lucy had said that the first night they'd met—when she smiled across the room, when they left the party only to get caught in the rain.

"Just like a movie," she'd said when he tried to shield her with his coat, when he suggested they hide under an awning. "And wet was wet." She'd spun. Acting out her little movie, he later realized. Playing the role of carefree and excited. He'd kissed her, falling for the scene, the romance she created, and thought—*Life would begin again.* That's what the moment meant. His heart had been broken just weeks earlier, but with one laugh, one spin in the rain, one kiss, Lucy had put it back together. Life had begun.

No. No. No.

Lincoln clenched his teeth. Stupid. Pathetic. Broken. Think of something else. Something. Anything. *Her.* Not Lucy. The afro-haired woman. The Nubian goddess. Not Lucy with her silky blonde hair and bright blue eyes: bluer than the sky, bluer than the deepest lake. Those eyes—not now. Not tonight. Not when he'd come so far.

But the woman he'd started seeing everywhere. Graceful. Determined. Fast. He could think of her, of the first time he saw her. It had been a night like this, one block from here. The rain poured down. And she'd come running—thighs flexing, arms pumping. He'd heard her before he'd seen her: The thump of her black boots on the pavement. The steady puff of her breath. He'd turned as she'd flown past him. She didn't yell for the bus. Didn't wave her arms. She just ran. And the bus, which started to pull away from the stop, slowed. He imagined the smile on her face, the sigh of relief, and wished he'd seen it.

A moment later he'd seen her face, barely. Foxy Brown— the 'whole lot of woman' 70s action queen—had been his thought while he watched her retreating figure, but as he glimpsed her face through the flash of wipers against wet glass, the comparison didn't do her justice. Not even close.

Steps away from his apartment, Lincoln walked past Joseph's car. He hesitated, looked in the back. A gym bag and protein bar wrappers. So that hadn't changed.

Upstairs, he stood in the entry and peeled off his wet clothes. One by one he let the items fall. Positives. He could leave them there as long as he wanted. He wouldn't, but he could, and no one would say a word. His boxers were the last to go: now dingy Calvin Klein's Lucy once thought were so spiffy.

Better.

Untying the bag that held his dinner, Lincoln stepped to the window. The city shone. Each light representing how far society had come: a view disorganized yet perfectly planned. Stop lights, crosswalks, buildings made to withstand the wind—when winter came, the snow.

Lincoln took a bite of his calzone, luxuriating in the freedom to stand naked in a window with no one to tell him not to. The city twinkled. It didn't look real. More like a set, like the idea of what a city would be. Full of its systems, its rules lived by, that worked so well, until they didn't. That kept most people safe, most of the time. That prevented utter chaos.

Lincoln took another bite, the hot cheese and sweet pineapple a burst of goodness.

All anyone had to do was obey the rules. Stop at a red. Pay your taxes. Slow at a yellow. Register to vote. Yield when directed. Don't sleep with your brother's girlfriend. Green means go.

Follow the rules and you got to live thinking everything was okay, got to believe that those years in between could be filled, could mean something. Break them, and—

Bang. Bang. Bang.

Lincoln dropped his takeout dish. Pizza sauce and bits of bacon and pineapple splattered the wall. The ball in his gut plopped right back in place from wherever it had drifted away to. He stood frozen.

CHAPTER THREE

The noise came again, three loud bangs. Lincoln looked at the spilled calzone.

Stupid.

He stayed frozen.

Stupid.

Romper trotted over to the spill and looked up at Lincoln.

"No."

The dog edged closer.

"No."

He slinked away.

Three bangs once more.

Lincoln moved to the door. But he was naked. There were steps to take: Get clothes on. Go to the door. Face them: Joseph and Lucy.

Another bang. "Lincoln?"

Not Joseph's voice. Certainly not Lucy's. "Lincoln, I know you're there."

Andrew. Only Andrew. "Just a minute."

A loud sigh.

Lincoln dashed to his bedroom and grabbed a pair of

sweatpants from a dresser drawer and a t-shirt from another. Back in the living room, he pushed the pile of wet and muddy clothes out of the way and opened the door just wide enough to stand in it. "Hey."

"Hey." Andrew's eyes widened. "What in the—?" He reached out and peeled something off of Lincoln's temple. A crumpled leaf. He held it out, left eyebrow raised.

"A truck got me."

"A truck."

"A puddle. You know. A ..."

"Whatever. Can I come in?"

"I'm kind of busy."

"Busy? You got a job?"

"No."

"A girl?"

"No."

"Then I'm coming in." Andrew pushed on the door.

Lincoln held it. "I'm working, okay? I'm eating dinner. Just ... what do you want?"

Andrew gave the door a shove. Lincoln stumbled back, then stepped aside.

"This, Lincoln, this is how you live."

It was a statement, not a question, so Lincoln didn't answer.

"You don't have to live like this."

"I like living like this."

"You don't."

Andrew walked through the living room. It wouldn't take long to absorb—couch, work table, crate, shoes lined up neatly by the door. He shook his head, then turned. "You practicing monk-hood? Rejecting materialism?"

Lincoln shrugged. He'd had everything in Lucy and his apartment in Montreal. More than he ever wanted, than he'd ever thought he wanted. When he left that life, he left it all. Every TV and designer tie and espresso coffee machine. (They had two.) And it felt good. Freeing. Those monks knew what they were about.

"You have your shares in the business. Why aren't you—?"

Lincoln stepped forward. "I'm not touching those shares."

"I'll get you a job then. You tired of office work? Is that what this is about? You can work on the floor. As a construction manager. Or on one of the crews? You used to love that when we were kids. Dad used to say you were better than some of his men, and Uncle Alex—"

"Don't talk to me about my Dad."

Andrew's mouth snapped shut. He nodded. "I could get you a job."

"If I wanted a job, I'd have one." Lincoln wanted to sit. Exhaustion rolled over him. But if he sat, Andrew would too, and stay for a while, get comfortable. "If this is why you came, you can go. I don't need a job. I don't want a job. But if I did, I wouldn't get one from him."

"From me, Lincoln. From—"

"They're all from him."

"You need to work."

"Who says I'm not? Who says work has to be what you think it is, what society thinks it is, what Joseph thinks it is?"

"Linc—"

"I'm alive, aren't I? I'm fine."

Andrew let out a puff of air. "For now."

"And now is all that matters, isn't it?"

Andrew frowned. "Whatever savings you have, they

won't last forever."

"I have a plan. A good plan."

Andrew scoffed. He pointed to the cut outs on the wall, the detailed lists of everything that went right and everything that went wrong, the table scattered with experimentation. "This, right? This is your plan?"

Lincoln leaned against the wall, hating this exhaustion, the fact that he couldn't stand up and say what he was doing mattered with verve, say that with every swing of the axe, every thrust of the hammer, he was getting his life back. Building it. But he couldn't say it, not with Andrew's face looking like that. He hated Andrew's face: Pity? Frustration? Sadness?

Andrew picked up the book on architecture, studied it a moment, then let it drop to the table. "I know what happened—"

"You don't know the half of what happened." Lincoln stepped back to the door. "You've offered me a job. Cleared your conscience. Now, can you go?"

"So you can get back to what? Eating dinner? That dinner?" He pointed to the calzone below the window, half out of its Styrofoam holder.

"You startled me."

Andrew laughed. The big, boyish one he'd had as a kid. The one that got them in trouble during sleepovers when Mom or Aunt Mindy would come in shushing them. "I'm not here to talk about a job." He picked up the calzone, put it in the container, and wiped his hands on a napkin. "I'm not even here to lecture you about living like a slob."

"I don't—"

Andrew walked around the table. "You get the invite to

Aunt Marilyn's sixtieth?"

Lincoln nodded.

"Rachel said you didn't RSVP."

Another nod.

"Man."

"You RSVP when you're going. I'm not going. So—"

"She's your mother, Lincoln. It's your mother's sixtieth birthday party."

Lincoln straightened. Eight months. He hadn't seen her in—"I'll send a card."

"You can't just—" Andrew crossed the room. He sank into the couch, legs spread.

Damn.

"I mean, Lincoln. Come on. She misses you."

"She—"

"She doesn't even know you're here. None of them do."

Lincoln walked to the window. The city twinkled on. He turned to face Andrew. The ball in his stomach pulsed. So heavy. "And they won't."

"I know. I know. You want it to be some big mystery. Some big secret."

"I want my privacy."

"They're your family. And they're worried."

Lincoln sent his mother an email once a month. Every month. The second Tuesday.

"Privacy doesn't exist when it comes to family." Andrew slapped his palm on the arm rest. "Especially our family."

Sunday made more sense, but the library was closed on Sunday. He used to send messages to his grandmother every Sunday, before she passed, and she forwarded them around to the rest of the family—no privacy.

But Lincoln had privacy now—he looked at Andrew—most of the time. "They know I'm okay."

Did his mother send Lincoln's Tuesday message around? Did Joseph see it? Did Lucy? Not that he told much: I'm okay. I'm fine. I saw a beautiful sunset or took a rejuvenating hike. Lies about the location of the sunset or hike. No indication of when he'd be back.

Andrew stared at him. Too long. Lincoln reached for the calzone.

"Aren't you lonely?"

Lonely? Nope. "You ever read David Potter?"

"Relative of Harry?"

"He talks about how in literature any story about a man's complete isolation from his fellow man—be it physical, psychological, whatever—is considered a horror." Lincoln took a large bite. Still warm. He wiped his mouth. "But it's not. Or at least it doesn't have to be. When you're alone you're ..." Lincoln paused. "Free. You don't have to account for yourself, for anyone else. You can just live."

"Lincoln, come on."

"People lie, Andrew. Have you ever met a person who didn't lie?"

"What's your point?"

"They lie. They disappoint. They cheat. Steal. Pretend."

"Yeah. People suck. So what? You suck, too. But your family still loves you. They still miss you."

"They're fine. They're better—"

"I miss you, man."

Lincoln's throat tightened. He shook his head. Andrew and he riding bikes, having their first cigarette, their first toke ... telling stories about the first girl they'd slept with, years before they had.

"But you're pissing me off." Andrew rubbed a hand through his hair. "Whatever happened, it wasn't your mother that ... well, whatever happened between the two of you, you work it out. You say sorry. Or I forgive you, or—"

"I'm not going to the party."

Andrew stood. "You're a selfish bastard, you know that? A cowardly selfish bastard." Andrew turned before he opened the door. "I'll keep your stupid promise. Act as if I didn't come here. Act as if I don't know you're minutes away, hiding out like a baby. And yeah, you're right. People lie. Even to themselves. Don't think you're some big exception."

When the door closed, Lincoln stared after it. At last, he picked up the calzone again. It was cold, but he wasn't hungry anymore, anyway. He threw it against the wall, then stared at what looked like a Rorschach splatter.

Even if Andrew couldn't see it, even if no one could see it, Lincoln was right. People were the problem. People who thought the highest goal was to have these biologically determined social networks. It kept babies alive, yes ... but beyond that? Once we were grown? People no longer needed tribes. That yearning to connect had been an evolutionary requirement to ensure we didn't die in the wilderness: so we could protect and clothe and feed each other. But through grocery stores and electric heating and running water, society created a world that enabled the individual to be just that, an individual.

What had the tribe done for him? Lincoln was tempted to hit something again. Throw something. But it wouldn't work, he'd just have more mess to clean. He closed his eyes. Lucy.

Lucy on the street corner—Haughty. Resistant. Lucy in

the hospital bed—outwardly so fragile, so precious, inwardly a cold, hateful vessel of recrimination.

This is your fault. She'd looked at him, her blue eyes like steel. *You killed my baby.*

Which was ridiculous, of course. The fall killed their baby. Lucy stepping backward down a flight of stairs killed their baby. But Lincoln was the reason she'd stepped.

Stolen from him, that's what the tribe had done, stolen everything. His joy, the things he'd loved about himself. A new life.

That's what social living had done. Stolen his passion for the outdoors, the ecstasy of burden-free love, his hopes for the future.

I never wanted your baby. His passion for working with his hands. *It probably wasn't even your baby.* His joy in being alive. *In fact, I'm sure it wasn't your baby.* His ability to trust.

Stolen it and morphed him into a man who lived for business. For appearances. For the bottom dollar. For a woman who stood for everything he thought he wanted and nothing he truly desired.

Lincoln opened his eyes. It had taken time alone to realize he'd never wanted her, not really. To realize she'd done him a favour. Not freed him, he wouldn't credit her with that, but led to his freedom. He was happier now than ... not than he'd ever been, but than he'd been in years. Than he'd been since he started following the path people, the tribe, laid out for him.

It had taken time to forgive himself for the death of the child that was either his son or his nephew ... though he wasn't sure he'd quite forgiven himself for that. Not yet.

He would see his mother again one day. His sisters. His

aunt and uncle and cousins. But not today, or tomorrow either, or at the party. Not until he'd created a solitude that was sustainable. Not until he knew they wouldn't suck him back into the life that had sucked away everything he loved about himself.

A cabin in the woods. A cabin in the sky. A parcel of land large enough and isolated enough that nothing and no one could touch him. That would be his answer. That's what he was working toward.

CHAPTER FOUR

The sun blasted through Lincoln's window the next morning, each ray pounding into his skull. His face scrunched and he slithered in the sheets. Filthy. Stinking.

There went his plans of heading out to the lot, spending the day cutting and hauling and clearing. Not gonna happen.

How many bottles of beer had he drunk last night? Six? Seven? The last bit of evidence sat sprawled on his bedside table. A trickle of Propeller Pale Ale beading right next to his clock radio.

It'd been months since he'd woken up like this. Six. Seven, maybe? In those first few weeks, it'd been a regular occurrence. Drink. Get High. Hide from life. Repeat. But then he'd bought the lot, concocted a plan, decided enough was enough. Apparently, enough was only enough until his past burst back into his life. Lincoln pushed himself onto his forearms with a groan. Romper, who lay across the room, not at Lincoln's feet per their usual agreement, perked his ears. He pranced over and did a little back and forth dance.

"Hold it," Lincoln grumbled.

A bark.

"Just—" Lincoln grasped the side of his head. He couldn't have had more than six. He'd only had a six pack in his closet, hidden away. Six and he felt like this? In the old days he could put away seven or eight with the boys or, in later years, after a successful acquisition, and wake up feeling spiffy. He chuckled, then held his head again. Spiffy. One of Joseph's favourite terms, typically used before getting ready for a night on the town. *Let's get spiffy, man.*

The pounding increased. He missed his brother.

Another bark.

Missed Rachel and his Mom and even Linda a bit. Lucy. Stupidly. Unbelievably. Pathetically. He missed Lucy.

Bark. Bark. Bark.

"All right, all right."

Lincoln swung his legs over the side of his bed. The distasteful smell he'd woken up with became unconscionable. Why would—? The truck. Muddy clothes, muddy body. Still, it was ridiculous that he stank like this. Showering hadn't been a top priority of late, but it had to be today. Romper followed Lincoln to the bathroom door, his eyes accusatory.

"I'll be quick. Two minutes. Three tops."

The dog settled on his front paws. Lincoln could let him out alone, but he wouldn't risk it. He bent and scratched between the dog's ears. The last thing he needed was this mutt disappointing him too.

Fresh out of the shower, and despite his pounding, fog-filled head, Lincoln held to the burst of energy the water granted. He swept the sheets off his bed, emptied his pillow cases, scooped up the sodden clothes from last night and threw them all, along with the pile from his clothes bin, into a laundry bag.

He gestured to Romper, who followed without making eye contact. It was at least two hours past when Lincoln generally took the dog out, but the instant they stepped outside, the sun—with its blasting rays—prompted complete forgiveness. Romper bounded up and down the street then settled on his favourite patch of lawn three houses up. Lincoln followed behind, impressed as always that Romper's preferred patches always had a garbage can nearby.

A look from a disapproving neighbour and Lincoln patted his thigh. Romper bounded toward him. Lincoln linked the leash he'd gotten a few weeks ago to the dog's collar. He'd take it off when out of the neighbour's line of vision, though Romper didn't seem to mind. It was Lincoln who minded. Something about putting a living creature on a leash ... it made him queasy.

After dropping his laundry at the Suds 'N Bubble, Lincoln headed to the Commons, a large green space in the middle of the city. A variety of young people and one old man—in his mid-eighties at least—roller-bladed on the large cement oval. A group of school kids played an awkward looking game of softball in one of the baseball fields, and a man played Frisbee with two young boys. Everywhere—people with people. Lincoln strayed far from the Frisbee players, scooped a ball out of his pocket, and sent it flying. Romper soared through the air with a leap of joy.

SPENT FROM FORTY-FIVE minutes of throwing a ball, but not even near tired of the sun, Lincoln picked up his laundry then decided to take the long route home. Romper pranced beside him.

Lincoln never did this in his old life—spent an afternoon in the sun, walked without needing to be anywhere and for no real purpose. He walked when Lucy wanted to walk. He had run for exercise. And even then, his mind never wandered. It calculated. It planned. It went over numbers and strategies and new initiatives.

Today it meandered. Today it felt free. People, as he'd told Andrew the night before, were awful—as individuals, as groups—people, as anything more than shopkeepers, and librarians, and garbage collectors, he could do without. But people just existing, going about in their own worlds, expecting nothing of him—that he'd miss.

The laughing teens with Popsicles. Popsicles! That old man who'd looked so able on his rollerblades, only to take them off, carefully put them in a bag, then hobble off with a limp, looking every day his age and more ... but he'd worn a smile, a sly one, like he'd pulled the wool over someone's eyes. Over life's?

That's what he'd miss. Life. People who gave the appearance, at least, that the world was beautiful.

If his plan worked, if he figured out a way to make it work, he'd miss watching life.

"Hi, there!"

Lincoln jumped. When was the last time a stranger on the street had talked to him, acknowledged his existence, even? A small round face, defined by a large gap to the side of her two front teeth, grinned up at him.

Lincoln stared.

The girl scrunched her nose then crouched beside the dog, digging her hands into his fur. "What's his name?"

"Romper."

"Romper." She laughed then waved over a little boy—about half her age and half her size, with three or four-inch dreads sticking up all over his head. The boy gazed at Lincoln, big brown eyes uncertain—Lincoln had seen him before, but where?

The boy shuffled over and touched the dog's head. Romper licked him, and the boy's face lit up like a firecracker. He put a hand on his cheek, as if marvelling, then threw his arms around the dog's neck.

A woman stood on the porch, eyeing them. "He safe?" She called in a booming voice.

Lincoln nodded.

"Don't be fretting him," she said to the kids. "No pulling his ears or tail. He'll bite ya." She seemed to hold back a chuckle as the girl waved a hand at her without looking back. The boy patted Romper with slow, cautious movements and stepped back a bit.

"He won't bite," the girl whispered. She looked again at Lincoln. "Will he?"

Lincoln shook his head and hefted the laundry bag higher on his shoulder. The boy was three, maybe four. Probably four.

He never used to think about these things, not until the last few months, when he'd had time to think, when he'd finally gotten over the numb shock that his life, as he'd known it, had disintegrated. Lincoln smiled at the boy. The little face looked up, then smiled back, before focusing on Romper again.

Lincoln's first son ... or daughter, if allowed to live, would have been about this age. He'd had no choice in aborting that child—the first woman to break his heart made that decision all on her own. His second child—potential child—with Lucy, the second woman to tear his heart to shreds, would be just a few weeks old now. Two children, never to see the light of day.

"Is he a puppy, or a grown up dog?" the girl asked.

His thoughts broken off, Lincoln focused on the girl. "I'm not sure."

"You don't know?" Her eyes widened.

"Well, he's not a new puppy."

"Hmm." The girl turned back to Romper, her brightly beaded braids clicking against each other. Romper sank to his bottom, his front paws still up. "Do you know how old you are?" Romper turned his head up to Lincoln, his patience wearing thin. For all his qualities, he wasn't one for indulging the whims of children ... unless they had a ball for him to catch.

"He can't talk, you know."

The girl glared at Lincoln then spun her head back to Romper. Click-click-click-click-click, went the beads. "I know."

Lincoln cleared his throat. "Maybe we should ... I mean I have to ..." Romper stood, ears at attention.

A car was coming up the road, two people in it, a man and a woman, arguing, the man's hand flailing as he spoke. A cat peered around the side of a garbage can—ah, that's what Romper was upset about. Lincoln reached for the dog's leash and was about to clip it when the cat bolted into the street. Romper leapt. The boy, his arms entangled with the dog somehow, catapulted over the curb as the car came onward. Lincoln's throat closed. He couldn't scream, couldn't move, as the car, the cat, the dog, the boy, all moved toward each other, faster than a blink but slower than a breath.

CHAPTER FIVE

Lincoln propelled himself into the street, on top of the boy, in front of the car. A screech not quite like the movies. Then silence.

Was it over? Had he died?

Noise hit him like a wave. The dog barking, car doors slamming. Feet pounding. Voices. Voices. Voices.

"Get up!" A woman's voice high above all the others. "Theo. Theo." Rage. Intensity. Fear. "Get up!"

Lincoln stayed inert. He could hear the words, but they made no sense. Get up? Impossible. His limbs were rigid. Locked. Curled around ... around a moving thing. A wriggling thing. A crying, wailing thing.

The boy.

The car. The dog. The cat. The car. He wasn't dead. Lincoln moved his limbs one at a time, unfurling. Romper's nose pushed at him, his paws ... pawed.

The sky was brighter than it had been. The world bigger. The bumper was inches from him. Had hit him. But barely. He could feel it, the spot on his back. But it was his ankle that throbbed, the pain erupting slowly then intensifying, spreading. A groaning, choking sound erupted from him.

The voices morphed into identifiable words. The boy was wrenched from Lincoln.

"Are you okay?"

"Is he okay?"

"He's okay. Look at him. He's okay."

"The dog ran out. He just ran out—"

"And the man."

"The boy."

The woman's voice was lower now. Soft whispers. Murmurs. Desperate. Searching.

Arms held Lincoln, started to lift him as the voices intensified. Another groan.

"Don't move him."

"Someone call the ambulance."

"Someone call the police."

"No. He's okay. Look. He's okay."

Romper's bark. Romper nudging him.

Lincoln was almost to his feet now. The weight of him seemed ten-fold. A third groan erupted and he was eased back down. A face materialized before his eyes as all those voices came into focus. A young man. A boy, really. Sixteen? Seventeen? The boy whose thin arms had been flailing in the car.

"You're all right? Hey, man." His eyes focused on Lincoln's—desperate. His voice cracked, again and again. Was he even sixteen? "Talk to me, okay? You're all right. Right? I mean, I barely bumped you." He turned his face away, looked up at the other voices and faces and bodies. "You saw that, right? I barely touched him. He touched me, my car, he jumped into the road!"

"To save the boy." The deep booming voice from the porch stood before them, Lincoln's laundry draped over her arm.

"Because of the dog," said the woman who had been in the car. "The dog—"

"Because of the cat!" Piped the little girl.

Lincoln put a hand to his head. It throbbed, but his ankle throbbed more.

"Yeah, the dog." The driver said, his voice cracking once more. "That's your dog, right? Right?"

Lincoln moaned. "You know you have to have your dog on a leash, right? You know that? It's illegal. Against the law. I was just driving. I was minding my own business and—"

"Stop." Lincoln put up a hand. "I'm not going to, it's fine, I—"

"Yeah, it's fine. Of course it's fine. You're lucky I'm fine. I should sue you. I should—"

The woman from the porch pushed the driver out of the way and crouched down. "Are you okay?"

A lump rose in Lincoln's throat at the sound of her voice, the concern, the genuine concern ... was he okay? He was alive. So he could be worse. But was he okay? He hadn't been okay in a long time. But that's not what she was asking. He nodded.

"Say it, are you sure? Scan your body. These things can be tricky, you think you're fine and then the adrenaline settles and—"

"I'm okay."

The woman put a hand on his shoulder. "Should we call an ambulance? Get you checked out?"

Lincoln shook his head and propped himself up—another

groan, a flood of pain. "I'm fine." He looked at his ankle, shifted it, then winced. "My ankle." Something wasn't right, that was for sure. "But that was the fall, not the—he's right, he hardly touched me."

Lincoln attempted to stand. The driver reached for him, guided him. Lincoln stood, ninety percent of his weight on his left foot. "It was an accident man," Lincoln sent the driver a smile, "could have happened to anyone."

"An accident?" The woman who was tending to the boy rose. She turned. Her. The woman from the bus stop. The library. The Nubian goddess. "That's your dog?" She pointed to Romper, who sat by the curb, ears down, looking shameful.

Lincoln shrugged. "Well—"

"That's your dog. You have a dog that chases cats and you were out here without a leash letting babies play with it?" Her whole body leaned forward. Vibrated. Her eyes focused, as if she could drill into Lincoln's soul if she tried hard enough.

"Well," the driver stepped away from Lincoln, his arm out, "I guess this conversation doesn't concern me. I guess I better get on my way."

The woman from the porch pointed her laundry strewn arm at the driver. "I've got your license plate number. You remember that. Any problems with this young man and—"

"It's not his fault." The female passenger spouted—half indignant, half whine.

"I saw the way you two were carrying on, his eyes not on the road."

"You've got that number." The driver smiled a nervous smile, a conciliatory one. He and the passenger opened the car doors and pulled away.

The woman with the boy kept her eyes on Lincoln. "I

asked you a question."

"Get out of the street." The woman from the porch ordered. "Or there'll be another accident."

The woman with the boy—who must be his mother, no woman could hold that kind of intensity without being a mother—eased her shoulders the slightest amount and helped the woman from the porch help Lincoln to the sidewalk. They led him to the porch and the owner gestured for him to sit. He shook his head, not wanting to look up at the boy's mother. He had eight inches on her, maybe nine, yet even with him standing, it seemed as if she towered over him.

"This your dog?"

An invisible weight pressed into Lincoln's chest. He wanted to disappear, dissolve, sink into the earth or slither away down some storm drain. Escape. "Sort of."

She stepped toward him, the boy at her heel with one arm wrapped around her leg, looking even more sheepish than Romper had. "He is sort of your dog?"

"He just kind of," Lincoln looked from the mother to the porch woman to the boy, and back to the mother, "came to me."

She leaned back. "Explain to me exactly how—"

"He showed up one day."

Her arms crossed, as if through no thought of her own. Her jaw clenched and unclenched, a little pulsing movement.

Lincoln leaned against the porch railing; his head seemed to tilt and whirl. His ankle throbbed. "And then he came again and again and walked with me when I went places and waited for me when I went inside and was there when I came out."

Her eyebrows rose. She bent and shifted Romper's

bandanna. "No collar?"

"No."

"Dogs don't just come to people. They have owners. People who own them. People who—"

"Do you actually think any living thing can own another?"

The woman's brows rose again. "Yes." She stepped back, the boy still clinging to her leg—the slightest smile on his face. "And if you don't want to think of it like that, think of it as family. This dog has a family. People who love him and miss him and—"

"If he loved them don't you think he'd be waiting outside their door, not mine?"

"Have you ever heard of the Humane Society? Or Rescues?" She shook her head, hurling Lincoln a look of disgust. "Find out. Maybe the people were travelling and the dog got out of the car, or maybe—"

"Are you upset about your son or about the dog not—"

"I'm upset about you being an irresponsible human being who just—"

"Stepped in front of a moving vehicle to save your son." Lincoln and the mother's head turned to the woman on the porch, who was rapidly folding Lincoln's laundry and stuffing it back in his bag. "Kali, this young man may have saved your son's life. At the risk of his own. Instead of lecturing the poor soul, don't you think you should say thank you?"

Kali's features shifted. She opened her mouth, then closed it. Her gaze fell to the boy. She was like a painting. A moving, breathing piece of art. "Thank you." Her chin raised and her gaze met Lincoln's again. "It was your fault to begin with. If you're going to have this dog with you, this stray dog you've acquired, then you should have it on a leash. You should train it and—" the woman on the porch cleared her throat. "But thank you. You didn't have to jump in front of that car." Kali's hand lowered to the boy's shoulder. She pulled him tighter against her. "Thank you."

Lincoln stared, his arms tingled, his head throbbed, his ankle ached, but he felt privileged almost, he'd saved *her* son.

"Anyone would have—"

"Anyone would not have." Kali pushed out her lips, the briefest of movements. "And you did. So thank you."

"That's better." The woman on the porch grinned. "Now, I have to take this one home," she gestured to the girl, who was standing nearby, watching it all, "and you," she gestured to Kali, "help this young man with his ankle. Give him a once-over to make sure nothing worse is wrong."

"Mrs. Martin."

"What?"

Kali glanced at Lincoln. "He should go to the hospital."

"I'm fine. I don't need the—"

"You can't force him. But you can tend to him, and see if he needs the hospital, rather than making him wait seven hours for someone to tell him what you can tell him in ten minutes."

"Mrs.—"

"I'll see you on Monday." Mrs. Martin set the laundry on the step. tweaked the boy's chin, and passed between Kali and Lincoln. "Come on now." She tilted her head to the girl who skipped behind her.

Kali leaned against the opposite railing. "You sure you're okay?"

"I don't need the hospital. My ankle's not great, but I don't think it's broken or anything."

Kali knelt before Lincoln and wrapped her hands around his ankle. She pushed his pant leg up and explored the area.

"You, uh, you a doctor or something?" Lincoln swallowed.

"I'm a nurse." Kali stood. "I think you're right, it doesn't seem broken. It's a bad sprain. Hold out your hands." Lincoln obeyed. "Those are some unpleasant-looking abrasions. You'll be sore."

Lincoln stared at the base of his hands. "I didn't even feel..."

"It's the adrenaline. The pain from the ankle."

Kali glanced at the boy. That profile. God. She was perfect. Sculpted. Not fragile or soft like so many women. Not even what you'd usually think of as feminine. But womanly. Exquisite. Made to be cast in marble.

She turned back. "You should go to the hospital."

Lincoln choked on his words. "So a nurse, huh? What kind?"

"Emergency."

"So you're just trying to give your pals more business?"

She sighed, a hand on her hip, annoyance clouding but not diminishing her features. "I don't ... if I took you to my place—"

"I'm a strange man and—"

"Well, it's not just that, but—"

"I live up the road."

"You live—" She stopped, stared at him. Shock. Shame? Homeless, she'd thought.

Lincoln nodded. "Around the corner. Not three minutes from here." He looked to his ankle. "Maybe five today. Maybe six."

"I'd need supplies."

"I have a first aid kit." Lincoln pointed down the street. "Fully stocked."

"Can you walk?"

Lincoln shifted to the hurt foot and winced. Kali's brow furrowed and her lips pressed together. Concern? Annoyance? Both? Lincoln picked up the laundry bag and grinned. "With help."

CHAPTER SIX

Lincoln was sweating by the time they made it to his building and up the three flights of stairs. "Days like this I wish I had an elevator."

Kali offered a tight-lipped smile as Lincoln reached for his key. He held it to the doorknob, but his hand shook. Kali put out her hand. "Let me."

Lincoln swallowed again. His body felt dry on the inside, like just being beside her sucked all the moisture out of it. His tongue felt like sandpaper. His clothes were soaked with the sweat of exertion and nervousness. If only he could do a pit check. At least he'd showered this morning. His deodorant boasted twenty-four-hour protection. If he stank, he should sue for false advertising.

Kali opened the door, turned to Lincoln, and offered her side to guide him into the apartment. Once inside, Lincoln dropped the laundry, hopped away from the door, and perched on the arm of the couch. Kali turned slowly then reached for Theo. Her eyes widened. Her body tensed. "This is where you live?"

Lincoln tried to see it from her eyes. Paint peeled on the

walls. Exposed plaster and spackling where some ambitious tenant must have begun the process of fixing the place up, then abandoned the effort. The floor boards were old and whorled, the wood buckling in places. But what was Lincoln supposed to do about that?

The room they were standing in was large, made more so by its barrenness. A large work table sat in the middle of the room. Saws. Planers. Scraps of wood. Branches. Attempts, on it and around it, to create models of his dream. One wall was covered with pictures. Tree houses. Dozens of them. Beautiful. Creative. Hopeful tree houses.

A record player he'd picked up at a second-hand shop sat in the corner on a milk crate full of LPs. Everything in the apartment was new ... or new to him. Nothing in the apartment was from his old life. He'd left it all in Montreal with Lucy.

He'd scavenged most of the items in the apartment; even the couch, which he'd claimed from a curb where it sat with a paper reading 'FREE' taped to it. An old-fashioned affair, it had wooden curlicue legs and a sheet covering the stains—not that Kali could see that. Lincoln's gaze travelled to the Rorschach splatter from last night's calzone on the wall under the window. That embarrassed him. Sparsity was one thing; disorder, mess, another. He'd meant to clean it. Wanted to clean it. Would have cleaned it before he'd left this morning, but Romper had been so eager.

It didn't make a good impression.

She gestured toward the pizza sauce. "That's not a lure for the rats?"

"I don't have rats."

"Mice."

"Never seen one."

Kali shook her head. "Lucky. I can't leave a crumb out." She walked to the work table, scanned its items.

"Popsicle sticks? You have a kid?"

"I'm doing models. Small scale for a larger project."

She glanced again at the tree-house-covered wall. "I see." Theo reached for a small saw. She yanked him away.

"It'll be amazing when it's done. Fully livable, winter and summer, with heat and electricity. I'm still working on plumbing."

"Plumbing?"

She took another look around the room.

"And you've lived here long or—"

"It's just a stopping place, until I, well—" He gestured to the wall of tree houses. "It's not the prettiest apartment, but I get a real steal on it. Three hundred a month."

Her head snapped toward him. "Three hundred?"

"Yeah." Lincoln shifted again. His back was starting to ache. "Could use some fixing up, but it's economical."

"I'd say." Kali rubbed a hand along her neck. "You said you have a first aid kit?"

"With the work I do," Lincoln gestured to the table, "it's important."

Her brow raised and her mouth opened, as if she were going to ask another question. He attempted to stand but she put out a hand to stop him. "Where?"

Lincoln slid off the arm and onto the couch. "In the kitchen. Second cupboard from the left." The kitchen. Clean. Tidy. But dingy, despite that. Repulsive to her eyes, most likely.

"You have an ice pack?"

"Ice cubes. And some baggies in the drawer to the right of the sink."

No response.

A moment later she entered, the kit in one hand and a baggie filled with ice in the other. A drying cloth hung from her shoulder.

She crouched in front of him but didn't make eye contact. "Has the pain improved any?"

"Not really."

She motioned for him to shift on the couch, so he could put his leg up with his ankle and foot dangling off the arm rest. Her hands were on his ankle again, assessing. Lincoln held back his winces.

"This is, uh, nice of you. I mean you didn't have to—"

"You saved my son."

"Yeah, but my dog. I mean if I hadn't been there."

"It's not your dog." Her jaw clenched again. Not the repeated movement of earlier, but more of a twitch.

"Still, thank you."

She looked up. Almost smiled. The closest he'd seen directed toward him. A muscle in his chest tightened. "You're welcome."

She reached into the kit and started wrapping his ankle. Silence surrounded them, and he could feel new beads of sweat forming, trickling down the nape of his neck. "I always thought doctor."

"What?"

"You, I always thought you were a—"

Kali's hands stopped, tensed. Her eyes scanned his. "Why … what do you mean, always?"

"I've seen you. Around. A couple of times. Once in scrubs.

48

I thought doctor."

She leaned back into a squat. "You spying on me?"

"No." Lincoln shook his head. He glanced at the boy—Theo—sitting in the corner with Romper. He'd never really noticed him. Just her. Always her. "I saw you. That's all."

"A couple of times?" Her hands relaxed. She went back to wrapping his ankle, though her movements weren't as fluid. "I've never seen you."

"You probably have. You just didn't look ... notice, you know? Most people don't."

More silence.

"When you dress like I do, I guess ..." He ran a hand over his beard.

She kept her mouth closed, her eyes on her task.

Lincoln did too, until the sound of their breathing, the cars passing outside, seemed too heavy. "He talk?"

She glanced at the boy. "He's only three."

"Only ..." Lincoln hesitated. "I'm not super familiar with kids. But he's big for his age, huh? I was thinking four. I have a nephew who's four and a niece who used to be. I don't see them a lot but—" *Stop.* "I seem to remember." *Just stop.* "I guess kids can be all different heights, right? Like adults. I mean. Of course, I guess. But there's shyness too, right? I mean because most kids are talking by three, aren't they?" *Shut up.* "Jake—my nephew—he was never shy but he had this friend, what was his name? Uh—"

She pulled the bandage tight. A meteor of pain shot up Lincoln's leg. He stopped.

She clamped the end of the bandage, tucked the makeshift ice pack around his ankle and leaned back on her haunches again. She looked at Theo, who stared right back at them, his attention drawn from the dog. "He can talk. He just doesn't. He chooses not to."

"Around strangers?"

Hands on her knees, she pushed herself up to standing. "You'll want to leave the ice on for ten to twenty minutes and reapply every couple of hours. Take the wrap off in about a day and a half."

Lincoln shifted onto his forearms. "He seems like a sweet kid. Romper doesn't let anyone touch him that long. He wouldn't let me."

Kali looked around the room, hands on hips. "Keep your foot elevated as much as you can. Especially for the rest of today and through the night. Prop some pillows up under it while you're sleeping."

Lincoln stared at her, but she didn't look at him. Wouldn't, it seemed. "I didn't mean to offend you. Lots of kids are quiet."

"Do you have crutches? Don't put any weight on your ankle for at least a few days. Three. Four, maybe." She picked up the bag she'd set on the work table. "When you start to walk, don't limp. Walk normally, even if it doesn't feel normal. That way the muscles will heal the way they're meant to."

"Is everything okay?" Lincoln glanced to Theo. "I mean—"

"You mean what?" She stepped toward him, looking ready to battle.

"Nothing." Lincoln reached forward to prop his leg up on a pillow. "So crutches, huh? Where can I get a pair of those?"

Kali's shoulders relaxed. She looked tired, suddenly. Worn. "I have a pair. My ..." she looked to Theo. "I ... they should fit." She motioned toward Theo to come. "After some errands, I could bring them over."

"You live around here?"

She nodded.

"Theo could stay if you wanted. I like kids all right."

Her shoulders tensed again. Her brows rose. "No."

Lincoln looked to Theo, whose eyes darted between Lincoln and his mother. "Yeah. I guess that'd be weird. Sorry."

"Two hours. Maybe three?"

"Sure."

"And no weight on that ankle." She leaned over and adjusted his ankle, propped the pillow against the arm of the chair, and had him scooch down so his foot was several inches higher than before.

Lincoln grinned. "Can I hop?"

Another smile, slightly bigger this time, there and gone so fast he barely saw it. "If you must, but carefully."

She lingered for a moment, her head turned to the second bedroom. The door was open, but all she'd see, Lincoln knew, was bare floor and a wall. Maybe a few dumbbells. "You live alone, then?"

"I do."

"You sleep on the couch?"

Lincoln tilted his head toward the hall. "I sleep down there. In a bed."

Her brows rose again—in surprise, envy. Not anger. "A two bedroom for three hundred?"

"It's subsidized housing. And as you can see, not the nicest place. It's not actually my place. Not according to the lease. A friend of a friend who didn't want to lose this rate, so I'm staying here for a while. Kind of keeping it for him."

Her head bobbed as she rotated in place. "You could make it nice. Nicer."

"Definitely."

She let out a noise, more of an inhale than a laugh, and stepped toward the door. "It's okay if it's unlocked?"

"Just fine."

"I'll be back in a couple of hours. I'll pop the crutches in and—"

"Maybe you could stay for dinner." What was he saying? Why was he— "I could order something. Pizza. Does Theo like pizza? Or Chinese?"

Her hand held the door. Theo was already over the threshold, but she straddled it. Her long, slender, naked fingers rapped on the wood three times. "I'll pop the crutches in and you can drop them off at Mrs. Martin's when you're done with them. I'll get them from her."

Lincoln propped himself up farther. "Sure. No problem. A day or two and—"

"You'll need them for weeks. Two at least. Don't walk without them for at least two weeks. I told you it was bad."

He stared at her.

"Do you hear me?"

He nodded.

"Okay, then." She was gone.

The apartment felt larger. Emptier. Lincoln settled back onto the couch, feeling as if his world had shifted.

CHAPTER SEVEN

Kali sat on the other side of the room, her gaze trained on Theo. His chest rose and fell, like nothing in life mattered but that. Her chest felt constricted. Twisted. Weighted. Her breath shook as she relived the moment.

Walking up the street, thoughts on how to get more shifts, how many she would need to qualify for full insurance, her need to move, her need to just do better, vanished, became nothing, as Theo tumbled in front of that car.

She placed her hand on her chest. Pushed. Harder. Harder. If she could touch the spot that ached, make it come alive, maybe it would leave her. She took a deep breath, the muscles in her arm strained with the pressure, yet the knot in the centre of her chest intensified.

She needed sleep.

But she couldn't close her eyes. Couldn't stop looking at him. He was her everything. If it hadn't been for that man ... she couldn't even think the words.

Kali rose from the chair and crossed to the bed. Theo was almost four. Too old to be sharing a bed with Mom, but she'd miss the day when she no longer felt his tiny warm body curl around her the way it did now.

Still, it wasn't right. This cramped apartment. Mould in the walls and mice, the occasional rat, scurrying along the floor so they never went barefoot. A three-year-old sharing a bed, a room, with his mother. Theo deserved painted walls with race cars or dinosaurs or balloons or whatever he wanted. He deserved a bed of his own. He deserved more than she had to give.

Kali nuzzled her face in the nape of his neck, revelling in her baby's warmth. He murmured in his sleep and she almost cried out. He could have been gone. He could have been lying in a hospital bed or in a morgue, not here with her. Two seconds, and her life, as she knew it, could have been obliterated.

Kali pulled back from the boy's neck and gazed at the ceiling. He was unnerving, that man. Odd in a way that made her wary. It wasn't just his clothes—he dressed like a homeless person—but the way he stood, despite that: Tall. Broad. Not the slumped shoulders characteristic of most men who dressed like him. He stood like he was used to being noticed. He spoke that way too, his voice deep. Resonant. The kind that pierces through walls. The type that's incapable of a whisper.

Something was off about him. His clothes, his hair, his apartment. Something was definitely off.

She'd done what she said she would when she went back with the crutches. Two knocks on the door, opened it, propped the crutches on the edge of the couch, and then vanished. She hadn't let Theo play with the dog. She'd barely looked at the man. Hadn't even asked his name.

Kali snuggled back into Theo. Morning would come too soon. Always too soon. She yearned for perpetual night, to hold Theo, safe in her arms. To let silent tears trail down her cheeks. To not have to be strong.

This hadn't been the plan: her, alone, like her mother had been. Like Kali had sworn she'd never be. Derek was supposed to be here. Supposed to cut the burdens in half and multiply the joys. That was the plan. The promise. The two of them a team. The two of them conquering the world, conquering their past. Building a future.

But he was gone.

The alarm sounded. Kali reached across Theo to turn it off, kissed his brow, and walked into her day.

"EGGS OR PANCAKES?" Kali kept her back to Theo as she stood at the counter. "Both?" No response. Kali closed her eyes, breathed. Endure, the psychologist had told her. Do the best you can. Advice her grandmother had given her countless times, but from a psychologist the words came at one hundred and fifty dollars an hour. "Maybe both, huh? After that big day we had yesterday, you must be ravenous." Use big words. Exciting words. Words that prompt curiosity.

Silence.

"Theo?"

If he has to communicate, he'll find a way. The psychologist looked so superior as she said those words. Like it was simple. *I know you mean well, but you coddle him. He doesn't need to talk because you talk for him.*

"Theo, honey, what—" Kali's voice cut off at the tug on her pant leg. Theo stood. Smiling. He held up two fingers. 'What does that mean?' she was supposed to say. 'Eggs or Pancakes?' She was supposed to force him to communicate. Show him the need. But that smile. Those eyes. So trusting. So open. Full of love. He *wasn't* doing this to be difficult. He had his reasons. He had to have his reasons. "Both, honey?"

Theo nodded, his smile growing even larger. He squeezed her side then retreated to his Lego table in the corner. It was second hand, of course. Missing some of the key pieces—a barn door, the roof on several vehicles, the panes for a windmill. Not that he cared. He clapped his hands when she had brought it home. Hugged her twice. Squatted before it, the way he was now, with elbows on knees, chin on hands, assessing.

At least the psychologist was smart enough to see Theo's lack of speech had nothing to do with his intelligence. Not like the daycare who forced him out, saying he wasn't developed enough to keep up with the other kids.

Monsters, the lot of them. Kali turned back to the counter and reached for the flour. That last day she'd found Theo in the corner. Crying. Shaking. The staff had been elusive, tiptoeing around the truth. But Kali knew the eyes of a mocked child, a tormented child.

Theo might be sensitive, but he wasn't stupid. And neither was she.

While the pancakes sizzled in the pan Kali put on gloves and went to check the rat traps. She had them in cupboards in the kitchen, bathroom, and hall closet—all places with child locks on them. The last thing she wanted was Theo seeing more death. More trauma, even of vermin.

The first time she'd checked the traps she'd gagged, ran to the toilet, and lost her breakfast. The mice made her sad. The rats made her sick. She didn't even bother with mouse traps anymore. They weren't such a big deal. But rats? Dangerous. Disgusting. Unacceptable.

The muscles in Kali's shoulders went rigid as she opened the cupboard under the kitchen sink.

Nothing.

She travelled to the bathroom next. Clear. At the hall closet her chest tightened. She opened the door. Bile rose in her throat, but she knew better now—check the traps before breakfast. This was the fifth rat in seven days. She squinted her eyes shut, clamped her lips closed, and reached.

"Theo, baby, stay at the table till Mommy says." No response, of course, but he'd heard her. Kali released the body, used a bag to pick it up, reversed it, and knotted it off. She then dropped that bag in another, knotting it off as well. She couldn't have this in her home any longer ... Not that this was a home.

Kali reset the trap and closed the hall door, making sure the child protective knob was doing its job, then ran out of her apartment and down the steps to the large communal dumpster out back. She threw the rat in, anger growing and bubbling with each new step.

What if one of these disgusting creatures crawled over her son in the night? Bit her son? She cleaned constantly—scouring the counters, the tables, everything the vermin could touch and infect. It was new for her. She'd never been an obsessive cleaner, and she hated it. But if one of them infected Theo. Bit Theo. Anything.

Kali stopped outside her apartment door and braced her head against it. Guilt settled in her gut for leaving her baby inside. Alone. Even for these few minutes. Guilt grew at the reason why.

She needed to talk to that jackass of a landlord again. He knew about the mould. He knew about the rats. He promised he'd do something.

But three weeks now since she'd seen the first rat. Five since she first told him about the mould—prompted by the burst pipe in the apartment above, the one she'd used to live in. And still nothing.

Remembering the pancakes, Kali rushed inside. A little darker than she'd like, but not burnt. Theo looked up when she entered, his smile serene.

"Almost ready!" she called, her voice falsely bright. "I hope you're hungry, Mister."

CHAPTER EIGHT

After dropping Theo off at Mrs. Martin's, Kali made her way to the bus stop. If she'd been more organized this morning, more efficient, she could have walked. This time of day she preferred the walk over the crowded bus, the forced interactions, the smiles she didn't feel like giving. Not that she had to smile, but inevitably some older person would strike up a conversation or look like they needed one. And Kali couldn't be the one to disappoint the day of someone who had few days left.

At the hospital, Kali checked her room assignments. Four at the moment. All occupied. She took the few minutes before the current nurse left to ensure all her rooms were fully stocked: suctions, CPR supplies, O2 working, and the list went on. Next, she familiarized herself with the patient charts. Kali sighed. Most days she felt ready for her shift—proud in advance of the difference she'd make. Today, though, she already felt wiped.

Yesterday's fear crept over her again. If that stranger hadn't been fast enough, had been distracted by a bird, a plane, had slow reflexes ...

"Morning."

Kali turned to Shelley, her shift supervisor and friend since grade school. The only person Kali regularly spoke to from her days in North Preston.

"Morning."

"Doing all right? You look run over."

Run over. Kali twitched at the term. "Good. Little tired. More rats this morning. Well, a rat."

"You have got to get that landlord of yours in gear. Or move. Why don't you just move?"

"I know." Kali pushed out a smile, regretting she'd said anything at all. "I should." Just move. Like it was easy. Simple. It would be for Shelley. When you have a husband with a full-time job, a full-time job yourself, and two sets of grandparents practically fighting to take care of your child, life was easier.

"Many shifts this week?"

"Three."

Shelley made a tut-tut noise. "Don't know how you manage. Still no luck on a new daycare? I mean we need you here. You're one of my best gals. I could get you full-time hours. Easy."

"No luck on daycare. You know that wouldn't cover twelve-hour shifts anyway."

Shelley nodded. "But Mrs. Martin, she could—"

"Any interesting cases this morning?"

Shelley scrunched her lips. "A few." Her expression softened. "There's a sweet old lady in room eight. Came in with complaints of heart palpitations, though she seemed more stressed than anything, and now she's worried about her dog at home alone. Says usually her daughter would watch it but she's on vacation or something. Gene has her, but you know Gene. Mind if I switch her room to you?" Shelley thought for a moment. "I'll give Gene the man with killer indigestion." She laughed. "Though his gas is the only thing that's killer."

"Sure." Kali set down the chart she was holding and headed for the next room. "I'll take her."

"Hi, there." Kali approached the woman with heart palpitations. She looked small in the hospital bed, which was saying something. The beds weren't big. A thin down of white hair covered the woman's head. Her eyes were shrouded by drooping lids, but Kali could almost see the woman she used to be. Regal. Poised. Or at least appearing so. "How are you feeling?"

"Flustered." The woman gave a little sigh. She raised her hands and let them fall gracefully. "It isn't pleasant, you know, to be out of one's comfort zone."

"It isn't." Kali approached the bed. "How are your pillows? All right?"

"I suppose, yes. Everything is all right. Everyone has been very kind."

Kali checked the woman's temperature.

"But I have a dog, you see? Sweet little Pomeranian. Do you know what I'm talking about?"

"Mmmhmm." Kali had no clue, but if she revealed that she'd be in the room for an hour. She took the woman's pulse.

"Ten years I've had her, so she's not the youngest."

So far all was well. Next, blood pressure. "But she is just the sweetest. And she needs me, you see. She's never away from me more than a few hours. It's silly, I know."

The image of the rat flooded Kali's vision. Its little tongue.

Its disgusting little tongue had been hanging out. Its eyes bulged. She hated killing it but hated more that it was in her apartment. Walking the same floorboards as Theo. As her.

"I sometimes even take her out with me. In my purse. Like in the movies."

Kali set the cuff aside. She smiled. "I bet she loves that."

"Oh, she does. She's just tickled by it. She pops her little head out and looks around. I imagine she feels like royalty. Like Cleopatra on her litter."

Kali checked the woman's respiratory rate next. Her chest tightened at the thought of talking to her landlord. He'd already moved her once, and that had taken some convincing. Would he have another apartment? What would getting pest control even mean? Could they stay in the apartment during it, and how long would it take? Mrs. Martin had no space for them. She'd squeeze them in perhaps, if she had to. But Kali couldn't inconvenience the woman more than a night. Maybe two. Shelley? Shelley was her boss, or practically. Shelley's life was full of her child and her husband and both sets of grandparents stepping in and out. Kali and Theo would be in the way.

Kali stifled a yawn and rubbed her eyes. She shouldn't be here after a sleepless night. Not that she'd make a mistake. She wouldn't let herself make a mistake. But still.

"I can't carry her too often anymore, though." The woman's voice lowered. "I get tired."

"I'm sure she's happy just to be with you." Kali rested a hand on the woman's arm. All her vitals were sound. A quick visit from the doctor and she should be on her way. "It sounds like she's lucky to have you."

"Oh, no." The woman smiled; the creases in her lined face

deepened. "I'm lucky to have her. She was a gift, you know. From my Harold. Two weeks before he died."

The woman looked to her lap. "It was like he knew. But he had a heart attack. He couldn't have known." She looked up. "But still, we hadn't had a dog in years. Not since the kids were in the house. But then he comes home with this little toy of a puppy. He would never have wanted a dog like that. He liked big dogs. Labs. Retrievers. The type of dog you could rough-house with in the backyard." She paused, looking at a life, a world, Kali couldn't see. "The pup was for me. So I wouldn't be so alone. I think he knew."

"He may have." Kali perched on the edge of the bed—she shouldn't. She was done in here. But a few moments wouldn't hurt. "Has he been gone long?"

"Well," the woman paused, "ten years. Ten years today, actually."

Kali's throat closed. Right, because the dog was ten years old. She squeezed the woman's hand again. "I'm sorry. This is a hard day for you."

"Ten years." The woman laughed. "It probably seems like forever to you, but to me it's a blink. I was with him for fifty-five years. I still wake up and expect him to be there. Still start to set out a second cup for tea." Her voice lowered. "Lie awake at night and wish for his arm to wander over, rest against me." The woman blushed. She waved a hand in front of her face. "Silly."

"No."

"The delusions of an old lady, someone the world has no use for anymore."

Kali rubbed the woman's wrist, her skin frail, like paper. Like her grandmother's had been. "Your daughter has use for you."

"I'm a burden. She wants to put me in a home."

"You have grandchildren?"

She nodded. "Great-grandchildren too. But they're all so busy. They get shifty. Uncomfortable around me. They yell, as if I can't hear. I hear fine." She paused. "I remind them of their mortality. They want to believe they'll live forever."

Live forever? No. Kali would slip away today if it weren't for Theo.

But that wasn't true. Not really. Though some days, days like today, it seemed a simple solution to the questions she had no answers for. "Well, I'm glad you're here. Not every patient is as sweet as you." Kali stood. Others were waiting. "And that Pomeranian. Think of how eager she'll be to have you back home."

"I'm all right?" The woman's eyes looked young. They searched Kali's. Fear and hope and trust.

Kali gave the woman her sweetest hospital smile. "I'll have a doctor check in on you, but I think you'll be on your way soon."

She nodded. Not relief, but resignation in her eyes. "Well, that's good then."

Kali returned the nod and left the room. A Pomeranian she carried in her purse. A child and grandchildren who had no need of her ... or at least gave that impression. An apartment that was home to rats and mould. A son who wouldn't speak. A husband who left too soon. Nights spent staring at the ceiling, wishing, hoping, and not always knowing what for. All these troubles in the world.

Kali shook her head. She didn't have time for sad, meandering thoughts.

As she approached her next room, a commotion erupted from the ER entrance. Kali rushed toward the sound. "MVA," Shelley yelled. "Three vehicles. Ten passengers. At least three critical. Let's go."

Kali swallowed. Her blood rushed. Her senses heightened. That old lady wouldn't keep her bed for long. Kali scanned the injured being rushed in. At least two children. One hollering, the other staring, wide-eyed. Both covered in blood. Theirs? Or that of the motionless woman rolled in after them?

All thoughts aside. Time to work.

CHAPTER NINE

L incoln stood at the work table. Two days, and the pain hadn't lessened. He puffed out a long string of air and clenched his jaw. Ten minutes he'd been here. Ten measly minutes, without even putting weight on his ankle, yet the ache grew and throbbed. Blood seemed to rush to the area, pool there. The intensity of it made his stomach turn. He straightened and his back screamed in protest, the pain rivalling the throb of his ankle. The woman hadn't lied. The sprain was bad. Worse than he'd realized. Two weeks without walking? Without building? Without heading to the lot? He'd go crazy.

Lincoln picked up the Popsicle stick model he'd been working on and threw it across the room.

Damn.

Now that would have to be cleaned too. He looked to the calzone remnants under the window. Romper had clearly decided Lincoln's command had an expiry date. Most of the bits on the floor were gone, but smears of sauce mixed with saliva in the grooves between the wood flooring and along the wall were still there. He needed to tackle it. Getting on and off the couch was hard enough. Getting on his hands and knees to scrub? Not yet.

And his back. Lincoln braced his hands on the table, careful not to put pressure where the skin had been scraped off. How he managed that he didn't even know. In the moment before he'd cradled the boy? That must have been it. The left hand was worse. He must have braced himself then curled.

Romper looked up with sad eyes. Bored eyes. Lincoln had managed to get down and back up the three flights of stairs twice each day. He directed Romper to do his business on the patch of lawn in front of the building, and Lincoln went no farther. Romper acquiesced, surprisingly. As a reward, Lincoln let the dog run up and down the street for several minutes while Lincoln perched on the steps, always calling the dog back when he strayed too far. Guilt plagued Lincoln as Romper cocked his head. The dog knew something was wrong. He must. Otherwise he'd be letting his frustration known in a much more aggressive manner. But still, he wasn't pleased. Each time Lincoln called him back he returned with reproach in his eyes.

Lincoln looked again at Romper. Was it normal to notice an animal's emotions like this? Or just lack of having a person's to notice?

He could let the dog keep running past the corner, let him stretch his legs. What was that saying? About letting someone go to see if they would come back? Well, Lincoln wasn't giving Romper the chance. If he didn't come back ... it wasn't something worth thinking about it.

The couch looked miles away. Not that the couch was great either. It meant lying on the deepest bruise he'd ever had. Two days.

Why hadn't Kali thought to bring him some painkillers? His First Aid Kit was lacking in that department. Had she checked his cupboard? Seen the small amount of food he had? Shouldn't she be worried?

Lincoln settled atop his crutches. He needed groceries. He needed meds. He needed to know this was just a sprain, that his back was no more than bruised.

Three options. Option one: Head across the harbour and make an appointment with his family doctor—who he hadn't seen in at least five years. But he didn't have a phone. And in that waiting room, he could see someone he knew. Someone who, if he sat across from them long enough, might see beneath the unkempt hair and tattered clothes.

Option two: Head to a walk-in clinic nearby. He couldn't think where any were, didn't know the hours, and couldn't look it up. He didn't have a computer. So that would require going to the library. But it was Monday. The library was closed. He could walk around aimlessly until he found a clinic. More time on these crutches. More time with his foot dangling, his blood pooling.

Option three: The ER. He knew where it was. He could take a bus there. It was always open. That was the reason to go. The option that worked.

In his mind's eye, he saw her again, the way she pushed open the door, brought the crutches in, said nothing, started to leave. His question stopped her but she dismissed it a second time, as if even the prospect angered her. Was it that outrageous? To come for dinner. To spend some time with an injured man. Was he that repulsive?

Lincoln stepped to the door and shook his head at Romper.

No dogs at the hospital. No dogs on the bus ... most likely. He actually didn't know the rule about that one. But no dogs in the hospital for sure.

Lincoln brought a book to the ER but didn't read it. Nausea coursed through him after the bus ride, as if he'd been on a rolling sea. In the ER waiting area, with sick and moaning people around him, it didn't fade. The nurse who did his intake assessment didn't seem impressed with his presence. Is this how the woman, Kali, that was her name, would have treated him, looked at him, scrunched up her nose at him?

"This happened three days ago?"

He nodded, noting the people travelling up and down the hall behind him.

"And you're just coming in now?"

He faced the woman, who seemed a few years younger than him. "My back seems to be getting worse, not better. And the sprain, if it is a sprain, seems exceptionally bad."

She raised one eyebrow.

"I've sprained my ankle before. It wasn't like this."

"It does look pretty nasty. You probably twisted it before. A sprain takes a while to—"

"Is Kali in? Kali said it was a grade two sprain."

"You've been in already?"

"No." Lincoln, whose gaze had wandered again, brought his focus back to the nurse in front of him. "She was there."

The woman appraised him, looking top to bottom. Looking, it seemed, for the first time. "You're a friend of Kali's?"

"No."

Another brow raise. "She was there. When the car hit

me."

"You were hit by a car?"

"I jumped in front of it to—"

"Sir?" She straightened. Reached a hand out—seeming confused and concerned. "Do you need to talk to someone? I must—"

"No. No." Lincoln waved his hands. "It wasn't like that. Kali's boy fell in front of the car. You see my dog saw this cat and—"

The woman set down her clipboard. "You jumped in front of a car to save Theo?"

Lincoln smiled. "You know Theo?"

"Yes, I ..." She waved a hand and glanced at the hall behind. "You saved Theo? Oh my God."

She glanced at the hall behind her again, looking angry. "Is he all right? Theo?"

"Not a scrape."

"Good. Well ..." she turned back to Lincoln. "As much as I'd like to progress things, you're going to have a wait. There are people here who—"

"That's fine. I expected that."

She tapped the clipboard on her lap. "Should I tell Kali you're here?"

"I ..." Lincoln hesitated. "I just came to get my back checked out. Make sure no real damage was done. I didn't mention it to Kali at the time. Didn't notice."

"The adrenaline."

"So she said."

The woman smiled now. Softened. "Are you sure? She's on for another hour."

Lincoln shook his head. "I don't know her. If she wanted

to check up on me she knows where to find me."

The woman stood. "We'll get you in to see a doctor as soon as we can."

"Any pain killers?"

The woman clenched her clipboard. Her lips tightened.

"Even Ibuprofen? I didn't have any at home and—"

"Three days?" The woman tutted.

"I live alone. Three flights up."

The same look of surprise crossed her face that had crossed Kali's. Did he look that bad? Lots of men had beards, unkempt beards even ... but maybe not the clothes. Maybe not the stink. That twenty-four-hour protection was forty-eight hours expired.

The nurse took a breath. "I'll see what I can do."

Lincoln picked up his crutches and returned to the waiting room. He eased into his seat. He shouldn't have mentioned the accident, mentioned Kali. He didn't come here for her. He came for the doctor. For drugs. For peace of mind. That was all.

PEOPLE FILTERED IN AND out of the waiting room, some obviously in a worse state than Lincoln, others not.

Every time someone came from the hall beyond, Lincoln raised his gaze, hoping. He wouldn't say he was attracted to Kali. Was he? More intrigued. Captivated. As if she weren't a person, a woman to pursue—not that he wanted to pursue her, he was done with all that. Rather, he felt drawn, like a moth to a flame—as ridiculous as that sounded—like her existence in the world meant maybe this globe we spun on wasn't all that bad. With her in it, maybe it couldn't be.

But even that. She'd come into his apartment. Helped him. Begrudgingly. He'd saved her son—inadvertently caused the reason to be saved, true. But still, he'd saved Theo. Risked his life. Injured himself. Was sitting here in this waiting room days later because he'd saved her son and yet she'd treated him like an inconvenience—couldn't wait to get out of his presence. Simply because he looked like he did? Because his apartment wasn't dripping with Ikea? Because he was broken?

Lincoln shifted in his seat. A baby wailed across from him. A man with his arm wrapped in bloody bandages sat a few seats over. A young girl curled into her father's chest, whimpering softly.

Lincoln had a long wait ahead of him.

Only he didn't. Forty-five minutes later the same nurse who'd taken his information called his name, ushered him down a hall, and directed him to sit in another small waiting area.

"Only a few minutes now." She smiled.

Lincoln nodded. From where he sat he could see another open area. A staff room of some kind. And there was Kali. She picked up a satchel and slung it over her shoulder. She wasn't in scrubs, but in old jeans stuffed into those combat boots of hers, a red top and a type of headphones he hadn't seen in years. No sleek ear buds for her. These things were massive. These things would drown out the world.

When she turned his way he raised his hand, stupidly. She saw him, he was sure she saw him, but she looked away. That same haughty look she'd worn when she first gave in to taking him to his apartment, and later when she'd returned with the crutches.

Lincoln swallowed, anger brimming. Not at her, of course. At himself. He shouldn't have told the nurse about them. She, like all the others, was not worth his time. Not even worth his thoughts.

Lincoln put his head back. See the doctor. Find out what was wrong. Get some pills. Do whatever physio or rehab he'd have to do to get better. Get back to the plan. That's what he needed. What he wanted. Before this accident, before these hours with nothing to focus on but the pain, he hadn't thought about Kali. Noticed her, sure, but then she'd leave his thoughts, leave his mind, until the next encounter.

Once he was working again, that's all she'd be. Something beautiful to notice, like a sunset. Or a raging storm.

The boy filtered into his mind's eye. She'd been so close-mouthed about him. Angry. Defensive. He was sweet. Quiet and shy, sure, but intelligence swam behind his eyes. A knowing. Could there be something wrong with him? Lincoln's throat tightened. Had something happened to him? Some man ...?

Lincoln suspected Kali was single. Was it for a specific reason? He'd never seen her with a man ... except the once. No way was she with that man, though, old enough to be her father. Worse off than Lincoln. But then he'd never noticed the boy before either. Perhaps, like he accused so many others of, he just didn't see.

His fist clenched at the thought of someone hurting that boy. Hurting her in the process.

"Lincoln Fraser?"

CHAPTER TEN

Lincoln raised his head at the sound of his name. A man stood across from him. "Lincoln, that you? What happened?"

"Brady?"

"Yeah, man." Brady put out his hand. Lincoln eased himself up and took it.

"You're a doctor?"

"Just about. Still putting in my hours to make it official." Brady dropped his hand. "But basically."

"Congrats."

"Ha." Brady paused. "Word on the street was you were living the life in Montreal. Heading one of your old man's offices or something."

"I was. Yeah."

Brady cocked his head. "Like that? No offence, man. But is that what corporate looks like these days?"

"I've switched directions."

"Switched directions?" Brady cleared his throat. "Saw your brother last week. Now he looked corporate."

"Corporate as they come."

Brady stared at him a moment before looking at his clipboard. Brady. Class clown. Royal screw up. Doctor. "So, I heard you jumped in front of a moving vehicle?"

"Yep."

"To save a kid? Kali's kid."

He knew her. Of course he knew her. "Uh huh."

"That's some heroic shit. You get a little?"

Lincoln flinched. His lip curled.

"I'm joking, man. She's not giving it to anyone, ever, from what I hear."

Lincoln leaned on his crutch and made a show of rubbing his back.

Brady glanced at the clipboard again. "Well, people are waiting, right? So, you've got the ankle and complaints of severe back pain. The car hit your back?"

Lincoln nodded.

"And you didn't come in that day? She didn't make you come in?"

"I didn't notice the back so much. My ankle was worse and," Lincoln hesitated, "shock, I guess."

"Yeah. All right. And the back's bad?"

"Worse than anything I've ever felt."

Brady turned and waved Lincoln to follow. "Let's get you into an exam room. I'll check out the ankle first and then the back." He looked back and grinned. "Seeing as you're an old pal and a hero, I may even send you for an MRI. Make sure everything's all hunky dory. If I don't and you continue to have intense pain you'll have to go through your doctor, which means the normal channels, normal wait. Three to four months at least."

"Sure, uh, thanks."

Two hours later, Lincoln was on his way with a filled prescription for painkillers. Brady warned him not to take them while operating any machinery and gave him directions not to walk on his ankle for at least another two weeks and then, as Kali had said, only walk as much as he could normally. No limping.

As to his back, the MRI revealed nothing but intense bruising. Lincoln hobbled away from the pharmacy. Once outside he stopped to take his first pill.

It'd been too long since he'd been lying down and the pain radiated all the way up his leg. The thought of those steps at home, of another night of ravioli or peanut butter on toast ... he clenched his jaw and opened the pill bottle while balancing on his crutches. He popped a pill and swallowed hard, then clamped the bottle shut and balanced on his crutches to get the bottle into his pants pocket.

Damn it.

Lincoln watched the bottle fall, bounce, and roll between the passing feet. His eyes burned and watered. This was shit. Absolute shit. How would he navigate? How would he get down the street, bend low enough to reach the bottle, and get back up again? And why was the hospital entrance so busy? Had every person in the city taken sick?

An oblivious passerby knocked the bottle with the toe of his shoe. The container bounced and rolled further away, landing perilously on the curb.

That pharmacist would never give him another bottle. She'd think he was an addict. She had already looked at him with shifty eyes. And Brady? He'd believe him, hopefully, but it would mean hours of waiting again. And what if he wasn't on shift?

Lincoln gritted his teeth and hobbled onto the sidewalk, his gaze glued to the pill bottle. Mother. The thought washed over him. The sight of her materialized in his mind. Here he was, a twenty-seven-year-old man, and what he wanted was his mother. His mother to scurry ahead, pick up the pill bottle, place a warm hand to his cheek, then usher him into her car and take him home, to the home he grew up in, the room he grew up in. She'd prop him up on pillows in his old bed and smooth his cheek once more.

She would too. Probably. Maybe. If he'd ask.

Lincoln weaved his way into the throng of people. Heartless, the lot of them. Blind. Couldn't they see he was struggling? These people were here to visit some other infirm soul or had become one themselves, and yet they—a woman bent ahead of him, her hand clasping the bottle. She was pudgy. The type of woman who, though not fat, probably spent her life perpetually trying to lose weight. She turned. Her face was blotchy. Plain. But angelic.

"These yours?" She smiled up at Lincoln.

"Yes, um. Yeah. Thank you."

"No problem." Her head tilted. "You all right?"

"Yeah. Sure. Fine."

She looked at him a moment longer. "Okay. Well, keep a grip on those!" She turned and continued toward the street. Lincoln clenched his fist around the bottle, the skin over his knuckles tight, and slid it into his pocket. He turned toward the bus stop and watched the one he needed drive by. He closed his eyes. He could get a cab. But that would require a phone. There were no pay phones anymore. Would some shop owner let him make a call? A hospital receptionist? Maybe.

He could wait and try to flag a cab down. Would it stop? Trust he'd pay? And for what? A five-minute drive, maybe less. Waiting for a cab, paying for a cab, would be stupid.

He tugged on his beard and glanced at the crowd of people milling around in front of the bus stop. Eight months ago he would have felt comfortable asking any of them to let him make a call. Not that he would have needed to. Of course he wouldn't have needed to. His phone had been attached to him like a limb.

He searched down the street for the woman who had stopped to help him. Long gone.

He scanned the faces within a ten-foot radius. No one made eye contact. One woman who'd been looking at him averted her gaze. Not meanly so, but uncomfortably. Nervously. As if she cared but not enough to offer help. As if she feared he'd ask for money and she'd have to make a decision—be kind and potentially feed a habit, be dismissive and turn away from someone who genuinely needed her.

He got it. He'd been there. Been that person. His shoulders slumped over his crutches—as they always did. He'd walk home. That was simplest. The painkillers would kick in soon. They had to. Then he'd be home. He'd lay back, maybe even take another pill, turn on some music and forget today.

Or no. He'd remember today. Remember the reason to get away. Leave the tribe. Escape. Cleanly. Perfectly.

Lincoln crossed the street and headed onto Trollope. Trollope. He'd never noticed the name of the street until he lived in the area. He bet the nearby high school students got a kick out of that.

A group of runners sprinted by. How long till he could run

like that again? Weeks? Months? Not that he'd been running much. He needed to get back to that ... when he could.

Just past the oval, Lincoln noticed one of the local bottle collectors. He stopped. Someone stood opposite him. Same satchel, same boots, same ridiculously large headphones. Kali.

She looked at the man tenderly, the same way she had last time Lincoln had seen her with him. She passed him something. The man, shoulders slumped even more than Lincoln's, took it. Kali kept talking. The man nodded, his head down, not looking at her. She laughed and the man looked up. Kali's smile softened. She raised a hand and placed it on the side of the man's face, just the way Lincoln had yearned his mother would put her hand to his face.

She hugged the man. Wrapped her arms around him and clung tight. He stood more rigid than he had before, arms at his side, face scrunched and averted as if she were hurting him. She stepped away and he must have said something; Kali nodded, looking sad, resigned almost. Suddenly she seemed the child, he the parent. She nodded. She smiled again—softer this time, put a hand on the man's shoulder, patted it, and said one last thing before walking past, straight toward the crosswalk ahead of Lincoln.

Lincoln backed up, shading himself behind a tree, and watched her go. Stride, really. He looked back to the man who was behind his cart now, pushing it in the opposite direction.

So it wasn't a fluke, a random occurrence the night several weeks ago when Lincoln had seen her in the park sitting with the man, by all appearances sharing a meal. Lincoln had assumed it was a random act of kindness. She'd been coming home with takeaway perhaps, seen him there and in a moment of compassion offered her meal. Lincoln had been surprised, but pleased. It added to the intrigue.

This added too, but in a different way. Not that it mattered.

He would get through these next few weeks, return the crutches, and get back to work. That was what mattered. That was the only thing that could matter.

CHAPTER ELEVEN

The next morning, life feeling bearable again thanks to the pills, Lincoln braved the shower. He couldn't stand without the crutches or bracing himself against the shower wall, and he couldn't exactly wash his hair with his hand against the wall, so the shower turned into an awkward half-bath affair, with the water streaming down around him. He couldn't work, and was tired of fiddling at the work table, so he grabbed his books. When his brain couldn't handle any more reading, he dropped the books to the floor and reached for Romper's leash. He took him for a walk, a decent walk, which ended at the library. Cheryl tutted as he walked in, full of concern. He smiled.

"My secret."

"Lincoln."

"Does it make me look pathetic?"

She nodded. He smiled again, then propelled himself to a computer. Figuring out the solar energy was the trickiest part for him. The rest he had some experience with, but wiring a house using only solar energy? And with the number of cloudy days this part of the world experienced, weeks could go by without any significant sunlight. Tricky, indeed. His options were some mechanism to store up the energy long term, or use some kind of generator—which, from what he knew, meant an alternative power source that would need to be replenished. Not an option he wanted to consider.

He could rely on wind power. This province had enough wind. But in the woods? It would mean clearing more land, setting up ... whatever had to be set up to get the power inside, and, from the little he knew, regulatory permits he'd rather not deal with.

So research was needed. Maybe this time of rest, time to let his mind work instead of his body, was a good thing. Better than rushing ahead, making mistakes that would be costly or difficult to fix. That was the attitude. That was the mindset to hold.

Without the intense pain, the crutches weren't too bad. Awkward, but not awful. And he could go at a decent pace too, without every attempted step sending spasms of torture through his back. Needing a break, Lincoln chuckled as he used the crutches to swing his body forward rather than simply walk with them. Was he high? He might be high. Outside the library, Lincoln gave Romper a nod. He should have taken him back to the apartment. He might be inside a few hours more. But the kids who made the library their second home would keep an eye on him, stand in defence if anyone came around vexed that the dog was allowed to roam free. Hey, one of the kids now! Lincoln waved. The kid waved back. What a good kid.

When did he take his pill? Just before he left. And at breakfast. And one when he woke up. Oops. Yep, he may be a little bit high.

Anyway, Romper wouldn't roam. He'd stay near the lawn like he always did. Content to be outside. Content to relax. So long as there weren't any cats. Lincoln scanned the area before heading back inside. Let there be no cats.

"Lincoln." Cheryl came out from around the circulation desk. "Are you okay, darling? I asked around, heard about the accident. Kids. Reckless."

"It wasn't the kid's fault. Romper—."

"Yes. Yes." Cheryl placed a hand on Lincoln's arm. "You all right, though, honey?"

Lincoln shrugged. "A few weeks."

Cheryl tutted. "Can I grab anything for you?"

Lincoln tilted his head to the computers. "Back to the grind."

Cheryl wrapped her arms around her middle. "Well, you raise your arm if you need anything or tell one of the children. Anything at all."

Lincoln nodded again.

Cheryl's expression transitioned to its usual semi-gruffness. "And be more careful, would you? Jumping out in front of cars." She winked. "You hero, you."

At the computer, Lincoln noticed the date. Tuesday. The second Tuesday of the month. Maybe he hadn't had a pill at breakfast. Maybe that was yesterday. Maybe he was just giddy to be out of the house, giddy to not be in such pain.

He let the cursor hover around the navigation bar. He'd come here to research, but he didn't feel so much like researching anymore, and it was the second Tuesday of the month. He navigated to Gmail. Outside of newsletters and advertisements, there were only four new messages. One from Andrew, sent before his visit. One from his sister, Rachel, probably for the same reason, and two from his mother.

Lincoln ignored the two from his cousin and sister. He knew essentially what they'd say. They could wait. But he opened the oldest one from his mother.

News of his father. Stable. He'd had a painting lesson that week and seemed to enjoy it. He was still carving. Nothing personal. Nothing about Joseph or his sisters. Next came the questions: How was he? Where was he? When was he coming home? After that, she loved him. Never forget that she loved him.

Having a second email was odd. His mother knew by now he wrote once a month. No more. No less. And she was good at waiting for that response. He let his hand hover, then clicked.

Lincoln,

Don't worry. No big news. No bad news. It's me who's worried about you. I know I shouldn't be, but a month is a long time. Longer for a mother than a son. Age seems to creep up on me lately. Oh, I'm not complaining. It could be far worse, couldn't it? But sixty soon. In some ways, I'm still a young woman. Or feel like one. In other ways, not. This week was one of those 'nots'.

I felt like some old sage, burdened with the knowledge of the universe. That knowledge was telling me things weren't okay. That you were in trouble or pain. That you needed me. Foolish? Am I a silly old woman making up things to worry about? Maybe. Hopefully.

I know your message is coming soon. I'm angry these are the rules you've established.

Let me know you're okay. As okay as you're capable of

being right now. And if you're not, remember I'm your mother. Remember that doesn't change.

Mom

Lincoln read the letter again. He was a bad son. He knew that. It'd been Joseph who betrayed him. Not his mother. And what was she supposed to do, abandon one son in defence of the other? She loved them both, she said, would be there for them both.

It was Lincoln who had abandoned her.

Still, the fact that Joseph sat across from her for family dinners, Lucy too most likely, and his mother allowed it, felt like betrayal.

And yet she'd known, felt his yearning for her that day. Threads that couldn't be broken.

Lincoln wrote a cheery letter. Last time he wrote he'd been travelling Europe. He was still there, he said, he'd just entered Italy. The Colosseum was amazing. She should really try to get there one day. He'd gotten a wretched sunburn. Perhaps that was the pain she sensed?

Lincoln stared at the keyboard. Why was he doing this? To protect her, or him? He continued. He wasn't sure how much longer he'd be travelling. He had the bug, though. When he returned to Nova Scotia, if he returned to Nova Scotia, she'd be the first to know.

He was playing a dangerous game. Joseph had walked by him last week. Lucy had seen him, he was sure. And Brady? Brady had run into Joseph recently. He could again, and if he did, certainly he'd mention he'd treated Lincoln. Maybe he already had. Maybe his mother knew. Maybe she played her own games of deception.

He missed her, he said. He loved her. He was glad to hear Dad found something new to enjoy. Was she doing all right? Was she taking enough time for herself? He knew she needed to visit Dad, but she needed her own time as well. Her own interests.

Lincoln stopped.

He'd been happy once. She'd been happy. They all had. Their whole family. And then in one moment, with one diagnosis, it'd fallen apart. And it kept on falling. Piece by piece. Long before Joseph and Lucy. Long before Lincoln forgot who he was and who he wanted to be.

Well, he wrote, he had to get going. The hostel charged by the minute for internet. But she should be happy for him, not worried. He was building so many memories. This trip, this change, it was the best thing for him.

He ended the email with love. He meant it too. Not all his words were lies.

A little boy with dreads ran by outside. Lincoln snapped to attention, waiting for the boy to turn, though he knew before he did that it wasn't Theo. Too tall. A little too broad. Yet Kali and Theo filled his thoughts once more. He wanted to know their story. Where was the boy's father? Who was the bottle collector? Why didn't the child talk?

Kali looked like a tower of strength. Maybe that was the appeal, when Lincoln, so often, felt weak.

The teens on either side of Lincoln both scrolled through Facebook feeds. Lincoln hadn't signed into his account since he left Montreal: an essential part of separating himself from the life he'd known.

He navigated to the site now. He felt like his sixteen-year-old cousin searching out a girl on Facebook. No, he wasn't sixteen. Nineteen now? Twenty ... three. Twenty-three. Lincoln should have known that. He did know it. When was the last time he'd spent time with the kid? Before Lincoln graduated undergrad, probably. Before he had become one-track minded about pursuing a life of success.

Lincoln didn't want to access his account, so he typed Kali's name into the public search function. Dozens of faces appeared, but most of the names had her name in a bracket at the end. Some term of endearment or nickname, perhaps? The others were variations. Kahlil, Kalincy, Kalid. And the site wouldn't let him see more than one page of results.

He glanced to either side of him again. The teens were engaged with their screens, not looking to see who he was creeping. He typed in his account information and, with a feeling like a kick to his stomach, signed in.

His feed flooded with images. A sickening amount of notifications and messages waited. He ignored them all and typed in her name again. Surely they'd have some friend in common. Brady, even. Facebook would recognize that, know who he was searching for.

And it did.

Lincoln took a breath. Her. Head and shoulders. Face turned away from the camera. It was literal ... her in profile. He could see no features, just that silhouette. But it was her ... the tilt of her head, the line of her neck, screaming defiance. He'd know that line anywhere. Her. Closed off. Inaccessible. Looking away from him. From everyone. It couldn't be anyone but her. But who was she looking at? Or what?

Lincoln clicked on the image, hoping to see more, but she only had that one picture. His eye roamed to her cover photo. A small moment of beauty—an icicle on a railing. Her news feed was empty but for cover photo updates: A piece of trash next to a flower. The Halifax harbour shrouded in mist. No pictures of her. None of Theo. All the images artsy, almost angry. Not as if they were taken to display, but to confront. Here. Look. See.

He smiled. As much as he wanted a glimpse of her life, he was pleased she hadn't given into displaying her every moment for the world to see. Of course, it was possible her privacy settings were high, that if he were her 'friend' the feed would be covered with happy, laughing photos. Posts displaying what she'd had to eat that day. A snap of her and her girlfriends out to lunch, all looking fabulous, all looking like life was the most wonderful thing.

Doubtful.

Lincoln x'ed out of the page. He typed in a search on solar energy conservation efforts and felt better ... a bit better.

CHAPTER TWELVE

Kali sat in the counsellor's waiting room. No. Psychologist. This wasn't any mere counsellor. This was a psychologist. Dr. Richards had specified the distinction at their first appointment when Kali said she wasn't the first counsellor Theo had seen. The woman looked to her notes. She was the first psychologist. A strong distinction, apparently.

Kali hated this part of the visits the most. Sitting here, separated, wondering. It didn't seem right. Three years old was too young for a child to be separated from his mother like this. Three years old was too young for a child to have mental problems.

Kali twisted the tails of her shirt in her hand. She pulled out her phone. Ten minutes passed. Twenty more until she joined the session. It felt like hours.

Twice a week. Three hundred dollars a week—the same amount that man paid for rent in a month—and right in the middle of the day, preventing her from taking a full shift. The weight that had been pressing in on her chest more and more frequently pushed again. Kali's eyes blurred and her head ached. She rubbed her hands over her face and sat straighter.

She looked at her phone. Eleven minutes.

At least this *psychologist* realized it wasn't a cognitive issue. Developmentally delayed. Kali hated those words. Hated the people who'd used them. That was not the problem.

Kali thought back to the day Theo's words had stopped. Theo had been like any other two-year-old. Happy. Laughing. Babbling away with new words every day, excited about each one. And then Kali had come home, just days before her University graduation. She'd walked in through her mother's kitchen and tossed her purse on the table. Exhausted.

"Ma?" The TV was on, so they must be home. "Ma?"

Kali poured herself a glass of water and rubbed her neck. It had been a long day in the clinic, and though she was excited to see Theo, she needed a moment to herself. She braced her hands on the counter. Things would be better soon. Easier. She had a job lined up—full hours, decent pay. She'd convince her mother to move into the city so Kali wouldn't have this commute every day. She'd already been dropping hints.

When Kali had moved out at seventeen she'd sworn she'd never come back here, but life didn't always work out the way you wanted. She'd married Derek at the end of her first year, believing his promises. Together, their lives would be different. Better.

"Ma?" Kali pushed herself away from the counter and entered the living room. Her mother's slippered foot peeked out from around the armchair. Kali's throat closed. She approached the chair, uncertain, then stepped around. Theo looked up at her. Eyes wide. Face wet. His body curled against his grandmother's chest. His hand grasped in hers.

Her mother's eyes were open, but she stared at nothing.

THE DOOR TO THE WAITING room opened and a woman in a business suit, a hand clasping the wrist of a boy who seemed wild, walked in. Kali had seen the pair before. She nodded at the woman. The woman pursed her lips in what could hardly be called a smile. Kali focused on the two, trying to draw her mind back from the memories. The coroner said her mother had been sitting there for at least four hours. Maybe longer. It was her hand clasping Theo's, not the other way around, so Theo had been sitting all that time—trapped. Four hours in the lap of a grandma who wouldn't look at him, wouldn't speak to him, wouldn't move.

Kali never heard his voice again.

And then, less than a month later, the explosion. The nursery worker—a sweet, dedicated woman who would forever be scarred—said she'd had a breakthrough with Theo. Said he had spoken his first words since the passing: *Thank you*. And as his mouth closed the blast shook the daycare. Children screamed. Adults ran and hollered, herding the kids as if they were frightened sheep. Fire blazed.

It created a connection in his mind, Dr. Richards said— though Kali came to that conclusion without any help. The moment Theo finally spoke, all hell broke loose.

Dr. Richards pushed her glasses up on her nose. *He sees a correlation*, she said. *Whether he thinks it's his fault, I don't know yet. We need to work to break that connection.*

Theo was almost four now, and not a word since. He

understood everything. Everything. And, for the most part, Kali understood him. Which is why Dr. Richards insisted the first part of their sessions happen without her presence, why she scolded and chided and made Theo's mutism, at least in part, Kali's fault.

"Ms. Johnson?"

Kali raised her head. The receptionist was smiling at her.

"You may come in."

Kali slung her bag over her shoulder, hoping today would be the day. The breakthrough.

THEO SKIPPED BESIDE Kali on the way home. One thing about those sessions, the majority of the time Theo was in a good mood when they left. Whether it was the sessions themselves or the excitement of being free from them, Kali didn't know. She didn't ask either. It was as it was.

"What would you like for dinner tonight?"

Theo smiled up at her.

"Any ideas?"

He kept smiling.

"How about pickles and cheese?"

He giggled.

"Or ketchup with apple pie?"

Another giggle.

Kali stopped. She crouched in front of him. "Can you tell Mommy what you'd like to eat? I bet I could make just about anything you wanted."

Theo stared at her a moment then looked away—as if she'd betrayed him, broken some trust.

"Honey?" His eyes stayed averted. "I just want to know

...” She stopped. “What did she even have at home? Pushing an answer would mean a trip to the grocery store if he wanted something that wasn't in their kitchen. Though it'd be worth it. It'd definitely be worth it to hear him request something. She gave him a little shake and squeeze, but he still looked away. “How about egg salad sandwiches? That sound good?” He turned to her and smiled, nodded. Kali stood and took his hand again. Egg salad sandwiches and then a talk with the landlord. Though it was too early for dinner. She'd talk with the landlord first. Maybe. What if he said no? What if he said, deal with it?

Kali looked to Theo. “How about a stop at the park?” His grin exploded.

As they approached their apartment complex after an hour at the park, Ronald, the landlord, stood in front talking to another tenant. The man seemed upset, agitated. He raised his arms and let them fall, shied away from Ronald's touch when he tried to put a hand on his shoulder, and grumbled something Kali couldn't hear.

Kali took a breath. This was her moment, unless he walked away, unless he turned and left without seeing her. But he would see her. She'd make sure of it. She was doing this today. Her chest tightened. Not from fear of talking to him— she could tell him her mind anytime, tell anyone—but if he refused to do something about the rats, the mould, or put her off again, what then? File a complaint. Go to the city. Sure. But the time. The effort.

Ronald shook his head as the man walked away, then turned. No smile softened his face.

“Kali Johnson.”

“Ronald Peters.”

"I was planning to come up to your apartment today."

"To fix the mould? Get an exterminator in for the rats?"

"Now, Kali—"

Kali stepped closer. "If that's not what you have to say, I don't want to hear it."

No grin. No challenge. "You need to hear it."

"No. You do. Listen," Kali positioned Theo to the side of her and leaned in toward Ronald, "it's been weeks. Weeks. And I've been more than patient." She crossed her arms. "But this has gone on long enough. I have a son. A child. And he's breathing in those spores, whatever's in the air."

"Kali."

"Rats crawl over our floors at night. Try to get into our food."

"Kal—"

"I can barely sleep with the sound of their scurrying, with the fear they'll crawl into the bed. Nibble on my son as he—"

"Kali." His voice was firm this time. Strong.

But she wasn't backing down. "Do you want that on your conscience? Do you want that to be your legacy? Maybe I should go to the media. Slum landlord. That'd make a fancy headline."

He smirked. Slightly. But it was a smirk.

Kali flared. "You think this is funny? You think it's amusing to make people live like this? I pay my rent on time every month. I was forgiving when those pipes exploded. Accommodating. I could have demanded you put us up in a hotel. But no, I moved to another unit, without complaint."

"Without complaint?"

"Without complaint to any authorities. And you clearly didn't fix the problem. You just let it fester." She shook her head. "Do you even have a conscience? Maybe you're the rat. That why it doesn't bother you that they've taken up residence on your property?"

"Do I have a conscience?" The man nodded. "Yes. Yes, I do. And I have a family. And that family needs to come first. Look out for number one, right?"

Kali faltered. "That doesn't—"

"I was going to try to be generous. Give you a month's notice. But seeing as you hate where you're living so much. I'll be kind instead. You have forty-eight hours."

"What?"

"Forty-eight hours for you to get the f—" the man glanced at Theo. "To get out of my apartment. My building. Forty-eight hours. That's as generous as I'm going to get."

Kali's arms shook, her fists clenched. The sound of a rushing wind seemed to swirl around her.

CHAPTER THIRTEEN

Lincoln made his way up Cogswell Street. The pills were a wonder. He knew the moment they started to wear off. The pain would creep and nudge. If he left it too long it would flare. As long as he took the pills regularly, though, he felt pretty good. Better than good, he was tempted to walk on his ankle he felt so good; he just needed to make sure he didn't take too many. Not again.

But he wouldn't, and he wouldn't walk on his ankle. He'd tried it once, not a great idea, and if he pushed it, was out and up on his feet ... foot ... for more than thirty minutes or so the pain would seep through the effect of the drugs, making him groggy and weak.

Two weeks. He'd give it that long before trying to get back to life. An injury could linger for years if not treated properly. And for the life he intended to live, that would not work.

Romper's ears perked. A low rumble emerged from his throat. A rat scurried between two buildings. "Stay." Romper obeyed, begrudgingly.

Before Romper, Lincoln wasn't sure he'd ever seen a rat outside of a construction site. But with Romper's keen sense, at least once or twice a week the dog would pick up on one. A city-wide problem, apparently. The papers had several articles in the past weeks about it. Especially with all the construction. A weird joining. Gentrification and rats. The two didn't seem to go together ... depending on how you looked at it. He chuckled. That had been him. Stuck in the rat race. Not anymore.

"Forty-eight hours?"

Lincoln looked ahead: Kali, not fifteen feet in front of him. The boy too. She stood talking to a man, yelling at a man, who looked twice the size of her.

"How in the world do you—"

"You don't have a lease."

Kali stepped back. Lincoln patted his thigh for Romper to stay close. He got near enough to hear clearly, then stopped.

"I ... I have a lease."

"You had a lease for Unit 407. You're now in Unit 307. You have no lease."

"But—"

"You've broken your old lease."

"Broken?"

"You vacated the premises."

"To move into one of—"

"Listen, Kali." The man looked worn. He shook his head. "I'm selling the building."

Kali stood silent. Lincoln wished he could see her face. Her shoulders sank. Her firm stance slackened.

"I don't—"

"I got a great offer. More than this piece of junk is worth. You have no idea the upkeep—"

"But ... what about all—"

"Those on a year lease are getting two months. Those on a month to month, a month. You don't have a lease. Several people don't have leases. The faster I get them out, the faster crews can start gutting the place."

"But ..." Kali's voice lowered. Lincoln crept closer. "Two days? How do you ...? What am I ...?"

"I'm not going to fix the mould, Kali, not going to do anything about the rats."

"I'll take you to court. To the tenancy board and—"

"And it'll be months to get a hearing. You don't have a lease. And in those months of waiting, the rats will get worse. The mould will get worse. Construction will start on other parts of the building."

Kali stood rigid. Her body shook.

"And you're right. You shouldn't be living here." The man glanced at Theo, who clung to Kali's leg. "Your son shouldn't be living here." He shook his head. "Consider this an opportunity. A push in the right direction."

"I've paid 'til the end of the month."

"I'll reimburse you."

"Where are we supposed to—"

"You're smart. You'll figure it out."

"My stuff."

The man sighed. "My cousin has a van. I'll offer you his services." He gave what was almost a smile. "I'm not doing that for everyone. Tomorrow night. He'll even help you lift." The man backed up the steps and toward the door.

"You can't!" Kali shouted—venom, hate, leaking from her voice.

"It's done."

"But—" Desperation now, so sorrowful it made Lincoln

wince. The man shook his head once more and slipped into the apartment. Kali stood staring, shaking.

Forty-eight hours. Lincoln watched her, her head held firm in the direction of the parting landlord. It couldn't be legal, to evict someone like that. She spun, as if searching for something, and her gaze fell on Lincoln. That venom and hate he'd heard spread through her features and focused on him. "What are you doing here?"

"I—" Lincoln stepped forward and leaned heavily into his crutches.

"You think this is a show?"

"No."

Kali eyed him. Her spine had regained its rigidity, but collapsed. "Forty-eight hours." She looked lost. Weak. All the times he'd seen her, not once had she looked weak.

"What am I going—?" Her hands hung limp at her sides. Theo still stood by her leg, his gaze locked on her.

Lincoln stepped closer. "Do you have family?"

She shook her head.

"Friends?"

"Not that ... no. I mean yes, but, no. Not—"

Lincoln was close enough he could have reached out and touched her now. He didn't, of course. "He wouldn't change his mind?" He gestured toward the apartment doors.

"It wouldn't matter. We can't ... if he's not fixing ... not taking care of ..." She hesitated. "We can't keep living with those rats." Her head scanned the street—looking for what, Lincoln didn't know. "I could go in a hotel or," a pause, "maybe some places would be open mid-month." She brought her gaze back to Lincoln. "Do you think?"

He shook his head. "I'm not sure."

"But my stuff. My ... a hotel, I mean—there's storage, right? It's probably expensive. Do you think it's—"

"I don't know." Lincoln's pulse quickened as he stood. Helpless. Pathetic. She stared past him. "What about my place?"

"Huh?" Kali looked to Lincoln. "Oh, to store my stuff ... that empty room? Would you mind?"

"To live."

Her expression was vacant. Shocked? Uncomprehending?

"To ... I mean, just until you figure something out. I have that extra room."

Her mouth slid open.

Lincoln raised a crutch. "If it sounds creepy, I'm not much of a threat."

Her eyebrows rose.

"And I could use some help. I mean, I've got painkillers now. Which is great. But it's still hard to get around. I still ... you could help, maybe. Get the groceries. Take Romper out if I'm ..." Lincoln shifted. "A short-term thing, obviously. But you need somewhere to go, and I could use ... someone to come."

She kept staring.

"You are a nurse."

She nodded. A sharp nod. "Okay."

"O—"

"All right. I'll pack up tonight. I work tomorrow, but tomorrow evening that dirt bag's cousin will bring our stuff over. Will you be home, to make sure we can get in?"

Lincoln swallowed. What was he doing? What had he said? He gave a quick nod.

"And you're not a rapist?"

He shook his head.

"A pedophile?"

"Are you trying to be funny?"

"Not in the slightest."

"I don't even know how to answer that."

"If you're not, you answer with a no."

"No."

Kali put her hand on Theo's shoulder. Her chest rose and fell. "This will work. I'll take out what I need, pile the rest in boxes. It may be cramped, but it will work. For a couple of weeks. Until ..." She paused. "It will work."

She focused on Lincoln again. "I'll see you tomorrow."

Tomorrow? At his apartment?

Lincoln stood, speechless, as Kali turned toward her building and walked up the steps.

CHAPTER FOURTEEN

Lincoln paced back and forth in his living room ... if propelling oneself on crutches could be called pacing. He had managed to get down on his knees to finally clean that pizza-sauce-plastered wall and had cleaned as much of the rest of his apartment as he could manage. Not that it was messy. He liked things clean, sanitary. But he'd been lax the past few days. Especially with the sweeping, something he still couldn't manage to do. Tufts of Romper's fur blew across the hardwood whenever a breeze passed by and settled in the corners.

Lincoln went over and over the scene in his mind, the words exchanged, whatever ridiculous force had prompted him to open his mouth and tell that woman and her son to move in with him. Now, a day later, it seemed like another person must have done it. This was the exact opposite of what he wanted, of what he'd been striving for. The one positive was his argument that she could help him out right now. Get the groceries. Travel down the stairs for Romper's quick visits to the lawn. Sweep the floor and stop allowing his apartment to feel like some desert riddled with tumbleweeds.

But was it worth it? To have that woman and her son coming and going? To live in exactly the scenario he'd been working to avoid? He looked at the clock on his wall. Even this. She hadn't said what time she'd arrive. Just, you'll be home, right? As if he had nothing better to do than wait around for her.

And what kind of a woman was she, to bring her son into the home of a stranger? He could be an axe murderer. She hadn't asked about that. Just a rapist or a pedophile. If he was one, did she think he'd admit it?

He looked to the clock again. 8:15. Thursday, at 8:15. She better come soon. If she didn't, too bad for her. Too bad if she needed help. He wasn't going to risk being on the street before that salsa class. He looked down at his crutches—not that he could help anyway.

Three taps on the door. Gentle. Unassuming.

Romper gave three answering barks and scurried toward the door, tail wagging.

"Just a moment." Lincoln hesitated. If he opened that door, if he welcomed them in, his life would turn into something completely other than it had been. He'd be invaded. It wasn't too late to say no, turn back on his word. He could say it was the drugs, say they'd made him loopy, unaware of what he was offering. He could tell her that the friend he was renting the place from was coming back and would need the room. He could leave a woman and her child on the street.

An image flashed in his mind: Kali and Theo standing in line outside some shelter. Would there be a line-up? Would they be allowed to stay in the same room? Each night, would they wait, uncertain whether the next night they'd have a place to sleep?

Lincoln knew nothing of how these things worked. Only what he saw in movies.

"Uh ..." Lincoln stepped to the door but stopped—handling the door knob was an awkward affair and he didn't want this moment, this first new moment, to be of him looking like a klutz. He stepped back. "It's open. Just ... just come in."

The door opened and she stood, her arms full of boxes. Only her eyes peered above the load. Had she walked up the stairs like that? Theo stood beside her, his arms wrapped around a teddy bear, a pillow, and what looked to be some kind of security blanket.

One more bark from Romper. He pranced between Kali and Theo then settled on Theo, circling the boy.

"I ..." Kali's voice seemed frail. Uncertain. Not at all the voice he was used to hearing emerge between those lips. Not that he was used to her voice, but he would be.

"Put your stuff anywhere." Lincoln spread his arm, trying to sound welcoming, cheerful even. His crutch threatened to tumble with the gesture, and he had to grasp it with a clatter and a grunt.

Kali stepped inside and motioned with her head for Theo to follow. She glanced around the room then set her boxes against the wall near the door. "To the couch," she whispered to Theo. He crawled up onto it. Romper followed.

Kali put her hands on her hips. She stood tall. "So, the movers—that bastard's cousin and a couple of guys—are downstairs. It's not a lot of stuff. I dumped some of it but," she glanced around the room, "I have a couch. I'll try to make it fit in our room." She stepped toward the half open door and leaned in. She stood back, a frown on her face. "Or not."

"We can figure that out." Lincoln stood about six feet from her, afraid to move. "The living room has space." He gestured. "Against that wall."

"Yeah." She brought her gaze back to Lincoln. "An armchair too. And all my kitchen stuff." She paused again. "I can leave most of that in boxes. I didn't want to get rid of too much, things I know I'll need when we leave again."

"Of course."

She looked back toward the bedroom. "The armchair will fit in there."

"Great."

"I don't want to invade your space."

"You won't."

"This is short term."

"Absolutely." Lincoln swallowed. "A stopping place. A transition place. It's that for me too."

"Mmmhmm." She stared at Theo. "Could he stay here while I go help the men?"

"Sure. Yes. Absolutely."

Kali stepped toward the spare room and stood inside the door. Assessing, he guessed. She came back out. "Okay. The couch won't fit there, but the armchair will. I ... I'll be right back."

She looked at Theo once more before exiting the apartment. Romper stood in the middle of the living room. His head lolled between Theo and the door. He knew something was up. He kept his gaze on Theo a moment then swivelled to Lincoln.

"Go on." Lincoln motioned to Theo. The dog gave a little hop and a leap over, then nuzzled his head into Theo's lap. Lincoln watched the two for a moment before turning his eyes on the door. He stood, motionless, as thumps and grunts of the men manoeuvring the old and uneven staircase sounded around them. He stayed standing as they entered, looked at him, then brought the couch into the apartment.

Kali was close behind, a different woman altogether from the one who'd just left. "Richard. Easy on the corners, will you?" She set down her new load of boxes beside the previous one. "Okay. Couch along that far wall. No, over a couple of feet." It went on like this for the next twenty minutes or so. Kali directing the men as if she owned the place. As if she knew in advance exactly where everything should go. No consultation with Lincoln. Hardly even looking at Lincoln.

When the men had left and the door had closed, Kali sat on her own couch. She looked to Theo. "Are you hungry?" The boy shook his head. "Thirsty?" Another shake. "Well, I'm parched." She pushed herself up and looked at Lincoln. "Can I get you anything?"

Lincoln shook his head as she disappeared into the kitchen. She emerged with an orange Fanta, certainly not something she'd found in his fridge ... or perhaps she had. But not something he'd put there.

Lincoln glanced between the two couches. He needed to sit. He couldn't believe he'd stood all that time. Only now did his body start punishing him for it. But he couldn't take another pain killer yet. What was better? To sit beside the boy or her, on her property. He opted for his own couch, where his own dog had curled up, and settled in a few feet away from Theo.

"It's a spacious place."

Lincoln nodded.

"You said you're renting it from a friend."

Another nod.

He could see it in her eyes, the urge again to tell him it could be spruced up. A fresh coat of paint, some real pictures on the walls. At least that's what he thought he saw. Would she do it? Take over? Would he come home one day to a place that looked like a home? She looked away. "I've never tried to get into a co-op, or subsidized housing, or whatever it's called."

Lincoln didn't reply.

"Maybe I should have."

Still, he didn't know what to say.

"I mean, I bet there are regulations. I bet if you had bed bugs or mould or rats, whatever agency was responsible for placements would make sure the landlord did something about it."

Lincoln coughed. "I imagine so. That would seem right." He fingered a hole in his jeans; a weight pressed against his chest. "I'm not legit here. I haven't contacted any agency."

"Right." She leaned back against the couch, sipping her Fanta. "Did I tell you about the bed bugs? That was the first problem. It was quite the process getting rid of them. We had to strip everything. Steam everything. They got all in our hair."

"Sounds awful."

"It was probably a ploy by the landlord, a way to get people out of their units so he could sell easier. A bunch of people did leave. And then the pipes broke. Or he broke them. That's when we moved."

"Moved?"

She looked to her lap. "Not sure how much you heard the other day. We moved to a different unit. That's why I didn't have a proper lease. I'm not just some stupid—" she stopped. "So, what's your deal? What happened in your life to land you here?"

Lincoln stared at her.

She gestured toward the table covered with all manner of construction items, to the smashed model house he'd picked up and let tumble among the other scraps of wood. "You said you're working on a project."

"Yup."

She pressed her lips together. "Not a big talker?"

He shrugged, swallowed, wanted to sink through the seat cushions and away into nothingness.

She crossed a leg, but not daintily. Her ankle rested across her knee, like a man's would. "You have your secrets. I have mine." Her voice softened. "That's best." She looked at Theo again.

Lincoln stared at the tree houses on the opposite wall, studying each one, imagining each one.

"This will be temporary. Really temporary. Maybe until the end of the month. I'll start looking for a new place tomorrow."

He glanced sideways at her. Oh, the weight. Where did it come from? How could nothing press against his chest so hard? "That seems best."

"And I'll pay you. Half for each day we're here."

He turned to look at her. "That's not necess—"

"It is necessary."

A tendril of fur blew across the floor. Lincoln pointed at it. "I'd be happy if you took care of those. Sweeping's hard with these things." He tapped the crutches.

"That's hardly worth rent. I don't want to owe you

anything. And I'm not a charity case."

"I didn't think—"

"And I'm not some ... there are reasons." She stopped again. "My mom was sick. I worked through school. All through school. She had medical bills. And I had plans. My life was supposed to be different. Supposed to be better. Some things you can't control."

"Of course."

She looked at Theo. "I know what you're thinking. But it wasn't like that." Her voice raised several octaves. "Theo, Sweetie, why don't you go check out our new room. You can choose what side of the bed you want."

Theo stood, his blanket trailing behind him. Her voice lowered again. "I was married. I wasn't some stupid girl who got knocked up."

"I didn't think—" Lincoln looked toward the no longer spare room. "Where's your husband now?"

"I don't have a husband now." She stood. "Well, I'm hungry even if no one else is. I brought the fixings to make spaghetti. You want some?"

Lincoln nodded. "Spaghetti sounds great."

CHAPTER FIFTEEN

Lincoln twisted in the sheets. He'd been in bed for two hours at least, his ears straining to hear every sigh, rustle, and whisper from the next room. All was silent after the first fifteen minutes, but still he couldn't sleep.

Dinner had been odd. Lincoln didn't have chairs for his table, which was a worktable anyway, not a dining table. He didn't have a dining table. But Kali did. She set it up in the far end of the kitchen, cramped against a wall. With only two chairs, she insisted on standing through the meal. Eventually, at Lincoln's urging, she perched on the kitchen counter. The fact that they were at the table at all felt strange. On the couch, staring out the window, was where he ate. Or, if he was in a particular mood, standing at the window.

The dinner was the first 'home cooked' one he'd had in months. The spaghetti brought memories of childhood. Not of his mother's spaghetti, but of his grandmother's. Ketchup in the sauce.

It wasn't high-end cuisine, but it was better than Kraft Dinner. Better than ravioli. It awakened something.

In his early twenties, Lincoln had gotten a taste for

cooking. In his old life, he had recipe books. He knew when an eggplant was perfectly ripe. He appreciated the superiority of aged Parmesan compared to those processed flakes that came in plastic bottles.

He baked bread and filleted steaks and had no processed food in his kitchen. Of course, as work demands grew, finding time to cook got harder. But that's what takeout was for—restaurants with real, whole, organic and free range foods. Cooking his own meals became a treat. An indulgence.

And yet it all, without even a thought it seemed, had been purged along with the rest of Montreal life. It wasn't until Lincoln sat at that foreign table, Theo casting him furtive glances, Kali looking uncomfortable, almost angry, that Lincoln realized he missed real food. Loved real food.

And what would he do in the wilderness? Catching or foraging enough food to live on wasn't likely. So he'd live off the land as much he could and travel to civilization for supplies when needed. Would living that way mean he had to say goodbye to culinary delights? Not necessarily. Maybe it would mean he'd discover new ones. Rabbit. Pheasant. Deer and Moose. Berries. Fruits of the forest.

Lincoln laid a hand on his stomach. It was soft now. Not firm as it'd been for most of his life. He didn't have anything close to a paunch, but his muscles had atrophied in the months of lying on the couch, drinking, numbing away his days. It'd only been a few weeks since he'd bought the lot, started clearing a way to the site he'd picked, and prepping the wood he'd need. Had he had a paunch before that? No way to tell now. Lincoln ran a hand along his arm, flexed. A lot less definition than he was used to. Seeing Andrew had made that clear. Lincoln had always been bigger, stronger. He wasn't anymore.

Did it matter? Should it? Lincoln stared at the ceiling. It had mattered before. Or was that only because Joseph believed it mattered? Joseph emphasized that your body represented your life. How you treated it, what you put into it, reflected what you deserved from life. What you were due.

The world thought the same thing. Beautiful people were the ones who made it. Look like you could take a man in the ring and you'd take him in a business meeting.

It had made sense.

And Lucy had liked his muscles, had run her manicured hands all over them. Her tongue. He'd felt like a god. Maybe that's why he hadn't noticed their slow disappearance. With no one to point his body out to him, with no tongue or fingertips delighting at ...

Lincoln stiffened with the memory. Sex hadn't been part of his new life, of his plans for his future one. And he hadn't thought of it much. Hadn't really missed it. But he wanted it now.

He closed his eyes, remembering snippets. The good times. The amazing times. The last time, which he hadn't known would be the last, and all the moments after. The implication that everything Lincoln had, everything he'd accomplished, was because of Lucy or because he was the boss' baby brother. The suggestion that it was her whispering in Joseph's ear, convincing him Lincoln was good enough, smart enough, encouraging Joseph to give Lincoln chance after chance to prove his worth.

Lincoln's need disappeared. The weight in his gut grew. He'd worked hard. He'd deserved the positions he rose to. It didn't come easily to him, so he'd worked. At first, following in Joseph's footsteps felt like wearing a hand-me-down funeral suit. Too tight. He wanted to wear it, though—out of respect, responsibility, because it was the right thing to do. Still, it squeezed, always, like a boa constrictor's grasp. Lincoln itched to take it off, to run free, slip into clothes that fit.

Until Lucy. Lucy stopped him from loosening that old tie and slipping off the coat. With Lucy, he slept in the suit, ate in the suit. Heck, he bathed in the suit and fucked in the suit. Lucy made him believe it was the perfect fit, believe it was what he wanted.

Lincoln gritted his teeth. Anger flooded over him. She was a liar, and she'd made him believe a lie. Want a lie.

A sigh sounded through the wall, long and feminine. Lincoln's thoughts tore away from Lucy. He felt exposed.

He froze, as if the woman on the other side of the wall could hear his slightest movement, his thoughts.

She was an intruder, but an invited one. How was he supposed to deal with that? She clearly didn't know how to deal with it—one moment taking over the space, making herself comfortable, the next seeming self-conscious and uncertain.

And then to bed. At eight-thirty. Leaving boxes everywhere. Leaving the apartment in a state of disarray.

Without a doubt, Lincoln had been invaded.

A whimper this time. From Kali, not Theo. He was sure of it.

Lincoln shifted toward the wall, put his hand against it. Was she awake? Lying there thinking ... what?

The rustle of sheets.

This was not good. Would not work. Lincoln stared at the

wall then shifted his gaze to the ceiling. He didn't know what he'd been thinking, inviting them here. Already he felt off-kilter, stressed, suffocated. He needed to get that woman and her child out of his life.

CHAPTER SIXTEEN

L incoln woke to shuffles outside his bedroom door, a woman's voice whispering, smells he'd missed. He sat up, then stifled a groan. The painkillers always wore off through the night—a good thing, he supposed, a way to judge his improvement from the day before.

Kali. Theo. He rubbed his head, an attempt to rub away the hours he hadn't slept, and looked at the clock. Six twenty. He reached for his crutches and made his way to the door. Stopped. No more coming out in boxers. Lincoln pulled on sweat pants and a t-shirt then opened the door. Romper bounded out of the room.

Lincoln followed the dog. "Oh, hello." Kali turned and leaned against the stove, looking like someone who'd been caught in the act. The act of what, though, making breakfast? "I'm sorry. We didn't mean to wake you."

Lincoln didn't reply. He looked at Romper, head snuggled in Theo's lap. Theo chuckled, one of the first sounds Lincoln had heard from the boy. Lincoln turned back to Kali. "Chocolate chip pancakes?"

"Our Friday morning treat. There's enough batter if you

want some."

She seemed different this morning. Softer. Shy, almost. Not like she owned the place.

Lincoln stepped closer. "They smell good."

Kali turned back to the stove. "Take a seat."

Lincoln felt an urge to wrap his arms around her, feel the curve of her waist under his fingertips. It was what you did when you woke up to a woman cooking you breakfast. But she wasn't his woman, and she wasn't cooking *him* breakfast. He was just getting leftovers. The urge fled quicker than it arrived.

Lincoln went to the cupboard next to the stove, keeping a respectable distance between his body and hers. He reached for a glass and his pills. Downed them.

She glanced over. "Still bad?"

"Not good."

"Getting better?"

"A bit every day."

She nodded. "Good."

Theo glanced between them. Did he wonder why they were here? What this strange man had to do with their lives?

"Morning, bud." Lincoln sat across from the boy.

Theo stared at him, his expression placid. He looked to his mother's back, then at Lincoln again.

"Sleep well?"

The boy's brow furrowed.

Lincoln looked to the table. A plate with three pancakes appeared in front of him. A plate with two in front of Theo. They were perfectly golden. "Uh, thanks."

Kali gave a slight smile then turned back to the stove. "I leave for work in about a half hour. I'll take Theo to Mrs.

Martin's. We'll be gone all day."

Lincoln took a bite of pancake. It was good. Delicious. On birthdays his mother always made chocolate chip pancakes. How long had it been since he had one—Six years? Seven?

"I don't have a key, so—"

"When will you be back?"

Kali turned to the window, as if it were a hard question to answer. "Eight. Maybe eight-ten."

"No problem." Lincoln took another bite. "I'll try to get out and get an extra key made."

She turned again. How did she do it, look so powerful, so in charge one moment and give a flash of uncertainty the next?

"Oh, I can do that tomorrow. Prevent you having to manoeuvre and—"

Lincoln raised a hand. "I go crazy if I stay inside too long. I'll do it when I take Romper out for a walk."

She turned.

"Maybe you can take him out to the lawn before you leave for work, though. If you can squeeze it in."

"Absolutely."

Lincoln finished his pancakes quickly, not wanting to see her perch on the counter again to eat. He left the kitchen when she came with her plate and retreated to his room.

He sat on the edge of his bed, the bedroom door cracked, and listened as Kali peppered the boy with questions he clearly wasn't going to answer. He listened to the sound of her opening the apartment door—Romper's happy little bark. Listened to Romper and her re-entering the apartment, of her directing Theo to get his bag and not wear those shoes, and then of the door closing, and silence re-entering his life.

Romper nudged the bedroom door open farther and cocked his head. He seemed perplexed by the fact that the door wasn't wide open. This would be one of many changes. When you lived alone, doors didn't close.

Lincoln shuffled down the hall and into the living room cautiously. The boxes. The furniture. They sucked up all the space.

He stood at the work table, determined to start on a new model. He looked at the door. He worked. He stood by the window, eating a tuna fish sandwich. He glanced at the door. He stretched out on the couch and read till he finished his book. He turned to the door. He walked from the living room to the bathroom and back to the living room to retrieve a book to read in the tub—his back needed the soak. Standing in a towel, he looked again to the door.

Would it open? It could, at any moment. She said eight. But what if she'd forgotten something? What if the boy was sick and she had to leave work early? Kids got sick all the time.

Would she knock? He'd left the door unlocked. Should he have?

Once out of the bath, Lincoln turned the lock. That was better. He'd have warning—today, at least. Why had he offered a key? Without one, he had some power over his own privacy. But he had offered. After a few hours more of distracted work, glad to be free of the boxes and furniture and lack of space, Lincoln, with Romper beside him, walked toward the library with the intention of finding a key cutter next.

Lincoln immersed himself into research, coming up with a way to safely heat the tree house in winter, and finding a device out of Switzerland that was supposed to be superior at storing solar energy. The key cutter wasn't far and so, with still two hours until Kali and Theo were supposed to return, Lincoln took Romper to the Commons. His back hurt too much to throw the ball, but Romper ran anyway, bounding ahead of Lincoln and then speeding back, his tail and tongue wagging. When Lincoln couldn't stand anymore, he settled on the grass and stared at the sky, with Romper beside him. He rubbed the dog's head then closed his eyes. When he woke, he waved down two runners to ask the time and arrived home fifteen minutes before Kali said she'd arrive.

Though unlocked, Kali knocked on the door. When Lincoln called out to enter, she ushered Theo in. She stood just past the entry and stared at the room. She didn't even acknowledge Lincoln. Her gaze passed over him as if he were another piece of furniture, another box not where it should be.

She removed Theo's backpack and stepped further into the room. "How was your day?"

"Good. Yours?"

Her chin, though set, quivered. She shrugged, "Fine," and helped Theo get his sneakers off. One of the laces was sticking. Shouldn't a three-year-old, even if he was almost four, have Velcro?

Lincoln hesitated. And why the quiver, why the shrug? *Leave it. Let it go. Just*—"Really?"

"Huh?" She looked up. So tired. But it was more than that.

"Your day. I mean," he leaned forward, "are you okay?"

Kali stared at him a moment. She put a hand on Theo's shoulder. "Why don't you go change into your PJ's. You can have your bath tomorrow." Theo looked at his mother, his head cocked almost the way Romper's did, then walked away.

Kali looked back at Lincoln. "I lost three patients today."

"Lost?"

"They died." She made her way across the room. "It's the ER. So it happens. But ..." That quiver again. "It's always so sudden. A shock. To have someone living, breathing, and then not." She trailed a hand along the work table, picked up his latest model, then set it down gently. "Today two MVAs and a boy who fell from a tree. He was only seven. You fight to make it better, you know? To fix them. But sometimes you can't make it better."

Lincoln swallowed, thankful for his sore back and twisted ankle—for only having a sore back and twisted ankle. "At least it's not you who lost them. I mean, it's the doctor's responsibility, right?" Stupid. Was that the right thing to say? Did that matter? "But even then. It's just, hard, I imagine. But life, right? And you save some?"

Kali stepped back from the table, her gaze sweeping the room once more. "Yeah. It's just life." At the entrance to the kitchen, she stopped. "It can be even worse being a nurse. You stand there, wishing you could do more. And there's a lot you can do. A lot *I* can do. But you're right. I'm not the one to call it. I'm the one to hold their hand as they lay terrified, not understanding why life is leaving, not able to tell their loved ones they love them or they're sorry or they forgive." Kali swallowed. She bit her lip. "Sometimes they tell me—ask me to pass the message on—if they have time, if they're that lucky, if, through the pain, they're even able to think those thoughts." She shrugged and slipped out of his sight.

Lincoln claimed he wasn't hungry when Kali offered dinner, saying he'd eat later. He would. And tomorrow he'd use some of the wood he had to make a chair. He didn't want her to feel she was in his way and didn't want to be in hers. While she put Theo to bed, Lincoln sat on the couch with a book on caulking natural tree limbs rather than using two-by-fours to build walls sitting on his lap. It seemed risky, relying on the unevenness of a natural limb or trunk against strong and bitter Nova Scotian winds. Perhaps a double layer. A base of practicality, an outside of beauty ... or the other way around, so he could enjoy the beauty while inside during those winter months.

Kali tiptoed into the living room and stood before him. Still tired. Still looking like she carried the weight of each death on her shoulders.

"Mind if I shower?"

Lincoln shook his head.

She came out, hair wrapped in a towel, just how Lucy used to wrap hers. Lincoln's throat clenched.

"Mind if I set up my TV?"

Lincoln raised his brows. "I don't have cable."

She pressed her lips. "Of course. Why would you? You don't have a television."

"Afraid not."

"And no internet?"

Lincoln shook his head.

"Maybe one of your neighbours hasn't locked their Wi-Fi."

She set up a small projection TV and connected her laptop to it. Lincoln hadn't seen a TV like that in years. In Montreal, a fifty-two-inch flat screen had sat in his and Lucy's living room. A forty in their bedroom. Not that they'd used either a lot ... or at least Lincoln hadn't. He was too busy trying to keep at the top of a world that always seemed to rise out of reach.

The Wi-Fi must have worked because the image on the screen came to life. Voices filled the room. Something about it made him angry, made him want to yell at her, tell her to turn it off, get it out, get out herself.

He left the room.

CHAPTER SEVENTEEN

Kali stood outside the apartment door. It was her seventh night with Lincoln. One whole week.

She had run out to buy some groceries for their dinner, for the first time leaving Theo at home with the man. Since tonight was Lincoln's last doctor ordered night off his ankle, her plan was to make something special. Tomorrow morning he could try walking—crutches free. After that, he said, they'd split the cooking.

Despite his protests, she'd made breakfast every morning. Dinner every night. And lunches the two days they'd all been home together. She was as helpful as she could be, as unassuming as possible, and hid her anger through it all. Anger that she needed to be in his apartment. Anger that she felt like an intruder—that he made her feel like an intruder.

Sometimes he'd get this look. This, *What have I done?* look. This, *Why are these strangers invading my life?* look.

Anger that her life, the life she'd planned, the life that was supposed to be so much better than the one she'd grown up with, had landed her here.

Despite the fact that he looked like a homeless person, it

was obvious by the way Lincoln stood, moved, and spoke that he'd never been homeless. That the face he was showing to the world was some kind of front. He was educated. He held the air about him of someone who had never wondered where the next meal would come from. If he didn't finish the food on his plate he threw it out, rather than put it in a container for a later day. He had kitchen utensils from Williams-Sonoma. He didn't need to live in this shitty three hundred dollar a month apartment. He was choosing to live here—for a reason she couldn't fathom—and that made her angriest of all.

Kali raised her hand to the door knob then dropped it. She couldn't let her resentment show. It didn't matter what she felt, what she wanted. She had to do what was best for Theo, and right now living in the apartment of this strange man was best for Theo. Right now, seeming pleasant, making sure she didn't do anything to screw up their welcome, was what mattered. Because the truth was, if Lincoln hadn't come along, she didn't know what she would have done. For now, at least, she needed him ... or, rather, needed his apartment.

In the past week she'd scoured apartment ads and seen half a dozen. Anything close enough to have less than a half hour's commute was more than she could afford or no better than the place she'd come from. She could get a room somewhere, rather than an actual apartment. But if she had to live with a stranger, why not Lincoln, at one-hundred and fifty bucks a month? What was that saying—better the devil you know than the devil you don't?

And better Lincoln than another slum apartment.

What she needed was more money. Then she could find a better apartment. Then she'd move her son once more. Kali sighed as guilt bubbled up in her—relief quickly mingled with it. Some days she was happy Theo didn't speak. It meant he didn't ask questions, meant she didn't have to explain any of this to him, just like she'd never had to explain the absence of his father.

She turned the door handle.

Laughter.

Lincoln and Theo sat on the floor. Lincoln with string ... no, shoelaces, looped around his fingers. He manoeuvred them almost magically. Cat's cradle. She hadn't seen it in years.

Theo reached his hands in and tried to take the strings the way Lincoln must have already directed him. His little tongue squeezed between his lips. He pulled the laces off Lincoln's fingers and onto his own. The laces unravelled and he laughed, his little dreads shaking around his face.

Lincoln looked up. "I'm trying to teach him—"

"Cat's cradle."

"Yeah." Lincoln looked back to her son. "Maybe next time, buddy. It's harder for you, your fingers are so small. Not these big monsters." Lincoln held his hands above Theo, as if threatening tickles. Theo crawled away, laughing more.

Kali tensed, then pushed her uncertainty away. It was innocent. Definitely innocent. She put on a smile. "Can I give it a try?"

Lincoln looked surprised. "Sure. Yeah. Of course."

"So is this what you do with your time? Instead of watching TV?"

"Not usually, no."

He held out his hands, an immediate tightness between them.

Had her tone been critical? Accusing?

Kali sat across from Lincoln. She looked at the laces, calling back this childhood skill, then inserted her fingers between his, pulled, and stretched her hands.

"Right on." Lincoln smiled, then took the laces off her hands. She examined them again, laced her fingers where they needed to be, and pulled. Theo clapped.

Kali looked at him and grinned.

Lincoln kneeled across from her and rubbed his beard. "This was always the trickiest one for me."

Kali kept silent. Lincoln caught the laces with his fingers, then pulled. The material flopped in his hands. Theo covered his mouth and giggled.

"You remember that one?"

Kali shook her head. Lincoln untied the laces. "I guess at a moment like this YouTube would come in handy, wouldn't it?"

Kali pushed onto her knees and stood. "I'll get started on dinner."

She left the two on the floor, swallowed, and looked back. He was so ... distasteful. With his hair and his clothes. He looked dirty, though he wasn't. He never smelled.

Still, she didn't want Theo getting close to him or thinking he was someone who mattered. But what was she supposed to do, tell the man who had jumped in front of a moving vehicle for her boy, then rescued them from living on the street, to stay away from her son?

Despite his offer, he clearly found their presence annoying—at times, at least. She peeked into the living room where Lincoln and Theo sat on the floor colouring. That first night she'd hooked up the TV, he hadn't said anything but the look, disgusted, like she'd taken a shit right in front of him.

That had disturbed her, made her wonder. But all week he hadn't said anything about her shows, just left the room. Not that she watched every night. She was cautious of that, just as she should be of him—cautious. She shook her head, remembering that look. It'd been a moment of frustration. Nothing, considering they had invaded his life, his space. And he'd let the frustration fade quickly. Still, it was enough, insulting enough, that she wanted nothing to do with this man past however many days or weeks she preyed on his charity.

Kali pulled out the chicken breasts and slammed them on the cutting board. She'd have to make it work. Do whatever she could, as best as she could, to make it work until she found a way to get out of here.

"Hey, Kali." She turned at the sound. Lincoln was smiling. "Anything I can help you with?"

Kali hesitated. "No, this dinner's for you." She turned back to the chicken. "Just relax."

KALI WOKE MOMENTS BEFORE her alarm. She switched it off and stared at the ceiling. They'd laughed at dinner. Lincoln had made Theo laugh. A lot. He'd made a third chair a few days earlier. Built it so the three of them could sit and eat their meals at the same time. A chair for Theo, he'd said, winking at the boy, his own special chair, and Theo had beamed.

At the end of the meal he had teased Theo, leaning forward as if he were going to walk without the crutches. Bending. Bending. And then Theo would wave his arms no, point to Kali, get her to tell Lincoln not yet. He had one more day. He had to be a good boy.

It was weird, this play acting. What was the source of

Lincoln's joviality? Getting free of the crutches—which he may still have to use from time to time? Or excitement about more freedom—being able to get away from her and Theo for longer? To drive again? Or, the worst option, excitement about getting his apartment back in only a few more days?

Before dinner last night, Lincoln had asked Kali how the apartment hunting was going. The end of the month was coming.

She'd lied. Great. Fabulous. She expected she'd found a place but others had applied too, so it was a waiting game to see who the landlord picked.

Lincoln smiled, looked pleased, said she must be eager to be done with him, have her own space again. She'd laughed, not telling him there was no apartment, that she needed to stay another month. Maybe two.

In reality, she'd stopped looking for an apartment. She was looking for a job instead. A solid job. And childcare.

She couldn't tell him. What if he said no, she couldn't stay. It was easier to say sorry than please, to hope he wouldn't throw a single mom and her son out on the street.

Kali rolled over. Theo's perfect little lips pursed in his sleep. His brow furrowed. What she'd give to slip inside of those dreams, see what he thought about, dreamt about. See what he'd have to say.

It was all so complicated. The job had to be nearby. Not necessarily this neighbourhood, but close enough that she could check on Marvin regularly. Close enough that Theo would know him, and that he could watch the boy grow. Kali pulled Theo close and wrapped her arms around the boy's middle.

Just as she hoped Lincoln wouldn't abandon them, she

couldn't abandon Marvin.

Kali kissed Theo's head then pushed herself out of bed. She watched him a moment longer. It was time for them to get separate beds—in a new place, with a new job and childcare. She'd make it happen, make life return to the path she'd always intended it to take.

Kali pushed open the door and padded down the hall. Coffee first, then a shower. She turned on the kettle and leaned against the counter.

"Morning."

Kali jumped and let out a yelp. "What are you doing there?"

Lincoln gave a half grin with a raised eyebrow. "Drinking some tea. Reading a book."

"You're usually asleep now." She pulled at the hem of her oversized t-shirt, hoping no sign of underwear showed through, then crossed her arms over her bra-free chest.

Lincoln looked to be stifling a laugh. "I couldn't sleep. Too excited, I guess, to move without those crutches."

Kali slid into the seat at the table across from him, eager for the cover it would bring. "And?"

"Weird. Very weird. My ankle feels stiff. Tender. But I'd say no pain."

"That's good." Kali laid her hands on the table then brought them back across her chest. "Be careful, though. Cautious. No running. No heavy lifting."

"No heavy lifting?" Lincoln put his mug down. "I was actually planning to do some serious heavy lifting. Wielding an axe then carrying away tree limbs and maybe a trunk or two."

Kali looked out the window. "It's your funeral."

"You're saying it'll kill me?"

She turned back, unsure of the joke. "It may cause further damage. Your back, too. I mean wielding an axe? What do you think you are? A lumberjack?"

"My back's been fine for a few days." Lincoln lifted his mug again. "The kettle's done."

Kali bounced out of her chair, pulled at her shirt bottom, and glared at Lincoln.

The mornings were hers. He never emerged until she had breakfast ready. Sometimes not even then. This was her time. She wouldn't talk to him about staying longer. She'd just stay. And he could deal with it.

She also wouldn't sit across from him drinking her coffee, letting him stare at her chest. Not that he was staring, his smiling eyes were on her angry ones. Kali grasped her mug. "Well, I'm off to the shower."

"With your coffee?"

"Yes." She paused. "With my coffee."

CHAPTER EIGHTEEN

Kali tiptoed out of the room, one arm still wrapped around her middle. Lincoln brought his gaze back to his tea. He'd seen it again: Anger. Frustration. But also insecurity. Embarrassment. She seemed just as mixed up about this arrangement as he was. He wanted them gone, wanted to get back to his life, to work on his models any time he wanted, and not worry about it interrupting dinner or, God forbid, their sleep. He wanted to come and go as he pleased. But he'd miss it, happening upon her in unplanned moments, like this morning. Seeing her at ease, unaware, until he'd broken the moment with his greeting. He'd miss knowing, in some small way, that he wasn't alone.

But he was alone. He always would be alone. It was what he wanted, what was best.

Lincoln finished his tea, grabbed a banana, two apples, three of the peanut butter cookies Kali had baked earlier that week, and the sandwich he'd made before she woke up. Maybe he wouldn't lug any tree trunks, but he'd swing the axe. He'd clear limbs. He'd make progress. At last, he was on his way back to the woods.

Lincoln rolled down the windows in the truck while Romper barked with delight at the wind whipping back his ears. The dog looked at Lincoln, barked again, as if to say thanks, then pushed his head out farther. The forty-five minute drive seemed to only take minutes. Lincoln grinned.

SEVERAL HOURS LATER, Lincoln stretched before calling Romper to the truck. He'd taken it easy, comparatively, but still he ached. His back throbbed, his ankle felt as if it had regressed almost a week. The pain would go away, though, would ease with rest. He'd pushed himself, but not too hard. Even though it meant cutting the day's intended work in half, he stopped before real damage could be done ... he hoped.

Still, it felt good. He felt good. Once back on the road, Lincoln laughed and slapped the wheel. It was like some strong and benevolent drug had seeped into his veins—better than the pain meds. He was back on track. He was working toward the life he intended.

And tonight he'd take advantage of the life he was living now, while he still had time. He stopped at a grocery store and, a basket on his arm, strolled the produce section. Eggplant. Zucchini. Fresh garlic. Onions. Orange, yellow, and red peppers. Carrots. Next, the meat department. Fresh, free-range chicken. Whole chicken, so the flavour of the skin would soak through.

Lincoln grinned again, feeling giddy. When was the last time he'd cooked for himself, not just thrown some packaged, processed, crap together? A week before Lucy's accident? Two? Maybe more.

Of course, in those last days in Montreal it hadn't been

cheap, packaged, processed foods. It'd been nothing but the best: take-outs full of fresh, locally grown ingredients. Business dinners at acclaimed restaurants. All as he tried to seal one of the biggest deals his father's corporation had ever had.

The one pleasure during those sixteen-plus hour days had been the food. And on a Sunday he could actually take some time off to cook for Lucy. For him. Candles. Mood music. Expensive wine. The belief in love. All before life, as he knew it, imploded.

"Find everything you were looking for?"

"Sorry?" Lincoln snapped to attention. A young, pimply faced cashier smiled nervously at him.

"Did you, uh," she gestured to the items she rung through the cash, "find everything?"

"Oh," Lincoln stared at the items. He was in the mood to say something pithy. *Do we ever?* But she wouldn't get it. Would maybe even think he was mocking her. "Sure." He smiled at the girl.

She nodded, keeping her eyes averted for the rest of the transaction. Lincoln noted his hands. Dirt coated them, each fingernail encrusted with black. He could only imagine what the rest of him looked like. Next, he took in the items the girl was bagging. An incongruous picture? Probably. He chuckled to himself and handed over his credit card, realizing he hadn't used it in a while.

Had groceries always been this expensive? Of course, in Montreal he got most of his produce at the market—Marché Sainte-Anne his favourite, with Jean-Talon a close second. He loved the haggling, the trips between vendors, the simplicity of it. The only simplicity, he realized, his Montreal life had.

Lincoln took the last of the groceries and headed to the car. Romper, head half out the window, gave a boisterous bark. Back at the apartment, Lincoln eased his way up the steps. The throbbing worsened. He hoped for peace, quiet ... though it wouldn't be awful to see Theo's smile or have him rush over, holding his latest painting like he had the other night—a picture of Lincoln, Theo, and Romper in a field, all smiling. Or to hear if Kali had saved someone rather than watched a life disappear. To see her smile instead of frown. That wouldn't be awful at all.

The apartment was empty. Most likely they wouldn't be home before seven-thirty. Plenty of time to shower and make a dinner that would wow. Wow himself. He was the one he was making this meal for. Still, after all the meals Kali prepared the past week, he hoped she would enjoy it too, enjoy having a meal waiting when she got home—back— when she got back, not home.

At eight-o-clock, Lincoln sat at the kitchen table. He tapped his fork on the rim of his plate. The food had been warming for over twenty minutes. He stepped to the stove. The vegetables looked wilted and pathetic. Would the chicken be dry?

It was stupid to not eat. To not enjoy the meal he'd made the way it was intended. Several times when he'd been out Kali had simply left food wrapped up for him to pop in the oven later.

Eight-o-five and Lincoln stood. She could be hours. Perhaps she'd gotten a double shift. Perhaps she'd eaten dinner out. Perhaps she'd found a new apartment. His plate full, Lincoln's gaze travelled from the table to his couch.

Eating at the table was Kali's thing. He stretched side to side. His back could use the couch. Soft. Inviting. Protective.

Moments after he settled into the cushions, familiar steps, followed by the sound of keys jingling, sounded outside the door.

Kali stepped inside, Theo's backpack dangling from her arm. She dropped the backpack on a pile of boxes and nudged at Theo to take off his shoes. Romper darted over, his tail wagging in front of Theo, who bent down to wet kisses. Kali raised her head, sniffing the air, and walked to the kitchen. "Lincoln?"

"Yep."

Kali spun, a hand to her throat. "I didn't see you there. What are you—"

"This is where I eat."

"Oh."

"Usually."

Kali stared at him.

"There's food left. I had extra, so—"

"Thanks." Kali smiled. She shuffled her feet. "Smells amazing."

"Now that I'm on my feet."

Kali smiled a moment more, a curious smile. "Theo, go wash your hands." She kept her gaze on Lincoln. "Good day?"

"Very."

"Wasn't too hard on the ankle? The back?"

"I'll be okay."

Kali stood there, staring at him. Lincoln shifted the cushion. She crossed one arm over her middle, her hand propping up her opposite elbow. She rested her chin against the other hand, staring at him.

"I kept it warm but it's not getting any warmer."

"Sure, yes. Of course." Kali turned to leave then stopped. "Not that you have to, of course, but looks like you just started. Want to join us?" She gestured her head toward the kitchen.

Now it was Lincoln's turn to stare. Did he want to? No. The couch was just fine. The couch was comfortable. His back was sore. And why should he be the one to adjust? This was his house. His kitchen. His living room. "No, not really."

Kali opened her mouth, leaned forward, then turned. Sounds of utensils, the tap, Theo's footsteps, travelled up the hall. Lincoln listened. Kali asked Theo question after question about his day. Silent answers. They'd be with his face, nods or shakes of his head, sometimes his hands, or, if he was annoyed with her, felt she was pushing too far, no answers at all.

Lincoln wanted to know.

He pushed himself off the couch, trying not to limp as he travelled toward the kitchen. He set the plate down and, using a hand for support, lowered himself into a chair. Kali and Theo looked at him.

"And Mrs. Martin said how many new kids were coming next week?"

Theo held up two fingers.

"You think they'll be your friends?"

He let his head wobble back and forth and shrugged, a hopeful smile coating his face.

Lincoln smiled at the kid, glad he was seeing the answers.

After dinner, Lincoln migrated back to the couch and picked up his most recent book on solar power. He'd done good work today. He was hurting, exhausted, but the pain and tiredness were worth the progress. And being home felt better than it had in weeks.

Theo's laughter, along with the sound of sloshing water, travelled up the hall. Lincoln kicked up his legs and stretched out on the cushions, enjoying the sound. He hoped the kids at the daycare would like Theo, be nice to him. The kid was different, and children were cruel. *Could* be cruel. Theo didn't deserve that.

CHAPTER NINETEEN

After her shift, Kali sat in the employee lounge scouring the computer for job openings. Jobs existed, but she didn't need just any job. She needed a job that would pay enough. She needed a job close enough to childcare that she wouldn't spend hours in transit. She needed childcare that would accommodate a nurse's long hours. She needed childcare that would be patient enough to work with a three, almost four-year-old, who decided not to speak. And she needed to not abandon Marvin. Marvin, who refused to leave the city with her, refused to get over himself and get a job, get his life back together. Let go.

After two hours and twelve minutes logged into the hospital's computer system, Kali sensed someone behind her. She turned. One of the older doctors smiled at her. He was a nice one. Bordered the line between harassment and affection sometimes, but nice.

"Looking for a new position, Sweetheart?"

Kali nodded.

"Finding much?"

"Not that fits."

He pulled up a chair across from her. "A friend of mine is looking for a nurse. It's not an exciting job." He chuckled. "Complete opposite of the ER."

Kali swivelled her seat so she was facing him straight on.

"It takes a strong person. But decent pay. Good hours. You're a single mom, yes? With a little boy?"

Kali nodded, certain whatever he was offering would just be another job she couldn't take. Good hours meant something different when you were a man, had a wife, and probably had the money for in-home childcare.

"And you're good with the elderly. Those in their last days or hours."

Kali sat up. He was stating those as facts, not asking a question.

The doctor leaned back. "It's out of the hospital system. A private retirement company. You'd be working with their palliative care residents. It'd be a one year contract covering a maternity leave, but once you're in with a place like that, if you do a good job, there would be a lot of opportunity for movement within the organization. Whether another maternity contract or even a permanent position."

"Are you talking about Westwood?" Kali leaned forward. "Isn't that crazy hard to get into?"

"They want quality people. These are high paying clients. People paying a premium rate to live out their last days well. And now those days are coming to an end."

"And the hours?"

"Typically eight-hour four-day weeks with one weekend a month of twelve hours days."

"Day or—"

"The role the director is looking to fill is days. And they

have child care on site—where the current clients you'd be working with are. Of course, clients change. So you could be moved, but the childcare is always available at the main site. It would just mean extra transit time."

Kali swallowed. Something would be wrong—like the job wasn't starting for months or—

"The contract starts the second week of August with a two-week unpaid training starting the second week of July."

"That's—"

"Soon. Yes." The doctor stood. "And would mean you'd have to take two weeks off from here. And if you don't get the job after those two weeks—it's basically a prolonged interview process, they'll be judging you during that time, two to three potentials, actually—you will have lost those weeks of pay for no reason."

Kali let out the breath she hadn't realized she'd held.

"But if you got it, which I feel confident you would, it'd be a perfect position for you. You're only part time here. I take it that's why you're looking?"

Kali nodded.

The doctor put a hand on her shoulder in a way that would make her yell harassment if he were twenty years younger. But he wasn't; he came from a different era, and he was offering her the opportunity she'd been waiting for. "I wouldn't recommend just anyone. When residents go into one of Westwood's palliative care wings, they know there's almost no chance they're coming out. So they need nurses with compassion, but also grit. Nurses who'll treat them like people, not lost causes. I've seen you here, with the hard cases. I think you've got what it takes."

Kali swallowed.

"Should I make the call?"

Her skin tingled. On-site child care. Day shifts. Regular day shifts. "Yes." The word choked coming out. "Yes, please."

CHAPTER TWENTY

Kali's cell phone had rung before she'd even made it back to the apartment. She had an interview at nine-o-clock tomorrow. She was scheduled to work, but called Shelley to switch her shift. This job could be the answer to her problems, could change her life. She'd make it change her life. She'd do such an amazing job they'd find a place for her after the maternity contract expired. Westwood Manor. It was the dream job. The place nurses joked about—an interview there akin to Prince Charming showing up at your door with a glass slipper. Her foot would fit.

Kali pulled the sheets up over Theo, brushed a hand across his forehead, then leaned in for a kiss. The boy shifted in his sleep but didn't rouse. She envied that, the way he slipped into sleep so quickly, so quietly. She stood in the doorway watching him. She'd come home determined to talk to Lincoln. In his mind, she had five more days before she was leaving. But she needed another month. Possibly two if this new plan worked. That whole just deciding to stay and letting him deal with it thing was no longer a good idea. She couldn't risk him kicking her out. She needed to know she could stay.

Kali closed her eyes and placed a hand against the door jamb, still gazing at her boy. She shook her head, pulled the door shut, then stepped out into the hall. She had to get the job. Had to wow them. Two weeks unpaid work when she was trying to save enough for first month's rent and a deposit for an apartment could seriously screw her over.

In the living room, Lincoln lay strewn across the couch. One hand hung off the edge and dangled, his fingers grazing the floor. His hair fell across his brow, just as Theo's always did. Exhaustion seemed to ooze from him.

Kali sat on her own couch and pulled out her laptop. The conversation could wait. If anything, it may make more sense to have it after the interview, after she got a sense for whether she'd actually get the job. If she didn't, she'd have to find another—leave nursing if that was her only choice.

Of course, maybe Theo would have a breakthrough. She'd get him in a preschool and not have to worry that either the kids or the staff would demean him. That could work too. She'd take more shifts at the hospital and be able to pay someone to watch Theo overnights. Mrs. Martin watched him for almost nothing in the day but overnights, she said, made her uncomfortable—a boy should be in his own bed, as should she. And for Kali, it meant finding someone she could trust. She shook her head, it was ridiculous to think about making plans based on Theo having a breakthrough. That may not happen for years, months.

Kali navigated to Netflix. Nothing. She checked the internet connection. Secured. Whoever she'd been stealing from had wised up and set a password. She closed the monitor and leaned back. Her life was meant to be different. She was meant to be different.

But then Derek had come along. Derek with his big dreams. Derek with his plans for the future. Derek, who sabotaged her plans with his shiny words, shiny smile, shiny ring.

Not that she regretted Theo. She'd never regret Theo, but ... *But.*

"You okay?"

Kali convulsed at the sound.

Lincoln was staring at her. "I didn't mean to startle you."

Kali brushed at the stray tear on her cheek. "I was just thinking, is all. Thought you were sleeping."

"I was."

Kali pushed herself up and pulled her legs under her. "Sorry if I woke you. I was trying to be quiet."

"It's fine." Lincoln sat so he was facing her.

She pushed out a smile, hating he'd seen her like that, seen her moist eyes. "Dinner was great. Thanks again."

He nodded.

"Where'd you learn to cook like that?"

"Self-taught, mostly. A little from my mother, though she tends toward heartier fair."

"Oh yeah?"

"I used to cook a lot."

"And then?"

Lincoln looked away from her. His chest rose and fell. "Life."

Kali made a noise of understanding. Life. She looked to her lap. He was awake now. She could broach the subject, say she needed another month—probably two. Most likely two. Two and a bit. June still had close to a week left after all.

"Can I ask you something?"

Kali's head shot up.

"You don't have to answer. I mean, I get ... it's sensitive and ..." Lincoln shifted, winced. His back was throbbing—he shouldn't have been wielding that axe. Stupid. "Theo. Is he, I mean." Lincoln swallowed. "He's obviously smart."

"Incredibly smart," Kali snapped.

"Yeah, so ... has he never talked or—?"

Kali took a breath, counted to three—there was no time for ten. She had brought her son into this man's life. And he was sweet to him. Patient with him. Welcoming. Kind. "He started to talk early, actually." She smiled, remembering. "He was advanced. Smartest little two-year-old I'd ever seen."

"And then?"

Kali rubbed her fingers across her lips. She looked up at Lincoln, smiled. "Life."

He nodded, turned his gaze toward the window.

Kali put a hand to her neck. "I was so stressed out all the time while pregnant. Those last months, especially. Angry. Worried. How would I do this alone? How would I finish school? How would—" She exhaled. Lincoln shifted toward her. "I had my mom back then. Or I figured I would. If needed. I'd moved out a few years previous. I never planned to go back."

Lincoln stayed silent. Kali rubbed her hands down her thighs, her mouth opening the moment the action stopped. "So, I wonder sometimes if all that anxiety seeped into him. Made him a skittish child. Prone to ... but it was more than that. Certainly more than that."

Kali kept her gaze straight ahead, not sure who she was talking to, Lincoln, or herself. Finally saying it. Even Shelley didn't know the details. "Mom had always been an anxious person. Growing up she never wanted friends over. Scared of what my father would or wouldn't do, would or wouldn't say. When he left she was scared of the judgement, of the way our life screamed lack." A thin bead of sweat trickled down the curve of Kali's back. "So I didn't have the chance to be anxious, to be scared. I was determined. And then I wasn't."

Kali's brow furrowed. The lights out the window looked so much nicer than the world they illuminated.

"And your mother?"

Kali spun her gaze toward Lincoln. Had she forgotten he was there? No. She just expected he'd remain silent.

"She passed a couple of years ago."

"Around the time Theo stopped speaking?"

Not around the time, *at* the time. "Mmmhmm."

"And your father?"

Kali raised her shoulders and let them fall. "Haven't seen or heard from him since I was a little older than Theo."

"Rough."

"Is what it is." Kali uncrossed her legs then leaned them side by side; her elbow pushed into the couch back, her hand on her head.

Lincoln's gaze was on her. She took it, placing her gaze right back on him.

"And Theo's father, is he—"

"Theo doesn't have a father." Kali pursed her lips. "Not anymore."

Lincoln nodded. "I'm sorry."

Another shrug. A slight smile. "Life."

A car screeched to a halt outside the window. A woman yelled a list of obscenities. Romper leapt toward the sound, his paws up on the sill, trying to see the commotion.

"And you were married?"

Kali looked to her hand, to the spot where the ring used to sit. Much to her surprise, she'd liked it there. She'd seen men traipse in and out of her mother's life, none of them bringing anything good, anything lasting ... except deeper debt. And the things they took—her mother's laughter, sense of self-worth, joy. Kali had no intention of letting a man take any of those things. She determined she'd stay single her whole life before she let that happen. And then Derek came along. And it'd been incredible.

She still had the ring. She'd sell it if she had to, if Lincoln kicked her out. Maybe it'd be enough for first month's rent. *And were you married?* He had asked. Kali curled her hand into a fist. "I guess I still am."

Lincoln's breath came out heavy. Stop, Kali wanted to say. Just—

"Was it an accident or ... was he sick? I shouldn't ... I ... he ... he must have been young."

Kali looked away, her chest clenching. "He was trying to be a hero. Had a hero complex, maybe. Out at Peggy's Cove. The waves were massive. And some stupid mother let her stupid kid get close to the rocks. And my stupid husband—"

Kali's voice caught. Her eyes brimmed with anger. That's what this liquid was. Anger. Not sadness. Not pride—which is how people expected her to respond to her hero of a husband. Her hero of a husband who jumped into the raging Atlantic with a wife who was four months pregnant. Who'd not even started to show. Who had put her trust in him.

Kali pointed to the large table in the centre of the room, the eyesore she walked around day in and day out. "What's with the tree houses? Are you trying to sell them? Is that how you make your income? Who wants a miniature tree house?"

Lincoln's gaze followed hers. "They're models."

"Models?"

"Yeah. They're not for money. They're for me."

Kali shifted. "You want a tree house? You don't even have a yard."

Lincoln smiled. He was looking away from her—at the desk? Through the window? She couldn't tell. "I have land. A lot."

"A—?"

"With the perfect tree."

Kali's mouth hung open.

"Hence the axe, the lugging of lumber."

He was weird. A grown man. A man who was educated, who had books on architecture, electrical systems, plumbing, and natural energy—stuff Kali knew nothing about. She had suspected he'd been an architect in his past life, or was studying to head back to school. "You're building a tree house ... as a place to retreat to? Kind of like a cabin in the woods?"

"Exactly like a cabin in the woods. Though not to retreat to. To live." He glanced over at her, then pulled his gaze to the table, his eyes scanning the items. "The big challenge is making it as self-sufficient as possible. Heating in the winter is key. I'll live off the land as much as I can, but heating in the winter and refrigeration in the summer. That'll be the trick, and to get both of them done safely."

"Right." He was crazy. Kali stood. "Well, I'm off to bed." Something deep inside her clenched. He wanted to live in the woods. In a tree house. In Nova Scotia. He was definitely crazy. Would any normal person, any sane person want that?

Kali picked up her laptop. Hopefully, at least, his crazy

was of the harmless variety. Two more months. Which meant she had time. Lots of time to talk to him about staying on into July. Into August. He hadn't asked her when she was leaving, so why should she tell? So long as he wouldn't kick her out—she didn't think he'd kick her out. So long as his crazy wasn't dangerous. She made her smile soft and welcoming. "Have a good night, Lincoln. Sleep well."

He nodded, his gaze still on the table, a look of contemplation on his face. Kali didn't know whether to hug him, tell him whatever he was running from couldn't be so bad, or to go running herself. She reached for Theo's backpack, which also held the book she'd been reading—something she'd need now that there was no Netflix—and stepped into the hall.

CHAPTER TWENTY-ONE

K ali rolled over and reached for her alarm. She'd forgotten to reset it. No seven a.m. shift today, but a nine o'clock interview. She squeezed her eyelids tight and pressed a hand to her forehead. Hammers? No. More like one hard hammer or mallet pressing against her skull, or like her brain had become that mallet and was trying to explode.

Kali pressed her hand harder, trying to push the pain away. She let out a soft moan and reset the clock. She should get up, take a long shower, prep for the interview. But perhaps another hour of sleep would take the pain away.

She'd been waking up with headaches off and on for a week now, and yesterday nausea accompanied it, but nothing like this. Not even close to this.

When the alarm sounded again Kali rolled over. Had she even slept? Her head throbbed, her stomach roiled. It made sense, the stress of the last few weeks, the move, the uncertainty of life constantly pushing in on her—no wonder her mind and body would try to push back.

Kali squeezed Theo into her, kissed his head, then crawled out of bed. The old, gnarled hardwood was cool on her feet.

She stopped a moment to enjoy it. Her home growing up had sticky linoleum. Her last apartment—well, it had old hardwood too, but with the consistent fear of rat droppings, she never went barefoot. Kali stepped into the hall. Her vision blurred and her head spun. She put a hand to the wall to steady herself and took several breaths, her other hand rubbing up and down over the side of her face. Everything seemed covered in lace. She blinked the haze away and stepped from the wall. Coffee could wait. She needed a shower—hot, then cold water to force her awake.

The water felt good. Amazing. Kali rotated under the stream. As she stood, the headache eased and her thoughts wandered. A tree house in the woods. Not to visit. Not as a retreat. But to live. What had happened to that man? She could get wanting to be alone, a place to escape to, but this was why he studied those books? Why his living room looked more like a workshop than a home? Why he had no job? And as he had no job, where was the money coming from? Three hundred a month wasn't a lot, but it was something—plus food, plus utilities.

Kali worked the conditioner through her hair. She didn't want to think about it. She shouldn't think about it. Obviously, he was still in the planning phases. He wouldn't be abandoning this place for a shelter in the woods any time soon. And that's all she needed. Time. Just a bit of time. His business was his business, and hers was hers.

Kali wrapped a towel around her. The shower had worked. That mallet pressing into her skull had subsided to a mere touch. Tension. Annoying, but nothing to ruin her day. Nothing to distract. She stood in the mirror. Should she pin her hair back, try to make it smooth and un-intimidating? No.

She wanted the job, but she wanted it as her. And this hair, this unruly afro, it was her. She rubbed a second towel through her hair and added some product. She faced the mirror again.

She could do this. She *would* do this. And today would change her life for the good.

Kali pulled on her clothes then made her way to the bedroom to awaken Theo. Only rumpled sheets lay on the mattress. She switched on the light, scanned the room, then passed through the living room to the kitchen. Theo sat in his chair, legs swinging.

"What you got there?"

Theo tipped up his plate. French toast? Kali turned to Lincoln, who stood at the stove. "Our roles reversed?"

Lincoln shrugged and flipped a piece of toast. "Thought you might be sick or something. You slept later than usual." He gestured his head toward Theo. "And this guy came knocking on my door, rubbing his belly.

Kali went to Theo. "I told you not to disturb—"

"It's okay." Lincoln cut her off and held out a plate with two pieces of French toast.

"These look good."

"Fresh baked bread. Makes all the difference. A fluff factor sliced can never get."

"Fluff factor?"

Kali sat at the table, staring at her food. "Don't think you have to start making meals now. I mean, we're not your guests."

"I don't." Lincoln faced the stove as he talked. Had he always been this tall? She supposed she wouldn't know. From the first moment she saw him he'd been limping, curved over.

And in every moment since then he'd had crutches under his arms. She could tell he had good posture before, just from the way he worked the crutches, from the way he stood when only leaning on one, but his posture now ... it was the posture of a man who knew his place in the world. But did he?

Kali watched him move. Despite the state of his pantry when she'd moved in, he clearly wasn't a novice in the kitchen. What had he done before ... this?

He turned, a smile on his face, and stepped to the table. Kali took her first bite.

"Shift change?"

She chewed longer than she needed. The truth? Some lie? Or just as much truth as he needed to know? "Uh, no. Well, kind of. Doing a half shift today."

"Oh, yeah?"

"Yeah."

"So, you have the morning off?"

"Well—" She glanced at Theo.

"I'm heading to the lot soon so you won't be in my way."

"These are really good." Kali took another bite. "Thanks. I see what you mean about fluff factor."

Lincoln laughed. He never laughed with her, only Theo. Sometimes Romper. "Thank you. I'd forgotten how much I liked food. How much I liked preparing it too."

Kali nodded. Forgotten?

"So, that apartment work out? If you need help moving I can help you, though I don't know if the two of us could handle that bed or dresser. You have someone else?"

"Uh ..."

"Or planning to hire? If it's not too far, a few trips in my truck may mean you don't need a van."

Kali stared at him.

Lincoln lowered his fork, tapped it on the ridge of his plate. "If you want. Maybe you have it all figured out already, but if you don't, I don't mind helping. Just glad to be behind the wheel again. Get my freedom back."

Kali bit her lip.

"Not that I used the truck a ton. I take it to the lot. On hikes. But when you can't do something ..." His words trailed off. "Are you okay? Did I? What's—?"

Kali swallowed, the bite she'd taken a lump in her throat. She reached for Theo's glass of milk, wishing she'd thought to get her own. "I'm, uh, actually, going to an interview this morning."

"Oh, yeah?" Lincoln's brow rose. "Well, that's good."

"Yeah." Kali took another bite. Lincoln's fork remained at the edge of his plate. He watched her.

"You nervous?"

Kali swallowed again. "A bit. It's a good job. A dream position." Again, how much to tell? Would he forget about the move? Could she just not leave? Better to say sorry than please, right? That's what she was betting on. Betting he wouldn't kick her out. He'd made them breakfast. Kali smiled. He couldn't be that desperate for them to leave.

Lincoln leaned back in his chair. "And this interview, it affects you taking that apartment? It in another location or ..."

That was true. The apartment she'd liked, the one she couldn't realistically afford but had seen anyway, was near the hospital. Her interview was across the harbour in Dartmouth, though she could be at any of the three main Westwood Manor locations. With no internet, she hadn't looked up which location had the staff childcare.

"Yeah. Exactly." The lies came smoothly. "I wasn't sure about the job, whether I'd even get the interview, and didn't want to lock myself into a one-year lease that would mean a crazy commute." Kali glanced at Theo, who ate slowly, his gaze travelling between her and Lincoln. Her throat tightened. She hated lying in front of him. Not that she hadn't done it before. "I should have told you. I was holding off, trying to figure things out, and that apartment's taken now."

Lincoln nodded. "So?"

Kali kept her face even, casual. Did she go into it all, say she couldn't pay him if he wanted her gone sooner than later? Couldn't pay him yet, at least. He didn't need details. And if she didn't get the job? Worse, if she got it conditional to the two weeks training and then failed to live up to their expectations? With no bump in pay and two weeks of no work, who knew how long she'd have to rely on his charity?

"So," Kali set her fork down, "if it's all right," she looked at Theo again, offered him a little smile, "if we could stay another month."

"Another full—"

"Two at the most. At the absolute most." She swallowed, this time nothing but tension blocking her throat. "I know it's an inconvenience. I know—" Her breath came short. Why? Why was she here? Begging to a stranger. Why had this happened? She pushed back the anger, the resentment that threatened to leak out and pour all over Lincoln. This wasn't about her. Wasn't about her pride. She looked at Theo again. It was about Theo, keeping Theo safe. And for now, at least, Lincoln's place was safe.

"It would really help." Her voice wavered. "I'm not sure what else—" She let out a thin stream of air. "I just—" She raised her hands, palms up. Don't cry. Do not cry. "We're in a bad situation here. But I'm trying to make it better."

Lincoln made a sound deep in his throat, then nodded. "Another month. Two at the most."

Kali inhaled sharply, relieved she'd held back her tears. It was okay. She wouldn't be sent to the street, or some homeless shelter, or worse—throw herself upon the mercy of some past friend, now barely more than an old acquaintance. For now, it'd be okay.

Kali looked from her plate back to Lincoln. "Thanks. That's, uh, that's great."

CHAPTER TWENTY-TWO

Lincoln held his axe high and let it fall against the large branch.

Another month.

He raised the axe again, his muscles taut.

Two, maybe.

He let the blade fall, and the limb succumbed. He stared at it, his breath coming in quick gasps, and wiped his forearm across his forehead. They hadn't discussed a specific length of time, a specific end date. But the assumption had been the end of the month. Time enough for her to find a new place. Time, so that she and her boy wouldn't end up on the street.

Lincoln lowered to bring the branch closer. He stood perpendicular to it and hacked away at the smaller branches and twigs. It was a good piece, a strong piece. Good enough to help form his wall. He dragged the cleaned limb to a pile he was collecting. Two more months. Two more months without his own space. Two more months of the confusion and disorder Kali's existence brought to his life.

He let the axe dangle and stood tall, taking in the land around him. His land. At least he had this. And maybe them being in his apartment would be stronger motivation to get the work done, make this land his home sooner. Lincoln surveyed the wooded area: free from disruption, free from disorder, free from Theo's smiles and laughter, from the curve of Kali's neck.

Lincoln chuckled, remembering the way Theo's eyes widened as Lincoln put the plate in front of him this morning, how he smacked his lips with exaggerated pleasure after each bite.

And Kali? She was a bother, sure. Always around. Always with her scathing glances, her looks that dripped of ... resentment? Which was ludicrous. He was doing her the favour. Not that it would be easy—taking charity from a stranger. Finding yourself in someone else's home and not quite knowing how to fit.

But there was the curve of that neck. And the fact that she was helpful. She cooked. She cleaned. One night last week when she'd thought he was asleep on the couch, she pulled a blanket up under his chin.

Lincoln stood beneath the tree that would hold his home. Soon, he'd build a temporary platform, clear away the branches that would get in the way of his planned structure.

Heart still pumping, Lincoln sank to a stump. How long had he been hacking away at the brush around the base of the trunk? Fifteen minutes? Twenty? He used to pump iron with his brother and their friends for an hour. Of course, they'd joke and laugh in between. Spot each other. When he was a teenager, summers working construction with Andrew by his side, they hauled two-by-fours for hours. They hammered away the afternoons. And, sometimes, still had the energy for a hike or swim afterward. Maybe he was getting old. Thirty wasn't that far away. Lincoln grinned in the stillness. Lucy had been terrified of thirty. Like it was a death sentence. Like when the day came she'd suddenly gain twenty pounds, her hair would gray, and her face succumb to wrinkles.

He'd teased her about it, secretly thinking she got prettier with each year. More the woman and less the girl. Not that thirty had been super close for either of them. Even now, he still had over two years to wait. Thirty.

The things he thought when he was young: By thirty he'd be married to a wonderful woman. Beautiful. Smart. Funny. As good a cook as his mother. He'd have at least one kid. Maybe two. He'd have his own business—like his dad had. Small, perhaps, but thriving. And with the knowledge he'd glean from his father's advice and input, he'd one day surpass his father's success. Or, a not so bad alternative, his father would retire and he and Andrew would take over the business. Partners. Joseph, he assumed, would pursue some other endeavour.

Lincoln leaned his head in his hands. Partners. When his father started to disappear, the dreams had shifted. No longer would Dad guide Lincoln through life. It was Joseph he turned to. Joseph who exploded the company, took it further, and made it larger than their father ever imagined. Joseph who groomed Lincoln. Who pushed him. Directed his path. Made them all rich.

Enter Lucy.

Lucy, who pushed aside any of Lincoln's resistance. Who persuaded him, when he'd considered going to school for architecture, that an MBA, as Joseph suggested, was the right choice. Lucy, who took his dream of a house just outside the city, built by his own hand, close to his parents' home but not so close they'd pop in daily, and transformed it into dreams of new and modern condos in cities far away. Montreal. Toronto. Vancouver. Wherever the business moved. Wherever Lincoln would have the most power. The highest salary.

He let her groom him. Let *them* groom him. Never suspecting there was more to their team effort. Believing the life they laid out was what he wanted—what he always wanted.

Lucy even had him collecting art, which he pretended to understand. Lines and corners. No feeling. No story. Like Lucy, like her beauty. Stunning, but sharp.

He should have seen it sooner, her lack of real affection. If he hugged her too tight, she'd chastise him for a wrinkled dress. If his kiss smudged her lipstick, she'd roll her eyes and pull out a compact. Did she do the same with Joseph?

Or had it been Joseph she wanted all along? Had she resented Lincoln because, out of deference to him, Joseph refused to go public, refused to come clean and commit?

Lincoln picked up the axe and hurled it. Romper convulsed, yelped, and sent Lincoln a look of accusation.

"It was miles from you," Lincoln yelled. Romper lowered his head, his gaze still on Lincoln. "Miles." Lincoln yanked the axe out of the trunk it had wedged in. He leaned his head against the tree. *It probably wasn't even your baby.* Lincoln had known something was wrong in those last months. Lucy, who in the beginning had encouraged him to work, encouraged him to devote his life to the business, started to resent it.

She encouraged him to go out, have fun. Encouraged him to make friends. Told him he needed a life, a life that revolved around more than his job, and more than her. But he couldn't. He didn't have time. She'd created him. Created his drive, his need to succeed. And success didn't come easy. Not for Lincoln. Joseph could do it all—win in the office and win in life. Lincoln had to choose. And he chose the office. Joseph was the full package. Lincoln was not.

He saw it, and so had Lucy.

Had that been when she decided she couldn't pretend anymore? Couldn't stand a life with the wrong brother?

She'd told him one day she was going off birth control. That she'd read an article about how bad it was for women, and why should she have to put synthetic hormones in her body that could cause irreparable damage when, instead, he could wear a harmless piece of rubber. He'd agreed. It wasn't like they were sleeping together too often by that point anyway. But had avoiding synthetic hormones been her only motivation? Had she been trying to trap Joseph—not Lincoln—into finally making a choice?

Lincoln turned from the tree. Not even close to a full day. Three measly hours. But he couldn't be out here. Not now. Not today, with all these thoughts. The ball in his gut landed with a thud. But what would he do when he was living here permanently. Where would he run?

Maybe it wasn't the location, but the work. His back was throbbing. He'd been pushing too hard, too soon. Lincoln crouched in front of Romper, willed him to come to him. Romper stared a moment, then, forgiveness granted, padded over. Lincoln cupped his hand behind the dog's head. Scratched, rubbed. He wrapped his arms around the furry body like a child would. He held on, one second, two, enough was enough. He stood.

"Come on." Lincoln gestured toward the trail leading to the car. "That's all today." Lincoln looked straight ahead. It made sense to take it easy. He was still recovering, after all.

CHAPTER TWENTY-THREE

On Canada Day, Lincoln took the steps to his apartment two at a time. He'd left early—before Kali and Theo had risen, before the traffic going out of the city became a burden. And he'd been right to return to the city in the late afternoon, while people were busy setting up their barbecues or heading to the park for free concerts, while the highways and roads were clear.

He'd had a good day of work, a great day. His body was finally getting back to where it was meant to be. The perfect holiday treat. Kali and Theo would be out somewhere, enjoying the festivities, and Lincoln would have the place to himself. He'd blare a record—even Sandy from downstairs wouldn't complain on a holiday—let the music and the water flow over him, and relax.

Romper barked and did a little dance when they reached the landing. Odd. Lincoln turned the key and opened the door. Kali and Theo sat on the living room floor, a large puzzle before them. Romper ran to Theo, who gave him a little pat, then moved his attention back to the puzzle.

"Hi."

"Hi," Kali looked up, "wow."

Lincoln looked to his clothes. Dirt stained. Sweat stained. His arms were no better. "Been working."

"At the lot?"

"Uh huh."

Kali nodded and brought her attention back to the puzzle. She held up a piece. Theo stared at it then pointed to a spot. Lincoln rubbed his arm, still standing in the doorway. It wasn't a big deal. With all the hours he'd been putting in at the lot, and Kali arriving home shortly after him the past few days, he hadn't had the place to himself in too long. But it wasn't a big deal.

Lincoln stepped toward them. "There's a concert at the Commons. Big bouncy castle too."

"Yeah. Usually is." Kali kept her gaze on the puzzle.

"Bet Theo would like it. You two should check it out."

"It's pretty crowded."

"Yeah, but—"

Theo pulled on Kali's arm. He did a little bounce.

Kali looked to him. "It's so noisy. Tons of kids. I don't think you'd like it." Kali made a crazy face. "And the concert. Drums. Boom, boom!" She clapped her hand against the floor.

Theo stared at her then dropped his gaze to the puzzle; he reached for a piece.

Noisy? So many kids? Shouldn't that be a three-year-old's dream?

Lincoln hovered over them. Kali looked up. "Good day of work?"

"Yeah."

He swallowed. Looked to the door. He couldn't kick them out. But he wanted his record. Wanted his space.

"Want to join us?"

"No, uh ..." Lincoln kicked off his work boots and headed toward the hall. "Going to shower."

When he emerged from his bedroom less than a half hour later, Lincoln went to the fridge. His head ached. Dehydration, most likely. A tall glass of water—he searched the produce drawer—with cucumber would do the trick. He closed the fridge door and jumped. Kali stood smiling at him, un-phased.

"You have any plans for dinner?"

"No."

Lincoln took the cucumber to the cutting board and set down the pitcher of water.

Kali leaned against the counter. "I was thinking something special—since it's Canada Day. Or at least a little special. I know you don't have a barbecue, so I asked the lady downstairs, Sandy. She's nice you know."

Lincoln didn't look up. She was so close. Why was she standing so close? "I know."

"She said we could use hers. I got freshly made burgers." She paused. "From the meat department." Her hand rested on the counter, just in his line of vision. "Partially so as not to buy a whole box. Didn't want to keep asking her."

"Smart."

"You in, then? As it's Canada Day?"

Lincoln shifted away. "Burgers sound great."

"I got some beers, too. For after Theo's in bed." She hesitated. He could feel her gaze on him. "Maybe indulge while looking out at the fireworks. You've got a perfect view here." She smelled good. What was it—shampoo? Some kind of body lotion? Lincoln shifted farther away. He glanced at her, lips pursed. She tilted her head. "You okay?"

"I'm fine."

"Sorry." Kali pushed off the counter, her easy mood gone cold at his sharp response. The tension shot from her like arrows. "I was just trying to be nice. I know you expected us gone by now. But if you have plans or you don't want to join us, you certainly don't have to."

Lincoln let the air stream out of his nostrils. He tossed the cucumbers into a glass and turned to Kali. "No, burgers sound great. I had no plans." He paused. "Thanks. For the invite."

"Sure." She shifted, arms across her middle.

"I'm heading to my room for a bit. Let me know when dinner's ready?"

Kali grabbed two glasses from the cupboard and sent him a false smile. "As you wish."

Meat drunk, and buzzed from three cans of beer, Lincoln lay against the couch. "Those burgers were good."

"You've said that." Kali grinned. "You know, this may be the first time I've had more than one drink in an evening since before Theo was born." She made a noise like a satisfied cat. "Since before I found out I was pregnant, I suppose."

"What's the occasion?"

She held up her can. "Why the birth of our nation, of course." Liquid sloshed from it.

"And that's your third. And you've hardly touched it." Lincoln laughed. "You're a lightweight."

Kali wiped drops of beer from her arm and smiled. Oh, that smile. This time, not in the least bit false. "I suppose I am."

Lincoln pushed himself up and set his beer can down. He glanced to the room where Theo lay sleeping. "So this afternoon, avoiding the bouncy castle. Noise is a problem?"

"Oh, no."

"What?"

"I'm not that drunk."

Lincoln reached for his can again. "I'm just asking." He took a swig. "I care about the kid."

Kali set her can on the top edge of the couch. "You do, don't you?"

Now it was Lincoln's turn to smile. "Hard not to."

"Mmm." A muffled blast sounded. Kali stepped to the window and pushed up the glass. The breeze ruffled her shirt and hair. "Ahh," she held her hands out, "how have we not had these open all night?"

"I like them closed."

"Sometimes." Kali twisted toward him. "When the salsa's blaring. That's when you like them closed." She waved a finger. "There's a story there. But I won't ask. Even though I want to know. Even though I love the sound of salsa."

She leaned her hands on the windowsill and stuck her head out. "I used to love fireworks. Canada Day was my favourite day. One year my mother took me down to Alderney Landing. I was maybe seven. And it was beautiful—all the people and the music. She bought us hot dogs and hamburgers. My mother never bought me anything when we were out. But that day she did." Kali twisted toward Lincoln, smiled, and turned back to the music. "And then the show started. All the lights. The colours. The sound that shot through me like a canon." She lifted her arms. "It was one of the best moments of my life." Her hands fell. Stayed there. Several more blasts sounded.

"Sounds like it was a good night."

167

"It was." She kept her back turned. "Something happened that night. I don't know what. Mom was gone for a few minutes. She told me to stay put. Then she was gone." A pause. "When she came back something had changed. She yanked me away before the fireworks had ended and we rushed toward the bus stop. She wouldn't talk to me. Would barely look at me. It was something bad."

"You don't know what?"

Kali shook her head, gaze still out the window.

"You never asked?"

Another shake. A succession of explosions, one after the other filled the room. She stared into the following darkness. "A sexual assault? Drug deal? News of my father? Maybe she even saw my father." Her knuckles gripped the sill. All the way across the room he could see her skin go tight. "No idea. I never asked. She never told." More bangs. Kali turned, a huge smile across her face. "Come to the window, Lincoln. You're missing it."

Lincoln took a breath and crossed the room.

CHAPTER TWENTY-FOUR

Lincoln stood behind Kali, his body close to hers. Not touching, he made sure of that, but close. Colours exploded over the harbour. Their brilliance lit up the sky and reflected in the black inkiness below.

"It's a good show this year." Kali's voice was wistful. Should he put a hand on her shoulder?

"Yeah. It's nice."

She tilted her head toward him. "Better in Montreal?"

"Yeah." He let out a little laugh. "Even better in Toronto. I bet Ottawa's best. The Capital and all."

"Probably." Kali pushed herself from the sill. "Want another beer?" She turned. "Damn it!"

Lincoln spun. Theo stood in the centre of the room—hands over his ears, tears streaming down his face, terror in his eyes.

Kali rushed to him. "Oh, baby." She covered his hands with her own and looked back at Lincoln. "The earplugs. I ... that damn beer."

"What?" Lincoln followed after them, watched as Kali urged Theo into bed, cradling him, holding him close. She reached one hand away and pulled open the top drawer of her bedside table, then inserted ear plugs into Theo's ears.

Theo didn't make a sound. Lincoln wanted to do something, make the pain stop, but he stood, helpless. Never had he seen anyone cry so silently.

Kali wiped Theo's tears and urged him to lie down. She wrapped her body around his.

Lincoln leaned against the door frame, hands stuffed into his pockets.

Kali sang.

Theo's rigid muscles softened. His body relaxed into the bed. Lincoln stepped away from the door and returned to the living room. He perched on the edge of the couch, elbows on his knees, waiting.

Less than twenty minutes later he heard the creak of Kali's footsteps on the hardwood. She stood across the room. Weary.

She slouched past him and sank into the corner of his couch. She never sat on his couch.

Lincoln shifted toward her. "What was that?"

She reached for a pillow. Shrugged. "There was an explosion."

"When your mom—"

"No, no. After."

"Okay?"

"At his daycare."

"Oh wow, uh—"

"Right as he spoke for the first time since my mom passed. It'd been weeks. Then he spoke. Then, boom."

Shit. Lincoln ran a hand over the back of his neck.

"It's like he thinks it's his fault. Like speaking makes bad things happen."

"That's, uh ..." Shit. "That's rough."

Kali laughed. "Isn't it?" She reached for a fresh beer. "But what to do, right? I'm paying three hundred bucks a month for a psychologist. No daycares will take the weird, developmentally disabled child who won't speak."

"Three hundred?" Lincoln shook his head. "And he's not ... I mean, he's smart."

"I know that." Kali drew out the words. "But I'm his mother. I'm biased." She set the beer down. "I know he's not weird. And he's not developmentally disabled or delayed or anything. He's just scared. He's hurting." Kali wiped a hand across her eyes. "It's not just me who knows this. The psychologist said he was smart, too. Advanced, even though he's choosing not to speak."

"And the therapy, it's not helping?"

"*She* says it's helping. But he still doesn't speak."

Music breezed through the window, loud and grating. 'Whoops' and cheers sounded along with it. A woman ululating. Was that what it was called?

Lincoln rose and started across the room.

"Stop."

"What?"

"Stop." Kali stood. "I want the music. I want the dancing." She crossed to the window. "It's louder than usual." She leaned out. "They're having a party!"

Lincoln stayed where he stood. Would Lucy be there? Joseph? Not likely. They'd be in Montreal—partying with the big dogs.

Kali stepped from the window, her hips moving, her arms swaying. Her feet ... doing moves he never could. She faced him. "Dance with me."

"What?"

"Dance." She came closer, her long red cardigan flowing around her.

Lincoln held his hands up. "I'm not a dancer. At least not like that."

"So learn." Her face was firm, almost frustrated. It eased into a smile.

"It's not that eas—"

She latched onto him. "Have you ever salsa'd?"

"No."

She adjusted his hand on her back, pressed to make the hold firm, and raised her other hand in his. "This is your frame."

"Okay." Lincoln swallowed. Her breath was warm; her hands, her body.

"I'll have to lead. Hold your frame firm. But let the rest of you relax. Move how I'm leading you to move."

Lincoln thought of one-two-three, five-six-seven. "Shoot." He stumbled over her feet. "Did I hurt—"

"It's okay." Kali positioned them again. "Relax. Then let me move you."

Lincoln closed his eyes, held the count in his head, and tried not to think of his feet.

"Good." A grin was in her voice. "I'd almost say you're a natural."

Lincoln opened his eyes. She was smiling at him. He tried to push down a blush, closed his eyes again. The song ended.

"Not bad." Kali looked up at him. New music rose. She took his hands. They went on like that. Two, three, four more songs. She taught him to move side to side, to push back. Two simple spins. She even showed him how to lead. The music shifted. His steps didn't work.

"What's—?"

"A cha-cha." She laughed, moving without him. "If you can walk, you can cha-cha." She backed away, stepped forward, all the while her eyes on him. All the while smiling. He didn't know she could be so light. "Try it."

"My hips won't move like that."

"They don't have to. Just your feet." She toned down the movement. "Like this."

Lincoln returned to the couch. "I'll sit this one out."

"Your loss." She closed her eyes, still moving. Swirling. Turning. With one smooth motion, she stripped off her cardigan, reached for a beer, and threw her head back, never missing a step.

"You used to do this a lot."

"Mmhmm. I taught for a couple of years. Before Theo."

"You must have been a teenager."

"Mmhmm." She turned away from him, swayed by the window, then stopped when the song did.

"Never thought of going back to it?"

She let out a hard laugh.

Lincoln stood and crossed the distance between them. "If you wanted ... I mean it's right next door. You could go see if they needed a teacher, or just go to dance. I could watch Theo."

She rested her hands on the sill; the muscles in her shoulders tensed.

"You could even go now if you wanted."

She turned. "Trying to get rid of me?"

"No." Lincoln stepped back, a lump rising in his throat. She smiled, looking at him like he hadn't been looked at in years, as if she saw a part of him he hardly remembered existed.

"Another dance?"

Lincoln didn't answer. He swallowed and brushed the hair out of his eyes. He should say no. He should definitely say—

He took her in his arms.

Though shorter, her body was bigger than Lucy's. Broader. Not that Kali was large, not even close. She was solid. Muscular. Firm, with the most womanly curves he'd ever touched. Lincoln tried not to look at her breasts—so close. His hand slid to her waist. Oh, the sway of that waist. His eyes had been on it half the night, on her hips, the way they moved as though hardly attached to her body.

The song faded then transitioned to a new one. "Bachata," she whispered. "This one's better close. Follow me."

He tensed as her leg slipped between his. But then he succumbed, lost in the movement. Lost in her. Half way through, she adjusted his hand so it rested against her shoulder blade and urged him to lead.

As the song ended he pulled her closer, put his hand beneath her chin to raise it, leaned in.

She pushed. "What are you doing?"

"I—"

"It's a dance, Lincoln. A friggin' dance."

Lincoln stepped back, extending the distance between them. "I know, I—"

"You know what?" Her body went rigid, her voice hard. "That this would be payment?"

"What? No."

"Is that what you want?" Her voice twisted. She pushed

her hips to the side, mocking a different kind of woman. "Payment? Will that make us even, make it so I'm not in your debt?"

"No." Lincoln moved farther back. What the fuck was happening? "That's not ... I don't want—"

"Look at you. As if," her voice faltered, "as if I'd want a loser like you. Someone who chose to be this way." Her eyes narrowed. "I know you don't have to be here."

"Kali—"

"Or maybe you do. Maybe you've gone crazy. Is that it? You've lost your mind, and so you're going to become a hermit in the woods. Or are you just some spoiled little rich boy who's throwing the biggest, stupidest tantrum ever? Daddy didn't love me so I'll show him by wasting my life and—"

Lincoln stepped forward. "Kali, what the fuck?"

"Get away from me!"

He backed up, hands raised. "I'm not. I—"

"What about when you're sick? Old? Will you still live in a tree?"

"I don't—"

"And here. In Nova Scotia. In friggin' Nova Scotia where the winters will probably kill you. Why don't you go somewhere warm? Somewhere where you won't end up some frozen corpse for people to find however many years later."

Lincoln stepped farther back, his mind reeling. He shook his head. Did she want an answer? He'd asked himself those same questions. Why was he here? Why was he trying to build his life of solitude here?

"This is my home."

"Your home?" She raised an arm, gesturing around the room. "*This* is your home? I thought it was some transition—"

"No, not here. Not—" Lincoln stepped toward the hall. "You're drunk and I ... I don't know what I was thinking. I shouldn't have—" He shook his head. "Happy Canada Day. Thanks for the burgers and booze."

CHAPTER TWENTY-FIVE

K ali flinched as Lincoln's door slammed. She stepped to the window then slammed the glass down.

Damn.

Damn. Damn. Damn.

She turned toward Theo and her room, listened for movement. If that slam had woken him again she couldn't handle it. Not now. She waited.

Silence.

Kali let out a long breath and wrapped her arms around her middle, staring where Lincoln last stood. So he tried to kiss her. Did that warrant what she'd said, how she reacted? She knew white boys thought dancing meant more—didn't understand the movement could be that and that alone. And had she lead him on otherwise? Maybe. Maybe she had looked at him like she wanted more. Had she?

No. Absolutely not. She'd just been tipsy with the dance and tipsy with the drink.

And he hadn't pushed it, hadn't forced a thing. He'd stepped away, looked genuinely sorry, genuinely embarrassed, yet she kept at him. Yelled at him. Mocked him.

He'd tried to kiss her, but that was it. Another man may have ... she shuddered at the thought. If he'd wanted to, if he'd been the type of man to insist, she couldn't have made him stop. But he'd stopped, and she'd torn him to pieces.

Kali stepped into the hall, staring at his closed door in the shadows. And now what? Should she go to his room? Apologize? Make sure she wouldn't wake up to find her belongings packed up, a note beside them—*Leave by tonight or I'll remove you myself.*

She stepped forward, then stopped. She couldn't knock on his door. She'd *never* knocked on his door.

It was stupid—getting drunk, letting down her guard, letting him think ... but she just wanted a night, one night to let go. To enjoy. Forget for a few hours that she hadn't heard back from the interview. Three days, and not a word. Forget that if she didn't hear back, she had no solid plan; without that job—hovering on the horizon like salvation—the future looked terrifying.

LINCOLN LAY IN BED. He hadn't heard feet in the hall, water from the bathroom, or the sound of her door close.

She was still out there. In his living room. In his space. And there was nothing he could do about it. Not a thing. Not until she was ready to leave. Not until he knew they'd be okay.

But her outburst had been good. Very good. A reminder. He'd let his guard down and he wouldn't again. He didn't need a woman—a woman *and* her child—screwing up his life.

Just because they shared the same space, that didn't mean they had to share each other's lives. And they wouldn't. Not anymore. He'd use their presence as motivation to get more work done. If worst came to worst, he'd be the one to leave. Leave her the apartment, and good riddance.

Lincoln let his tense muscles ease. Yes, tonight was good. Her outburst was just what he needed. She didn't want him, which was wonderful because he didn't want her either. The music, the beer, had been a slip. Nothing but a slip.

IN THE MORNING KALI woke with another raging headache. Different this time than the last. Worse. The pressure was there, that weird feeling like her brain was trying to explode. But along with it was an old familiar ache. Her head was foggy. Her vision was foggy. Her mouth tasted like cotton balls.

She wouldn't call in sick. Not for a malady of her own creation. Mostly of her own creation.

Theo had woken three times in the night, whimpering and shaking from the nightmares. She flicked off the alarm and checked on him. He was sleeping soundly now. She tiptoed out of the room. The sight of Lincoln's closed door brought it all back. Her rage. Her stupidity. The possibility that she may have destroyed the safe haven they had here.

The urge to go to him, apologize, returned. She stood with her fist poised at his door.

No.

Waking him up would not be the way to offer an apology. Food, perhaps? An awesome breakfast, and then she'd play it by ear, judge his mood.

Kali showered, changed, and had pancakes with fresh fruit ready—even though it wasn't Friday. She glanced toward Lincoln's door when she went to wake Theo.

Still shut. And no sound of Romper, whimpering at the door to get out.

After breakfast, with still no sign of Lincoln, Kali checked the front door. His boots were gone.

She glanced around the room. Her stuff was all where she'd left it. No note waited. So, it could be worse. Maybe he had forgotten. Maybe he didn't really care, or maybe ... three sharp taps sounded from the kitchen.

Kali entered the room. Theo smiled up at her then pointed to the stove.

"You want more?"

He nodded.

"Can your stomach fit more?"

Another nod—a big one.

"Well, all right then."

KALI ROLLED HER shoulders and stretched her arms. Her back ached. Her feet ached. Her eyes ached. Her brain felt like it was about to self-destruct, and she was battling her stomach to keep the day's meals inside of her.

Two car accidents, both with one of the drivers over the limit. Over a dozen injuries from drunken hijinks. And then the usual flus and food poisonings and sprains. The ER had been swamped when Kali walked in that morning and only slightly less swamped when she walked out. As much as she enjoyed a holiday, the repercussions in the ER were hardly worth it.

"Up to much last night?" Shelley questioned as they changed out of their scrubs.

"BBQ at home. A couple drinks." She hesitated. "Bit of dancing."

"You?" Shelley pulled her shirt over her head. "Drinks and dancing? You still remember how to do that?"

Kali forced a laugh. "Apparently."

"Well, that's good." Shelley pulled off her sneakers. "Where'd you go? And who'd you get to babysit? Isn't Mrs. Martin 'all children should sleep in their beds and I should too'?"

Kali turned to whip her shirt off and quickly pulled on a tank top, forever alarmed at how Shelley could stand in her bra like that, knowing any stranger could walk in. Even in junior high, when most of the other girls hid their developing bodies, Shelley walked around the locker room, half naked, like she owned the place. "Just at home."

"At home?"

Shelley slipped on a blouse but left it unbuttoned as she stepped toward Kali. "I've been meaning to ask you—I heard your building's been bought. You all right? Found another place?"

"Oh," Kali shimmied out of her pants, one eye on the door, "I already moved, actually. A temporary place."

"Why tem—"

Kali groaned inwardly. She might as well get it out. If she didn't, Shelley would pry until she felt satisfied. "I moved in with this guy. Just until I find a place."

"A guy, huh?" Shelley grinned. "About time."

"Not like that." Kali grabbed her satchel and slung it over her shoulder. "The guy from the accident. Turns out he had an extra room. Crazy low rent."

"The homeless guy? Kali, you're not—"

"He's not homeless. He just," Kali paused, "looks it. Besides," Kali pulled on her boots, "it's really short term."

"He could be a rapist or a pedophile or—"

"He's not."

Shelley finished buttoning her blouse. "If you were that desperate we could always squeeze you in. For a bit, at least."

"I'm not desperate." Not yet. "What about you? Good celebrations?"

"Family picnic. With the cousins and kids and in-laws. Screaming babies. Too much sun. It was a ball."

Kali edged her way to the door. "Sounds great."

"Seriously, Kal. You know anything about this guy?"

Kali let her shoulders fall. "We've been there a couple of weeks and—"

"Weeks!"

"And we've been fine so far. He's—" What was Lincoln? Weird. An introvert, clearly. Focused. Driven. "Decent. A very decent guy."

"Well, watch yourself." Shelley slipped on her pants and shoes. "And especially watch Theo."

Kali hesitated before pushing open the door. "I will."

IN THE PSYCHOLOGIST'S office Kali stared at the white walls, the painting of a coastal scene. That's what she wanted—to step right into the canvas, walk through into a new world.

Escape.

"Miss. Johnson?"

"Yes?" Kali turned.

"Dr. Richards will see you now."

Kali stood and nodded at the receptionist, who led her down the plushly carpeted hall.

She sat in the chair across from the psychologist. "Thank you for fitting me in."

"It's a pleasure. Though I only have a few minutes." She looked to her computer. "You said there was an episode last night?"

"The fireworks."

"Ah."

"I meant to put earplugs in for him before he went to sleep, but I forgot. He was pretty shaken up about it."

She nodded.

"I just wondered if—" Kali's voice caught. She shook her head and sat straighter. "You think it may have caused any lasting damage? Worse damage. I mean. He had nightmares again last night but then seemed fine this morning."

The doctor tilted her head and gave a motherly smile. "Kali."

"I've read about it. Post-Traumatic Stress Disorder. Repeated exposure to the stimulus can—"

"Children have nightmares."

"I know, but—"

"Outside of his speech delay, his aversion to loud noises, Theo is a well-adjusted young boy. He's bright, active. Reasonably sociable."

"Sociable? He hardly interacts with other children."

"The girl at—" Dr. Richards looked to the file on her desk,

"Mrs. Martin's. They seem to get along well."

"They do, but—"

"Have you been encouraging him to speak, rather than enabling his decision not to?"

"I try, but—"

"It's simple, Kali. You don't allow him to use actions. You act as if you don't understand. You make him realize that without words he won't get what he wants."

"If it's so easy, why don't you do it? Huh? Why hasn't he talked for you?"

"I told you." Dr. Richards wore that smile again, like Kali was some stupid child. "My office needs to be a safe environment. An accepting environment. I do coach him, but you're the one who's with him the most. I see him for two 45 minute sessions once a month."

Kali glared at the doctor. "You don't know what it's like. He doesn't even get angry. He gets upset. Sad. Like I'm betraying him."

"You're not meant to be his friend."

"I'm meant to be his mother!" Kali stood. "What do you expect me to do, not feed him if he refuses to talk? Watch him walk away hungry?"

"If he's hungry enough, he'll say what he wants to eat."

"You're ridiculous."

"Don't starve him, but push him."

Kali turned to the door.

"Come back."

She faced the doctor but stayed where she stood.

"I have homework for you. It's over a month away so you'll have time to mentally prepare for it. And to help Theo prepare for it too."

Kali crossed her arms.

"On Natal Day I want you to take Theo down to the harbour for the fireworks. Talk to him about it beforehand. Often. Not about the noise, though do let him know it's loud, but about the light, the excitement, the beauty. Explain what the noise is, that it's safe. Show him pictures, videos."

"I don't have TV."

"Use the internet."

Kali adjusted her satchel. "I don't have that either."

Dr. Richards pursed her lips. "You have a library card. Either way, I'll show him videos too."

"I don't know."

"Well, good thing you have time to think about it. It would be good—for his noise issue at least, to show him that not all loud bangs are scary. That some are great."

Kali stared at the doctor. Swallowed. She wanted to get angry. Was angry. But none of this was the doctor's fault.

"The world's a noisy place. Do you really want to raise a son who can't step out into it?"

And what if he had a breakdown out in that crowd? What if the nightmares got worse, if the explosions scared him so much he never spoke again? "I'll think about it." Kali reached for the door handle. "Thank you for seeing me on such short notice."

CHAPTER TWENTY-SIX

Kali stepped out of Dr. Richards' downtown office and into sunshine. Take Theo to the fireworks. Was the woman crazy? But she should take him to do something, get him out more. They hadn't left the downtown core in almost a month. Besides quick runs to the store, she hadn't driven in almost as long. She had tomorrow off. A beach trip would be perfect. Play in the sand, lounge in the sun, maybe even find some nice kids Theo could play with. And get out of Lincoln's way.

She'd tell Theo about that, get him excited about that. Not fireworks.

Kali's bag vibrated. She reached into the satchel. A blocked number. She hesitated. "Hello?"

"Kali Johnson?"

"Yes." Kali listened to the voice on the other end of the line, answered when she needed to, hung up when the person said goodbye. She held the phone to her chest and closed her eyes. She'd got it.

The Westwood job. She got it!

Well, she got the two-week long training interview. It

started in less than two weeks, and she'd rock it, be the best nurse they'd ever seen. Get the job. Get the childcare. Find a new place to live.

Kali practically ran to Mrs. Martin's. This would be it. This would get her life back on track. Maybe in a year or two, once they'd hired her full time, she'd have enough for a three bedroom apartment. A nice three bedroom apartment. Her, Theo, and Marvin too. She'd convince him. She'd make her life work, their lives work.

Marvin. Kali slowed her pace. With the fireworks last night, her hangover, the impromptu psych meeting, she'd forgotten tomorrow was the day she was supposed to take Theo to see Marvin. He wouldn't go to the beach, at least not a public one, but if she went to one of the secluded coves Derek had shown her, maybe he'd be convinced. Theo could play with kids another day.

KALI BREATHED DEEP the scent when Theo jumped into her arms. Nothing smelled like him. "How's my boy?"

He squeezed her tight then pulled back for a smile.

"Were you good for Mrs. Martin?"

Two big nods.

"And did you have fun with Cherie?"

Another nod.

"What'd you do?"

He looked to Mrs. Martin, who stood behind him. "They were trying to build a tree house, just now."

"A tree house?"

"A miniature one. For the birds. With Popsicle sticks."

Kali lowered Theo to the ground. "And whose idea was

this?"

"Who knows with these two." Mrs. Martin put one hand to her hip and waved the other, as if exasperated. "I said if it was for the birds it was a birdhouse, but no. They insisted it was a tree house. Adamant about that fact."

"Oh." Kali looked to Theo. "Like Lincoln."

A nod and a big smile.

Tightness spread through her chest. "Well, thank you, Mrs. Martin. I don't work again until Sunday."

"I'll see you then!" Mrs. Martin came out to the porch, waving as they made their way down the steps and to the sidewalk. It was just a tree house. Any kid would be intrigued with a tree house.

Nervousness and exhaustion washed back over Kali. Lincoln was likely home, unless he was specifically avoiding them. He could be at the library. Or taking Romper for a walk. Just let him be taking Romper for a walk. Let her have a few minutes to not fear his thoughts over last night.

A bark sounded from behind the door. Not a walk. But still, he could be gone. Once, he'd left without Romper. Kali put her key in the lock. The scent of bacon and onion and garlic wafted around them.

"Hey, boy." Kali bent to pat Romper, who barely gave her a glance of acknowledgement, his focus on Theo. Kali left the two at the door and stepped into the kitchen. Empty. No pots or pans with warming leftovers waited on the stove.

She walked down the hall and rapped gently on Lincoln's door. Nothing. Well, damn. Was he going to be this much of a child about it? She was about to knock harder when the toilet flushed. She stepped away from the door.

"Oh, hey." Lincoln appeared and stepped around her to

get to his room

"Hi." This wasn't her. Cowering. Not speaking her mind. "Whatever you made for dinner smells good."

"Yep." Lincoln put one foot over the threshold then hesitated. "Leftovers are in the fridge. I ate a couple of hours ago and wasn't sure when you'd be back."

"Great. Thanks." Kali stepped forward. "About last night."

Lincoln sighed and turned.

"I just—"

"Listen. Last night was stupid. A mistake. I'm sorry I—" He gestured toward her. "But maybe it was good. Get us to stop acting like we're ... anything, I guess. You're boarding here. A tenant. Whatever. We should keep our distance." He paused. "Like you said."

"No." Kali bit her lip. She wrapped her arms around her middle. She didn't want to be standing here. Hated that she needed him, needed to apologize for telling a man not to kiss her ... though that wasn't what she actually needed to apologize for. "I mean, it's not like we need to be best friends or anything but it's been nice, the way things have been going. I shouldn't have said," she pressed her lips, "the things I said."

"Kali—" Lincoln stood to his full height.

"I was upset. Stressed. I hadn't heard from that job, which I thought meant I didn't get it." She smiled. "But I did." Sort of. Lincoln didn't need to know it was tentative training.

He nodded. "Well, good. You start mid-August?"

"Officially, yeah."

"So we keep to ourselves as best we can. You start looking for an apartment. And the sooner we go our separate ways the better, for both of us."

"Lincoln."

"I liked my life the way it was. And I'm sure this isn't the ideal situation for you."

Kali stared at him. Of course it wasn't the ideal situation. But that didn't mean—

"I have reading to do. Have a good night."

The door closed behind Lincoln. A sound down the hall made Kali look up. Theo stood watching as Romper walked toward Lincoln's door. Had he heard? Would he even understand? Probably not. Maybe not.

"Hey, Sweetie. You hungry?"

Theo's head tilted to the side. Romper whimpered at Lincoln's door.

"Come on." Kali waved Romper up the hall and entered the kitchen in search of leftovers.

AN HOUR LATER KALI was sitting in the living room reading Theo stories.

"Was that a good one?"

Theo nodded. He held the book up to her. "No. Not again. We'll get some new ones from the library tomorrow."

He pushed the book toward her face.

"Theo." She tickled him and he squirmed. "Four stories is enough for any boy."

He held his hand up.

"Five? No, not five." She held her fingers up. "Four."

He shook his head and waved his hand, pointed to himself, held up four fingers. Then he pointed to the book. Four fingers again. Pointed to himself. Five fingers. To the books. Five.

"Ahh," Kali laughed, "four books because you're four, but you're not four yet. Soon. But when you turn five can you have five books?"

He nodded, his grin the one that clenched her heart. Kali leaned down to him. "We'll see. But what about when you're fifty?"

Theo raised both hands in a shrug and cocked his head to the side.

"How about we make a deal? If you still want me to read you stories when you're fifty, then I'll read you fifty stories." She paused. "For your fiftieth birthday."

Theo nodded vigorously. He stuck his hand out for a shake. Kali grasped it.

"Deal." She shifted him closer. "I have a surprise for you."

Theo's eyes widened.

"We're taking a trip tomorrow. To the beach!"

Theo pressed his lips together for a moment then raised his arms as if swimming. He put his hands together and mimed a dive.

"Yes." Kali clapped. "And not just the ocean. We'll play in the sand and lie in the sun AND—" she paused for effect, "we'll do our best to convince Grampie to come with us."

Theo's eyes widened again. He looked skeptical.

"I bet you could convince him. Tell him you really, really want him there."

Theo pulled back, a look of impending betrayal settling over him.

Kali's heart clenched again, this time for a different reason. "You could draw him a picture of all of us at the beach and give it to him, then give him a little tug so he knows you want him to come."

Theo scrunched up his face and put his hand to his chin. Kali couldn't help but smile. If he never spoke, at least he could have a career as a mime one day ... not that she wanted that.

Theo held out his arms and pushed forward.

"His cart?"

A nod.

That was a problem. It wouldn't fit in her car. "Maybe one of his friends could watch it." Did Marvin even have friends? "Or maybe we could empty everything out into the trunk and if he lost the cart, he could get another one."

Theo seemed to consider this for a moment. He jumped off the couch and ran to the corner where his paper and crayons were. He held a sheet up.

"No." Kali gave him a smile. "Not tonight. You can draw Grampie the picture tomorrow morning when I'm making breakfast."

Theo held up the paper again.

"Tomorrow."

He set it down.

"Bedtime now. Let's go brush your teeth."

KALI RETURNED TO THE living room and pulled a book out of one of the boxes she'd yet to unpack. She wanted to watch a movie, not read. Wanted to lose her thoughts in some comedy. But with no internet, her computer felt useless.

Kali was three pages into the novel when she looked up. "God." She gasped. "You startled me."

"Sorry." Lincoln approached, then stopped about five feet away. "Theo has a grandfather here?"

Kali sat up.

"I wasn't eavesdropping. I was in the kitchen."

"He does."

Lincoln shifted. Something wasn't right. "Then why didn't you move in with him?"

"What?"

"If Theo has this grandfather who you're obviously close enough with to take to the beach, why didn't you move in with him? He didn't have a couch you could squat on?"

Kali clenched her teeth. "He doesn't have a couch. He doesn't even have a house."

Lincoln stared at her. His expression shifted as recognition seemed to fall on him. "The bottle collector?"

Kali swallowed. She nodded.

"He's your—no. Your husband's father?"

"He is."

"Geez." Lincoln moved to his couch and sat. "Well, that explains it. So you two are still close?"

"He matters. He's Theo's grandfather."

"How did he—" Lincoln stopped.

Kali searched his face. What was going on in his head? Would whatever money he had that let him live here without working, let him think he could build a tree house in the woods to survive the winter, run out? If it did, he'd probably end up like Marvin. Only from the lack of visitors he'd had so far, Kali doubted he'd have someone like her to look out for him.

Marvin had been normal once. Had a house and a job and a family. And then he hadn't ... and he'd broke. "How did he what?"

"How did he end up like that?"

Kali closed her book and stood. Lincoln wasn't her

concern, he'd made that clear, and she and the things that mattered to her weren't his. "Didn't you say it's best we kept to ourselves? That means not asking questions about my family."

Lincoln didn't respond, and Kali left the room.

CHAPTER TWENTY-SEVEN

Over the next week and a half, Lincoln hardly saw Kali—which was good, which was the way it should be.

And then she started training.

She was home in the mornings when Lincoln got a later start to his day. Home in the evenings when he returned from the lot or, if the weather wasn't good, returned from a day researching at the library. And she'd have supper made. And she'd offer him to join them. He could have said no and taken his food to his room, but the one time he had, Theo had spent the next few days sending him curious glances. Once, when Lincoln was about to leave, just after finishing the last bite on his plate, Theo grabbed Lincoln's pant leg and smiled. It was some magical power, that smile. So he sat. He interacted with Theo and chatted with Kali. It wasn't that bad. And when he needed to get away, at least he had his room. He always had his room.

"Lincoln?" Kali stood outside his bedroom door. "Can I come in? Can we talk?"

Come in? She had never come in.

Romper perked up, shifted his head between Kali and Lincoln, then settled it back down. Lincoln gave the dog's head a rub. "Uh, sure."

The room was sparse. A bed. A bedside table. She stepped in, closed the door behind her, and stood.

Lincoln rubbed a hand along the back of his neck. "What do you want to talk about?" She held a paper in her hand. Hands. Clenched it, almost. It was the last day of her training. Had things not gone well? Was she losing the job? Would she have to stay longer?

"A couple of things." She gestured to the foot of the bed. He nodded and kept his mouth shut, though he wanted to tell her to get on with it, say whatever she had to say. She sat. Minus the day after Canada Day, it'd been weeks since Kali had been timid. Not that she'd walked around like she owned the place, more like it was her place too, like she knew he wouldn't tell her she'd overstayed her welcome.

"I was planning to talk to you about Theo." She stopped.

"Theo?"

"Yes, well, I don't know if I explained it before but this training, it was a two-week thing. A trial."

"A—?"

"But that's all good. I got the job. It's just that the job doesn't start until the second week of August."

Lincoln's brow furrowed. "Okay?"

"So I need to get what shifts I can back at the ER ... to make sure I have enough for a deposit and first month's rent. So I can get out of your space as soon as possible."

"You don't have—"

She held up her hand. "I do—it's just with me gone, with them knowing I'm not coming back, I couldn't get all day shifts. I'll have to do some nights in the next few weeks and Mrs. Martin, well ..." she shifted, moving more of her body onto the bed, "would it be all right if I left Theo with you? I wouldn't be starting until seven thirty so you'd just have to get him to bed. Really, it's only about two hours of watching him and staying here through the night. I'd be home in time to wake him up."

Lincoln furrowed his brow. Was this why she was nervous? Where did he ever go in the night? And he'd read Theo his stories three nights the past week, while Kali studied the training manuals for her new job.

"That's fine."

"Good. Great." Her smile rose then fell. She turned her gaze toward Romper. "I took one of my patients on an outing today, to see her niece in a play." The muscles in Kali's throat convulsed. "At a community centre in Cole Harbour." She opened the paper in her hand and held it up. "I'm pretty sure it's Romper."

Lincoln leaned forward. He didn't need to look at Romper to compare. Same scruffy black hair. Same left ear permanently bent, as if the cartilage had been damaged in some fight. Same red bandanna tied around the neck. Same contented smile. "That could be any dog."

"It could."

"I've had him for over four months. If someone was looking for him—"

"They are looking for him. They have been. In Cole Harbour. Dartmouth. They didn't think he would have gotten as far as Halifax—two towns and a harbour away." Kali offered a closed-lips smile. It's been four months and they still have these signs up."

"Romper's my—" Lincoln looked to the dog, who looked right back at Lincoln.

"Maestro!" Kali patted her lap. Romper's ears perked. He gave a bark. "Come here, Maestro." Romper padded over to her. Another bark.

Lincoln's throat tightened. Something within him felt like running. "You patted your lap. You said, 'Come here.' Any dog would—"

"You try it. A different name."

Lincoln sat motionless.

"Try it."

He cleared his throat and raised his voice an octave. "Daryl." He patted his lap. Nothing. "Daryl. Come here, Daryl." Romper looked to Lincoln. Lincoln patted his lap again. "Come here."

Romper slinked around the bed, then sat in front of Lincoln. Lincoln rubbed the dog's head. Kali said nothing. Lincoln let his hand drop. "I need him."

"Maestro," Kali called again. The dog bolted toward her and nuzzled under her outstretched arm.

Lincoln's jaw clenched. He wanted to be alone, yes. He wanted solitude. But those days working long hours out at the lot ... those days without Romper?

He had the main support for the floor—the first floor—up now. Had constructed a rubber filler around the trunk, going out three feet. It would provide insulation in winter, could be removed in summer if he wanted more air flow, and allowed for trunk growth. His dream felt within reach. But without Romper to toss a stick to during his breaks, to walk with through the woods, to sit beside when he needed to think— that wouldn't be solitude. It'd be loneliness.

Kali kept her head down, her gaze on the paper. "I called the number. The family happened to be at the Centre. Their little girl was in the play too."

Lincoln stared at Kali, his teeth clenched.

"The dog is actually their son's dog. He's thirteen. They got Ro—Maestro for his tenth birthday." Another soft smile. "You should have seen his face when I told him I thought I knew where his dog was."

Lincoln's whole body felt squeezed. So what if Romper was their dog? They'd lost him. They'd lost—Lincoln looked at Romper, who came back to him, pushed his muzzle into Lincoln's thigh, cocked his head, and kind of smiled—the most amazing dog he'd ever seen.

"How would they know it's him?"

Kali rubbed a hand across her chin. "He's micro-chipped." She let the hand fall. "The parents thought for sure he was dead. They asked why you wouldn't have taken him to the Humane Society or a shelter, somewhere where it could have been scanned."

"How would I know—"

Kali raised a hand. "They won't make a fuss about it. They're just glad he's okay."

"He didn't have a tag on his collar. If you care about your dog you have a tag on its collar."

"But with the chip."

"What about Theo? Theo loves that dog."

"Lincoln." Kali shook her head. "It's not your dog. It's certainly not Theo's dog." She shifted off the bed and stood. "And Theo would be losing the dog when we move out anyway."

Lincoln stared at the section of wall Kali's head had

blocked moments before.

"What right did you have to call? What right did you have to anything?"

Kali shrugged.

If he'd seen the sign would he have called? Or would he have torn it down and gone looking for any others to dispose of? He clenched his teeth. "So what's the plan? I take him to the SPCA or something? See if it's actually their dog?"

"You could." Kali passed Lincoln the flyer. "But they're fairly eager to have him back. Do you honestly have any doubt it's him?"

Lincoln held the flyer in his hand. Lots of dogs looked similar.

"The boy said the inside of his collar has a pale blotch on it."

"A blotch?"

"Apparently he thought he'd tie-dye it one day. His mother stopped him in the process."

Lincoln unclasped the collar and turned it over. He closed his eyes.

"I'm sorry."

Lincoln inhaled. He raised his head and waved a hand. "Just a dog, right?" His throat tightened. "I can always get another dog." He put a hand to Romper's head. "It would just suck if he thought I didn't want him."

"He remembered his name. He'll remember his family."

Lincoln passed Kali back the flyer. "This is their address?"

She nodded. "Now?"

"Might as well."

CHAPTER TWENTY-EIGHT

Theo sat on Kali's couch, his eyes wide and moist, glaring at Lincoln.

Lincoln sat on his own couch, legs spread wide, back bent over them. Every few minutes he glanced at Theo and offered a smile before letting his head fall again. Romper. The dog's head had perked up when Lincoln pulled his truck into the family's driveway. When the front door opened, he barked joyously and leapt out of the cab the moment Lincoln opened the door. He tackled the boy, who fell back onto the grass, and smothered him with kisses. He hadn't licked Lincoln, not once. The parents came out then, along with a little girl. Smiling. All of them smiling, like Lincoln wasn't dying right in front of them.

The little girl laughed and jumped. The father shook his head, a grin plastered on his face. It was almost a minute before anyone acknowledged Lincoln.

He took a step toward the excitement. "Well, I guess it's your dog."

It was the father who looked over. "Yes." He looked back to his children. "That's our dog." A pause, where Lincoln was forgotten again.

And then the mother looked over, her eyes bright. "Thank you for—"

"No." Lincoln waved his arms in front of him. "Sorry, I ... didn't know about the chip. If I had—" Would he have done anything? Romper pranced into his life, following him, insisting on being loved at the exact moment Lincoln needed someone to care for, someone to care for him.

Drunk. Angry. Wondering what was the point of life and half passed out against a tree, a damp nose pushed itself against Lincoln's cheek. And Lincoln had seen him—hungry, tired, ridiculously mangy looking—in need of a friend.

He'd taken Romper on a hike through the woods a few days later. On the drive back he'd seen the land for sale sign. The dog gave a reassuring bark, and Lincoln had known. That land was what he needed. That land was what would heal him.

"He looks healthy." Another grin from the father.

Lincoln fought to keep it together, to push back the moistening of his eyes, not let his hands shake, not scoop the dog up in his arms, jump in the truck, and drive away.

"Well," Lincoln raised a hand to the level of his head and stepped back, "I guess that's that." The parents' heads turned toward him, more nods, smiles, murmurs of thanks, while Lincoln opened the truck's door.

Romper's head shot up, his attention pulled from the boy. He looked at the scrawny teen, at Lincoln, back to the teen. His head tilted. "Bye, boy." Lincoln's voice came out deep. Hoarse.

Romper stepped away from the boy, and the family tensed.

"Maestro." The boy's voice held a hint of desperation.

"Maestro." The father's held gruff command.

Lincoln's chin trembled.

The dog came toward him and nudged his nose against Lincoln's thigh. Lincoln looked to the family, his eyes wide, helpless.

Another nudge.

What would the dog do if Lincoln cocked his head toward the seat, as he had so many times before, indicating it was time to go? Lincoln stood rigidly, his gaze darting from the dog to the family. He could try. Cock his head, see if Romper jumped in, and if he did, Lincoln could pull away, shout out an apology as he gunned it up the street.

But if Romper didn't jump in? If he looked at Lincoln as if he were pathetic, shook his head that Lincoln could think, actually think, he'd choose him over the family who raised him?

Lincoln sank to his knees and wrapped his arms around the dog's body. Romper pressed his head against Lincoln's and then, when Lincoln stood, Romper stood as well, and took two steps back.

Lincoln hopped into the truck and slammed the door. He turned on the ignition. Romper sat, the boy and his family all standing a few feet behind him, like a picture. Lincoln glanced in his rear view mirror and inched out of the driveway, his chest tight. Maestro sat watching. Sat. Didn't follow. Didn't bark in confusion. When Lincoln pulled onto the street, Romper stood. He took a couple of steps forward and gave one bark. One happy bark. Lincoln switched into drive. Before the turn at the end of the street, he looked back. Maestro had turned and was following his family into the house.

Lincoln raised his head. Theo was still glaring.

"How about pizza?" Kali asked as she stepped into the living room. "To celebrate."

"Celebrate?"

A tear trailed down Theo's cheek. He wiped it away angrily.

"That I got through the training, that the woman I'm replacing had nothing but good things to say, that I got the job." She smiled at Theo. "I know today was hard." She turned to Lincoln. "But you did the right thing. Not that you need me to tell you that," back to her son, "and Theo, baby, you'll understand one day. I promise. One day when you have your own dog."

His eyes widened in a moment of hope.

"Not any day soon. But maybe one day. Probably one day." She stepped further into the room. "So, pizza? My treat."

"Sure." Lincoln stood. "Would be great to celebrate you getting one step closer to all of us getting our lives back."

Kali's lips pursed as he passed her. He hesitated, debated rephrasing his words, hated himself a little, and walked on.

Later that night, after she put Theo to bed, Lincoln watched Kali enter the living room. "How's he doing?"

Kali looked over at Lincoln, a soft smile on her face. "He'll be all right." She shrugged. "Kids are supposed to be resilient, right?" She curled up on her couch—the first time she'd sat out here with Lincoln in days. If he was in the living room, she was in the kitchen. If he was in the kitchen, she'd be in the living room or her room. He stayed in his room often, so she wouldn't have to worry about it.

"Right." Lincoln watched her, the way she rubbed her head, how her eyes seemed squinted. "Are you all right?"

Another smile. Did her eyes glisten in the light more than they should?

"A headache. No big deal."

He shifted toward her. "Bad?"

"More that I've had it so often." She dropped her hand. "Mornings usually. This pressure." She raised her hand again and pressed her palm against her forehead. "And my eyes. They're blurring. Too much hitting the books."

"You've been studying those manuals every night."

"I know." Another smile—for her this time, not him. "Not tonight, though. I need a break." She scanned the room. "The apartment feels empty, doesn't it? Without his nails clicking across the hardwood. Without his smell."

"He didn't—"

"Not bad. It was a good smell. A very doggy smell."

She closed her eyes and rested her head against the couch. One minute. Two. Lincoln kept his eyes on her. She breathed deeply. "You know, Theo never wanted to go with anyone else as a baby. He clung to me. Even my mom—it took a while before he would settle in her arms."

Lincoln kept silent.

"It's always taken him a long time to warm up to people. At the daycare, before it exploded, there was only one worker he connected with. He clung to me, tears streaming down his face the first time I left him with Mrs. Martin." Kali opened her eyes. "But not you." She shrugged. "Maybe it was Romper."

"You mean Maestro?"

She gave a sad smile.

"Theo certainly wasn't a fan of me tonight."

"Me neither." She tilted her head toward the ceiling. "It kills me—how he can't express himself. I wish he'd yelled at us tonight. I want him to throw a tantrum, question, let me see what's inside. Instead, it's all hidden. Bottled up." She looked at Lincoln, her eyes pleading, searching for an answer he didn't have.

"He'll talk if he needs to." Lincoln hesitated. "When he needs to."

"Sure." She nodded. "One day. And I'm doing all I can. I'm doing the best I can."

"Absolutely." Lincoln rubbed his hands on his legs. His throat went dry. He didn't like this—them, talking. Them, so close.

"They teased him, you know, the kids at the daycare. Not so much the first one. The one that—" She stopped. "But the next one. The older kids. They called him stupid and weirdo and freak. And the workers. They spoke so politely, so clearly, like I was stupid. Like I couldn't hear or understand." She spoke under her breath. "Like he was stupid."

Kali made her voice go loud and higher pitched. "*We're sure your son will learn one day, but he's just so behind the other children. It's a distraction. Disruptive.*" She shook her head. "Can you believe that? Silence disruptive. *We don't have the resources for one on one care. We don't want to see him singled out. It's better if you take him elsewhere.* Bitches."

Lincoln made a noise of agreement.

She said something, barely a whisper. Lincoln leaned forward. "What?"

"I'm so scared."

"Scared?"

"This new daycare. What if they don't take him? I talked to the administrator. Told her he had ... Mutism." She shuddered to say the word, as if it tasted vile in her mouth. "And she said it was fine, that all children were unique, but what if the workers don't feel that way, what if the children ...?" Kali turned her gaze to the floor.

She looked so small on the couch. Looked like she needed to be held. He wanted to take it all away—her pain, her fear. She pulled her feet up under her and he marvelled, for probably the hundredth time, at how small they were. Outside she hid them away in those big combat boots, even on the hottest days. But he got to see them.

"Children always find something to make fun of each other for." Lincoln offered a smile. "Always. Theo's at a disadvantage because he can't say anything back. But when it comes down to it, lots of kids can't say anything back."

She laughed. "That supposed to make me feel better?"

"No. I don't know." Lincoln let a few breaths pass. He shouldn't say anything more. Shouldn't ask a question. Shouldn't take in the line of her neck or the curve of her hip. "Did anyone die in the explosion?"

"No. The worker, the one he liked, who liked him, was badly burned on one arm. A little on her face. Some smoke inhalation. She lost some of the use of her hand. But besides that, besides her, just minor injuries."

Lincoln nodded. "Maybe enough time has passed. Maybe being in the new daycare will help him heal and being around all those kids who are talking will let him see it's not such a big deal."

"Maybe." Kali shifted, her body angled toward him. "I'm sorry about Romper. Truly."

"It's not your—"

"I know. But if I hadn't been here you'd still have your dog."

"And a thirteen-year-old boy wouldn't have his."

She stared at him the way she had that night—as if she saw something in him that didn't often reach the surface. Lincoln raised a hand to his chin and rubbed the scraggly hair there. He pursed his lips, wanting to inch toward her and wanting to flee.

She edged toward the end of her couch, closer to him. "What happened?"

"Hmm?" She was so close—he could reach out and graze her arm if he wanted—and so woman. Alarmingly beautiful in the fading light. He didn't think about it often, her beauty. It was strong. Almost an affront. Almost offensive, like she didn't have the right to look that perfect.

But the dim light softened her beauty, made it seem more of this earth, made it seem like maybe if she weren't sitting in his apartment because she had nowhere else to go, she could be sitting here because she wanted to be. That they could share one couch.

"Lincoln?"

His limbs tingled with the need to close the distance between them. Three steps is all it would take.

"To you." Her voice sliced through him. "What happened to you?"

CHAPTER TWENTY-NINE

"Kali." Lincoln kept his feet firmly planted. He stared at the ground, wanting her to un-ask the question, change the subject, not make this night worse by digging into the past.

"Something happened. This hasn't always been your life."

Her words flung him back to reality. They weren't friends or lovers sharing an intimate moment after a mutual loss; they were strangers, thrust together only until they'd be thrust apart.

"And you were right when you said our lives should be separate."

Kali looked away. "They will be. I promise that. But tonight—" She met his gaze, her eyes shaded by lashes he could hardly believe were real. "Fine. I'll answer a question you asked me. His name's Marvin. My husband's father." She leaned her head against her hand. "Even when I first met him he was a little off. He still had a home then, but not a job. He'd lost it a few years earlier. A few years after he lost his wife." She hesitated. "I say home, but he lived in an apartment. He'd sold the home the boys grew up in. Couldn't afford it." She wore a wistful smile. "He blames it all on himself—his wife's death, the boys growing up without a mother. She died when Derek was sixteen, but she'd been sick years earlier. Marvin was the smoker but all he got was a gravelly voice. That, and watching the woman he'd loved since he was twelve years old die of lung cancer."

Lincoln grasped at the one thing he could think to say. "Boys? He has another son. Wouldn't he hel—"

"He jumped in the ocean after Derek."

"Whoa."

"Yeah. Whoa." Kali closed her eyes. "After that, Marvin fully lost it. Moved out of his apartment. I didn't see him for months. He didn't show up at the funeral. I still don't know where he was or what happened during that time. I thought he had died, maybe killed himself." She stopped, her gaze on the hardwood. "Then one day I saw him. I tried to get him to move in with me. If he cleaned himself up, cleaned his mind up, he could find a job again."

"That's not so easy."

"No." She shook her head. "It's as if he doesn't believe he deserves a home—him smoking inside, insisting on smoking inside, is what killed her. I guess in the early years she'd asked him not to, said she hated the stink. He thinks he's a failure as a husband, a failure as a father, a failure as a man. But he raised good men. Kind, generous men. That means something." Kali paused. "There. I answered one of your questions."

"Not a question about you."

She bit her lip. "True. He's why I'm here, though, why I haven't tried to start over somewhere else. Theo's the one thing that gives him any joy. The one thing to make him smile."

"I'm pretty sure you give him joy."

"What?" She let out a small laugh. "I plague him. Always trying to get him to change his life."

"I've seen you two together. He doesn't view you as a plague."

"You're some stalker." She smiled. A light, easy, comfortable smile.

"I'm observant. Not the same thing." Lincoln stood. He couldn't see that smile again. Not tonight. "Congrats on the job." He paused, offered a half smile. "Really." Another pause. "I'm off to bed."

Kali stayed on the couch. He was right. She hadn't told him anything truly personal. She was just hoping for a moment of connection. Just a moment. A moment where, perhaps, she could be strong for someone else instead of always having to be strong for herself. A moment where she could stop thinking about her own life and focus on someone else's.

Kali closed her eyes and let darkness settle over the room. Something was wrong. She knew enough to know that. The headaches. The blurred vision. The nausea. But it didn't mean she had something to worry about. She'd seen dozens, hundreds of patients come into the ER scared about the symptoms she was experiencing. Stress could be the cause. And she was stressed. A vitamin deficiency. Diabetes, perhaps, though she doubted that. Some bug her body was slowly fighting off.

Two and a half more weeks. Then she'd be on Westwood's benefits plan, and if it was something more serious, something she'd need medicine for, she'd have eighty-five-percent coverage. She could get through two more weeks. She opened her eyes to the shadowed room. Even one night away from the books and her vision was sharper. Maybe that's all it was. She hadn't read so much in years.

ON NATAL DAY KALI woke with a smile. No pain. She hadn't worked the night before and wouldn't work today. Not good for her bank account, but good for her boy, for the decision she had to make. Dr. Richards had shown Theo photos and videos of fireworks over the past month, had explained how it worked, and where the noise came from. Had told him maybe he'd get to see them one day.

After every appointment she asked Kali if she'd talked to Theo about the fireworks yet, if she'd made her decision. She hadn't. Maybe, she thought, she'd let Theo stay up. Give him ear plugs. Stand with him at the window. Safe. Protected. Maybe that would be enough.

Kali stretched. The apartment was cool. She crossed the hall and closed the living room window. A glance toward the door told her Lincoln had left. He'd gone to his lot less since Romper went home. Maybe three times in the past week and a half. Yet he was gone every day. Where he went, she didn't know. Boots gone meant the lot. Sneakers gone meant somewhere else. Once, she'd seen him in the library. Once, she'd seen him making his way toward Point Pleasant, the large park on the tip of the peninsula.

Wherever he was, he wasn't home. He was almost never home. Yet, after the night she'd told him about Marvin something shifted. They hadn't gone back to the way things were before she'd yelled at him, but they were easier around each other. Lincoln, when he was home, tried even harder to make Theo laugh or offered to take him to the park. He asked her polite questions about work, and she asked him polite questions about the tree house—which actually sounded like a complex and highly technical endeavour. She wanted to see it but felt weird saying so.

They were roommates. Nothing more, nothing less.

EVERY NOW AND THEN, if the wind shifted just right, Kali heard the sound of children laughing, of music. She'd spent the early morning doing a puzzle with Theo, then reading him a book. The city's Natal Day festivities started at ten. Most of the events were at the Commons, but the library was doing something, and the community garden had a face painter. They had options.

But it was 10:24 and still they were in the apartment. Who was more afraid of the noise and the people—Theo or her?

Theo laid stomach-down on the couch, a comic book Lincoln had bought splayed out in front of him. It was far too advanced, but he poured over the pictures.

"Want to see if Cherie would like to go to the park with us?"

Theo looked up, a large smile on his face.

"You could maybe get your face painted. And listen to

music."

The smile remained, shrunk, grew. Theo held both arms up then clenched and unclenched his fingers while puffing out bursts of air with his pursed lips.

Kali inhaled, her smile on tight. "Fireworks?"

He nodded.

"Fireworks happen at night, Sweetie. It's day."

Theo tilted his head to the side. Blinked. Looked at her like ... like she was the one who didn't get it. He rolled off the couch and marched to the door, collapsed in front of it, and pulled his sneakers on with vigour.

Don't let them tease him. Please, don't let them tease him. Kali pulled on her boots.

She knocked on Mrs. Martin's door. The woman opened it with a huff; the scent of fresh biscuits and baked apples wafted out around her.

"You're not bringing him today. You said you had today off."

"Oh, I do." Kali kept Theo in front of her, a hand on each of his shoulders. "We're going to some of the festivities and thought Cherie might like to join."

"Cherie's off with her parents today."

"Oh, maybe we'll see them there, then."

"No, they went to the Valley to visit her father's people. Coming back here tonight for dinner and the fireworks, though." Theo tugged on Kali's shirt. Mrs. Martin bent down toward Theo. "I'll tell her you were by."

"Thanks. Thank you." Kali lingered a moment longer. It smelled so good. Not that she couldn't bake herself. She could. But to sit with a family, to eat food she hadn't prepared. Home-style food, not the fancy stuff Lincoln made.

214

Mrs. Martin did a lot for her. Too much. She couldn't ask to join her family's celebration. "That's nice. Having them over. Your other grandkids coming too? Your son?"

"Sure are." Mrs. Martin placed a hand on her hip. "So I better get back to cooking. You two have fun."

"Thanks." Kali stepped back from the door, trying not to let her disappointment at the dismissal show. "Enjoy your day."

"Will do, Sweetie."

Kali took Theo's hand in hers and led him down the steps. "Face painting!" She grinned at him. "This will be so much fun."

And it was fun. And not one kid said a nasty word. Not to his face, at least. His lion-painted face. A few friendly kids tried to talk to him and seemed slightly perturbed when he didn't talk back. Several asked their parents about it. Two asked Theo about it. He just smiled his sweet smile. To one, he'd given a silent happy roar.

CHAPTER THIRTY

After the face painting event, Kali and Theo went to the library just in time for a puppet show, then on to the Commons, where a band was playing. Women with big smiles, one with a big belly, were giving out freezies. A huge bouncy castle, shaped more like a pirate ship than a castle, drew children from across the lawn.

"Wanna go?" Kali asked.

Theo nodded—his fast, vigorous nod—and dragged her down the path. He stood in line, his feet firmly planted, and inched forward every few minutes. He'd look up at her when they moved, grin. And she grinned back. He kicked off his sneakers and crawled inside, looked back when he realized she wasn't coming with him, hesitated. Kali waved him on.

"Go ahead, Sweetie." He looked at her, at the castle, at her. "It's for the kids, no adults allowed. Go on." And he did. Bouncing. Laughing. She imagined sound was coming from that laugh. Loud, boisterous sound, instead of the barely audible giggles that sometimes escaped him. She stood as his little form rose in and out of view, as his eyes sparkled, and felt, for the first time in as long a time as she could remember, that she was living a normal life. That Theo was a normal, happy, well-adjusted boy. That they were just your average family. And that they might be okay ... soon.

She'd have a job with regular hours. A substantial pay increase. She'd rent an apartment with two rooms and get Theo an amazing bed. A race car or some animal or a space ship. She'd seen a space ship bed on Kijiji last year for fifty dollars. In a few weeks she could actually afford that, knowing there'd be money, consistent money, coming in.

The psych visits would be covered up to fifteen hundred a year. But he'd stop needing them. She could feel it. When their lives were settled, when he had his own room and didn't see her stressed all the time, when she smiled real smiles and laughed real laughs—ones without fear behind them—he'd stop being afraid. They'd be fine.

Theo ran to the back of the line the moment his turn was done. His cheeks were flushed and pushed high with a smile. He raised his eyebrows, his eyes lit, a question in them.

"Yes," Kali laughed, "you can go again."

Feeling frivolous, she bought each of them ridiculously overpriced hot dogs and Fantas, even though she could get them for half the price at the corner store two blocks away. They sat on the grass, licking the ketchup and mustard off of their fingers and letting the music flit over and under and around them. It was a kids' band Kali had heard about but never heard, though every other parent and child around them knew the words. When they finished eating, Theo jumped up and danced with a group of children—shaking his hips and wiggling his arms and smiling so big.

Kali held back her tears. She clapped. She cursed Derek. This was the life they were supposed to be living. This was the life he'd promised.

WHEN THE BAND LEFT the stage and the bouncy castle started to deflate and other families trailed away from the park, Kali took Theo's hand and turned toward home. A glint flashed in the corner by some trees. Marvin. She waved.

He raised his hand about two inches then let it fall.

"Look. It's Grampie."

Theo released her hand and ran across the field. He stopped a foot away from the man, who bent down to pat the boy's head. Theo looked back at Kali and waved an exaggerated arm at her, urging her to hurry up.

Kali hastened her step.

"I saw him—" Marvin cleared his throat then looked at Theo. "I saw you dancing." Something of a guttural noise, the closest he usually came to a laugh, escaped his throat. "You've got the moves."

Theo waved his hips then put a hand to his mouth in a silent giggle.

Kali rubbed her hand on Theo's head. "You should have come over."

"Oh, no. No." Marvin stepped back from them. "They don't like it. Me. Around. Days like today. Just trouble."

"Not if you were with us. Not if you left—"

"I don't leave the cart."

"I know." Kali nodded. He didn't leave it for the beach that day, despite her offer to put everything in the trunk. He wouldn't leave it for dancing and hot dogs. She touched a hand to his shoulder, remembering the days when he'd hug— awkward hugs. But he'd give them. Receive them. After those missing weeks, any touch, especially sudden ones, seemed like they burnt.

"It was nice to watch." His eyes darted between Kali and the boy. "His daddy used to dance like that. Like he meant it."

Kali remembered. Derek had danced like that as a man too. The first night they met he'd been dancing. Dancing like he meant it, not like he was trying to impress.

Theo reached a hand out and gave Marvin's leg a tug. Marvin looked down. Theo gave him the lion face he'd been perfecting all day—fierce silent roar—or so Kali suspected. It must have been fierce; Marvin jumped back. He put his hands to his face and peered up over his eyes. "D-don't h-hurt me. I'm afraid of lions."

Theo's arms dropped beside him. He tapped his hands on his chest. Kali could picture him smiling—assuring his grampie with his kind smile and his big brown eyes that it was okay. It was just him.

Marvin looked relieved. He held a finger up at Theo and shook it. "Don't you scare me like that."

Theo's hands went to his mouth—she couldn't hear the giggle.

"You should come home with us." Kali stepped forward, feeling brazen, desperate. Today she'd been a family. And he was their family. "I can pick up some burgers from the store and one of our neighbours would let us use her barbecue."

"Store's closed, Kali."

"Right." She pressed her lips together. "Well, we have other food. It's a holiday. Come for dinner."

"Kali."

"You can meet Lincoln."

"Kali."

"I know I've complained about him a bit but he's not that bad. He's—"

"I know he's not that bad. He's helping you out. I'm thankful."

"You know I'm moving soon."

"I know."

"And I want you to come. It's just across the harbour."

"Kali." He raised his hands above his shoulders and looked to the sky. "This is my home." He grinned. Winked at Theo. "I don't like roofs."

"In the winter you—"

"I do what I have to do."

"This winter you'll move in with us. I'll have an apartment by then. A good apartment."

Marvin took hold of his cart and started to manoeuvre it out from the shade.

"Stop it. Why is some shelter better than me? Than us?"

"Kali."

"Stop saying my name!" She closed her eyes, bit her lip, then looked up, her voice even. "You can't keep living like this."

"I get by."

Kali held her hands over Theo's ears. "You'll die. One day I'll come looking for you and—"

"People die, Kali."

"I said stop it. *Kali. Kali.* Like I don't understand. You don't understand. Maybe this isn't about you. Maybe it's about us. You're all the family we have left and—"

"That's not true."

Kali grabbed for Theo's hand. "Say goodbye to Grampie."

Theo waved.

Kali held back a scowl. "I'll check in soon."

"You have a good night, Sweetness. Okay? Go see the—"

"Don't talk to me about the damn fireworks!"

CHAPTER THIRTY-ONE

Kali hauled Theo along beside her and gave him a slight tug as he turned to wave toward Marvin. Before they had even crossed the street her pace slowed, her anger fading. She shouldn't have yelled like that. It wasn't Marvin's fault he was broken, wasn't his fault some part of his grandson was.

But Theo was different. Marvin was a grown man. Yes, shit had happened. But shit happened to Kali too. And she kept it together. Kali may not have lost her son, but she'd lost a father—been abandoned by a father—she'd lost her mom. She'd lost a spouse. Not in the way Marvin had, not at all. But the end result was the same.

And what if she just decided to give up? She couldn't. She didn't have that luxury. And Marvin shouldn't either.

Kali trudged up the stairs, yearning for that happy feeling of just minutes before. A happy, worry free afternoon—destroyed. But she could have a happy life. A decent life. Maybe Marvin wouldn't be part of it, but her and Theo's life could be better. *Would* be better. Would be great. Kali looked to Theo and smiled. His eyes widened in shock. She looked ahead and clutched Theo against her.

"Hi?"

"Hey." A man sat in the shadows on the top step outside Lincoln's apartment door. "You here to see Lincoln too?"

"No." Kali stepped to the landing, keeping Theo behind her. She could see now that the man was dressed casually, but nice, like he was on his way to a party or coming from golf. His muscles bulged out of the sleeves of his collared t-shirt. His smile was easy, the smile of a man who was used to being smiled at.

Should she open the door with him standing there? He obviously knew Lincoln, but if he was sitting outside the door either Lincoln wasn't home or wouldn't let him in.

"Then what are you doing here?"

Kali raised her chin. "I live here."

"You—?" The man looked shocked, frustrated, dejected. "He move?"

"No."

He ran a hand through his hair. "Then—" He looked from Kali to Theo and back again. "You live with Lincoln?"

Kali edged closer to the door. "I'm his roommate." She held Theo against her. "We are."

"Oh, uh, wow. Okay." He nodded, a look of amazement washing over his features. "Well, uh, mind if I wait inside? I have another thirty minutes to kill before enough is enough."

Kali stared at him.

"Sorry, uh, I'm his cousin. Andrew." Andrew stuck out his hand. Kali hesitated. "I swear." He raised both hands, wore a smile that was confident but kind. "I come in peace."

"I guess." Kali put her key in the door. "Just a half hour."

Andrew stepped in after her with the casual, accustomed

stance of someone who'd been there before. He didn't blink at the work table in the centre of the room or the cutouts of tree houses on the far wall. Kali's shoulders relaxed an inch or two. "The new furniture is yours, I take it. Lincoln didn't suddenly attempt to make this place a home."

"I'd hardly call it new."

"So he put an ad out or something? Single man requires young woman and child for roommates?" He chuckled.

Kali did not. She turned to Theo. "Why don't you grab your colouring?"

Theo scrunched up his nose at Andrew then walked across the room, glancing back every few steps.

"Cute kid."

"Can I get you something?" Kali took off her satchel and stepped toward the kitchen. "Water? Lemonade? Milk?"

"Any beer?"

"No."

"Lemonade, thanks."

Kali returned to Andrew sitting on Lincoln's couch, legs spread like he owned the place. Kali passed him the glass and retreated to her own couch. "You're his cousin?"

"For as long as I can remember."

She half-smiled. "I didn't think he had any family. At least not around here. He's never mentioned anyone."

"Pretty sure I'm the only one who knows he's back in town."

"He wasn't?" Kali sipped her lemonade. "I mean he left?"

"You guys don't talk much. Do you?"

"No."

"Well, who am I to tell someone else's story?"

Kali swallowed. This was her chance to find something

out about the stranger she lived with. "Well, you clearly don't visit often. Why?"

"He doesn't want visitors." Andrew looked to Theo, who re-entered the room, and let out another small chuckle. "But I wouldn't have thought he wanted roommates either. So what do I know?" He turned to Kali. "Seriously, he put out an ad?"

"It's more like he's doing us a favour. We were in a tight spot."

"Ah," Andrew nodded, "that big heart he tries to hide away." He leaned forward. "So, how's he doing? Is he okay?"

"I'm not sure."

Andrew made a worried noise in his throat. "Guessing that's a no." He gestured to the wall of tree houses. "He still all about that?"

Kali nodded.

"That where he is today?"

"Probably."

"He tell you it's his birthday?"

"No." Kali shifted. "Really?"

"Twenty-eight." Andrew pulled a small thin package out of his pocket and set it on the arm of the couch. "In case I've got to go before he returns. A little something. A running joke." He stared at the package, his jaw clenched, his brow knitted, then looked at Kali. "He a good roommate?"

"We're making do."

"How old's your kid?"

"Almost four."

"He's cute."

Kali smiled. Andrew smiled. Theo coloured.

"No idea when he's returning?"

Kali tilted her head from side to side. "Usually by seven.

Sometimes later."

Andrew sighed. "I can't wait that long." He stood and stuffed his hands in his pockets. "Tell him I came? Tell him I wish him a happy birthday?" He nodded to the package. "And tell him to come to his mother's god-damn birthday party."

"What?"

"Sorry. Sor—" Andrew glanced to Theo and gave an embarrassed shrug. "His mom's birthday party. Just ... tell him to get over himself and come." Andrew paced toward the window and back. "His dad's getting a pass from the institution for a couple of hours and, yeah, Joseph and Lucy will be there but so will like fifty other friends and family. He can avoid them." Andrew stared at Kali. "You have no idea what I'm talking about."

She shook her head.

"It's probably pointless, but tell him to come, okay? He knows when it is. Convince him to come." He looked to Theo. "Maybe you could do a better job than me. Use the kid. Tell him what it would feel like if your kid was a bridge away and didn't come to your sixtieth birthday party. Tell him what a selfish prick he's being."

Kali stood. "I don't know."

Andrew puffed out a blast of air. "Well, tell him I came. Maybe I'll try again sometime. Though I doubt he'd let me in. Been ignoring my emails."

"He doesn't have internet."

"Yeah, but he has the library, right? Isn't that his new hangout?"

Kali kept silent, feeling any answer would be a betrayal.

"Happy Natal Day." Andrew lingered at the door. "You

out to enjoy the festivities tonight?"

"Maybe."

"Try to make sure he has some fun. I mean I don't know if you have any sway, but it's the guy's birthday. And he's out in the woods with no one but that mangy dog. Then what, a night at home picking his toenails?" Andrew shook his head. Angry? Sad? Both? "He deserves more than that."

Kali made no promises, not bothering to tell him Lincoln didn't even have the dog anymore, and watched Andrew leave. She closed the door behind him, more curious than ever, and formulated a plan.

CHAPTER THIRTY-TWO

Several hours later Kali heard Lincoln's boots on the stairs outside the apartment. "You remember what I told you?"

Theo grinned.

"And you remember, big booms, but they're okay. They're safe."

He gave her an exaggerated thumbs up. Kali nodded. She'd give them all what they needed tonight. Conquer all of their fears.

"Hey." Lincoln stepped through the door but barely glanced at Kali. His shoulders were stooped. Dirt smeared across his face.

Kali stepped toward him, uncertainty tingling through her. "Are you okay?"

Lincoln put a hand to his beard. "A rough day."

She stepped in his path. "Want to talk about it?"

He rubbed his temple. "I miscalculated. About a week's worth of work, and me along with it, fell from the sky."

"Oh my gosh!" Kali gasped and put a hand to his shoulder, the nurse leaping within her. "Are you hurt?"

"Miraculously," he shrugged out of her grasp, "I landed on a huge piece of rubber."

"Oh." Kali stepped back. "Good."

"Bruised. Angry. Feeling like a fool. But no worse hurt than that." He shook his head. "Gonna hit the shower."

"I wanted to talk to you."

He groaned.

"After the shower. That's fine."

Theo stood with his arms crossed, a pout on his lion's face.

"You'll show him later, Sweetie. He'll love it." She glanced around the room. "A puzzle while we wait?"

No response.

"Or trucks?"

Theo walked toward the bucket that held his dollar store and thrift store vehicles. He hauled out the flattened TV box Lincoln had drawn a roadway on last week. In less than two minutes all of the trucks and cars lay across it.

Lincoln emerged a half hour later, looking slightly less haggard. Kali raised herself up off the floor.

"Whoa. Lion."

Theo popped up and did his practiced silent roar. "You've got that down!" Lincoln smiled and put a hand to his chest. "Don't sneak up on me with that growl or you'll give me a heart attack."

Theo smirked.

Lincoln gravitated toward the kitchen. "You happen to make anything for supper?"

"No." Kali stood. Lincoln bent to open the fridge, his head lost inside it. "I thought we could go out."

His head appeared. "Oh yeah? Well, I'll scrounge something up."

Even his eyes looked tired. Dejected. They disappeared behind the fridge door again. "No." Kali shortened the distance between them. "I meant *us*. All of us." Lincoln rose. "Head down to the harbour, get some street food, see the fireworks."

He shut the fridge door. "That's not—"

"Look," she stepped so there were only inches between them and looked back to Theo, "it's not for me. The psychologist thinks it's really important for Theo not to be afraid of loud noises. That getting over that may be a huge step back toward speech."

"Okay, but—"

"And I can't take him down there alone. All those people. What if he freaks? What if he runs or ... not only that. If we can't get a good spot, if people are crowding around us or something, you could lift him up on your shoulders, make sure he gets the best view. So—" Kali looked to the floor. Her words needed to come smoother. "So it will be amazing for him. So it will help."

"They're fireworks. They're in the sky. Everyone can see them."

"Please." She raised her gaze to Lincoln. "Please. It's taken me a whole month to decide if I'll do this. What if it makes things worse? What if ...?" She shook her head. "I need someone there with me. And you're all I have."

"That nurse."

"She's at a cottage with her family." She smiled and bit her lip. "It'll be fun. Just a few hours. It'll be nice."

Lincoln looked over her shoulder. Kali turned to see Theo standing behind her, making the explosion motions with his hands. He let out puffs of air, almost the sound of a soft explosion. Almost. She looked back to Lincoln, who was grinning.

He shook his head. "Yeah. All right. I'll come."

LINCOLN STOOD IN FRONT of his closet. It'd been months since he thought about what to wear. He dressed for the weather. He dressed to get dirty. He didn't dress for people, not even himself.

In Montreal, he'd had a closet full of expensive clothes. Stylish clothes. Clothes for every occasion.

He pulled out his least torn pair of jeans and a t-shirt that could barely be called threadbare. The last time his birthday had fallen on Natal Day was when he was twenty-two. It was the first summer after undergrad and his whole life seemed ahead of him. Dreams of architecture, of making his own way, still swam in his head.

The time before that he'd been eleven and Dad had taken Linda, Rachel, and him down to the harbour. And danced. Actually danced. Not much, but their father had raised his hands, swung his arms, and stomped his feet. Linda had begged off with her friends, rolling her eyes, only checking in every half hour or so. Rachel had asked to go off too, but their father had said no. She was thirteen and her friends could join them if they were so desperate to see her. Joseph, at seventeen, had pulled out of their driveway in the early afternoon and didn't return until after the fireworks had finished and Lincoln was in his bed. Lincoln couldn't understand it—why choose anyone else when they had their father's undivided attention?

He walked beside his father, a big mountain of a man, excited for the noise and the crowd and the way his father called him champ and put him up on his shoulders, even though they both knew he was too old for it.

That was the last truly good day. Shortly after, Alexander Fraser started to disappear. To get angry. To think Lincoln was his brother, not his son. At first they hadn't known what it meant. They'd teased and joked and lived as if everything would be okay. His father was young, how could he get such an old man's disease?

Lincoln pulled open his door.

"You ready?" Kali's smile was bright, almost too bright, almost manic, as if everything that mattered hung on this night. He wanted to see that smile relax, see it come naturally.

"Yep. How about you?" He turned to Theo and gave a little dance, his arms waving in the air. "Fireworks!"

Theo jumped up and down.

"Get your jacket," said Kali.

Theo's head swivelled from shoulder to shoulder.

"Get your jacket. It's not cold now, but it will be. I'll put it in my satchel."

He acquiesced, running across the room and coming back with the coat held high. Kali took it and stuffed it in her already full bag. Lincoln held open the apartment door. Theo, skipping by, gave him another silent roar. A ball of warmth, a feeling he'd almost forgotten, spread through Lincoln.

The night was humid, with an ocean breeze that promised the temperature would shift as the sun set. Lincoln glanced at Kali. She'd told the boy to grab a jacket, but the cardigan slung over her arm was thin.

"Just a sec." Lincoln bounded back up the stairs and grabbed a sweater. It'd be a pain to carry it around all night, but a worse one to see her shiver.

The streets thickened with people as they neared downtown. Kali had wanted to go across the harbour to Alderney Landing—the concert, the official launching spot for the fireworks, the place where both of them had had such memorable days—but they'd see the fireworks just as well from this side of the harbour. And what if Theo did freak out? From the Halifax Harbour they could walk home, rather than wait for a ferry or try to manoeuvre one of their cars through all the traffic across the bridge.

And those reasons were true. It was also true that at Alderney Landing he'd be sure to see old friends. Maybe even his family—Rachel lived a fifteen-minute walk away. At the Halifax Harbour, the chances were less. He rubbed a hand along his beard. At the Halifax Harbour, with a few beers in them, people might not notice him. Might not question.

CHAPTER THIRTY-THREE

Lincoln laughed as Theo stomped and wriggled in front of a group of buskers. He laughed harder as he was pulled into the group. Kali watched, the feeling from this afternoon easing back over her. It would be nice having a man in Theo's life.

They'd gotten weird looks all evening. A few nasty looks from black women who, probably, were thinking she should have known better, that she should stick with her own, and if she didn't, to *choose* better. But Lincoln *was* better than most, if you looked past the surface, at least. He was dressed half decently tonight, but his hair and beard still made him look like he couldn't afford a decent cut, let alone a home. One woman actually shook her head and kissed her teeth at the trio.

That woman and all the rest could go to hell—or at least back to the eras that raised them.

Kali hadn't chosen Lincoln to be in their lives, not in any sense of the word. But for now, for tonight, she was glad he was with them, dancing with her son, making Theo laugh. Theo spun, his grin so big she wondered if it hurt. He waved her toward the dancers. She shook her head. Not that she didn't want to dance. She did, but she wanted more to watch him, see her boy smiling, standing in a flock of people, unafraid. She hadn't known he was capable of it, to be in a crowd and not stand out. To just be a boy—happy.

Kali's eyes darted to Lincoln. She bit her lip. The beard wasn't so bad. It suited him—with those dark eyes, thick lashes, large, almost feminine lips. If he tidied the beard up a bit, trimmed his hair, he'd be ... well, he'd be gorgeous—in a rugged, woodsy kind of way.

Theo waved his arms again. When she didn't budge, he ran over. Feigning resistance that made him giggle, Kali let Theo pull her into the crowd.

Giggling and exhausted, they stopped in front of a kiosk that sold fish and chips. Despite her protests, Lincoln treated. They sat behind the small restaurant, away from the streams of people on the boardwalk, and shooed the seagulls away.

"Stop feeding them." Kali shook her finger at Theo. "I see you under the table."

He opened his eyes wide and shook his head.

"You are."

He shook his head again.

"It might make them sick. Fries aren't good for them. Fries are people food."

Theo twisted his lips. He picked up a fry and planted it in his mouth. After several angry squawks, the seagulls plagued another table.

Lincoln tensed, his bite of fish halfway to his mouth.

Kali glanced around. "What?"

"Nothing." He stood, his shoulders hunched. "Switch with me."

"What?"

"Just—" He slid onto the bench beside her. She slid out and kept her mouth shut, wanting to ask but not wanting to anger him, ruin the night. Several more times it happened throughout the night—tensing, shifting out of the way or keeping his head down. She looked for cops. She looked for people who looked shady, but Lincoln was the shadiest person in view.

Darkness crept upon them. And Theo smiled. He laughed his silent laugh. He kept close, a hand constantly clinging to either Kali's or Lincoln's as they walked. Sometimes both. When they reached a volleyball court converted to a massive sandbox, they decided it'd be the perfect spot to wait for the fireworks. Theo played apart from the other children but looked at them, shared some smiles. Every twenty to thirty seconds he'd turn his head to Kali and Lincoln. That was normal, though. Children checked to make sure their parents were there. That's what they did. She rubbed her arms as darkness settled, then waved Theo over and slipped him into his jacket. They found a better spot to wait for the show, though about five rows of people had beaten them to it. At least it meant they'd be sheltered from the wind. She rubbed her hands over the thin sleeves of her cardigan. Typical. She'd thought to bring Theo a jacket, but not one for herself.

Kali jumped as hands touched her shoulders. She turned to see Lincoln's coat draped over her. "I don't need—"

He shrugged. "Neither do I."

Theo looked up at them and made his fireworks symbol. "Soon." She pulled out her phone. "Fifteen minutes."

Theo settled onto Lincoln's lap, his head snuggled against Lincoln's chest. Kali started to reach for him, not liking

Lincoln and Theo's closeness, but stopped. Theo would be okay when they moved. He'd be fine.

They stood a minute before the fireworks were scheduled to start. Theo made his hand motions, again and again. The sky lit, the first boom reverberated through the air. Theo screamed.

His hands flew to his ears, his body collapsed on the pavement. Kali's heart constricted. She sank beside him, fear and anger coursing through her. "It's okay," she whispered beside his covered ears, her arms wrapped around him. "You're safe. It's o—"

Hands reached between them. Theo's body lifted off the ground.

"What are you—" Kali yelled uselessly as the night exploded around them.

Lincoln pulled Theo's hands away and held him up, his little feet kicking. He yelled in the boy's face, "It's okay. You're safe. Watch," and swung him in the air and onto his shoulders, forcing Theo's face to the sky.

Theo's hands shot back to his ears like magnets. Kali reached for him, but Lincoln stepped away. The boy's face contorted. Kali reached again, but Lincoln shook his head. Theo's eyes widened. His mouth opened. His brow softened. His hands fell away.

Kali breathed.

The sky went dark. It lit again. Sound thundered against them ... and Theo smiled. He wrapped his arms around Lincoln's forehead and bounced. He released his hands and clapped. The sky lit with a multitude of colours, the explosions coming fast, faster, one after the other, and Theo's face glowed, transfixed. Kali saw it in his eyes, the reflection of it all, and joy, relief, thankfulness shot through her.

Lincoln's hand was on her waist, drawing her near, turning her toward the lights. The opposite hand rose up to steady Theo as he leaned down to whisper in her ear. In the still between explosions, she heard him. "This is for you, too."

THEO'S BODY SPRAWLED against Lincoln's chest. His arms and legs bounced as they walked the blocks back to their apartment. He whimpered and shifted as they trudged up the stairs. He settled with a smile as Lincoln lowered him into bed, pulled off his sneakers, and drew the sheet up over him. Kali stood back as Lincoln stepped away from the bed. Should she go to her boy, kiss his sleeping face, or follow the man who'd brought him in?

She turned to Lincoln. "Thank you."

"Mmhmm."

"No." Kali put a hand on his arm and followed him out of the room. "I ... I would have ruined it. I would have carried him out of there, just as afraid as he was. I would—"

"You didn't."

"I know." Her hand still rested against his bicep. "Thanks to you." She paused. "He's going to remember tonight." Her voice came out raspy. "It was amazing."

The slightest smile crossed Lincoln's face. "He deserves it."

Kali nodded. "And you? Did you have a good night? Did you have fun?"

"Yeah." He rocked onto his heels. "It was all right. Great, even." He glanced toward his room.

Kali's lips pressed together. She glanced down the hall,

238

following his gaze. "Just wait here or ... you coming to the living room?"

"I can. Give me a minute."

Kali grabbed the wrapped box from its hiding spot, along with the gift she'd found in the time between Andrew leaving and Lincoln returning. She stood in the living room, sat on the couch, stood again, waited. Lincoln stepped into the room. "Here." Kali stuck out the hand with Andrew's package. "Happy Birthday."

"What?" Lincoln stared at the package like it was a piece of spoiled meat. "How?"

"Andrew was here. He left this for you."

"Oh." He stepped forward and took it from her then slipped it in his pocket.

"You're not going to open it?"

"I know what it is?"

Kali raised her eyebrows.

"He's been getting me the same thing since we were fifteen."

She held out her package. "You don't know what this is."

"From?"

"Me."

He took the gift from her, a curious look in his eye. "When did you know?"

"Today. Open it."

He peeled off the wrapping. "Thoreau?"

"*Walden*." She stepped toward him. "See, *Life in the Woods*. I asked Cheryl what book would be good for someone who spent a lot of time alone."

"Cheryl? Librarian Cheryl?"

"Yeah, and—"

"You told her I was in the woods? What did you—?"

"No. I didn't mention your name. I just asked her and this was one she suggested and I thought—perfect."

Lincoln's brow furrowed.

Stupid. Stupid. She should mind her own business. Stay out of his life, like they'd agreed.

He stared at the cover, the frown deepening on his brow.

He hated it. He thought she was saying all he was, was some hermit. She stepped toward him. "That guy up on Gottingen who sells basically everything, he was open and— that's why it looks so ratty. It's used, but it's a holiday right, so—"

"Thank you."

Relief washed over her.

"This is really nice. You didn't have to, but thank you."

Kali retreated. She sank onto the couch. Lincoln's couch. He sat on the opposite end, the book in his hands.

"I've heard about this."

"Yeah?"

"Yeah." He flipped some pages, seemed to read a few lines, closed the cover. "So thoughtful." Lincoln turned his head back to the book, gripping it with both hands. "Andrew came to drop off the present?"

"Uh huh."

"You let him in?"

"Yup."

"He say anything else?" His knuckles turned white.

Kali shifted toward him, her back against the armrest. "He mentioned your mother's party."

"And?"

"He wants you to come."

"What else? Did he talk about anything else?"

She offered a slight smile. "He said you were a prick. And that a bunch of people would be there. Over fifty. He said your dad would be there too, for a couple of hours. That he had a pass."

Lincoln's head rose. "Really?"

"Yeah."

His head fell again. "If he comes back, tell him I can't go."

"Why?"

Lincoln's jaw twitched. He looked in pain. "It's complicated."

She should shut up. Leave him alone. This was none of her business. Just like his birthday was none of her business ... but he liked the gift and, maybe just a little bit, maybe just for tonight, she could make it her business. "It's just a party, though, right? Go for a few hours. Wish your mom a happy birthday. Leave."

He shook his head.

"What's the worst that could—?"

He started to stand. She reached forward and placed her palm on his forearm, pushed. He settled beside her, closer than before. "Okay, maybe I should shut up, leave you alone, but obviously something happened. Whether you did something, she did something, I don't know."

Lincoln shifted so he was looking at her.

"I think of Theo. A birthday's just a birthday, that's true. But it's also, not, you know? It's a day you want the people you love around you. And there's nothing Theo could do that would make me not want him near me. If there's anything I did that made him feel that way, I'd hope he could remember the good days. You're a good man, you know how to be with a child, I imagine you got that from her."

Lincoln opened his mouth, inhaled, and closed it again.

"So that means even if she was a shitty mom at times, or did something, she also must have done a lot of good. I just know I hope, no matter what, Theo would come if he could."

Lincoln swallowed. He leaned back against the couch. "She wasn't a shitty mom."

"Yeah. Exactly."

"Andrew put you up to this." He raised an eyebrow and grinned.

Kali leaned against the couch, a smile on her face. "Yes."

He laughed, then let his head fall in his hands. "You don't know the situation."

"You're right."

"She can't see me like this." He rubbed his beard.

Kali smiled and laid a hand on Lincoln's knee. "It's not so bad. Comb your hair. We can go get you a new outfit. Or not. Go as you are."

"We?"

What was she doing? Coming on to him? No. She was being a friend, doing his cousin a favour. That was all. Kali pulled her hand away. "If you want. Or not." She stood. "I've done my job."

He reached for her hand. "Sit with me."

Kali tensed. Things were good right now. She could be friendly, but not too friendly.

"Let me finish my birthday not thinking about this. Not talking about this. Talk to me about something else." Lincoln pointed to the clock across the wall. "Twenty-seven minutes. Then it's done." He let out a half smile. "Then you're free."

Kali grinned, remembering the other part of his present.

"Wait here a minute."

She rushed to the kitchen then returned holding two cupcakes, one lit. Lincoln's eyes crinkled.

Kali sat next to him and held the lit cupcake forward. He leaned back and inhaled. "Don't forget to make a wish."

He halted his breath. "I'm twenty-eight."

"And I don't believe in wishes." Kali shrugged, a weird tightness in her chest. "But I wished anyway, and you came along, and I'm not on the street with my three-year-old boy. So give it a shot."

Lincoln closed his eyes and blew.

CHAPTER THIRTY-FOUR

Lincoln opened his eyes to Kali's smile. "You make a wish?"

He nodded. A lie. How could he wish, when the thing he wanted, he absolutely did not want? Her hand was inches from his. When he reached for the cupcake their fingers grazed, and it was more intense than the entire fireworks show combined. Touch. He missed it. His skin tingled with want. It'd been creeping up on him these last weeks. Not even in a sexual way. Or, not only in a sexual way. Theo reaching for his hand to lead him to a puzzle, snuggling into him and holding out another book and then another. The other night he'd wrapped his arms around Lincoln's legs when he returned from the lot. Dirty, probably smelly, yet the boy hadn't cared. That touch was like a salve.

Kali's touch, though, was entirely different ... or entirely more. A salve too—her hand on his arm, his knee. His hand at the fireworks, reaching to draw her close so he could whisper in her ear. It took that wanting, the want of touch, to a whole other level. A base level. A level that made the weight in his gut grow at the thought of leaving her, of her leaving.

Solitude. Escape. A life with no expectations. That's what he wanted. What he needed.

Yet at the lot these past weeks, without Romper beside him, he filled the silent moments wondering what Kali's day was like. Had she watched someone die? Had she helped save a life? And Theo, would today be the day he spoke? The day he let go of whatever fears kept his voice chained away?

Would they be home when he arrived? Would Kali smile at him, or frown? Would they chat like friends or walk past each other, silent. How much of tonight's outing was for Theo, and how much for him?

"These are good."

"Double chocolate. From a bakery, not the grocery. I splurged." That grin. That smile that came easier now, that was directed at him.

"Worth it."

She leaned her side against the couch, her body turned toward him, her knees just inches away. She seemed so comfortable in his space. Even the fact that she'd sat on his couch without asking, it didn't bother him anymore. Not at all. Not even the slightest. He almost loved it.

"Any luck with an apartment?"

Her lips pressed together. Her brows furrowed. Damn. She thought he was asking how soon she'd leave. He wanted to know how long she'd stay.

"A couple possibles. I'll start looking more now that I have mostly night shifts. I needed a couple of days to recoup from that training."

"Yeah, absolutely. No problem. No rush."

"I'll find something, though."

"Really, no rush. It's fine."

She bit her lip. Shifted away.

No rush. It's fine. Did he mean it? Could he want them and not the rest of the world? Could he want them and his house in the sky?

The words hovered on his lips: *Stay.* Maybe not forever, but for now. *Stay.* But what did that mean? Did he want to date her? Call her son his own? Or was it her presence, the consistency and familiarity, the illusion that with them here he wasn't alone?

"Two minutes."

"Hmm?"

Kali pointed to the clock. "Two minutes left of your birthday."

"Ahh."

Her voice was soft, weighted. Her eyes heavy, her blinks long. "Was it an okay birthday?"

The minute hand clicked forward. "Moments."

"Mo—?"

"Moments were great. Moments were perfect."

"Good." She kept her gaze on the clock. When the hand shifted again she braced her hand on his knee and pushed up.

She stood over him and he wanted to reach out again, tell her not to leave, tell her ... what? "Sleep well."

She smiled and was gone.

Lincoln's thoughts shifted away from her. In the darkness he thought of his mother: how she viewed his choices, whether she was angry, how pathetic he'd look showing up now, after all this time, admitting he'd been here all along, that his travels were a lie. Because if he went to the party, he couldn't keep lying. Over email was one thing, but to her face? No.

And Joseph would know. And Lucy. And his sisters, his cousins, his aunts and uncles. Or maybe he could lie. Say he just came home. Came home for his mother's birthday—wouldn't that be admirable? People would think, oh that Lincoln, devoted son. But then they'd ask about his travels, and he'd sound like a fool making up stories of elephants in Thailand and the Scottish moors.

What are you doing now? they'd ask. *What are you doing next?* Would he lie, or tell the truth? *I'm building a tree house in the woods.* They'd look askance, but slightly interested, at first thinking it was a business venture. And then, as he continued, they'd shift away, step back. Say they were hungry or needed to make a call or, look, there's cousin Peter, who they haven't seen in ages.

They couldn't understand. They wouldn't. But what did it matter?

Kali was right. His mom would want him there, would want to know he was safe, okay. That was what mattered.

SEVERAL DAYS LATER Lincoln stood in front of his closet yet again, knowing it was hopeless. The moment had felt so empowering, when he'd packed up all his suits and loafers and wrinkle free dress shirts and taken them, in three large bags, down to the nearest Salvation Army. He'd wanted nothing of the life that destroyed him ... but could keeping a jacket or two, some khaki pants even, have been such a bad idea?

He'd have to shop, as Kali said. He looked to the mirror in his closet door and rubbed his beard, gave a tug at the long locks falling down over his face. He could cut it all off, trim his hair, become the man he once was—in appearance at least.

But did he want to? He couldn't go like this; that was for sure. His mother would break down. But a trim, some shaping of the beard—enough to look like he made an effort, not enough to let old acquaintances recognize him on the street—that he could do.

THAT AFTERNOON, LINCOLN returned home with a respectable outfit. Not something he would have worn to a business meeting, not even to a night out with the guys, but respectable. Jeans. A button up flannel shirt. Something a traveller would wear.

His beard was two inches shorter, his hair trimmed and even. He held a wrapped present. A bracelet his mother may not love but couldn't hate. Pretty. Simple.

He waited for Kali. She hadn't mentioned the party again. He hadn't mentioned her apartment search. She'd asked him if he thought he'd get another dog when they left. He hadn't known what to say.

He wanted her to know he was going to the party. Wanted to know, no matter what happened tonight, that she would be here, hoping it'd go all right, rooting for him. Lincoln swung his arms. He picked up a book. He glanced in the mirror, adjusted his new style, not able to wait any longer, and left.

The party started at five. He'd decided he'd get there at seven-thirty. Late enough that people who came for the food would have left. That his father, who had to be back in the home by seven, would be gone.

He hadn't RSVP'd, so it didn't matter when he arrived.

Cars lined the street of the home he'd grown up in. Too many. Uncle Albert and Aunt Gertie walked past his truck, arm in arm, laughing. Two vehicles left and another one came. One of his mother's curling friends? An hour passed. Two. And Lincoln stayed seated. Stupid. Stupid. Weak.

He hadn't even been the one to do something wrong. Why was he the one who felt paralyzed at the thought of seeing his family?

But he had done something. He'd yelled at his mother. Cursed her for not disowning Joseph, for saying Lucy made a mistake, it'd been wrong, but that didn't mean he could talk to her like that. For telling Lincoln that Lucy was in pain, a pain Lincoln could never understand—as if Lincoln didn't hurt just as much, as if betrayal hurt less than loss. Not that he hadn't lost ... He had lost everything.

But it was more than that, more than his mother, hardly his mother. He'd failed, and everyone knew it. He'd been ... cuckolded, and everyone knew it. Made a joke by the two people he'd loved most.

Lincoln stepped out of the truck. The house was three lots away. Music trailed along the evening breeze. Laughter. A couple left through the front door and strolled down the driveway. "Lincoln? Lincoln Fraser, is that you?"

He held up a hand and gave a tight-lipped smile without stopping. The woman whispered as he passed.

The majority of the guests would be in two places—the kitchen and the back porch. A few would be in the living room—the older ones, or the ones who'd had too much to drink and weren't the best at holding their liquor.

His mother could be anywhere, doing anything. She wasn't one to sit around.

The ones in the living room hardly noticed him, though Great Uncle Richard raised an arm. "Looks good on you, son. Not so prissy like the boys today."

Lincoln nodded.

Aunt Mev appeared in front of him. "Lincoln, baby, is that you? I thought you were in Malaysia or Venezuela or some such place." She laughed. A liquid laugh.

He shrugged and accepted her embrace. "I'm back."

He kept walking. Find Mom. Say hello. Give her the present. Give her a hug. Leave.

"Lincoln, that you under all that hair? You look just like your daddy when he spent that summer in the woods."

Lincoln turned. "What?"

"The summer before he met your mom. Spent it cutting lumber and came out looking like you."

"Oh."

"You back for good?"

"Not sure." He kept walking.

His mother sat in the backyard, Linda's youngest on her knee. Laughing. He stepped over the threshold and onto the porch.

"Lincoln?"

He dropped his gaze to the manicured hand on his forearm. He didn't need to look up to know who it was.

CHAPTER THIRTY-FIVE

Lucy stood in front of him, a nervous, not-quite-smile on her face. "We didn't think you'd come."

"Why would you?"

He met her gaze, her beautiful blue-eyed gaze. She looked away. "I ... that was you that night, wasn't it? On Brunswick Street."

Lincoln followed her gaze—Joseph talking with Rachel.

"Wasn't it?" Her hand was still on his forearm. It felt like a vice grip though she barely touched him. "I should have said something. I should have come back, but I didn't know where I'd find you, if I'd find you ... if you wanted to be found." She paused. "I told him I didn't like it, didn't want to salsa anymore." She let out that little uncertain laugh he used to love. "Was he angry about that." She made her voice go deep, the same voice they used to use together to mock Joseph. Was it the voice she used with Joseph to mock him? "*First you beg me to go to salsa. Beg me. And then you don't want to go back?*"

He turned his gaze to her. Her hand fell, and he was there again, almost a year ago, just outside the Square-Victoria metro entrance, yelling after her, telling her to stop. Telling her he'd been a fool and they could keep the baby, they *should* keep the baby. Telling her they'd make it work, if that's what she wanted.

She'd turned to him, her eyes like nothing he'd ever seen before—fear, anger, joy, and something he couldn't decipher. She'd given him the finger, stepped toward the first step leading to the underground, her gaze still on his, and catapulted into the depths.

"I should have come." She rubbed a hand along her collar bone, the place he'd kissed so many times, and the image melded with the sight of her body lying at the bottom of those steps, legs and arms askew, hair spread every which way, her child's life already starting to seep out of her. "I should have looked for you, to see if you were okay." She stopped, her gaze swivelled across the yard to Joseph, laughing, and back to Lincoln. "I care, you know. That you're okay." She swallowed, the delicate tendons in her neck convulsing above the scar. He'd put his hand over that spot, blood running through his fingers, and screamed for help—heart racing, body shaking, terrified the woman he loved, the woman he thought loved him, was dying on the cold hard tile with commuters rushing past or hesitating as they avoided her, unsure what to do.

Lucy smiled. "It wasn't all bad."

Wasn't all bad? Lincoln's throat tightened. Of course it wasn't all bad. He'd loved her. He'd fucking adored her. And she'd been fucking his brother—for years. Lincoln stepped back, his fists clenched. "I'm here to see my mother."

"Lincoln." She stepped in his path, her voice the placating little whine she so loved to use.

252

"Move."

"I'm sorry. I never meant to—"

"Sleep with my brother?"

Her mouth hung open, her eyes wide.

"Lucy, out of my way before I move you out of my way."

She stepped aside. Lincoln strode down the porch steps, across the lawn, past the people who chatted, laughed, called hello.

"Hey, Mom."

Marilyn Fraser turned. She stood, setting her granddaughter on the lawn. "Lincoln?"

Her arms were around him. Squeezing him, holding him. "Oh, baby, you're okay. You're all right." She pulled back, her arms still around him, then raised a hand to his bearded cheek. "You look just like your daddy." She pulled him to her again.

"I just wanted to say Happy Birthday. I can't stay long."

"Lincoln." She pulled back again. "Is everything okay?"

"Sure. Yeah." He pushed out a smile. The tendons in his neck throbbed ... Lucy's open mouth, Lucy's shock—as if he'd been inappropriate, bringing such a thing up.

Rachel, Linda, and Joseph stood to the side. Lucy sidled up to Joseph. He didn't put his arm around her. He didn't look at Lincoln. He puffed his chest out, but kept his gaze averted.

Marilyn glanced at them. "All my babies." She gestured to Rachel. "Thank you, darling, for getting him home."

Rachel shifted awkwardly. Was she angry? Concerned? She'd sent emails. Fifteen emails. And he hadn't responded to one. Linda's face was pissed. Joseph's was unreadable—Lincoln wondered what it would feel like to put his fist in it.

He lifted a hand to his sisters. They didn't wave back.

"Uncle Lincoln?" Linda's six-year-old—was he six now?—looked up at him. "That you? Mom said you'd gone to hell."

Linda reached for him. "Could go to hell," she snapped. "I said he could go to hell."

"Linda." Marilyn shook her head. "Sweetheart."

Lincoln stepped away from his mother's grasp. He pulled the present out of his pocket. His hand shook. "Here. It's just a little something."

"I'm sure it's lovely."

"You can't just do that to people. Just disappear." Linda's voice rose. "No matter what happens."

"He was travelling," said Marilyn. "It's good for a young man to travel."

"Yeah, right."

"Anyway," Lincoln spoke low to his mother, "I can't stay. I just wanted to wish you a Happy Birthday. You have a good day?"

Her grip tightened on him. "It's been wonderful. And it's better now. But what do you mean you can't stay? Where would you go?"

"I have a place."

"A hotel? You're staying here."

"No. A place. My own place."

"You bought—"

"I'm renting."

"So you didn't just get back," Linda wore a smug grimace, "from your travels."

"I have a place in Halifax."

Marilyn nodded. Her grasp loosened. "There are a lot of people here. And we need to catch up." She looked to her other children then back at Lincoln. "You come back sometime this week." She clasped her hand. "Okay? Sometime this week. And we'll catch up."

Lincoln wanted to say no. Wanted to tell her there was nothing to say. She had her children. She'd made her choice. He wasn't a prodigal son. He was just the one who'd failed at the life she wanted for him, the life everyone had wanted for him. He nodded. Rachel opened her mouth and stepped forward. She closed it.

"Dad was here."

Lincoln looked to Linda.

"You knew about the party, right? So you got Rachel's emails. You knew Dad would be here. You knew *when* he'd be here."

He'd known, but not from the emails. Of the fifteen, he'd only even opened the first two.

"When's the last time you saw him, huh? Long before—" she gestured toward Joseph and Lucy. Joseph turned toward the house, leaving Lucy standing there stupidly.

Linda continued, "What's your excuse for that?"

Lincoln put a hand to his mother's shoulder, mouthed the words, Happy Birthday, and headed for the fence. He wasn't about to walk through that house again, wasn't about to get a step closer to Joseph. His fist would land on his face for sure, and his mother's party would be ruined. His fist clenched, imagining.

He turned to open the door of his truck, but a soft touch on his shoulder stopped him. Rachel. "Hey."

"Hey."

He lowered his head. "Sorry, I—"

"Stop it."

"Okay." Lincoln's shoulders hunched. "How'd I do? Good party crashing?"

"You were invited."

"Yeah."

"So it's not exactly crashing."

He gave a half smile.

"I knew you were in town. Have probably been in town since you disappeared from Montreal all those months ago."

"Andrew?"

"A guy I went to school with mentioned he'd seen you, that you were all scraggly and homeless looking. I got the rest out of Andrew."

"And Linda?"

"She got it out of me."

"Mom?"

"She thinks you were gallivanting."

"And you never came to visit?" Lincoln pulled at his ear, gave a close-lipped smile. "Drop off a casserole to your wayward brother?"

Rachel exhaled. "Andrew wouldn't tell me where you lived. If he had, I wouldn't have brought a casserole."

"I kept in touch with Mom."

She shook her head. "What they did—"

"I don't want to talk about it."

"And then him firing you—"

"Rachel!"

"I'm just saying. It sucks. It's wretched. All of it."

"But you still sit with them at Sunday dinner."

"He's my brother. Yours too."

"Yep. Well—" Lincoln pulled open the door. He reached forward and cupped her head in his hands, kissed her

256

forehead. "Have a good night."

"You visit Mom next week."

"Will do."

"I'll find you and I'll cut you if you don't."

He grinned. How many times had she sworn that in their childhood? "I'll be trembling in my boots."

"Come here, you idiot." She wrapped her arms around him. "And answer your bloody emails." She punched him in the arm.

He rubbed it in mock pain. "Don't send so many."

She pulled out her phone. "What's your number?"

"I don't have one."

She let out a long sigh and threw up her hands.

He shrugged. "I'm leaving now. Watch your toes."

She stepped back.

Lincoln waved. He drove down the street, passing all the homes he knew almost as well as his own.

His pulse started to calm. It could have been worse. His mom had been happy. Annoyed, but happy. His ruse was blown, but he'd avoided deep questioning. He'd seen Lucy and hadn't spit in her face or broken into sobs. He'd seen Joseph and hadn't stabbed him with a makeshift shiv.

Kali would be proud ... if she cared.

He tried to recall if she worked tonight—must not, or he'd be at home watching Theo. He hadn't told her he was going to the party, but he'd tell her he went and was pretty sure it'd make her smile.

CHAPTER THIRTY-SIX

Lincoln heard movement as he approached the door to their apartment. Not only was Kali home, she was awake, and unlike his family, she wouldn't look at him like he was a disappointment.

He opened the door and stared. Half of the boxes that had spent the past weeks lined up and piled against the wall were in the centre of the living room. Kali sat amidst a pile of items, packing tape around her.

"Oh, hey!" Her eyes widened. "Look at you. A haircut. New clothes. Was tonight the party?" She braced her hands on her knees and stood. "You went? That's great."

"Uh, yeah." Lincoln kicked off his new sneakers and closed the door. "What's going on?"

"Packing. Tell me about the party. Was your mom ... did ... did everything go okay?"

"She was happy to see me." Lincoln stepped into the room. "What are you doing?"

Kali grinned. Grinned. She hardly ever grinned ... though she had been more lately. "I didn't want to tell you until I knew it was a sure thing, but I found a place." A happy breath of air escaped her. "It's only three blocks from Westwood's main campus. A twelve-minute walk. This nurse is taking a job in Ontario and she needs to go now. So I'll technically be subletting the last couple of weeks of the month and my lease will start in September." She reached for a pile of old yearbooks. "Why do we keep these things? Crazy." She dropped the pile into the nearest box.

"So you're leaving when?"

"I'll move in tomorrow after work." Another grin. "My first non-shadowing day!"

"Tomorrow?" Lincoln sank onto the arm of the nearest couch. "That's uh—"

"Soon. I know."

"And isn't the job in Dartmouth? What about Theo? I thought the daycare couldn't take him for another week. Wasn't Mrs. Martin supposed to watch him until—"

"No." She perched on a box. "They can take him right away. A space opened up. I didn't want to jinx it until I knew for sure it was happening. Really happening, you know?"

He gave a half nod. "But it's sudden. Is he ready?"

"He'll be ready. I took him over today to introduce him to the place. This one little girl kind of claimed him. Walked him around, introduced him to the other children. He'll be okay."

"That's great. That's uh," the room seemed to grow around Lincoln, as if she'd already left, as if the space she left behind were a chasm, "super."

"Super?" She let out a laugh. "Okay, Mr. Rogers."

This was too fast. Too soon. He wasn't ready. "You don't have to leave yet. You don't have to rush, I mean. Moving's rough, right? Take your time, move over slowly."

"No." She reached for another item. "This was the agreement; as soon as I was able, I'd be gone. I'm able. So, I'm going."

"Yeah, but—"

"But what, Lincoln?"

"I don't want you to feel like I'm kicking you out." He laughed. "Sure, of course I want my place back, but a few days, a few weeks, it's not a big—"

"A few weeks?" Kali turned from him as she gathered some items on the other side of the room. "This has been kind of you. Incredibly kind. I appreciate it. But we're not staying a few more weeks."

"Okay, well," Lincoln ran a hand through his hair, "I'll make sure I'm home then, tomorrow night, to help you take the first load over."

"Oh, it's no problem." She taped the box with Theo's dinky cars. "I hired movers. That's why I'm packing up tonight. By tomorrow at this time it'll look like we were never here."

"Movers? But I can help. You don't need to—"

"You've done enough." She smiled. Happy. Eager to leave.

"Okay, well." The room grew and grew, and Lincoln felt lost in it. Her face: Excited. Resolved. She'd walk out and never look back. "Sure. Yeah. That's great."

"I really do appreciate it."

"Of course. Yeah."

Lincoln passed by her. "Congratulations. I'm happy for you." He turned, pushed out a smile. 'Cause he should smile. This didn't matter, her going. Or if it did, it was a good thing. "Bet you're relieved to be getting out of this dump."

She shrugged. "It's not so bad."

LINCOLN KEPT WALKING. In the hall, once out of view, he put a hand against the wall, steadying himself. What was happening? Why did he feel like his world was crumbling? It wasn't. It was going back to the way it should be. He'd have his space back, his life back, he'd stop being blinded by the illusion that Kali and Theo were what he needed, what he wanted. They weren't.

By tomorrow they'd be gone, just like they'd never been here. He could put these last few months behind him, put *them* behind him, and finish the tree house. If he worked hard and fast, he could start living there soon, living his dream. If he started small, focused on a compact insulated room, maybe he could even live there through the winter, then work on expansion next spring. That could work. Yes. It would work. It'd be perfect. And no one would find him there. If he wanted to visit his family—for their sake, not his—he could, but he'd be the one in control. He'd give them no address. He'd hide away. Escape.

Yes. This was good. Just what he needed. What he wanted.

CHAPTER THIRTY-SEVEN

The next evening Lincoln watched as Kali directed the men stomping through his apartment, telling them what to take and what to leave. He stood in corners and shifted along walls, trying not to get in their way.

Theo skipped among the mayhem. "A new place," Kali told him, "with fresh paint and big windows, and your own room." His eyes lit. "Your own bed, too." At this he seemed a little wary. "But you can sneak in with me whenever you like."

The skipping resumed. With Kali's couch and the boxes that had lined the living room wall gone, dust bunnies tumbled across the floor.

An old familiar pressure situated itself on Lincoln's chest. *Say something. Do something.*

The apartment grew larger with each trip the men took down the stairs. Their footsteps echoed. Their voices boomed. Kali told Theo to play with his trucks on the couch then hauled out a broom.

"You don't have to do that," Lincoln told her.

"I do." She corralled the bunnies.

Should he ask where she was moving? What if she forgot something? What if he needed to get in touch with her?

She swept the bunnies into a dustpan and walked past Lincoln to the garbage under the sink. She turned back. "With moving in early I'm a little tighter than I hoped. Can I get my portion of the rent to you in a couple of weeks?"

He shook his head.

"I can't?"

"No. I mean you don't need to."

She rested a hand on her hip, "Of course I need to," and stepped past him. "I don't take charity."

Lincoln followed her. "Maybe I can stop by sometime, see your new place. Pick it up then."

"Oh," a glance, "I can drop it off. That's easier."

Lincoln stepped out of her way. "Sure. Absolutely." A wall had shot up between them. Her wall. Was this all it was, all it ever was—she'd needed him, and now she didn't, so that was the end.

She passed him once more, pulled out his couch, peered behind it. Theo giggled and she gave him a wink.

Would she let some other man into their lives? Would he be a good man? Would he teach Theo to throw a ball— Lincoln had taken him out a few times, the kid had potential—or how to talk to a girl ... once he decided to talk?

Would *she* teach him? Marvin wouldn't. So who else was there?

Theo glanced at Lincoln, his smile lit like a sparkler. The smile faded. His brown eyes looked deep into Lincoln's, searching, searching. Could Lincoln handle not seeing those eyes again?

"Will you do anything with the spare room?"

"What?" Lincoln turned to Kali.

Kali smiled. "Now that you have it back. Maybe find a use for it?"

"Oh, uh, move the weights back in. Maybe storage." He cleared his throat. "I'll be amping up work on the tree house. It'll mean buying a number of supplies. Safer to store them here I suppose."

She nodded, stepped into her old room, swung open the closet door, and peered inside.

Footsteps thumped up the stairs. The movers, arriving for their last load. Kali grabbed her satchel, Theo's backpack, her car keys. "Well," she raised her hand in an easy half sigh—it was a movement he'd never seen on her, "I guess this is it."

Lincoln stepped forward, though at least five feet stood between them.

"Thank you." She closed the space between them, one hand outstretched. "You saved us."

He took her hand, his vocal chords frozen.

She released his grip. "I wish you," a soft smile, "well. I wish you well, Lincoln."

"Anyone would have done it." The words fell out of him, like an unexpected burp.

"What?"

"Anyone would have, I mean I had the space, so—"

Her eyes laughed. "No. Anyone would not have." She adjusted her satchel and rested a hand on Theo's shoulder. "Tell Lincoln goodbye."

He looked up at her, the little tilt of the head that Lincoln knew he'd miss seeing every day. The boy's brows furrowed, his face questioned.

"Lincoln's not coming with us to the new apartment. He's

staying here."

A shake of the head. A tug on his mother's shirt.

"You need to say goodbye now. We might not see him again. Let Lincoln know you were glad to stay, but it's time to say goodbye."

Theo tucked his head against Kali's hip and wrapped his arms around her leg. He stared at Lincoln.

Lincoln crouched down. The pressure against his chest tripled. "I liked having you here. Getting to know you." He glanced up at Kali. "I hope I get to see you again soon. Maybe go to the park. Maybe play catch."

The boy's eyes brightened. He nodded.

"That sound good?"

Another nod.

"Can I get a hug goodbye?"

Theo flung his arms around Lincoln and squeezed. Lincoln let go first. He stood. Kali's lips were pursed.

"What?"

"I just..." She shook her head.

"Yes?"

"Never mind."

Lincoln glanced to Theo then back to Kali. "It'll be nice. Give you a break if I take him out sometimes."

She adjusted the strap of her satchel and left both hands on it. "Sure. Absolutely. Well, you have my number." She started to turn, then stopped. "I was thinking. You and your tree house. It sounds really complex. It seems like you've thought it all out, put a lot of work into it."

"Yeah."

"So, there's this whole community of people who adore tree houses. For some, it's connected to the tiny house movement."

Lincoln stared at her.

"Really, a whole movement. Are you on Pinterest?" She shook her head, laughed. "Of course you're not. But look it up at the library. There are all these images. All these people dreaming." She adjusted her satchel. "Your plan is to generate what income you'll need through woodworking, right? Chairs, tables, shelves? Odd jobs." Lincoln nodded. "And that's an all right plan I guess, but you have something more to offer, something, uh, more lucrative." She gave a half smile. "People would buy your plans. Some maybe even contract you to design it for them. It could mean travelling." A pause. "It could mean good money."

Lincoln didn't know what to say.

"It's just an idea." Another smile—a shy smile.

"That's uh ... interesting."

"Yeah. So you could build them for others or come up with a patent, a manual, something. Maybe even your own full-fledged business one day." Her words came fast. "Though maybe that's not what you want. But I was just thinking, with the specialization for colder climates, how you'll make it self-sufficient, sustainable, and beautiful too—isn't that what you've talked about? That it won't just be practical, but beautiful?"

"Yeah, but—"

"It's just a thought." She smiled, one shoulder shrugging. "Most people probably won't want to live in them all the time like you. But for vacation homes, for reading rooms. For a place to escape. People would want them. People would love them."

"Okay."

"Okay." She drew Theo against her. "I just—I don't want you freezing to death out there. Or ... you'll need money."

"I'll be okay."

"Okay." She stepped backward until her hand reached the doorknob. "All the best, Lincoln. Take care of yourself."

Theo waved. First she, then he, disappeared behind the door. It made a quiet click. Lincoln swallowed. He was alone.

He stood in the space, remembering what it was like in those first months before Romper. And then before Kali and Theo. He stood, and though the walls seemed to spread, he felt suffocated. He crossed to the door, yanked it open, and ran down the stairs.

CHAPTER THIRTY-EIGHT

"Kali."

She turned on the sidewalk, her hand inches from the back passenger door. Lincoln could almost hear the words coming out of him.

'Stay.'

Her brows would rise, then furrow. 'What?'

'Stay.' He'd shrug. 'It's comfortable. It's nice, this thing we've got going here.'

She'd cross her arms, probably adjust her satchel one more time. 'It's too far from work.' Or, 'This is a shit neighbourhood.' Or, 'Are you kidding me? I've been counting the days until I could get away from you.'

He wouldn't know what to say then, to any of it. Maybe he'd tell her they could watch out for each other, or suggest how much money she'd save by paying only one-fifty a month or paying nothing. He didn't need her cash.

Lincoln took the last steps down the porch. "Watch out for yourself. Be safe."

She let out a laugh, close-lipped. Almost more a hum or faint chuckle. "That's what I do. What I've always done." She opened the door and ushered Theo in, secured him in his booster seat, then walked around to the driver's side. "See you, Lincoln. It's been swell."

The moving truck pulled from the curb. A girl and her dog walked down the street, Kali pulled her car into traffic, and the salsa music from next door blared.

What uselessness.
What beauty.

Two weeks into her new job, and a day short of two weeks waking up in her new apartment, Kali's heart pounded. The pressure in her head had been coming off and on for weeks. Intensifying.

But the job was great. The apartment was wonderful. She was no longer spending hours poring over her training manuals. She had no reason to be stressed. And yet almost every morning she woke with this pain. This nausea.

Today the pressure had intensified mid-day. The pain and sickness fogged her vision, like looking through lace. From time to time her ears rang. Kali didn't know what it was, but it was something. It was real. She'd been reaching for her client's medication and, pain throbbing, nausea making her vision blur, couldn't figure out which was which. She squinted, reached for the one she felt sure was right, and opened the cap.

"Kali?" Dianne, the coworker whose shift she'd been taking over, touched her elbow. "That one is for the evening."

"Right. Right." Kali rubbed her temple, recapped the meds, and laughed it off. "Momentary lapse."

Dianne's brow furrowed. "You can't have momentary lapses. Are you okay?"

Kali nodded. *Was she?*

Her heart started to pound. And now, nine hours later, after she'd finished her shift accident-free, dropped off Theo at Mrs. Martin's, and sat waiting in her doctor's office, it still pounded.

"Kali?"

Kali stood and followed the receptionist she'd known since she was a girl into one of the clinic's patient rooms. For probably the hundredth time she went over the possible causes for her symptoms. Most harmless. Many easily fixable. It was those few that weren't harmless, that couldn't be easily fixed, that made her palms sweat ...

She rubbed her hands on her pants.

Dr. Pickles shuffled into the office. His name had made her giggle when she was a girl. He still had several cartoon pickles and images around his office. Some had been there longer than she could remember.

He'd retire soon. Probably. His hair had greyed further in the ten months since Theo's last checkup. His shoulders were slightly more stooped.

"Miss Johnson, how's that young man of yours?"

"Good."

"Speaking?"

"Not yet."

He tutted. "Well, it'll come." He settled into the chair behind his desk. "The psychologist's not helping?"

Kali shook her head. "At least not in any way I can see."

Dr. Pickles leaned forward, his knobby, loose skinned elbows pushing into the desk. "But you're not here about Theo."

She shook her head again and described her symptoms in clinical detail—from their first occurrences to their present intensity. While Dr. Pickles seemed relaxed at the start, his body shifted toward the end, leaned forward. He questioned her deeper, asking things she wasn't certain of. *Thump. Thump. Thump* went her heart.

"What else? Tingles?"

Had there been? Yes. But ... the kind he was describing? *Thump.*

He listed symptoms off. Confusion. Weakness. Loss of

consciousness.

Thump.

Spasms. Nausea. Numbness. Loss of hearing.

Thump.

Reduced motor function. And then there was the vision. So much about the vision.

Thump. Thump.

She'd had some of the symptoms he listed. More than she'd realized. But not all. Not even nearly all. Still, his brow furrowed. He rubbed his bottom lip, just the way he'd rubbed it before they found out her mother was sick.

"So?" Kali swallowed. *Thump. Thump. Thump.*

"It's most likely nothing." He smiled. "Often, innocuous and unrelated causes can show up at the same time, making symptoms seem worse than they are." He rubbed that bottom lip. "But you know that."

"I do. That's why I took so long to come in."

He made that sound all doctors seem to make. Deep at the back of their throat—showing agreement, concern, uncertainty. "But we also want to be safe. Rule out something potentially more serious."

Kali knew the word that was floating through his mind. It floated through hers, but she couldn't say it. Couldn't even think it. Not that it was an automatic death sentence, not necessarily. Not always.

He grabbed a prescription pad and wrote something. He passed the paper to her. "For your nausea."

"It's not all the time."

"Then take it when you need it."

Kali nodded.

Dr. Pickles stared at her a moment. "Cover your eye."

"What?"

"Your eye. Just put one hand over—"

"Which one?"

"Either."

Kali raised her hand over her right eye.

"Anything?"

"What do you—"

"Your vision is clear?"

"Yes."

"Now the other."

Kali swallowed. She shifted her hand and gasped.

"Kali?"

"It's blurry. Everything is ... like a veil, like ..." She stopped. "How could I not notice?"

"One eye will compensate for the other." Dr. Pickles gave a little sigh. "I'm sending you for a CT scan." He turned to his computer, navigated the mouse and tapped several keys. "I can get you into the VG tomorrow."

"Tomorrow." Kali squeaked. Patients often waited months for a scan. If the referring doctor thought it could be serious, maybe weeks. *Thump. Thump. Thump. Thump.* "I work tomorrow, but—"

"You'll call in sick or find a replacement."

Kali nodded. How could she not have noticed, how ... those early mornings, when she'd rubbed her head, her eyes, had this been the veil all along?

"Don't jump to conclusions." Dr. Pickles leaned forward. "We don't know anything yet. Not for certain."

Now Kali made the noise in the back of her throat. Cautious was two months. Cautious was getting her into an ophthalmologist within the week. There was no doubting it now; the word that floated in her mind floated in his. And though that word didn't have to be as serious as people thought it was, clearly Dr. Pickles believed, in her case, it could be.

CHAPTER THIRTY-NINE

The first three nights after Kali and Theo left, the silent apartment pressed in on Lincoln. He'd open the window, aching for the sounds of the neighbourhood to pierce through, but, despite the shouts of children playing, cars revving, and mothers hollering, the silence lingered. On the fourth night he stayed in the woods. The silence there less hostile. He worked until his muscles ached. Day after day, after day. He constructed sheaves. Hammered and cut and hauled. Came up with the idea of a dumbwaiter, not only to lift items from the ground, but to use once the multiple floors were built. He considered the idea of a turret, reaching above the highest branches, to survey the land as far as his eyes could see. He decided on rain gutters made of cut copper pipes that he'd shine to glint in the sunlight. With Kali's suggestion of marketing his plans, his ideas seemed endless. Not that he'd necessarily need them all for himself. But to try them out, to make sure they worked—why not?

The tree house, almost as if it had a life of its own, grew. On the tenth day, the seventh of living in the woods, he stopped. He wasn't done, not even close, but to do more would require material he couldn't access for several more days. He'd checked the shipment two days before, during a trip into town to restock his food supply.

Lincoln climbed down from the tree he'd called home for almost the past two weeks and took several steps back. The tree house was bare, free of the intricate woodwork he'd add before he called the project complete, and smaller than the finished design would be. But it was beautiful. Livable, even, at least until the weather cooled.

With the shipment, the most important component being the solar panels he'd ordered custom made from a German facility, he could get started on the electrical work, heating, and insulation. The plumbing would take some more experimentation. Not that it was necessary, of course—but if he planned to live here all winter, during a week with the cold or flu it'd be pretty awful having to climb down the ladder to squat in the snow, which, eventually, would create its own problem. He was thinking some sort of pipe system along the base of the tree, behind the ladder, to not be an eyesore, and directed to a composting toilet perhaps. The technical aspects still needed work. He'd already figured out a water collection and filtration system so he didn't have to always trek to the lake. He considered pumping it in, but that seemed too easy, too modern. He wanted a different kind of life, a life with as little impact on the world around him as possible, not one merely an adapted version of the life he'd left. Still, figuring it out would be interesting, and he might, if he followed Kali's suggestion, find an alternate way to support himself while helping others' dreams of solitude (if only as a retreat) come true.

Each day and night he'd worked until exhaustion hit, then fell into his hammock and woke with the sun. Tonight, though, he had hours until the sun would set, and even more until sleep would find him. Already, in the few minutes since he'd stepped back from his work, thoughts of Kali, and of Theo, flooded over him.

Lincoln went to his pack and pulled out the book Kali had given him for his birthday. *Walden*. He knew little about it beyond the fact that it was about some writer from the mid-1800s who'd decided to build a cabin in the woods and live there, away from society. He'd leafed through the introduction the night Kali gave him the book, as she stood watching, and through those few snippets he gathered the endeavour was about a man determined to meet himself face to face. Lincoln liked that. Could see himself in that.

His 'cabin' was in the sky, and now that his first level was built, he had a view of a lake, not more than a two-minute walk through the woods. He'd barely thought about the book since that night, always reaching for one of the texts that would help make his tree house exactly what he envisioned it to be, but now it called to him.

He walked toward the lake and sat in one of those tree limbs that curve out over the water, as if the sun and the lake and the tree itself had conspired to make the perfect resting place. He put his back against the trunk of the tree and his legs straight out in front of him. Eyes closed, he savoured the exhaustion that settled over him. He could sleep. Maybe he should sleep. The breeze danced over the hairs on his arms and legs, birds chattered in the boughs above. This is what he wanted. This is what he missed, what he'd loved as a child after a day of racing through the woods with Andrew, the way they'd sit at the end of it, if only for a few minutes before heading back home. Tired, but content.

He opened his eyes and flipped through the book's introduction, choosing instead, to dive right into the author's words. Lincoln read as if those words were consuming him, and not the other way around. The words seemed written for him.

Part of the machine, Thoreau insisted, that's what so many men were. Crunching numbers, greasing the gears, while the part within them that was still human lived a life of quiet desperation.

Is that why he hadn't known Lucy was cheating on him? Why he never knew his brother, every day, with every word of encouragement and clap on the shoulder, had been lying to his face? Lincoln had been desperate, chasing a life that never could have given him the satisfaction he wanted.

He read on. And on.

I went to the woods because I wished to live deliberately ... and not, when I come to die, discover that I had not lived ...

Lincoln lowered the book. For the first time in as long as he could remember, he felt connected. Understood. Like his need, his yearning to escape finally made sense to someone other than himself.

But was this living—deliberately or otherwise? These past days he'd spent labouring with nothing but him and the birds and the wind and the howling wolves at night. He was alive. He was creating something. Building something. And once it was made he'd have more time for moments like this. As much time as he wanted. He could read all the books he'd wondered about—both the classics and the blockbusters. He would start woodworking again—the entire tree house would be a work of art. And maybe, with Kali's suggestion, he'd help others create their own works of art. He liked the idea of manuals better than contracting: that felt too much like business. Like what he'd been doing before.

But beyond that? Would it be enough? Without Kali's smile? Her eyes when angry, unsure, laughing? Or without Theo's silent grin?

Thoreau wasn't alone. Not really. Not as much as Lincoln planned to be. They both had the animals, though with Romper gone, Lincoln didn't have the one animal he wanted.

And Thoreau had visitors. He walked to the village or a neighbour's almost every day. Lincoln could have visitors. He could make that work. The edges of a smile crept across his face. Theo would love it here. Love climbing the ladder. Love swimming in the lake. Lincoln looked to a nearby tree whose branches stretched out over the water. He could tie a rope there, or even a big rubber tire, and Theo could swing. Kali could relax. Really relax, without mindlessly streaming Netflix shows. Not that he didn't understand that. He'd done it too, on late evenings after work when Lucy wanted to go out and all he'd wanted to do was lie down and disconnect his mind.

And he could have other visitors too. One day. Maybe. His mother. Rachel. Perhaps even Linda and her kids. Though he couldn't imagine Linda climbing up that tree, not ever. She'd probably tell her husband to buy an RV for the sole purpose of a visit. He shuddered at the tracks that thing would make, at the trees that would need to be cleared to get it close enough. No, maybe not Linda.

His imagination travelled. The design as it was now was about one-hundred and twenty square feet with a fifty square foot loft for his bedroom area. But he could expand up. Build a whole second floor and even a third, or half a third, if Theo ever moved in. He'd want his own space and Lincoln could build it ... and a turret. He'd decided, a turret was a must.

Lincoln returned to the pages. He read until he couldn't see the words clearly, then returned to his house in the sky.

He woke with the sun the next morning and went for a swim in the lake, another habit he'd started. After lying in the morning sun to dry, he gathered some water, a compass, the survey to his land, the book, a lunch, and hefted his pack over his shoulder. He hadn't explored since Romper was with him, and that was never more than twenty or thirty minutes away from his site. But he had a lot more land to discover. Sixty acres of this wilderness was his. He wouldn't mark his territory with fences or keep-out signs, but he wanted to know it.

After about thirty minutes of walking, Lincoln stepped out into a large field flooded with wildflowers. Pinks, purples, yellows, and whites. As the sun beat down, sending up the scent of warm honey, a breeze ruffled the blossoms, making the flowers dance. Fat and fuzzy bees flitted from bright coloured blossom to bright coloured blossom. A large boulder sat on the opposite side of the field.

Lincoln crossed to it and sat, transfixed by the waving colours. Kali would love this. He sat straighter. But would she? Did he know her enough to know? She'd scoffed at his endeavour. Well, maybe not scoffed, but hadn't seen the beauty in it, had looked at him like he might be crazy. At first. That last day she'd had respect, had encouraged him to make something of it—saw that others had similar dreams to his own. And she'd bought him the book.

He reached into his pack and flipped to the last page he'd read. The hours passed, and when he came to the end he looked up, for probably the fortieth time since he'd started. He was travelling in the direction of his dreams, he had literally begun work on his castle in the air, just like Thoreau.

He flipped several pages back to read those lines again. Was it ludicrous to take Thoreau's words as gospel? Did this obscure man who lived over a hundred and fifty years ago know something the rest of society didn't? And what did it mean when he said the castle he built needed a foundation? *I left the woods for as good a reason as I went there. Perhaps it seemed to me that I had several more lives to live, and could not spare any more time for that one.*

Lincoln read the words once, twice, three times. He wasn't ready to leave the woods. He didn't know that he needed to in any kind of concrete way. But as good as these past few days had been, as much as he felt he could breathe in a whole new way, free from the noise and the machinery and the smell of all that life in the city, he also needed more. He needed her. His life didn't have to be the woods and nothing else. He could live parallel lives. One here. One there ... whatever that would mean.

Theo needed someone. She needed someone. And so did he.

CHAPTER FORTY

K ali nodded.

"You understand, yes? I need to know that you're hearing me, that you comprehend—"

"I understand." Kali spurted the words. She closed her eyes—*Breathe. Just breathe*—then opened them wide. How could she ever close her eyes again, knowing one day when she opened them—

"Kali, are you—"

"I'm fine."

"I know this is so little ... nothing really, but—"

Kali snatched the pamphlets Dr. Pickles placed before her and stuffed them in her satchel.

"I'm sorry." Dr. Pickles closed the file that held her CT Scan results.

He did look sorry. He looked close to tears. A mound rose in Kali's throat and she swallowed it down.

"This isn't a death sentence. There's no reason to—"

"I know," she snapped. Kali looked to the desk then took a breath and met Dr. Pickles gaze. This man was not her enemy; he'd cared for her, her mother, her son. Kali blinked away a tear and tried again, her voice calm. "I know. Thank you." She stood. She smiled.

"Next you'll see the neuro-ophthalmologist. She'll perform visual field and visual acuity tests, then probably pass you along to neurosurgery, or perhaps radio—" Dr. Pickles cut off. "She'll be able to tell you more."

"Next week." Kali gave a curt nod, the smile still pressed on her face. She clenched her calf and thigh muscles repeatedly, refusing to let herself faint.

LINCOLN PACED. HE looked up to the apartment complex. It was new. Five years old at the most. It housed dozens, maybe hundreds. It had to be, what, fifteen floors high? And somewhere within all those rooms sat Kali and Theo.

And what did he want from them? To say hello? To go for a walk? To beg them to come back and live with him? Each option seemed equally ridiculous. He was nothing to them. And they were nothing to him, except for the fact that they were.

Lincoln held two baseball mitts in his hand. One large, one so small it seemed more for a doll than a boy. They were his excuse, his reason for being here: to teach Theo to catch a ball, to improve his throw.

Inside the small enclosed section before the building's foyer, Lincoln scanned a digital list of names. But what would he say when he buzzed? What would she think? If only she'd forgotten something, that could have been his excuse—his legitimate reason. But to show up where she lived, to not even call first, it was weird. Disturbing. That's what she'd see, Lincoln the stalker.

Why hadn't he called? Because he was scared she'd say no. Tell him they'd moved on—both literally and figuratively—and he should too. He had his hand poised to press her buzzer when the foyer door opened. He smiled at the woman exiting and slipped through before the door closed.

Less than a minute later his hand was poised again—this time to knock at apartment 912.

"Lincoln?" Kali pushed the heel of her hand under her right cheek. Her eyes widened then slanted. "What are you doing here?"

"I—" The slant wasn't just from anger or confusion, her eyes were red and rimmed. "Have you been crying? Are you hurt?"

She waved a hand. "What are you doing here?"

He held up the gloves. "I thought I'd see if Theo wanted to play catch."

Her face twisted. "So you just show up? Why didn't you call?"

Good question. "I was in the area and I thought, well, if you're busy that's fine. If it's a bad time or—"

"How did you even know where I live?"

"Mrs. Martin."

She stared, then sighed. "I don't know. It's not great, but, come in."

He walked through the small entryway. Shoes were strewn across the area. Pictures and prints hung on the wall, ones he'd never seen. Theo in various stages of life. An older woman who must be her mother. Kali.

Why hadn't she hung these in his apartment? Should he have asked, offered her the chance to make the place feel like home?

The furniture he recognized, with a few extra additions. They passed through the kitchen and into the living room where Theo lay sprawled across the floor with Kali's laptop in front of him. Some game with bright coloured creatures flashed across the screen. Theo turned and his face exploded in a smile.

Before Lincoln could blink Theo's arms were wrapped around his legs, squeezing.

Lincoln rested a hand on the boy's head and turned to Kali, his heart clenching. "Guess he remembers me."

Kali stepped back, her arms crossed. "I guess so."

Lincoln pulled the boy off of him and crouched down, his hands on Theo's shoulders. "You miss me?"

A nod and a grin.

"Good." Lincoln grinned back. "I missed you too. Like a bear misses honey."

Theo giggled.

"You been taking care of your mom?"

A huge nod.

"You like your new apartment?"

His head wobbled this time—a bit of a nod, a bit of a shake. He put his hand on Lincoln's chest.

"It looks like a fabulous place to live. And you have your own room?"

This time the nod was ecstatic.

Lincoln stood and looked to Kali, whose hand was on her chest. "Are you okay?"

She shrugged.

He stayed where he stood, scared by the urge to reach out, to draw her to him, to tell her whatever it was, he would help. It would get better. "The place feels so huge without you two."

"But that's good, right?"

Lincoln inhaled. Now he was the one to shrug.

"Anyway, things with us are wonderful." She spread an arm to the side. "This apartment is wonderful. The job is wonderful. Life is wonderful." She bit her bottom lip, halting its tremble. "Thanks, again, you know. For giving us the time I needed to get here."

Lincoln willed his feet to stay still, his arms to remain at his side. "What's wrong?"

"Nothing." She snapped, then waved a hand between them. "Nothing big. Just, uh ... been having some trouble sleeping. And the job is wonderful, but a little intense. Settling into a new life, you know. Things are busy." She looked to Theo. "And he needs time to adjust. You coming here, confusing him, isn't the best thing."

"I didn't mean to—"

"But it is confusing, right? He loved being at Mrs. Martin's. He, for some reason, loved your place. And now all these new things to get used to and you come here, stepping right into them. What if he thinks he's going back with you? That we're going back with you?"

Theo tugged on Kali's shirt.

Kali looked down at him. "We're not." Then back to Lincoln. "You see?" Her voice was strained. "Maybe it's best if you don't come around." She stepped to the island separating the kitchen from the living room and leaned against it, almost as if she needed the support.

"Kali?"

"What? God!" She turned away, one palm pressed hard against the island, the other against her forehead. She looked up with a forced smile. "You should be happy. I know we were a bother. I know we messed up your way of life. So go back to that. How is the house coming, anyway? Lots of improvement?"

"It's coming." And it was, but that didn't seem to matter right now.

"That's great. That's perfect."

She was fighting. Tears. Kali was fighting tears. Lincoln stepped toward her. "What is it? What happened?"

"Can you leave? Please. Just—" She was shaking. Literally trembling. Lincoln crossed the space between them and took her in his arms. She clung to him.

"What is it? What—"

"No." The word came out in a growl and she pushed him away. "Just go. Please. It's nothing. I'm fine. Everything is fine."

"Kali."

"Leave my apartment now."

So he did, with a wave to Theo, whose eyes were wide. He stood outside her door. She was telling him to leave, but did she really mean stay? Should he have, no matter what she meant? For that brief moment, she'd clung to him like a drowning woman. He put his hand on the doorknob to go back inside. It was locked.

CHAPTER FORTY-ONE

K ali sank to the floor against her apartment door. She put a hand to her mouth and stifled a moan. Theo stood in front of her, terror in his eyes.

"It's okay, Sweetie. Mommy's okay." She cradled him against her. "I've got a headache, that's all." She squeezed him and brushed the hair out of his face to kiss his forehead. "Go back to your game." She lifted him off of her and he stood, uncertain. "It's okay. Really. Go." He shuffled away, eyes still on her. "Baby, go. Mommy needs some alone time."

She kept her smile on until Theo was out of sight then let it collapse, both palms to her forehead.

"Meningioma." The neuro-ophthalmologist had explained, not that Kali needed an explanation. She'd seen patients live and die with it. She knew the word. What it meant. What it *could* mean.

It was the other words that left her reeling. The possibilities. The specifics of her case.

A brain tumour could be nothing. An inconvenience, or not even. But those other words. Inoperable. Blindness. Death. Not likely, but possibly, death. Those words left her gasping. Not that Dr. Manning had brought up death, nor Dr. Pickles either. Kali had brought up the word to each of them, and neither had said it was an impossibility. Unlikely, highly unlikely, but ...

Kali didn't know what to fear more: blindness or death. No. She knew. Death. Obviously, death was worse. Of course it was worse. But blindness, or legally blind, even? She was twenty-four. She had an almost four-year-old and no one else, except an old damaged man who refused to come inside, refused to live even the semblance of a normal life.

How would she support herself? How would she support Theo? Would Marvin step out of his self-inflicted prison to take care of them? Was that even possible?

Kali's head fell. She was getting ahead of herself, seeing a future that didn't have to exist.

"Your condition is rare," Dr. Manning smoothed back some stray hairs, "very rare." But sometimes, she said, as if reciting from a textbook, tumours have intense periods of growth. Some suggest these periods can be triggered by stress, hormonal imbalances, sickness, but really the cause is something we can't pinpoint. The theory, though, is that after the triggers are gone, the growth can settle, slow.

If Kali was lucky, that's what the recent weeks of sudden symptoms had been: intense growth triggered by stress. She'd lived with rats. She'd lost her apartment once, then twice. She'd moved in with a stranger. She'd faced the fear of being kicked out any day.

And now that the stress had faded?

Only it hadn't faded. How was she supposed to relax with this diagnosis looming over her? How was she supposed to relax when she knew if she didn't the tumour might not settle? Not that the doctor had said that ... it was Kali's own thoughts, own paranoia; she'd seen it in patients countless times, taking a suggestion, a thought, and turning it into the end of the world.

What Dr. Manning said was that though Kali's recent symptoms over such a short period of time may suggest fast growth, they couldn't know the rate of growth without more tests, and that growth could slow. That, possibly, some of the symptoms she'd experienced could fade. It could be months, even years, before a strong growth phase happened again. She could be fine—for now.

But a year from now, two, twenty, the tumour could rear its debilitating head again, even with treatment.

Always there. Always waiting.

Her sight seemed fine at the moment—looking straight ahead at least. But if she closed her right eye? Anyway, she didn't have to close it. So it was fine—besides the fact that the peripheral vision in her left eye was disappearing, besides her pounding head and teary eyes. This pounding, she hoped, was from the tears, not the tumour. The tumour made her head feel full of pressure, her brain too big for her skull, made her head ache. It wasn't this pounding pain. Or was it? A new development, perhaps?

This would be her life—trying to determine what pains were natural and what meant life as she knew it was slowly ebbing away from her. Already, her life would never be the same. Dr. Manning never said the tumour wouldn't grow. She just said it could take years before the growth became a major problem. And already, a significant amount of her vision was lost.

Kali could feel herself in the clinic room again, a woman

she'd worked with as a colleague sitting across from her. But there were no jokes today. No smiles or words of support or encouragement from either side about a job well done.

Kali had rubbed her hands, squeezed, rubbed.

"We'll keep a strong eye on this, Kali." Dr. Manning looked uncomfortable. Uncertain. She looked like she'd rather be anywhere else. "Monitor you every week for the next several months. Hopefully, the growth ceases or slows. We have no reason to think it won't."

And no reason to think it will.

"In the meantime, we'll certainly look into treatment. It's getting to the tumour that will be a problem." Dr. Pickles had hinted at this, but Dr. Manning went into detail, about the way the tumour had attached itself to just the right spot ... or wrong, between Kali's optic chiasm and optic nerve, affecting both her field of vision in one eye and peripheral vision in the other. How rare this all was, how usually this type of meningioma presented itself either on the optic chiasm or the nerve, not both. "Junctional Scotoma," she said. And, as a result, Kali's vision, though not gone, was going.

"So rare."

"I get it," Kali snapped.

Dr. Manning cleared her throat, smoothed the now non-existent stray hair. Honestly, she said, Kali was lucky her symptoms weren't worse. But she should watch for more. Lack of balance. Increased nausea. The list went on.

And yet the risk of surgery was higher than the risk of letting the invader grow. Surgery wasn't an option, but there was treatment. She'd send Kali to a radiation oncologist to discuss that. There was hope.

And then the questions started, more intense than those of

Dr. Pickles. Dr. Manning tensed when Kali told her about the medication the other day, almost giving a patient the wrong pill. But Kali couldn't keep it secret. Her job was not worth someone's life. And if she'd given that sweet old lady the wrong med at the wrong time ... well, the woman probably wouldn't have died. But another mistake, with another patient; It could be deadly.

"That's the only time something like that happened?"

Kali nodded.

"You must keep track of that."

Another nod. Did Kali look like Theo, nodding like that but saying nothing? Did her eyes widen the way his always did? Is this what it was to have so much you wanted to say, needed to say, yet the words wouldn't come?

"At this point I don't think there's a need to take away your license—"

Kali tensed.

"Or even to tell your employer. After the next couple of scans, that may change." Dr. Manning looked to her notes, more, Kali was sure, to avoid looking at her. "It's possible, if the growth progresses faster than I anticipate, you may wake one morning with vision loss that's substantial. That doesn't return." She looked to her notes once more. "Which is why we're going to get you an MRI as soon as possible, an appointment with a radiation oncologist, and I'll book another appointment to see if there is any change in your vision in a week or two."

Dr. Manning took a breath, her lips squeezed tight. "Your visual field is already decreasing in your right eye, and well, you know about the left. The coming and going you mentioned, the blurriness, that's likely unrelated. Strain.

Tiredness." She looked up from the notes. "Yet ..." She shook her head. "I don't think it's necessary to start preparing for more intense vision loss; you have enough on your mind—and hopefully treatment will halt or even reverse what you've already lost, to some degree—but know that day may come. The day to prepare." She pushed out a smile. "Some people find it helpful, comforting, to start taking some steps, or to at least think about them. Making sure your home is as safe and accessible as possible. Even closing your eyes sometimes and trying to navigate that way. Make a game out of—"

Kali's expression must have stopped her. Dr. Manning formed a fist over her mouth and coughed. "This isn't my area of speciality, but the CNIB has fabulous services. Do you have someone at home to help if need be?"

Kali lied. And shortly after she left Dr. Manning's office.

THAT WAS JUST HOURS ago. Less than two hours. It seemed like a dream.

Kali squeezed her knees to her chest and pressed her back into the door, needing the firmness of it, needing something in her world to be solid. This could be nothing. All of it. An inconvenience. An annoyance. Treatment. Regular checks for a while and then, if all was good, maybe once a year. Just an inconvenience ... until it stopped being an inconvenience, because unless something else killed her, there was a chance that one day her tumour would grow. She closed her right eye again. It wasn't nothing. Not at all. She had already lost a significant amount of vision, and she may never get it back.

That future loomed before her: Dark, terrifying. And if it came sooner than later she'd never see her son as a young man, as a father, never look into his eyes the moment after he'd looked into the eyes of his own child.

She was getting ahead of herself. Again.

Kali pressed her head against the door, almost tempted to open it, to run down the hall after Lincoln, and tell him what? She was terrified? She needed him? Ridiculous. He'd laugh. He'd run in the other direction.

She didn't need him anyway.

She'd figure it out. Always had. Always would.

Not that she should have to, not on her own at least. For the millionth time, she cursed Derek. Cursed his hero complex. Cursed him for jumping into that ocean. For thinking strangers meant more or as much as family. For everything that came afterward.

Protect your own. That was the way to live. He'd made her fall in love with him, convinced her to marry him, put his child inside of her, and then abandoned them. He'd made his choice. He hadn't protected his own. And now she was alone.

CHAPTER FORTY-TWO

Lincoln sat in his truck as cars rushed by. He'd pulled over to the side of the road. Something was wrong. Obviously. But whatever it was Kali didn't want him to be a part of it. And why would she? He was a stranger she'd lived with for a few months. Nothing more. Except he *was* more, or she was ... or they were, together. He turned to the mitts on the passenger seat. Kali and Theo had awakened something in him he didn't think could be awakened, hadn't wanted to be awakened.

But there it was.

He didn't want a normal life, the nine-to-five, the city, the streets, the people. But he wanted them. Kali wasn't about to live in a tree in the woods. She wouldn't want his life. But his friendship? She might want that ... if she could get over herself for ten minutes. *That* she might want or need.

Lincoln's heart pounded, strong thumps against his chest. And he wanted her, wanted them. If only as a friend, fine. That may be all he could manage.

He ran a hand through his hair. Maybe he was just lonely, or not as evolved as he thought. Maybe he needed someone and needed that person to need him too. And Kali and Theo catapulting into his life was just good timing, showing him that lack. Maybe, but he didn't think so.

Another question: did he deserve them?

What Kali definitely didn't need, what Theo didn't need, was someone who would flit in and out of their lives. They needed someone reliable, who would help take care of them, rather than someone who needed taking care of.

Her stances. Her resistance. Her offhand comments. She believed the world was out for itself. And besides that one act of kindness, had Lincoln ever given her a reason to think differently? All he did was live for himself. First in Montreal and now here. He'd run. He'd hid. He'd lied. He hadn't even kept his word to visit his mother.

Lincoln stifled a groan; His mother. He turned the car on. One visit had fallen to pieces today, but perhaps another one wouldn't.

LINCOLN WALKED UP steps so familiar he could jog them blind.

The door opened before he knocked. "You need a calendar?"

"Mom."

"No, really." She gestured behind her. "I have an extra in the den. You can take it. No charge."

"I'm sorry."

"Well, you're here now." She winked then stepped aside so he could enter.

"How was the rest of your party?"

"Kind of died down after the prodigal son returned then

vanished again." She raised a hand then let it fall. "Not much could top that kind of excitement so no one bothered trying."

"Prodigal son, huh?" He didn't think it was a good analogy, but he'd play along. "So where are my riches?"

"Ha." Lincoln's mother walked to the kitchen. "You've got your riches if you want them." She lifted the kettle. "Coffee or tea?"

"Green?"

"You bet ya." Marilyn sat across from him. "So how'd you do it? Google maps? But sometimes you mentioned smells, tastes. You read other people's travel blogs?"

Lincoln set down his cup. "The girls told—"

"I'm not stupid." Marilyn sipped her tea. "I know my boy."

Lincoln looked away. His gaze fell on the assortment of framed photos on the wall, and lingered on a new one— Joseph and Lucy. "Really?"

Marilyn followed his gaze. "A Christmas gift."

"That would look great in the attic."

"It's my son and his fiancée."

Lincoln closed his eyes.

"You didn't know?"

He shook his head.

"She's pregnant, too. About three months along."

Lincoln's arms tensed. His chest tingled.

"I'm not trying to hurt you. I just thought you should know. Sooner than later. If you happened upon her when she was showing."

"She know who the father is?"

"Lincoln."

"What, she didn't last time. Once a cheater ..." His voice

trailed off. He saw Lucy again in that hospital bed, so vulnerable. So aching. He'd gone after her that morning to tell her not to have the abortion, not if she didn't want to. To tell her he wanted the baby, career plans be damned. To apologize—for asking, for assuming. He should never have thought she'd want to abort it, to have told her she *should* abort it, that that's what made sense. So he chased after her to apologize, to say he'd changed his mind and he'd support her whatever she decided.

She'd called him an ass-hole, backing away from him, backing right down those steps. And the option of an abortion disappeared.

Not until he heard her say it, had it even occurred to him that the child might not be his.

"What they did was wrong."

"Really? So you agree."

Marilyn pressed her lips together. "But they're together now. And they seem happy."

Lincoln stared at his mother. How much did she know? Did she think it was a one-time lapse? A moment of weakness? Or did she know it all? Know that Lincoln had shaped his life around Lucy. Done everything for her and what she wanted. Changed the course of his life for her, and what she thought was best.

Did she know that first night Lincoln brought Lucy home to a Sunday family dinner, after almost a year of dating—the night Lincoln had a touch of the flu and left before dessert—the affair had begun? Know Joseph's offer to drive Lucy home—so she could stay longer, get to know the family better—hadn't been kindness?

Or the fact that several months later, when Joseph offered

Lincoln a job at the Montreal office and Lucy decided to move with him, the expectation of stolen moments of lust and betrayal were almost certainly part of the equation?

Did Marilyn know that the first weekend in their new apartment, the apartment furnished with Lucy's taste and Lincoln's money, when Lincoln was late at work, trying to wrap his head around the business, the numbers that were such a struggle to conquer, Lucy was wrapping her legs around his brother?

Lincoln's heart pounded.

Did his mother know that so many of the nights Lucy encouraged Lincoln to work late, to make sure he was on top of the game, Lucy was on top of the wrong son?

What Lincoln couldn't figure out was why Lucy had stayed with him at all. Why not end it after that first cheating kiss?

Why not tell him she wasn't happy? Why move with him? Pretend she wanted a life with him, a future? Why mould him to be the man she wanted him to be, when the older, taller, more successful version already existed?

And why did Joseph let her? Would it have been that much harder to stab Lincoln in the front than the back?

He knew the answer. Guilt. Cowardice. Perhaps touched with a desire not to hurt him.

But they weren't idiots. They knew they couldn't keep up the facade forever. It must have been Joseph's idea, continuing the lie. And Lucy must have hated it.

It probably wasn't even your baby, she'd spouted, with hate and vindication, and something like revelry in her voice.

Then Joseph walked in and the angry, hurting revelry bloomed in her eyes.

Like a child, Lincoln had thought Joseph was there for him, to support him.

One look at his brother's face, at the way his eyes searched Lucy's, at how her anger at Lincoln turned to the sorrow of mutual loss, and the truth fell all around him.

Shattered.

Joseph had repeated the words, over and over—*we never meant to hurt you*. Lucy had stared at him, her eyes cold. The two people he loved more than anything. One full of hate and accusation, the other of meaningless words.

We never meant to hurt you.

But they had. And they'd meant it. You didn't accidentally fall into a person's pants. You didn't slip and, whoops, your penis was inside someone.

"Lincoln?"

He drew his gaze back to his mother.

"Why are you here?"

"You asked me to visit."

"That's not what I mean."

Of course it wasn't, but what was he supposed to say? He didn't know why he was in Halifax, across the harbour from the family he wanted to avoid.

He could be anywhere in the world. But he was here. And Lucy was pregnant. Again. Lucy, forever, would have a tie to his family. To him. Even if Joseph and she broke up, the womb that was meant to hold Lincoln's child would now hold his brother's. He'd be the baby's uncle. Forever. Not father. Uncle.

So why was he here? Here, where he knew, eventually, he'd come back. Here, where he could happen upon Joseph and Lucy at any intersection.

"I don't know."

"Lincoln."

Did it matter where he was? People sucked everywhere, people, everywhere, couldn't be trusted. But the land. That he got. That he knew.

"It's home?"

She made that noise he couldn't describe, the noise that was decidedly her and full of her love, that sliced through him. He focused on her—her slight smile, her mussed hair, the crinkle around her eyes.

"I'm sorry, Mom."

She nodded, the look that accompanied the noise still in her eyes. "I understand."

"I shouldn't have lied to you. I should have at least told you where I was. I just needed—"

"I know." She placed a hand on his. "It's been rough."

He let out a little laugh.

"What have you been doing with your time?"

He told her about the tree house. He told her about Kali. He told her about Theo.

"Building a tree house in the woods." Marilyn shook her head. "That sounds like the Lincoln I remember."

"Hmm?"

"Using your hands. Creating. Not that business stuff."

Lincoln rested his head on his hand. "You didn't think I should be doing the business stuff?"

Marilyn's eyes crinkled. "Not that you shouldn't, but I could tell it didn't come easy—that it was what you thought you should do, not what you wanted to do. You were doing marvellous, though. Joseph even said so, how impressed he was, how even if you weren't his brother you'd be rising through the ranks."

"Really?"

"Really. But that doesn't mean it was right for you. You're a physical person. You always have been." She squeezed his hand again. "Born to build. That's what your father used to say. From blocks to Lego, to using whatever you could find around the house or yard. You remember Rachel's dollhouse?"

"Uh ..."

"She wanted an extra room. You built a sun room with a walk-out porch above. You couldn't have been more than eight." She shook her head. "Meant to create. Just like your father." That smile again. "Joseph creates too, in a way. But building, that's what you're made for."

Lincoln looked up at her as she walked toward the kettle. "You think so?"

Marilyn glanced back. "You don't need me to tell you. You just needed some time to figure it out."

"And when the tree house is done?"

"Then you'll move on to something else." She winked. "Maybe make others' tree house dreams come true."

Lincoln looked away, his brow furrowed. He hadn't told his mother Kali's suggestion. The fact that his mother seconded it made the entrepreneurial spirit he'd seen in his father seem to leap inside of him. He didn't want to live on the family money, which now felt like his brother's money. And while he'd enjoy woodworking, he knew it wouldn't always be easy to bring in enough on that to survive—especially once he got older, or sick.

Marilyn poured the hot water into two mugs. "And this woman. Sounds like you were there for her during a rough time."

"I guess."

"Not everyone would do that, invite a single mom and her child into their home." She glanced back with a smile. "No romantic element?"

"I had space. She needed some space."

Marilyn nodded.

"And she's doing great now. Fabulous, she says. New job. New apartment. New life."

"And you miss her." Marilyn crossed her legs and put a hand to her chin, an action he'd seen her do countless times. "Do you love her?"

"Love?" Lincoln shook his head. "I barely know her." He waited, but his mother didn't speak. "It's more like ... like ..." Lincoln stopped. "I can't even explain it. It's like she's worked her way into my pores."

"Right."

Lincoln shook his head. "Did I just say that?"

"I believe so."

"At first I wanted her gone, them gone. They'd invaded my life, my space."

"By your invitation."

"I know."

"And it could just be that you're lonely. It could have nothing to do with them specifically."

Lincoln nodded, but that wasn't it. He knew for certain that wasn't it.

His mother's knowing look. "I doubt it. Try again. Maybe call this time. Go slow." She set the mug of tea in front of him. "And build your house, whether you ever live in it or not. Get it done."

Lincoln laughed and reached for the tea. "You're the first person who hasn't thought I was crazy."

"Of course you're crazy." She smiled. "But lots of amazing people have been crazy, and they've gone on to create amazing things." She stood. "You build your house. Make it safe. Sturdy." She laughed. "Insulated, please. Exquisite, too." She paused. "That was the most amazing thing. How you always wanted to find the beauty in everything you built. Now some of that beauty was outside of my taste." She gave him a wink. "But it was still beautiful."

Love welled up in Lincoln. Guilt for staying away so long. "I'm sorry, Mom."

"Another sign that you're not too far gone." She leaned over and squeezed his chin between her thumb and forefinger. "Your dad would be proud too." She looked away. "How he'd like to see you, all grown up, to know it was you. How he'd like to see that tree house."

Lincoln closed his eyes, not wanting to go there. His throat clenched.

"You'll visit when you're ready."

He looked up.

"I just hope for your sake you don't get ready too late." Marilyn let out a small laugh. "My two sons. One in a mansion big enough for five families. The other in a cabin in the sky."

"And your daughters?"

"Oh, they're both doing fine. Linda, anyway. Rachel's holding back. Something's just waiting to burst out, direct her life; she just hasn't discovered what it is yet, where it's meant to take her."

"And do you know?"

Marilyn patted his hand and stood. "Your revelations are for you, Rachel's for her." She walked to the fridge, still just as covered in photos of children and grandchildren and extended family as always. "You'll stay for supper." It was spoken as a statement, not a question, yet she waited for a response.

Lincoln nodded.

"All right, then, let's see what we've got."

CHAPTER FORTY-THREE

Lincoln stood in the library. He didn't want to make the call here. It was part of why he hadn't called last time. The week before, someone had cut the cord of one of the few pay phones left in the neighbourhood. Why someone would do that, he couldn't figure out. He picked up the handset, dialled Kali's number for the first time ever, and pulled the phone as far down the hall as he could without snapping it.

The phone rang. Two, three, four times. He was about to give up when a voice sounded in his ear. "Hello?"

"Kali, hi."

"Hi."

"It's Lincoln."

"I know."

He swallowed. Why did she sound like that? What was her problem? He kept his voice friendly. "Sorry for showing up like that the other day. I know I should have called."

"Yeah."

"It seemed to be a bad time. Are you okay now?"

Silence.

"Kali?"

"Yeah."

"You're okay?"

"What do you want, Lincoln?"

He stepped back, as if her words, or her tone, rather, had spit in his face. "I just wanted—" He hesitated. "I miss you."

More silence.

"Both of you, I mean. And Theo. Has—"

"What? Has he asked about you? Has he magically started talking about you? Are you the key to unlocking the mystery?"

It was his turn to be silent. She sighed.

"Look, I'm sorry, okay." Silence. "He drew you. He ... he misses you too, I guess."

"Yeah?"

"He doesn't have a lot of men in his life."

"Well, I was thinking maybe some time, it doesn't have to be today or anything, but maybe sometime this week I could see him? Take him to the park, or to play catch or—"

"Why?"

"I told you."

"I'm not interested, Lincoln. If that's what this is about. I know there was that one night, but I thought I made it clear—"

"Look, I'm asking to take your son to the park, not to date you. Okay? I wouldn't mind being your friend—and don't go telling me you have more than enough of those because I know you don't—but if you don't want my friendship, at least let me have Theo's." Lincoln paused. "He's a good kid. And I'm a good man, and as you said, he doesn't have a lot of men in his life."

"He doesn't need—"

"Maybe he doesn't. Maybe you're enough for him. You probably are. You're amazing. I get that. But that doesn't mean you don't deserve a break from time to time, and that doesn't mean he couldn't benefit from having someone in his life beyond you."

Her voice came out ragged, almost raspy. "And when you get bored?"

"I won't get bored."

"Or move out into the woods to live your hobbit life and forget Theo ever existed?"

Lincoln grinned. "My hermit life?"

"What?"

"You said hobbit. I'm not going to shrink."

"Huh? What? Oh." She laughed, and it was a like a gift. "Yeah, hermit."

"I'm already living in the woods."

"What?"

"For almost the last two weeks. But I have a truck. I come into town." He hesitated, thinking of the words, of Thoreau's visits, of his visitors. "It's forty-five minutes. Living out there doesn't mean I have to cut myself off from life or from people. If you want some guarantee I won't drop Theo or get bored, or busy, or forget, I'll give it to you. Once a week. Twice. Whatever you want. I'll make a pact."

More silence.

"Kali?"

"Why?"

"Why ...?"

"Why are you so interested? Why do you care?"

"Have you met your son?"

He could almost hear her smile in the silence. Hear her giving in. "Okay. How about Monday? Three-thirty to six ... I'll probably be free far before then, but—" she paused. "That will give you two some time." A deep breath. "I planned to take him to Mrs. Martin's, but he can hang out with you instead."

Lincoln hesitated. "No sooner?"

"I just ..." Kali sighed. "That way you'd be helping me out too."

"You want me to pick him up?"

"You still have your old place?"

"Yeah."

"I'll drop him off."

They said their goodbyes and Lincoln put the phone back in its holder. It was a victory. A small one, but a victory nonetheless.

ON MONDAY LINCOLN had the baseball gloves out and was waiting on the steps to his apartment ten minutes early. She hadn't mentioned it, but it was likely Theo wouldn't have had dinner when he arrived. They'd toss the ball around at the Commons then get something to eat on Quinpool Road. Maybe that gourmet burger joint. Lincoln could imagine the way Theo's eyes would grow as the server laid down a burger half the size of his head in front him.

Lincoln tossed the ball from hand to hand, amazed at the excitement that surged through him. He'd been weak in Montreal. Weak in letting his life be ruled by others, determined by others. He was done with that. He didn't understand in exactly what capacity, but he knew what he wanted now: a life not ruled by schedules, numbers, and all of society's expectations. A life with Kali and Theo in it, in some capacity at least. Some regular capacity.

Thinking she'd move to the woods was crazy. But weekend trips? Possible—at some point in the future. For now, whatever she was willing to give, he'd take, and adapt his life to make it work. He wasn't willing to give up the woods, the house, the life he'd been dreaming of. Not yet. Not entirely. But he'd figure it out. Somehow, he'd merge their existences.

Every time a car came down the street Lincoln had his eye on it. When at last that car was hers, he stood and waved. Kali pulled up to the curb and turned off the engine. She didn't look at him; she was turned around, saying something to Theo. After a few moments she unbuckled, stepped out of the car, and around to the back passenger side. Theo had undone his booster seat and had one hand up against the glass, the other one waving frantically at Lincoln. When the door opened, Theo bolted across the sidewalk and slammed into Lincoln's legs before Lincoln even had a chance to think about crouching down to catch the boy in a proper hug.

Lincoln pulled Theo away enough to lower down and let the boy wrap his arms around his shoulders instead.

"Let me guess?" he asked when Theo finally pulled away. "You missed me."

Theo nodded.

"Like this?" Lincoln spread his thumb and forefinger apart about half as far as they'd go.

Theo shook his head and spread his arms so far back his chest popped out.

"Oh, well that's good." Lincoln laughed. "'Cause I missed

you like this." He imitated Theo's motion. "Times fifty."

Theo wrapped his arms around Lincoln once more. Lincoln swallowed and raised his gaze to Kali. Her back was against her car, an unreadable expression on her face. Sadness? Wariness? Confusion?

"Hey."

"Hey." She reached into the car and pulled out Theo's backpack. "I packed a sandwich for—"

"No," Lincoln waved a hand, "don't worry about that. We'll have a dinner date."

"Okay, well." She passed him the backpack. "A sweater and one of his books. Some water."

"Great."

She looked to the car, chewed on the corner of her lip, then turned back to Lincoln. "I'll be back by six."

"You going to be around here? If not, I could always drop him off. We could throw his booster seat in my truck and—"

"No. I'll be here. Six." She rubbed her forearm. "You still don't have a phone, do you?"

"No."

"A watch?"

"I'll ask people."

"Ridiculous." She closed her eyes and shook her head. Her throat convulsed as she swallowed.

"Kali?" Lincoln stepped forward. "What's going on?"

"Nothing!" She softened her voice. "Nothing. I'm fine. Come here, Sweetie." She knelt and motioned for Theo. "Have fun, okay?"

He nodded.

She kissed his forehead. And then she was back in the car. Lincoln watched until the vehicle turned out of sight, then he looked to Theo. "You wanna play ball?"

A nod and a grin.

"Race you to the Commons?"

Another nod and they were off.

KALI STEPPED INTO HER car and slammed the door. She closed her eyes then opened them, greedy to see the people passing by, the trees, the cars, everything. Her vision blurred. She wiped her eyes frantically. She didn't have time for this. She needed to get home, see Theo, hold Theo, memorize Theo.

She pulled into traffic. How many more times would she be able to do this? And when she couldn't? Kali indicated and merged into the roundabout on the way to Mrs. Martin's. Every aspect of driving required sight. Good sight. Clear sight.

And what if Theo never spoke? What if she couldn't see the way he tilted his head, each movement meaning something slightly different? The way his eyes widened or squinted, how a smile could mean so many things?

She turned down Cornwallis and waited at the light. Turn. Turn. Turn. She almost hit the gas and then eased off. If she got a ticket now, no one would believe it had nothing to do with her vision. She eased through the intersection then swung right onto Maitland. She took Mrs. Martin's front steps two at a time and banged on the door.

"I'm coming. I'm coming." A voice hollered from within.

Mrs. Martin appeared, a baby on one hip and a mixing bowl in the other.

"Child."

"Theo." Kali looked past the woman. "Theo, come on!"

"Kali?"

"Mrs. Martin, I've got to go. Can you get him?"

"Theo's not here."

"What?"

"You called me, said you didn't need—"

"Damn."

"Sweetie." Mrs. Martin set the bowl on a door-side table and grasped Kali's arm as she tried to turn around. "What's going on?"

"I just forgot ... I ... sorry."

"You know where he is?"

"Yes. Yes. He's with Lincoln. I have to—"

"Oh, that nice young man. Odd, but—"

"Mrs. Martin." Kali looked to her arm.

"You all right, Sweetie?"

"Yes, I—"

"You're not. Kali, what—"

Kali pulled out of the woman's grasp. "I've got to go. I'm sorry. I—" She turned and held a hand out in parting as she ran back to her car.

Kali ran up the stairs to Lincoln's door and pounded. Waited. Pounded. "Lincoln." Pounded again. "Lincoln!" Damn.

"Kali?"

Kali turned to see the bottom floor neighbour, Sandy, shuffling out in her house dress. "Kali, is that you? What's going on?"

"Nothing, I—"

"Such noise."

"I'm sorry."

"Don't think Lincoln's here."

"I know. I—"

"If you know, why are you banging on the door?"

Not now. She couldn't handle this right now. "Well, he's not answering, so now I know."

"Oh." Sandy shook her head. "Better just come back."

"Mmhmm."

"But no more banging."

"No more banging."

Kali waited until the woman had shuffled back into her apartment then rifled through her satchel. She pulled out a pen and her notebook. *Ended early. Going out to look for you.* She paused. And then what? She'd been in and out of the doctor's office so fast it was only quarter to five. She started again. *Ended early. Thought I'd head home and get some work done. Please bring Theo home after all.*

She ripped off the bottom half of the page and tried to slide it in the door. The paper drifted to the floor. She could leave it there, right in front ... but what if he didn't see it? Damn Lincoln. Who didn't have a phone?

She rifled through her purse again and pulled out a pack of gum. It was gross, but so what? She popped a piece in her mouth and chewed rapidly. Once it seemed pliable enough she pulled out the wad and stuck it on the door. She stared at the note. Guilt bubbled up. Lincoln would have to scrape that off. The building might be a dump, but Lincoln kept his place clean, orderly.

She had to do it. She couldn't just stay here. Just wait. For over an hour. She couldn't be anywhere right now except her own space. She looked up and down the street, hoping, then got back in her car and pulled away.

CHAPTER FORTY-FOUR

Theo's hand slipped into Lincoln's. He looked at the boy and smiled. "Was that burger rockin'?"

Theo nodded.

Lincoln grinned. "I can't wait to take you out to play catch again. You were so good. Like superstar good."

Theo puffed up his chest, then pretended to wind back and throw. He lost balance and tugged on Lincoln's arm, eyes wide.

"I got you." Lincoln squeezed Theo's hand. "You excited to tell your mom all about it?"

Theo's head lolled from side to side, a half smile on his face.

"Or show her. Act it out."

He nodded.

"I bet she'll be impressed. I bet she'll be really impressed." They reached the steps to Lincoln's porch. "Wait here?"

Theo plopped down on the top step.

"She should be here any minute." The clock at the restaurant had read 5:45 when they left. For Lincoln it was no more than a ten-minute walk, but with Theo in tow, fifteen was more like it. Lincoln actually expected Kali to be here when they arrived, hoped she wouldn't be angry. He settled in beside Theo. Cars passed. Children passed. Mothers with strollers. A stray cat.

"Excuse me, Miss," Lincoln called to a young girl captivated by something on her cell phone. She tore her gaze away as if it physically hurt. "What time is it?"

"6:18." She walked on.

"Thanks."

Theo looked up, his eyes wide.

"Don't worry, buddy." Lincoln wrapped an arm around Theo's shoulder. "She probably got held up. She'll be here soon."

A firetruck, lights off, passed by; Theo jumped and waved. Another cat. Two male joggers with skin-tight shorts and nothing on top. Half a dozen cars. "Sir?" The man must have been pushing his nineties, he walked with a cane and a smile. "Do you have the time?"

He turned his wrist. "6:32."

Theo leaned against Lincoln's side. Lincoln put a hand to his head. Theo looked up at him. "Don't worry, buddy. It's okay."

"She coming back?" The words were lower than a whisper. His little body shook.

"What?" Lincoln's heart raced. Calm. Be calm. Don't scare him. He leaned down, so his ear was closer to Theo's mouth.

"Is Mommy coming back?" Terror rested in Theo's eyes.

"Of, course, buddy. Yes. Of course."

"She sad. She cry and cry."

"Your mommy?"

Theo nodded.

"Why's she crying?"

He shrugged.

"Just once or every day?"

Theo looked to the side, he wrapped his arms around his middle.

"Buddy?"

"'Cause I no talk?"

"No." Lincoln shook his head. "No. That's not it. I'm sure of it."

Theo stared away from Lincoln.

"I have her number upstairs. We'll go get it and then see if Sandy will let us use her phone. Okay? We'll find out what's going on. Sound good?"

Theo nodded. He stood and reached for Lincoln's hand.

From the second landing, Lincoln saw something white on his door. At the top, he tore it off.

"Oh, man."

Theo tilted his head. "Your mom was here early. She's gone home. She wants me to drive you."

Lincoln looked to Theo. "All this time we've been waiting for her and she's been waiting for us."

Theo furrowed his brow.

"Isn't that silly?"

He shrugged.

Lincoln started down the stairs. A booster seat. Damn. He jogged back up, unlocked the apartment door, then scanned the living room. "Wait here."

He picked up the one throw pillow on his couch and jogged to his bedroom—shoes still on, Sandy would be pissed—and grabbed two pillows from his bed.

His arms full, he smiled over the load at Theo. "What do you think of this?"

Another shrug, accompanied with a scrunched up nose.

"Makeshift booster seat. That's what this is." Lincoln kept his smile on, disappointed the boy didn't talk. But he *had* talked. He'd do it again. And whatever Kali had been stressed about, been crying about, this news would certainly make it seem like nothing in comparison.

Lincoln started the drive with question after question and threw in an observation or two. When he looked in the rear view mirror to see Theo staring out the glass, a serious expression on his face, he kept quiet.

Kali's voice sounded almost the moment Lincoln hit the buzzer.

"Come up."

She was standing in the hall waiting when the elevator doors opened. She ran to Theo and scooped him up. "What took so long?"

"Sorry, I—"

"Six o'clock, Lincoln. I told you to have him back by six o'clock."

"Six o'clock at my place."

"So you should have been here by six-fifteen. It's almost seven."

"I know, but—"

"And what was I supposed to do? You don't have a phone so I couldn't go back over there." She carried Theo into their apartment.

Lincoln trailed behind. "Listen."

"No, you listen." She was almost shaking now. Her eyes glistened. "Anything could have happened. Anything. You take someone's kid, you make sure you have a way to contact them. I should be yelling at myself, letting you—"

"You're right."

"What?" Kali turned to Lincoln, her arms still wrapped around Theo.

"You're right. I'll get a phone. I was back by six. We were back. But we waited on the curb for you. It was nice out, so—"

"Oh." She set Theo down. "Oh, that makes sense, I—" She bent down, smoothed a hand over Theo's brow, kissed him, stared at him. Really stared. "I didn't think of that." She took a deep breath. "You have fun, Sweetie?"

Theo looked from Kali to Lincoln, eyes wide, seeming frightened. With his gaze back on his mother, he nodded.

Kali put both hands on his shoulders. "I'm sorry I was yelling. I was just so scared. And I missed you." She hugged him again. "Okay?"

Another nod.

"You played catch?"

That firecracker smile lit his face. He stepped back and mimed the action.

"That's great. You catch them all?"

His head tilted side to side with a little half grin.

"He caught most." Lincoln stepped forward. "He's definitely a natural."

The half grin blossomed to a whole one.

Kali kissed Theo again, both hands on the side of his face. Her lips stayed on his forehead longer than Lincoln had ever seen. Something was up.

Another hug. "Go say goodbye to Lincoln, then brush your teeth and change into your PJs. I'll be there soon."

Theo made a little dash and wrapped his arms around

Lincoln's legs. Lincoln crouched down. "I'll see you again, soon. K, buddy?" He glanced at Kali. She stood with her arms crossed, no answer in her eyes or stance. "I had fun. Up high."

Theo jumped to slap Lincoln's outstretched hand.

Lincoln stood as Theo ran down the hall. "Again, I'm sorry. I didn't mean to—"

"I get it." Kali leaned against the wall. "I should have waited. That would have been the smart thing to do."

"Why didn't you?"

"Are you judging me now?"

"No." Lincoln stepped back. "I just—" He ran a hand through his hair then took several steps toward her. "Are you okay?"

She nodded.

"Kali." He reached out to put a hand on her shoulder but she thrust it away before he could make contact.

"God, Lincoln."

"I'm sorry, I—"

"You can go, okay?"

"I want to know what's wrong."

"Why? You think you can come in here and fix all my problems? Well, you can't. Some problems don't get fixed."

Lincoln's brow furrowed. His mouth went dry. He could see it all over her. The hurt. The fear. She pulsed with it. "Tell me what's going on. Maybe I can't fix it, but maybe talking—"

"Go. Please. Take a hint and—"

"He talked."

"What?" Kali stepped forward. "What do you—"

Lincoln smiled. "When we were waiting. He asked if you were coming back."

"He did?" Everything about her softened. Her eyes practically beamed with hope. They misted. "What else?"

Lincoln gave a little shrug. "He said you were sad. That you cried all the time."

"He—" She swallowed.

"He was scared it was because of him, because he didn't talk."

Kali glanced toward the hall. She wrapped her arms around herself. "He finally talked and that's what ..." She looked back at Lincoln. "Anything else?"

"No. I tried. Peppered him with questions in the car, but no."

Kali let out a little gasp. "But he talked. He actually talked." Her shoulders shook and she looked away.

"This is good. Right? Really good."

She laughed. "Amazing. It's—" She put a hand to her head and let it trail down her face. "He'll do it again. If he did it once, he'll do it again."

"Definitely."

She turned back. She was beaming now. At him. Lincoln fought the urge to reach out and hug her, share in the joy.

"You should celebrate."

"What?"

"I didn't really talk to him much about it. I was nervous to scare him out of it, you know? But maybe a big celebration would be good. Did the psychologist say anything about that? What you should do when he finally—"

"No."

"Okay. Well," Lincoln grinned, but it was shaky, "how about tomorrow night? I can take you both out for dinner somewhere nice. Or fun. And we can let him know how proud of him we are. How great it is. Maybe Marvin could even—"

"No, Lincoln." Kali put a hand out. "I'm not sure what I'm supposed to do. I'll call Dr. Richards, but whatever it is, whatever I'm supposed to do, I'll do it." She let the hand fall. She bit her lip. "Thank you for giving him a fun night, and for telling me. But this is between me and my son."

"Okay." Lincoln pushed out another smile. "That's fine. That's great. I'm just happy—"

Kali gestured toward the door.

Lincoln nodded. "I'll get that phone. And I'll give you a call. Maybe in a day or two."

"I don't—"

"You said consistency, right? That if I wanted to be in Theo's life it should be consistent."

Kali opened her mouth then closed it. "Okay."

CHAPTER FORTY-FIVE

KALI BREATHED DEEPLY—keeping her eyes opened. The best news in the past two years and a strong contender for the worst of her life, all in the course of an hour.

The water from the bathroom sink cut off. Footsteps padded across the hall. Her good boy. Her precious boy—getting ready for bed and going to his room, just like Mommy asked. Is this what she'd have to rely on for the rest of her life, hearing him? Always attuned to every step, every sigh, every smile. Could you even hear a smile? What about a silent tear?

But he'd spoken. If he'd done it once, he'd do it again. That's what she'd cling to. He'd talked once. He'd do it again.

She wanted to pepper him with questions, let him know she knew. But if he wanted her to know, if he was ready, he'd say something, wouldn't he?

Kali peeked her head into Theo's room, her face all smiles. "Hey, baby. You ready?"

One huge nod.

"Pick a story?"

He held one up.

"Oh, I *love* that one." Talk, baby. Talk.

Theo smiled up at her and Kali nearly broke in two, his voice forgotten—how could she live without seeing that smile?

She climbed into the bed, savouring the warmth that emanated from Theo's little body, savouring the scent of him. That distinct smell had faded as he grew, would one day cease to exist, she imagined. But tonight she breathed it in. The scent of Theo.

He snuggled over and she curled an arm around him, nestling him close.

"*There was a mother who had a new baby and she piiicked it up and rocked it ...*"

Theo tilted side to side, his gaze on the page. How would she read to him? Kali smoothed her hand over his cheek. Did children's picture books even come in Braille? The words were always dispersed across the page. Would he have to guide her fingers?

"*And flushed it down the toilet.*" Kali shook Theo, "*ju-ju-ju-ju.*" He giggled. "*Sometimes the mother would say, 'This kid is driving me craaazy.*"

Dr. Manning had shaken her head, the MRI results in her hand. *I was wrong, Kali. You need to start making plans.* Plans. But not an answer. Not a solution. Just plans. *The growth is rapid.* Rapid. The word wasn't used lightly. Kali knew that. When a disease's progression was rapid, hope often flew away. *Your life is about to change.* But life always changed, right? And people adjusted.

"*I'll love you forever, I'll like you for always, as long as you're living, my baby you'll be.*"

Months of vision, she said, if Kali were lucky. Possibly weeks. But it could be days. Days. What could Kali plan for in days?

"*She would pick it up and rock it, back and forth, back and forth ...*"

Kali rocked Theo here, as she always did. But would she be able to when he was nine? Fifteen? Twenty-four?

Tell your employer as soon as possible. For now it's fine to work, but you'll have to monitor your sight carefully. And you need to let them know.

And what if they thought it wasn't fine to work? Would their liability cover a nurse who was going blind? Would their insurance cover the bills to come if they tossed her aside? *We'll keep with your weekly appointments for now. The growth may slow.* May. May. But not likely, the doctor's eyes said. Not at all.

Any change in vision, any at all, you need to document. Kali had nodded. *You'll see me weekly until you can start treatment, which will be soon. As soon as possible.* Another shake of Dr. Manning's head. *Four millimetres in just under two weeks. Soon, maybe at your next visit, I'll likely have to take your license.*

That had hit like a smack in the face. Kali was a nurse. Outside of being with Theo, nowhere did she feel more whole, more her, than when she was helping people. And she was good at it. Damn good.

Kali? Dr. Manning had stared at her. *Kali, are you—*

Sure, sure. Kali held up her chin. *I'm fine. I only spent five years in University, half of those as a single mom, juggling tests and clinic hours with diaper changes and late night feedings. And in one moment it'll all be gone. I'm just fine.*

Dr. Manning's brow had furrowed. She opened her mouth, closed it, spoke. *There may be capacities in which you*

327

could remain a nurse. Not direct patient care, obviously, not like you're doing now. But with support, assistance ... She hesitated. *I meant your driver's licence.*

Kali had nodded. It wasn't worse. But close.

Theo tugged on her shirt sleeve, a question on his face. Kali forced out a chuckle. "Sorry, Sweetie. Where were we?" She focused on the page. "Ah. *And it had straaange friends, and it wore straaange clothes ...*"

Once those things were gone—her license and her career, or at least her current career—the weekly vision appointments would stop. What would be the point? Her disease wouldn't be at risk of destroying any lives, except her own of course.

Dr. Manning shook her head when Kali brought up surgery again. She wanted this tumour out of her, though she knew ... knew the risks. Surgery, Dr. Manning reiterated, was no option. Not with the location of the growth. But, she reminded Kali, she'd see the radiation oncologist soon. She wasn't sure what the treatment protocol would be, stereotactic radiotherapy, perhaps. It wasn't her speciality. But, she said, Kali should have hope—maybe of renewed vision, definitely of a relatively normal life outside of that. A cessation of growth. Stabilization. Which was why it was so important to act fast. Hopefully, years more to watch her son grow ... figuratively if not literally.

It was a waiting game. Wait to lose her job, wait to lose her license, wait to lose her sight. Wait to see if this treatment could transform her fate. Perhaps, wait to lose her life.

Kali paused the reading and kissed Theo's forehead, smoothed her hand across it once more. He tapped his finger on the page.

She couldn't bring herself to even formulate the thought,

process the steps she'd have to take for her son, to make sure he was cared for, to ensure she could care for him, and if she couldn't ...

More urgent taps.

"*Back and forth, back and forth, back and forth, and sing ...*"

Several pages later Theo's fingers were on her cheek, wiping away a tear. She rubbed the heel of her hand across her face. Laughed. Smiled. Kissed him.

"Mommy's so silly. I'm just thinking about the story. About how much I love you. How you'll grow so big."

She sang. "*I'll love you forever ...*"

Would Theo sing the song to her one day? If she made it that long, if she survived in a dark world. And would he have to hold her in his arms, not when he was a full grown man, but sooner? Would he be forced to grow up too fast, to guide her, care for her; would he have his childhood stolen?

She was being stupid. Blind. She could figure it out. There was no need to think about any of this yet. She had time. *Months. Weeks. Days.*

Lincoln. He popped into her thoughts like a Jack-in-the-box. Lincoln kept showing up in their lives, infusing himself into their lives. Theo loved Lincoln. And Lincoln, she was sure, loved Theo. Could he help her through this? Be the answer she was looking for, a better answer than the one that made most sense?

Lincoln wouldn't just take her son, pledge to care for her son, if she couldn't. But if she could make him fall in love with her before revealing what that love would mean ... She could see it in his eyes, he wanted her. Yet want and love, want and caring, were two very different things.

Could she do that to him?

No. Lincoln was good. Kind. The type of man who might actually stay because he believed it was the right thing to do, not because he wanted to. The type of man who, if she let herself, she maybe could love. But she'd been down that road before and she wasn't about to travel it again.

And guilt, or obligation, or whatever would make him stay, only lasted so long. He would run eventually. That's what men did. Kali gave herself a mental shake. She didn't need Lincoln. She'd work it out. And her son, her sweet boy, he'd be okay.

"... *back and forth, back and forth, back and forth. And sang, 'I'll love you forever, I'll like you for always, as long as I'm living, my mommy you'll—*"

Kali couldn't finish. The words caught. Theo was staring at her, she could feel it, but she didn't look down. Couldn't look down. She forced herself to finish the story, her voice shaky. She closed the book and still she couldn't look down. Theo tugged on her arm. Once. Twice. Would he talk for her? He'd talked for Lincoln. Maybe if she did what the psychologist said, refused to look at him. Forced him. "What, baby?"

Another tug.

"Tell Mommy what it is."

A hard yank.

She gave in, letting their eyes meet. He wrapped his arms around her neck and kissed her tear stained cheek. Kali clung to him. When she pulled back he wore a soft smile. A smile too old for him. A smile that carried *her* pain.

ABANDONING HIS PLAN to return to the woods in order to get a full day's work in the next day, Lincoln turned his truck toward the Brunswick Street apartment. The look in Kali's eyes—terror, desperation, sadness—it was none of his business. But he wanted it to be.

He'd get that phone. He'd try again, tomorrow even. He could say it was to ask about Theo, see if he'd talked. He didn't care what she said, something was going on. Something bad. And as far as he could tell, besides a three-year-old boy and a damaged old man, he was the closest thing to a friend that woman had.

CHAPTER FORTY-SIX

K ali woke with a start. Something was different.

The pain.

She wasn't in pain.

She wasn't in pain? She took several slow breaths, assessed. No, she felt fine. Another breath. This wasn't a reason for joy. Not likely. Science may not back it up, but with the hours she'd logged witnessing patients' ebbs and flows, she knew it was more likely a reason for fear.

LINCOLN HEADED OUT first thing in the morning to get a cell phone. Something simple. A phone, not a mini computer. The salesman was practically livid, treating Lincoln like he was some pariah—or a mental patient. Lincoln just smiled. He understood. He'd been that guy. Lived and breathed that guy, intent on following protocol, on making the biggest sale possible—though Lincoln had dealt with transactions in the hundreds of thousands, not hundreds. But he stood his ground through all of the salesman's slick, persistent talk and walked away with a simple phone. No internet. No data. But a carrier who boasted the best signal strength in the province—assured to get reception even at his castle in the air.

He resisted the urge to call Kali immediately and spent the day lying in the sun, walking the harbour, and imagining a life where she'd let him take her in his arms. He hardly let his thoughts travel further than that: to wrap his arms around her, fully clothed, to offer comfort. That'd be enough for now.

When he couldn't wait any longer, at five-thirty on the dot, Lincoln dialled Kali's number. Two. Three. Four. Five rings. Then her voice, an octave or two higher than normal, saying she'd get back to him as soon as she could.

Apparently, that night, she couldn't.

The next day he tried again, at 5:45 this time. Again, she, apparently, was not able to return the call. At nine, his truck loaded up with the shipment he'd picked up earlier that afternoon, he returned to the woods.

He decided to wait, to have some patience, and at six two days later, his muscles aching, the birds praising his efforts, he pulled out the phone once more. He didn't leave a message but stepped into his truck and navigated the access road he was wearing down a little more with each trip.

In the foyer of her building he buzzed. Once. Twice. Three times. Anger rose with each push. He'd let Kali live with him for almost three months. Had been good to her. To her son. And she couldn't even return a call? Have the decency to tell him to get lost if that's what she wanted? And she probably did want it, he got that. But she also told him he could call, told him he could see Theo again. He pressed the buzzer once more.

"You looking for that new gal, the one with the sweet little boy? The quiet one?"

Lincoln turned. "Yes."

The woman looked like Lincoln's grandmother. An older, more tanned version of his mother, with skin that defied age and tight white curls covering her head. "I'm afraid she's not here. Can only hope she comes back soon."

Lincoln stared.

The woman seemed harmless, a look of concern covering her face but a twinkle of joy at being the one to know the gossip.

"Why?"

"Mmm." She shook her head. "An accident."

Lincoln's chest tightened. Kali, or Theo, or both?

"I was there. It's like she didn't even see the truck. I don't know. Maybe she was taking the boy to the park across the way." She pointed, and Lincoln followed her gaze. "She looked both ways, too, which is the weird thing. The odd thing. And then she stepped out like she didn't see the truck barrelling toward her. Lincoln's palms moistened. He tried to speak, but no sound escaped.

He swallowed. "Is she? Are they?"

"Oh!" The woman exclaimed, a half-smile behind her alarm. "They'll be fine, I would say. Just fine. The driver saw her, thankfully. A horrible screech. A yell or two. She was shaken up. Very shaken up. The little boy saw the truck, I guess. Anyway, he must have been trying to yank his mother out of the way and took a tumble. Not even a bad one by the look of it. But," the woman paused, "she's a nurse, did you know that?"

Lincoln nodded.

"Said she thought he fractured his arm." The woman put her hand on her flower-patterned chest.

Lincoln breathed.

"The odd thing was, she called a cab to take them to the hospital. And she drives. I've seen her."

Lincoln stepped back. "Maybe she was shaken up?"

The woman nodded. "Maybe. Well, she was. All pale like, well as pale as we get." She laughed. "But at the same time she had the sense enough to go to her car and get his booster seat. So she couldn't have been *that* shaken up." The woman put a hand to her chin; several wiry hairs stuck out of it. "Seems a sweet gal. You're not her man, are you?"

Lincoln shook his head.

"Hmm. Well," she elbowed him, "maybe if you cleaned yourself up a bit, you could be. Working man?"

"Huh?" Lincoln looked toward the park. The intersection before it was a simple one: no sharp turns, no big trees blocking the view from the crosswalk.

"You a labourer? Just come from a site?"

Lincoln glanced at his dirty arms. "Yeah, uh ... kinda. When did this happen?"

"An hour and a half ago? Maybe two?"

"Thanks." Lincoln stepped out of the foyer and looked up and down the street. So distracted she didn't see a truck? Something was definitely going on.

He tried her number once more and almost threw the phone when he heard that high octave voice.

He could wait, or he could try to find her.

She'd most likely be at her old ER. And they may push her through, but not likely, which, unless it was a really slow night, meant a fractured arm would be a long wait. So if he left now, she'd almost certainly be sitting in one of those uncomfortable chairs, waiting.

LINCOLN TAPPED HIS fingers on the steering wheel as light after light turned red seconds before he approached each intersection. Parking his pickup in the city was rarely simple but, as if fate finally cut him a break, a large spot was free as close to the hospital doors as anyone could hope to get. As he walked the short steps to those doors, his pace slowed. What was he doing? And what did he expect?

Kali had been ignoring his calls for almost a week. She didn't want him around. Stalking probably wouldn't change that. He hesitated, painfully aware of the stares. Since his mother's party, his hair didn't scream homeless quite the way it used to, but his clothes were filthy, his arms, his shoes.

A woman in a business suit shook her head as she passed him. An old man out with his I.V. and a cigarette cast him a sly grin. Most avoided looking at him at all.

Lincoln strode through the automatic doors and into the ER.

No Kali.

He surveyed the room, not sure what to do next. She could be driving home now ... in some cab. She could be in the bowels of the building. He pulled out his phone again, shook his head, and slid the device into his pocket.

A familiar face walked by.

"Hey!"

The nurse who'd admitted Lincoln several months ago clenched her clipboard to her chest and tried not to cringe.

Her expression relaxed as he came closer. "Oh, you're that guy, aren't you?" She smiled. "The one who saved Theo."

Lincoln nodded. "Are they here?"

"Yeah." She looked to her chart. "Just a sec." She stepped to the side of him, called a patient, disappeared a moment, then was before him again. "Kid's got a fracture. Nothing too serious, but he's waiting to get it set."

Lincoln looked past her, hoping to see ... he didn't know what. "How long will they be?"

"I'm not sure. An hour. Maybe two. I could probably get you back there, so you could—"

"No." Lincoln shook his head. "No, that's okay."

The woman stared at him. "You two close now? Kali told me she was staying with you for a bit. She seemed pretty shaken up. Worse than Theo." She let out a heavy sigh. "I tried to get her to take a sedative but," she stepped closer, "maybe it would help. You being there, if—"

"No, I—" Lincoln rubbed a hand along his neck. "Maybe just tell her I was here? Tell her if ... if she needs anything to call, or to call either way, or—"

"Yeah, sure. I'll do that." The woman looked to the waiting room, at her chart, then back at Lincoln. "You know what's going on with her? She seems off. I mean I know there's been a ton of changes—the new job, the move. But a move's good, right? It's awesome she's out of that dump of an apartment. And the job's great. But still ..." The woman's voice trailed off.

"Yeah, still." Lincoln rubbed his chin. "What's your name?"

"Shelley."

"Thanks so much, Shelley, for your help. If you can tell

her I was here, ask her to call, that'd be perfect."

Shelley wrapped her arms around the clipboard again. She nodded and smiled as Lincoln backed away.

Outside, Lincoln ran his hands through his hair. Trickles of sweat broke out at his temple and the back of his neck. She wouldn't call. There was almost no way she would call. And something was wrong, even her co-worker noticed it.

Would Kali talk to him if he were standing here when she came out those doors? Would she turn down a drive when he had his keys in his hand ready to take her?

There were any number of doors she could come out of, but this was the one she'd most likely use to get a cab. Lincoln navigated to a bench at the side of the courtyard. His legs bounced. He rested his hands on his knees in an effort to still them, but a few minutes later they were bouncing again. He stood. Shelley had said an hour, maybe two. He could spend a half an hour walking around the Commons, maybe even pick up something for them to eat, and still be back in time.

CHAPTER FORTY-SEVEN

At the Oval, teens roller-bladed to top 40 hits. An elderly couple, hand in hand, glided along beside them. All the baseball fields were full. A man tossed a Frisbee to his dog, a black shaggy-looking dog, and Lincoln looked away.

A cart glinted by North Park Street. Marvin. Lincoln quickened his pace. "Hello!"

Marvin caught sight of him then struggled to turn his cart in the other direction. He shook the thing and grumbled as he tried to get it off of the grass and onto the sidewalk.

"Sir." Lincoln came up beside him.

"This is mine." Marvin grasped the cart and crouched against it.

Lincoln stepped back. "Oh, I know. I—"

Marvin's eyes narrowed. "You're the man that was with my Theo." He yanked the cart away from Lincoln. "What do you want?"

"I'm a friend. A friend of Kali's."

"But not of mine." Marvin, his cart free, turned from Lincoln and started down the sidewalk. Lincoln ran in front of the cart. Marvin made a gasping noise and backed the cart up.

"I just want to talk to you. You care about them, right?"

Marvin stopped, his eyebrow raised.

"I care about them too. And they're in the hospital right now."

"The—"

"They're okay." Lincoln put his arms out. "They're fine. Theo fractured his arm, but he's going to be fine."

The man's shoulders relaxed. His voice was gravelly, like he didn't use it much. "What happened?"

"Kali stepped out in front of a truck."

"A—"

"Weird, right? The person I talked to, a witness, said she looked both ways and then stepped out."

"You don't think—" Marvin's eyes widened. "Oh, Kali." He put his hands to the side of his head and pelted himself. "Kali, no. Sweetness, no."

Lincoln eased around the side of the cart. He rested a hand on Marvin's shoulder; the man's head shot up as he shuffled away.

"I don't know. I don't think so. I can't imagine ... but Theo said she'd been crying and—"

"Theo said? Theo talked? The boy talked!" Marvin's face lit. "He talked?"

"Yeah," Lincoln let out a chuckle, "a bit. But the thing is I think something is wrong. Something big. I've been trying to talk to her," Lincoln passed a hand through his hair, "but she shuts me out."

Marvin nodded, suddenly seeming ... normal. "She'll do that. Shut you out. She shut my Derek out, time and again."

Marvin grinned. "Not me, though. Doesn't shut me out. Must be 'cause I'm so sweet or," his smile faded, "well," he held his hands out and gestured to himself, "why push away a lost cause?"

Lincoln pressed his lips together. He took a breath. He needed one. Whether it was Marvin or his cart, he didn't know, but he commended Kali for hugging the man.

"So she does this, pushes people away?"

"She's stubborn. Tough. So stubborn and tough it makes her stupid, even though she's not." He looked away. "Kinda like me. Probably why I've always liked her so much." He turned back to Lincoln. "But at the same time, she's kind of an open book. If you think something's wrong, then something's wrong. And you can push and push but until she's ready," he made the lips-zipped-tight motion across his mouth.

"Any way to speed the process along? Her being ready?"

Marvin laughed. His face went serious. "But she likes you. Or she trusts you."

"How do you—"

"You had her Theo. Not just anyone gets her Theo. No man, especially." Marvin leaned toward Lincoln. "You like her?"

"Uh ..."

"I mean really like her, not want to," Marvin looked sideways, "you know, but really like her. Like her like a man likes a woman. Not a boy, who only thinks he's a man."

The ball landed in Lincoln's gut. "I care about her. And I care about Theo."

Marvin put his fingerless-gloved hands on the handle of his cart and leaned against it. "That's good. And you must be some kind of decent. You wouldn't be here talking to me if you weren't." He rubbed his thumb and forefinger across his chin. "She has no one. No one but me anyway." A gravelly laugh. "Which equates to the same thing." Marvin's hand clamped onto Lincoln's shoulder. "She's worth it. And when she decides to love, she can love hard." His bony fingers clenched down. "Be worth it. If you let her, if you prompt her, be worth it." He let go. "Maybe you already love her."

Lincoln stepped back. What was he supposed to say to that? What *could* he say to that? To a stranger, especially. He didn't love Kali. Theo, maybe, but not Kali. She made life more ... livable. That was all. It'd felt hard to breathe since he saw Lucy in that hospital bed, learned his child was dead before it had even lived, learned it may not have even been his child. When Joseph entered that day, his gaze on Lucy not Lincoln, it was as if all the air had been sucked out of the room, out of the world; but from the moment he first saw Kali, slowly, it had come back.

Marvin loosened his grip and patted Lincoln's shoulder. He smiled the smile of a man who would have been handsome once. "Yeah. I feel you." He nodded, his head bobbing just short of maniacally. He dropped his hand. "She's worth it. Not easy. Nothing with her will be easy." A chuckle. Marvin put both hands back on the cart. "She's stubborn and she's scared and kinda broken too. Derek made her worse. You'll have to fight her just to stay around. But stay around."

Lincoln looked toward the hospital. "I'm going there to wait for her, to see how Theo is. Come with me."

"No." Marvin started to push the cart away. "No one wants me around."

"Kali will." Lincoln put a hand on the cart. Marvin tensed. "Trust me."

Marvin shrunk back. One arm wrapped around his middle and the other clenched the cart handle. Lincoln waited. Marvin glanced toward the hospital then back at Lincoln. "Just to make sure the boy's all right."

"Just to make sure he's all right." Lincoln smiled, and the weight in his gut fluttered a little. The pain and uncertainty in Marvin's eyes felt scarily familiar.

LINCOLN RETURNED TO the bench at the side of the courtyard. Marvin waited up the street, the tip of his cart visible behind a gathering of trees. Lincoln sat with his back straight, his eyes on the door. He slipped out his phone and a sliver of unrest shot through him at how easy this habit came back to him. But there were no stocks he was eager to check, no scores, no business news. Just the time. He was only checking the time.

It had been a little over forty minutes since he exited the ER, which meant Kali and Theo could still be another hour. More, even. His stomach grumbled. He wished he'd remembered to pick up some food. But his stomach could wait. Catching Kali, confronting her, forcing her to open up, was more important than food. A grin slipped through. She was tough, Marvin had said. Stubborn. So was he. Or at least he could be.

He pictured her—the way she looked at Theo, her persistence with Marvin, her ploy to make his birthday something he'd enjoy. She wasn't just tough, she was caring, once she let you in. Devoted.

The minutes passed. After two more phone checks, Lincoln resolved not to pull it out again. It wouldn't make them come out sooner, and unless Shelley was far off, there was little chance he'd already missed them.

He focused instead on watching the people entering and exiting the building and wondered what their stories were. And then there they were. Kali's face was drawn, exhausted, like she hadn't slept in a week and had been crying half of that time. Theo's body was slung across hers, his arms and legs dangling at the sides of her small frame. His booster seat dangled from the arm that wasn't grasping her boy.

Lincoln stood, waved a hand to Marvin, and approached.

"Hey."

Kali's head lifted. Her mouth opened, the slightest sigh emerging. She shook her head and walked on.

"Kali."

"What?"

Lincoln stepped beside her. "You need a ride?"

"No."

He put a hand on her shoulder. She stopped, licked, then bit her bottom lip, but didn't turn.

"You do need a ride."

"I called a cab."

She spun and dropped the booster seat. "How do you know I need a ride? You actually stalking me now?"

The clink and rustle of Marvin's cart approached them. Kali glanced from Lincoln to Marvin then back at Lincoln again. "You? Why?" Her shoulders slumped.

"Hi, Sweetness." Marvin sidled up to her.

"Hi."

Marvin put a hand out to Theo's sleeping head. He didn't touch it, just let the hand hover half an inch above the boy's dreads, then gestured to the cast on Theo's left arm. "How is he?"

Kali adjusted Theo with a little jerk and held him tighter. "He's fine. He'll be just fine. How are you?"

Marvin shook his head. "Where's your car, Sweetness? Why didn't you drive?"

Kali's lip trembled. She bit her lip again and looked up and away from them. Her chest raised and the air streamed out slowly.

"Sweetness?"

She looked to Marvin. "We need to talk."

Marvin shifted toward her. "Okay."

Kali looked to Lincoln, then back at Marvin. "Not here, okay? And I need to get Theo to bed. Just this once, come with me."

Marvin's gaze lingered on his cart—eyeing it as if it held riches, or a life.

"Marvin." A plea was in Kali's voice.

"I'll take you. All of you." Lincoln stepped closer. I have a tarp and some cables in my truck. We'll put the cart in it. It'll be safe."

Kali opened her mouth as if to protest then turned to Marvin.

He rubbed a hand on the scraggly curls of his beard.

"Will you come? If your cart comes too?"

"I can bring you back here after." Lincoln reached for the booster seat. "Or anywhere you want to go."

Marvin looked from his cart to the truck then back to his cart. He nodded.

CHAPTER FORTY-EIGHT

Back at Kali's apartment building, Theo barely woke as Lincoln peeled him out of the booster seat. He smiled then plopped his head on Lincoln's shoulder. Lincoln held him close.

Kali stood, a hand on her hip, then reached for the booster seat. "Bring him up, then wait for Marvin down here."

Marvin, who'd spent the drive in the front seat, one hand clasped to the door, the other to his armrest, crawled out of the cab and edged his way around the truck. "Why don't you take him up, then come on down and we'll talk?"

"Marvin," she spoke slowly, her voice tight, "I can't leave him upstairs alone."

"No?"

"No."

Marvin looked to the tarp that contained his cart. "I suppose it's not likely anyone would look under that?"

"No." Lincoln looked to Kali. "No one will touch your stuff."

"And Lincoln will watch it."

Marvin shook his head. "Let the boy come up, Kali. Then

he'll take me home."

Kali flung her arm. "Fine."

Lincoln carried Theo to his bed and set him down gently. A part of him didn't want to let go. As long as the boy's limbs were around him, Kali couldn't exactly kick him out. Theo murmured as Lincoln pulled off his shoes and pulled the covers up around him. It felt familiar. Good. He turned to see Kali, a look of pure pain in her eyes.

"Accidents happen. He'll be—"

"I didn't see the truck. I looked but—"

"It's okay." Lincoln stepped to her.

She backed up. "It's not okay."

Kali walked away. Lincoln switched off the light and followed her. Marvin stood in front of the couch, a roll of paper towels in his hand. He tore them off, one by one, and laid them on the cushion.

"Marvin!"

He looked up, sheepish. "Your couch is so new. So clean."

Kali leaned against the counter separating the living room from the kitchen. "It's only new to me."

"Well." Marvin continued his preparation then sat gingerly on the edge of the cushion, careful not to let his shirt touch the backrest.

Kali shook her head, a hand to her chest. "I don't care about the damn couch."

Lincoln hesitated between her and Marvin.

Kali closed her eyes. "If you're staying, you might as well sit."

The ball of fear grew in Lincoln's stomach. Her eyes looked dead. She was here, but not. "Kal—"

"I have a brain tumour."

Lincoln lowered into the chair behind him. Marvin looked to the floor, his head shaking.

Kali stepped between them and perched on the coffee table across from Marvin. Lincoln wanted to say something, tell her to stop. It wasn't right. She wasn't about to comfort him. Not now. She shouldn't take care of—

"Marvin." She reached for the older man's hand. "It'll be okay. Or ... well, I don't know. But we'll figure it out."

Marvin's gaze ping-ponged around the room. "No, Kali. You're confused, or the doctors are. You're young and—" He zeroed in on her. "You're confused. It's a mistake."

"It's called Meningioma. And it's growing fast."

"You're not—" The blood drained from his face.

"Hopefully not for a long time. A very long time. And maybe not from this." She kept her eyes on Marvin, spoke to him as if Lincoln weren't even in the room. "I'll need help. Not yet, but soon maybe. I know it'll be hard, but if you could ... Things are going to change, probably sooner than later." She stopped, her back straight, her arms steady. "I've already started to lose my vision—"

Lincoln leaned forward. "You didn't see the truck."

Kali's head fell.

"You didn't see the truck, even though you looked. And that's why you didn't drive. But can you see now?"

Kali's shoulders rose then fell. "I can't see you, not really. I can see Marvin. But sitting where I'm sitting, with you sitting where you are." She looked up, her eyes on Marvin, but her voice for Lincoln. "I should be able to see you. It's starting with my peripheral on my right eye. On the left, it's kind of a haze that I guess is getting hazier and hazier. But my left eye compensates. I can't tell unless I close it."

"The headaches. It wasn't just your studying?"

She shook her head.

Marvin finally looked up. "You're such a good girl."

Kali smiled.

His head shook in fast little spurts. "Derek. Derek would know what to do, how to help. If Derek were here then—"

"Derek's not here." Kali's voice was firm, hard. "He's not here, and he's not coming back."

"But—"

"Derek's gone. He's not coming back."

"But—"

"Marvin, we talked about this."

Marvin nodded.

"That's why I need you." Kali looked at Marvin, the way you'd look when trying to convince a child something bad could be made better. "We can get a place with an extra room."

"No." Marvin pulled his hands free. "No."

Kali wrapped her arms around her waist and straightened again.

Marvin's head kept shaking. "I told you. I need to be outside. I need—" He stood and paced. "I'm sorry." His hands went to his head. He cradled it as he rocked forward. "I can't."

Kali stayed where she sat, her gaze to the floor. Marvin looked back at her. "I'm sorry, I ... I can't. I tried, Kali. You know I tried. Beatrice, if she were here she could do it. She could help. But I can't."

"Marvin." Kali's head was still down. Her voice was low.

"I couldn't help her either. I tried but still she left. Still. And Derek. And Jason. Everyone leaves and I can't help. I—"

"Marvin."

349

"But Derek. Derek could help. He could help you and Theo. That's his job. To help you and Theo. If you could—"

"Marvin." Kali bounced up like a Jack-in-the-box, though not a happy one. She grasped Marvin's shoulders. "Stop talking about Derek. Derek is gone, okay? He's gone."

"Derek's gone." Marvin nodded. "Gone."

"And I'm going to be okay. I'm sorry, I shouldn't have ... you don't need to worry about me. I'll be okay."

Marvin's body relaxed. He raised a hand to Kali's cheek. "You're going to be okay, Sweetness?"

She nodded.

"And you're not going anywhere?"

"Not for a long time." Kali let out a smile—a costly one. "I just need to know you'll be okay. You need to do better. Take care of yourself. Go to the shelter when it's cold, or here, you can always come here. Remember to eat. You need to do that for me so I don't have to worry about it. So I don't—"

"I can do that." Marvin nodded like a child would. "I'll do better."

"Okay." Another smile, easier this time. "One day I may not see you anymore—"

A look of shock, then acknowledgement, on Marvin's face.

"Literally see you." She rubbed her hand along his arm. "So you'll need to be around, to tell me you're okay. To describe how Theo looks. All right?"

Another nod.

"I didn't mean to upset you."

The Marvin Lincoln had talked to an hour or so earlier, the man who seemed almost normal, who had some sense of wisdom or foresight, crept back. "I'm sorry, Sweetness. I'm sorry to ... I just—"

"It's okay."

"I'll try." He offered. "I'll try to help. I'll do my best."

"I know you will." Kali's shoulders sagged. "That's all anyone can ask, right, for people to do their best."

Marvin nodded. He looked to Lincoln. "He's the one to ask for help. He'll do good, won't you, son?"

Lincoln cleared his throat. He tried to speak, but Kali got her words out first.

"Lincoln will help by taking you back, then he'll be done."

Lincoln stood. "You can't drive anymore?"

Kali sighed. "I don't know. I have an appointment tomorrow morning. My license is going. I don't know whether it's going yet."

"Well, I'll drive you to the appointment."

"There's the bus. Cabs."

"I'll drive Theo to daycare and you to the appointment, and to work after if you're going."

Kali's eyes flashed. She shook her head, then said, "Okay."

"Okay?"

"Okay. Just tomorrow. Just until I figure things out. I'm not a charity case."

Lincoln couldn't smile, but he nodded. "Of course not."

Kali's eyes were on him. "I'm going to lose my job."

Another nod.

"I don't know when, but unless a miracle happens ..."

"You should get to bed. What time's the appointment?"

"Ten." She wrapped her arms around her middle once more. "I'll drop Theo off late tomorrow. Can you be here by nine?"

"Yes." Lincoln looked to Marvin. "You ready to go? I think Kali could use some sleep."

"Just wait." Kali rushed to the kitchen. She came back a minute later with a bag and passed it to Marvin. "Some chicken salad. Apples. A banana. And those granola bars you like."

Marvin sank into himself again. "You don't have to, Sweetness. I get by. You know I—"

"Don't give me anything else to worry about." Her voice was firm as she pushed the bag toward him.

He took it and shuffled toward the door. Again, Lincoln resisted the urge to wrap his arms around her. He also resisted the urge to flee, to tell her he was wrong, he couldn't come back tomorrow, he couldn't come back ever again.

He rested a hand on her shoulder, pleased she didn't yank it away. "I'll be here tomorrow. At nine. Not a minute later."

She nodded, and a combination of emotions he'd never seen in her before settled in her eyes. Fear. Affection. Hope.

CHAPTER FORTY-NINE

Marvin didn't speak on the drive back to Halifax. Again, his hands were clasped tightly to the door and armrest. As they crossed the bridge, Lincoln looked over. "Where am I taking you?"

Marvin stared straight ahead.

"Marvin, I—"

"Where do you live?"

"Brunswick."

"Brunswick's fine."

"I can take you any—"

"Brunswick's perfect."

Lincoln turned onto Gottingen Street without another word. On Brunswick, he looped his truck around to park in front of his house. Marvin's hands settled on his lap. He looked over. "I lost my head a little there. It happens." He looked down. "Sometimes."

Lincoln pushed out a smile. It wavered.

"I wasn't always like this. I used to be ... okay, you know?"

"I'm sure—"

"I was a school teacher. History."

"Oh yeah?"

Marvin nodded. "My wife was too. The kids loved her. Not just our kids. The students."

Lincoln tapped the wheel. "She sounds great."

"She was. Beautiful. Sweet. Perfect." Marvin let out a little laugh. "Not perfect. Nobody's perfect. But she was perfect to me."

Lincoln offered a close-lipped smile.

"She taught English and Music. She sang like an angel." A long pause. "But I was a smoker."

Lincoln turned to him. "Kali told me. I'm sorry for your—"

"Kali told you? She talked about—"

"Just a bit. Just the gist, you know?"

"Oh, it's okay. I don't mind." A stronger laugh. "My life is an open book." His head fell again. "Beatrice would be so disappointed in me. I did my best for the boys. I kept it together as long as I could. As best I could, anyway. And then they jumped in the ocean." He paused, all signs of the unhinged man who'd paced Kali's apartment gone. "At least I raised me some heroes. That says something, wouldn't you say?"

"Yeah." Lincoln's heart raced. This man had watched the woman he loved die. Witnessed the day by day victory of a disease. And it destroyed him.

Would Kali's death be similar? Maybe not, maybe not even close. But it'd be hard. Her life would be hard, as would his, if he forced himself into hers.

"I stopped the day she got the diagnosis. The very day. Never picked up another cigarette."

"Kali told me that too."

"But it was too late."

"Where are you staying tonight, Marvin? I have an extra room. Why don't you—"

"No. No." Marvin opened the truck door and stepped down like a man much older than he was. "Today was my first day in a car in four years. The first time in someone's home too. That's enough."

Lincoln untied the tarp and pulled Marvin's cart off the truck bed. Marvin grasped the handle as if his life depended on it. "You still want her?"

"Huh?" Lincoln knew exactly what Marvin was asking, but wasn't sure how to answer.

"If you do, make sure you know what that means. If you don't, get lost now. Get lost fast."

Lincoln grimaced.

"There's programs and such, right? She'll figure it out. Won't end up like me."

"No. No, she won't."

Were there programs? And if Lincoln were to walk away, was this man the only person Kali would have?

Marvin pulled his cart to the curb. "Thanks for the ride, son. I hope I see you around."

Marvin clanked down the street and turned the corner. Once the man was out of sight, Lincoln walked the steps to his apartment's door. The feeling of wanting to flee came back—different this time. He wanted to run away from this place, straight to Kali's building, up her stairs, and bang on her door. He wanted to convince her she wasn't alone, convince her somehow things would be okay, her life would be okay.

Terror coursed through him. At least he had the answer to Marvin's question.

KALI WOKE THEO WITH a smile. "How's my brave little man?"

His arms reached out and she cuddled him against her.

"In much pain?"

He shook his head.

She ran a thumb across his forehead. *Speak. Just speak.* "Hungry?"

A large nod.

"All right. Pick out some clothes and I'll go make you breakfast."

He grinned.

She stood, then bent down again and kissed his face, her smile on strong. Kali fluffed her hair and jutted out her chin when she stepped outside his room. She could do this. She had no choice but to do this.

What she wanted was to stay in Theo's room, crawl into his bed, and stare at him for hours, memorize him—every curve of his features, every eyelash, every perfect little tooth.

But she couldn't. She had a life to live. The doctor's warning didn't mean anything, or didn't *have* to mean anything. Not yet. She could still have weeks, days, years until her vision became a real problem ... probably not years, but stranger things had happened. Miracles happened.

It wasn't a Friday, but Kali made pancakes with chocolate chips. Would she be able to do this if she was blind? Would the treatment Dr. Manning referenced work? Would she get it in time?

Most likely, even if her vision left entirely, she could manage to measure out all the ingredients, to locate those ingredients—each item would need its own place—but what about knowing the perfect moment to flip each pancake? How would she know the bubbles had popped?

Kali looked at the clock. Eight-thirty. She should call a cab. Lincoln may not show. Not that she even wanted him to. A cab would be easier. Simpler.

"Hey, baby!"

Theo shuffled into the kitchen. He pointed to his arm.

"It starting to hurt now?"

A nod, with the sweetest little smile.

"Sit there. As soon as the pancakes are ready you can have a pill that'll make it feel so much better."

He climbed up into his chair, the one Lincoln had made. Kali flipped two pancakes on a plate for Theo and brought it to him. How would she tell him her sight was going? That she had a tumour in her head? How would she make him understand? Be sure he understood?

Kali sat across from Theo. Only when he tapped his plate then pointed at hers did she take a bite. When they'd both finished and Theo had taken his pill, she cleared the plates. 8:48. Lincoln definitely wouldn't show. Kali called a cab.

At 8:55, when the buzzer hadn't rung, Kali held out Theo's backpack and walked to the elevator.

She pushed her way out into the sunshine, one hand grasping Theo's booster seat. Lincoln. Standing against his truck, a smile travelling across his face as he saw them. He walked over, something in his hand, and bent to Theo. "Hey, buddy." He held up a marker. "Anyone sign it yet?"

Theo looked to Kali, a question on his face, then turned

back to Lincoln and shook his head.

"Sweet. Then I'll be the first." Lincoln drew a big smiley face then wrote: *Get better soon. We've got a ball to toss!* He read it to Theo and the boy grinned. Lincoln stood, uncertainty on his face. "Morning. How are you?"

"Fine. Thanks."

Kali opened the back door of the truck and helped Theo in. Lincoln pulled the truck into the street as Kali called the cab company and cancelled. Lincoln looked over but didn't say a word. She started to direct him to Westwood.

"I know where it is." He kept his eyes on the road. "The main campus?"

Kali glanced at him. "Yeah." Had he stalked her there, too? She gave herself a mental shake. He grew up in the city. Of course he knew the place. She looked out the window.

With Theo dropped off, the silence in the truck seemed louder. Kali stole glances at Lincoln. He stared straight ahead, his jaw set. Did he regret picking her up? Was he coming up with an excuse not to pick her up after her appointment? Not that she cared. She could take the bus, no problem. So he could give his excuses and it wouldn't matter to her. She could do this on her own. She *would*. All of it. Handle all of it.

Most likely Dr. Manning would say she was being overly cautious, not driving. Some people drove with one eye. She could drive with reduced peripheral vision. No problem. If it was a problem, her license would be gone.

"Has Theo talked again?"

Anger bubbled. Kali glared at him. "No."

"Did you look into it? Talk to the therapist?"

"I've been a little preoccupied."

"Yeah. Right. Of course." He tossed her a small smile.

358

"You want to talk about it?"

"I'd rather not talk at all."

Lincoln returned his gaze to the road. Kali leaned her head against the back of the seat and turned toward the window, hiding the tear that escaped down her cheek. She was a bitch. Why was she being such a bitch? She wiped her face. Whatever. If there was a day she had a right to be a bitch, this was that day. Still. She turned to Lincoln, opened her mouth to apologize, looked away again, her gaze focused on the water sloshing in the harbour far below.

What if Lincoln was all she had? What if she needed him? And what if he ran?

CHAPTER FIFTY

Lincoln had a phone now, so Kali could call him. That was the plan, the agreement, for Kali to go to her appointment then call Lincoln to come get her when she was done.

But he waited. In a spot with a view to the door. She'd called a cab this morning, and he didn't trust she wouldn't again. But she didn't need a cab company right now, she needed someone she could rely on.

An hour and three minutes after he dropped her off, Kali emerged from the clinic doors, sunglasses on before she even stepped outside. More bad news. She stared into the street then up and down it. She stepped out from the shadow of the building, adjusted her satchel, and looked to the sky. If he could freeze time, right in that instant, he would. Her standing in all her unearthly glory, unearthly beauty. It seemed cruel and wasteful that someone this beautiful wouldn't be able to see the beauty around her.

Kali reached into her pocket and punched in a number. Him? A cab? She was near a bus stop; she could be calling to see when the next one would arrive.

Lincoln waited for the vibration. Waited. Waited. She was talking to someone. He wanted to see her eyes, to know if the smile that coated her lips was real. He doubted it.

The call was too long to be a cab company. Shelley, perhaps, the friend he'd met at the ER? Maybe she'd be someone Kali could rely on. Or Mrs. Martin, Kali calling to ask about babysitting?

She pulled the phone from her ear and stared at it. She raised it again and his buzzed.

"Hey."

"Hi." Her voice was resolved. Firm. "I'm ready now. Can you—"

"I'm already here." He honked. She looked up, waved, and slid the phone into her satchel. When she stepped up into the cab of his truck her expression was grim.

He looked over, offered a smile, and started the engine. What did you say when someone came from an appointment with a neurologist, or ophthalmologist, or whoever she'd seen?

Could an appointment to check the progress of a rapidly growing brain tumour ever be good? He could ask her how it went but what could she say? Awful. Devastating. Horrid.

While stopped at the third light in a row, Lincoln looked to Kali again. All he could see was her profile, the lines that defined the face that captivated his dreams. "Still have your licence?"

She didn't look at him. Her chest rose then fell. "Yes."

"Well, that's good."

"She didn't take it, but strongly recommended I don't drive. Just in case."

"Oh."

"Sometimes, as happened with the truck, people like me

lose parts of their vision before they realize it. I could be driving, think I've checked my blind spot, when really ..." Her voice trailed off. "You get the picture."

"Yeah." Lincoln positioned both hands on the wheel—perfect ten and two. "So, you'll just have to be extra cautious then? Extra aware?"

She shifted her satchel higher on her lap. "I'll drive if it's an emergency. A necessity. And yes, I'll be extra aware. I have another appointment in a week. Each time she'll reassess." Kali turned away from him, her gaze out the window. "As the doctor stressed several times, I'm lucky. I live in a city with public transportation. Not everyone is as lucky."

Lincoln pulled through the intersection and made his way to the bridge. "Well, I guess that's true. Small blessings." Damn. Why did he say that? A trite expression of the church ladies, he'd heard it countless times growing up, and he'd always hated it.

Kali let out a bitter laugh. "Yeah. For sure. It's only been two years since I could afford a car. I don't use it a ton, so there were times I wondered if it was worth it. Then I'd remember Theo as a baby. Lugging him everywhere. Lugging that stroller everywhere. To appointments, to get groceries. It's not easy—getting all that onto a bus. And the good times—taking him to the beach, going for a drive in the country and stopping at vegetable stands." She shook her head. "At least he doesn't have a stroller anymore."

Lincoln almost said it again, small blessings. He caught himself before the words slipped out. His gaze caught on her, the way her slim-fingered hands clasped her bag, how she looked straight ahead, to the side, but not at him. Never at him. "As much as I can, I'll help out. I can take you to get groceries. To appointments."

"From your cabin in the woods? Oh," she glanced at him and rolled her eyes, "I mean tree house. You're going to drive up here every time I have an appointment or need some food, right? Become my chauffeur?"

Now it was him who looked ahead. Would he do that? Should he? He wanted her in his life, wanted them, but did that mean he wanted his life to revolve around her?

"I said as much as I can. It may take a bit of planning, but I'd need groceries too. Supplies. We could plan it on a day you have an appointment. I pick you up, take you to it, we do a grocery run after."

She scoffed. "What do you think you're doing?"

He tried to smile. "Driving you."

"Why?" She yelled. Her voice settled, her arms wrapped tight around her. "Why are you here? I don't line up with your plan. Your stupid little plan. A tree house in the woods." She shook her head. "Do you have any idea how naive that is? How childish? I get why you're doing it. I don't know how or what exactly, but I know why—someone or something hurt you. And now you think you can escape it. Now you think you can live this idyllic little life where no one will hurt you and nothing bad will happen. But that's shit. Go as far as you want, never see another person again but it won't change anything. You can't escape. There's no escape, Lincoln. None."

He glanced over. Her gaze was ahead again.

"Life sucks." Kali let out a harsh laugh. "Do what you want. Go where you want. But you can't escape."

Lincoln drove through three intersections. At the fourth,

he eased the car to a stop in time for the red light. "You're right."

She looked at him. For the first time on the drive, their eyes met.

"I thought I could escape. I wanted to escape. But life's there too. You're there too."

She raised an eyebrow.

"I mean thoughts of you. Of Theo. You reminded me that life is more than ... I don't know ... than escaping. Than trying to live entirely for myself. You brought me back into the world, to wanting to be in it."

She swallowed—that little convulse of her beautiful throat.

"I've changed in the few months since we met, in the past weeks since you left. In the past years, too." Lincoln drove through the green light. "When I saw you and Theo outside that dump of an apartment I wanted the woods, craved it with everything in me." He looked back over. "Needed my castle in the air."

Her brow furrowed.

"I still want to finish it, still want to live there, but it doesn't have to be to the exclusion of everything and everyone else."

Kali sat silent a moment. "And what about next week, next month, when you change again?"

"We can change, but not backwards. At least I don't think so." Lincoln glanced over again before turning his gaze to the road. She was staring at him. "I'm just asking you to let me help you. Maybe we found each other for a reason." After two more turns, he pulled into the Westwood roundabout.

Kali didn't move to unbuckle her seat. She shifted toward him. "If you want to help, if you're determined to help, then fine, help. But don't expect more than that. Don't expect more from me than ... than thank you."

"Okay."

"You helped us out during a time when we needed it. But it wasn't charity. I'm paying you. Soon. And you'll take the money. It's better if we leave it at that."

"Why?"

"You're not going to help your way into my bed. If you think I'm some charity case who'll throw herself all over you because you take me to get groceries, because who else would want a single mom with a brain tumour, a blind single mom with a brain tumour, think again. Because it doesn't matter who else would want me. I don't want anyone or need anyone."

"Understood."

"You say that."

"Yes."

"But you'll get bored. You'll walk away. You'll realize being the hero isn't all it's cracked up to be."

Lincoln held in a laugh. "I'm not anyone's hero. I'm not trying to be a hero."

"Well—"

"And if you recall, I wanted you and Theo in my life before I had any idea about your," he paused, "health condition."

"Brain tumour. You can say it."

Lincoln gritted his teeth. "Brain tumour."

"And now that you know?"

"I'm terrified."

The swallow again. And a softening ... maybe. She looked to her lap. "Me too."

"I might not be able to handle it, whatever you're going to go through, as well as I'd like. I ... I've been a bit broken."

Her gaze stayed lowered. "I could tell."

Lincoln's heart pounded. "I can promise I won't walk out on Theo. I won't stop calling or visiting out of nowhere. Nor you. I can promise, for now at least, if you call me and you need me, I'll come. Until things get settled. Until you figure out how to make things work."

Still, her gaze stayed lowered.

"Kali?"

"And then?"

"I don't know. If you tell me to go, I will?"

She nodded.

"So how about until then, until you figure things out, you stop," he grinned, "or at least *try* to stop treating me like some criminal who's trying to worm his way into your life?"

The smallest of grins. Another nod. "You heading back to the tree house tonight?"

"Haven't decided."

She looked up. "You can come for dinner if you like. While I can still see to cook."

A tremor of warmth spread through Lincoln. "Sure. Want me to pick you up after work?"

"I'm not going to let you become my chauffeur. I can take the bus."

"Yeah. But tonight, since I'll be in town, heading to your place."

She unbuckled her seatbelt. "I'm working late, to make up for a bit of the time away. Six o'clock?"

"Six o'clock."

She opened the cab door and stepped out, but her hand

stayed on the handle. "And Lincoln?"

"Yeah?"

"Thanks." She slammed the door, and this time it was Lincoln who swallowed.

CHAPTER FIFTY-ONE

L incoln spent the rest of the afternoon on the Dartmouth Common, watching the clouds and the ships in the harbour stream by. He thought of Romper, how if he were here he'd lay his head on Lincoln's thigh, or urge him to get up and toss a ball, Frisbee, stick ... whatever was available.

And then he thought of Kali. Kali, who despite the growth in her brain, despite her resistance, her anger, still had the power with even half a smile to make Lincoln feel he was exactly where he was meant to be.

It'd be hard. Even without the ... what was it, Meningioma, it'd be hard. With it? Who knew.

But he hadn't promised her forever. And she'd promised him almost nothing at all. Day by day, he'd have to decide this was what he wanted, whatever *this* was. He'd have to fight: Himself. Life. Maybe her.

LINCOLN RETURNED FROM Theo's room to find Kali with her feet up on the couch and curled beneath her. He started to head for the chair across from her, then went to the other end of the couch.

"He go down all right?"

"Squeezed an extra story out of me."

Kali nodded. "He likes you."

"I like him."

A slight laugh. She looked up under those dark long lashes. "I'll never live in the woods with you."

"I didn't ask."

"Well, I'm just telling you."

"I bet you never thought I'd be sitting here in your new place."

"That is true."

"You thought you'd never see me again when you left."

"I thought it wasn't likely." She pulled her feet up closer. "Don't ask that next question."

He wasn't about to. Even if some part of her had wanted to see him again, she wouldn't admit it. At least not yet.

"People care for themselves and their own first. They have to. If they didn't, they'd die."

"That sounds like something you've said again and again."

She shrugged.

"Well, maybe you could be 'my own' one day." He winked.

Her body shifted away from him. "You barely know me. You think you want me, but you don't."

"I told you, I'm not asking for anything." Lincoln smiled. "Except a thank you."

"I'm not blind yet."

He looked away. "Want and expectation are two different things."

"But you admit want. So what do you want? To be my boyfriend? My lover? My provider? You think because we spent a couple of months in the same apartment and managed not to kill each other that means we're compatible? Soul mates?"

"No."

Her lower lip curled into her mouth. She bit it. "Then why are you here? What do you want?"

"To know I'll see you often. Not in a romantic way. Not necessarily."

Her eyes widened, almost rolled, she started to speak but he held out a hand.

"To be near you, and Theo. That's all."

"Near us. What does that even mean?"

"It seems pretty self-explanatory."

"Or bizarre. And if I decide I don't want you near."

He shrugged. "You do. You're just scared."

"Really."

"I'm here, aren't I? Invited in. And I'm offering you the most I can give."

Her brow rose. A signature move.

"Me."

"Get it through your head. I do not want you."

"You need me."

"I'm fine."

"Today."

"So what, you'll be back tomorrow?"

Lincoln shifted to the edge of the couch. "Or the next day, whenever." He pulled out his phone and gave it a little shake in front of her. "We talked about this. When you need me, you'll call, and I'll come." He stood. "And you'll call."

She looked up at him, strong and fragile all at once.

"And if you don't, I won't stalk you. I promise. I may check in." He slid the phone back in his pocket. "But if you tell me, once and for all, to get lost, I'll listen." He met her gaze, amazed at the fear and hope he felt in his smile. "So don't tell me to get lost again, unless you mean it."

Her mouth opened, closed, opened once more. "I don't get it. You had this dream, this goal of solitude. What if I need you every day?"

"You won't, at least not for a while."

"And then?"

"Then we'll figure it out. I know, right now at least, if it comes down to it, I'd rather be here. I'd rather be in all this, than in a tree in the woods without you."

Kali closed her eyes and shook her head. When she looked back up at him, his breath caught. There it was again. Hope. Fear. Affection. He felt half-drowned.

"All right." She moved to the edge of the couch, closer to him. "If you're going to be here, be here." She paused. "I hardly know you, so tell me something."

Lincoln grinned. "How about I start with something you helped teach me. That book. *Walden*. Reading it was like ... reading my life. There's this line when Thoreau talks about how people are born into lives of expectation—inheriting farms, houses, barns. And he asks the question, 'Why should they begin digging their graves as soon as they're born?'"

Lincoln sank onto the coffee table, his knees inches from the cushion that held hers. "I read it and ... well, not as soon as I was born but maybe as soon as my father stopped being my father, I started following my brother instead, and I felt that burden. Like I was working to dig my own grave and I didn't even know it. When I left, it was as if I'd been unshackled. And when I read those words, I understood why."

Kali nodded, her gaze intent on him. "When your father stopped being your father?"

Lincoln felt the breath travel through his lungs and down to his belly, right where that familiar ball made its weight known. "Maybe that's enough sharing for one night?"

"I know what it is to have a father walk away. To leave you."

Lincoln faltered. "He didn't leave."

"He—?"

"Vanished." Lincoln put his hands on his knees and stood. "It's getting late."

Kali reached out a hand but didn't touch him. "Don't leave yet." He remembered this scene, the roles reversed. He sat beside her.

The corners of her lips barely rose. "How about something lighter?"

Lincoln folded his hands and waited.

"You were some big business hot shot, right?"

"Trying to be."

"So where'd your wardrobe go? How'd you transition to ... to ... that?"

Lincoln looked at his threadbare jeans and grinned. "Laying aside those fancy clothes was laying aside a whole life."

"And this is what you decided to pick up instead?"

He chuckled. "I tossed everything before I moved. Almost everything." Everything Lucy had helped pick out, everything she'd liked. "I only kept the worst, what society would call the worst. The clothes I used to work in." He held out his hands. "Really work in, I mean, when I made something."

"On your dad's construction crew?"

"Mmhmm." Lincoln looped a finger through one of the holes in his t-shirt. "It had another purpose too, this wardrobe—people didn't look at me, not really. I could hide in my own city."

"And you wanted that?"

"I wanted that."

Kali looked past him. "That's the scariest thing, that people won't look at me, that they'll stop seeing me as a person, and I won't even know it."

Lincoln held back the hand he wanted to stretch out.

After several minutes Kali shifted away from him. "You're right. It's getting late."

"It is." Lincoln held his breath. "Would you like me to stay? On the couch, or—"

"No." She shook her head.

"I can. I will."

She stood. "No."

Lincoln smiled. "Okay." He rose. "I'll be back, though. Just call and I'll be back."

Kali didn't look at him, but she nodded, reached for his hand, gave it a squeeze, and let go.

It was enough. For now, at least, it was enough.

THANK YOU!

Hello,

I hope you enjoyed *Behind Our Lives*.

Lincoln and Kali's story isn't over. Book Two in the *Behind Our Lives Trilogy* will release in the spring of 2017. While you're waiting for the rest of the story, I'd greatly appreciate it if you took the time to leave a review of *Behind Our Lives*. Reviews are incredibly important, especially for independent authors like myself. They let other readers know whether or not it's worth taking a chance on an author and helps us get marketing deals, which can extend our reach and mean we're able to provide you stories for years to come! Head over to your favourite retailer and/or Goodreads to leave your review today.

To order your copy of Book Two in the *Behind Our Lives Trilogy* visit http://www.charlenecarr.com/Book2Trilogy

Thank you so much for taking the time to read *Behind Our Lives!*

All the best,

Charlene Carr

ACKNOWLEDGEMENTS

A huge thank you to my husband for constantly supporting my work. To my mother, for her keen eye on the many versions and revisions - this would be an entirely different process without you! To my beta readers, who read my works in their early form, with metaphorical bloomers showing - your feedback is invaluable.

I would also like to thank the staff and clients of the CNIB St. John's, in particular, Lynsey Soper, who has been a superstar in getting me contacts and connecting me with people who have made Kali's experience in the early days of her diagnosis as realistic as I could manage. Thanks, as well, to Dr. Linda Magnusson, Dr. Teri Stuckless, and Dr. Leo Edward, for your medical consultation. If anything in the story does not make sense medically, that is wholly based on my lack of attention to detail or failure to ask the right questions. Your help and generosity with your time has been a gift.

Finally, thank you to my readers. You're the reason I do this. You give me the motivation to keep on when it feels too hard.

ABOUT THE AUTHOR

Charlene Carr is a lover of words. Pursuing this life-long obsession, she studied literature in university, attaining both a BA and MA in English. Still craving more, she attained a degree in Journalism. After travelling the globe for several years and working as a freelance writer, editor, and facilitator she decided the time had come to focus on her true love - novel writing. She's loving every minute of it ... well, almost every minute. Some days her characters fight to have the story their way. (And they're almost always right!)

Charlene lives in St. John's, Newfoundland and loves exploring the amazing coastline of her harbour town, dancing up a storm, and using her husband as a guinea pig for the healthy, yummy recipes she creates!

Charlene's first series, *A New Start*, is Women's Fiction full of thought, heart, and hope.